PENGUIN CLASSICS

NOTES FROM UNDERGROUND
THE DOUBLE

FYODOR MIKHAILOVICH DOSTOYEVSKY was born in Moscow
in 1821, the second of a physician's seven children. His mother
died in 1837 and his father was murdered a little over two years
later. When he left his private boarding school in Moscow he
studied from 1838 to 1843 at the Military Engineering College
in St Petersburg, graduating with officer's rank. His first
story to be published, 'Poor Folk' (1846), had a great success.
In 1849 he was arrested and sentenced to death for participating
in the 'Petrashevsky circle'; he was reprieved at the last
moment but sentenced to penal servitude, and until 1854 he
lived in a convict prison at Omsk, Siberia. Out of this experience he wrote *Memoirs from the House of the Dead* (1860). In
1861 he began the review *Vremya* with his brother; in 1862
and 1863 he went abroad where he strengthened his anti-
European outlook, met Mlle Suslova who was the model for
many of his heroines, and gave way to his passion for gam-
bling. During the following years he fell deeply into debt. In
1867 he married Anna Grigoryevna Snitkina (his second
wife) and she helped to rescue him from his financial morass.
They lived abroad for four years, then in 1873 he was invited
to edit *Grazhdanin*, to which he contributed his *Author's
Diary*. From 1876 the latter was issued separately and had a
large circulation. In 1880 he delivered his famous address at
the unveiling of Pushkin's memorial in Moscow; he died six
months later in 1881. Most of his important works were
written after 1864: *Notes From Underground* (1864), *Crime and
Punishment* (1865–66), *The Gambler* (1866), *The Idiot* (1869),
The Devils (1871), and *The Brothers Karamazov* (1880).

FYODOR DOSTOYEVSKY

Notes from Underground
The Double

TRANSLATED
WITH AN INTRODUCTION BY
JESSIE COULSON

PENGUIN BOOKS

PENGUIN BOOKS

Published by the Penguin Group
Penguin Books Ltd, 27 Wrights Lane, London W8 5TZ, England
Penguin Books USA Inc., 375 Hudson Street, New York, New York 10014, USA
Penguin Books Australia Ltd, Ringwood, Victoria, Australia
Penguin Books Canada Ltd, 10 Alcorn Avenue, Toronto, Ontario, Canada M4V 3B2
Penguin Books (NZ) Ltd, 182–190 Wairau Road, Auckland 10, New Zealand

Penguin Books Ltd, Registered Offices: Harmondsworth, Middlesex, England

Notes from the Underground first published as
Zapiski iz Podpolya 1864
The Double first published as *Dvoynik* 1846
This translation published 1972
23 25 27 29 30 28 26 24

Copyright © Jessie Coulson, 1972
All rights reserved

Printed in England by Clays Ltd, St Ives plc
Set in Linotype Juliana

CONTENTS

TRANSLATOR'S INTRODUCTION

WHEN the young Dostoyevsky began work on his second novel, *The Double*, in the May or June of 1845, he was glowing with the excitement and delight, the 'sort of shy rapture' of what he still thought of thirty-two years later as the most wonderful moment of his whole life, when the great critic Belinsky had said to him: 'Cherish your gift, remain true to it, and you will be a great writer', and he had come away in an ecstasy, stopped in the street and vowed to himself that he would remain true, he would be worthy of such praise. *Poor Folk*, the novel that had aroused the enthusiasm of Belinsky and of the poet Nekrasov, almost as influential in the Russian literary world, was not published until January 1846, and meanwhile Dostoyevsky basked in warmth and admiration, 'drunk with my own fame'. The sobering morning after had followed soon enough; *Poor Folk* was less rapturously received by the general public than its author had been led to expect by the attitude of literary and fashionable St Petersburg, and the reception of *The Double* when it appeared only a fortnight later was a mixture of positive hostility and profound indifference. Dostoyevsky, who had been declaring in his letters to his brother that his new novel, usually referred to as 'Golyadkin', was ten times better than *Poor Folk*, now 'felt disgusted with Golyadkin. A great deal of it was written in haste and fatigue. The first half is better than the second. Alongside brilliant pages there is trash and rubbish that turns the stomach; one can't read it.'

He was now being as excessive in decrying his own work as he had earlier been extravagant in his expectations of it. The book is the production of a writer too young and inexperienced to be anything but derivative in plot and manner – and yet – as Belinsky had told him – possessing the direct intuition of the artist and capable of becoming great. Its most obviously striking quality is perhaps its immense readability; it demands to be swallowed in one gulp. The style may be modelled, not entirely successfully on Gogol's, but it flows as swiftly as a river in flood, and conveys a feeling of urgent excitement and apprehension.

The 'Gothic' subject of a man haunted or possessed by his exact double must have seemed conventional enough at the time: it might have cropped up in the work of Gogol or as one of the tales of the still-popular Hoffmann. The choice of a government clerk as hero was also almost a formula of the age; Makar Devushkin, too, the hero of Dostoyevsky's first novel, was a clerk in the government service. But there is nothing stereotyped or commonplace about the handling of the theme or the character of Mr Golyadkin. *The Double* is unmistakably Dostoyevskyan in its ability to see everything that happens from inside the skin, so to speak, of its hero.

Mr Golyadkin finds himself snubbed and derided by his superiors in the official hierarchy and in society, and it is at the end of a humiliating day that began with high, if not entirely confident, expectation that he first encounters his double. The double not only resembles him physically, he bears the same name and comes from the same part of the provinces. Almost at once, this 'Mr Golyadkin junior' becomes the most important factor in Mr Golyadkin senior's life, inspiring his enemies (Mr Golyadkin senior feels that he is surrounded by enemies), working against him, usurping his place, appropriating his work and the credit attached to it, and finally driving him mad. But is this really what happens? Does Mr Golyadkin junior exist in cold fact? Perhaps the real horror of Mr Golyadkin's position is that he unconsciously knows that his double is simply that side of his own nature that he disapproves of and fears? The vehemence with which he assures himself that he is 'no different from anybody else' and that there is nothing out of the ordinary in his strangest actions, the anxiety with which he rehearses the things he will say or the letters he will write, the curious ambiguity of his early encounter with Dr Rutenspitz, the vaguely menacing quality of this apparently mild and benevolent gentleman, all afford us hints and glimpses of dark shapes moving in the depths of the pool whose still and shining surface is all that meets our eyes at first. Some of the later episodes in the book produce almost the effect of being extracts from the classic studies of split personalities which were not written until half a century later.

It is perhaps not surprising that *The Double* did not recover from its unsuccessful start during Dostoyevsky's lifetime; the great gap of his arrest, imprisonment, and exile was too wide to be easily crossed. Critics and students of Dostoyevsky in this country, with some exceptions, have tended to lump all his early works together as mere juvenilia, too remote from the great productions of his maturity to merit much attention. Yet Dostoyevsky himself remained convinced that the 'idea' of his book had been valuable and was worth re-working; there is evidence in his notebooks that during the sixties he was planning to add new episodes and perhaps largely rewrite the book for its second appearance, in the first collected edition of his works up to that time. Although the additional episodes were not used some rewriting was certainly done, but the impact on the general public remained slight. It is not, however, altogether fanciful to think one can hear echoes from the themes and scenes of *The Double* recurring again and again in Dostoyevsky's later works down to *The Brothers Karamazov* itself.

The Dostoyevsky who wrote the short novel *Notes from Underground* had already achieved fame as the author of *Memoirs from the House of the Dead*, the fictionalized account of his experiences as a convict and Siberian exile. *Notes from Underground* appeared in 1864, and its author's dying friend, the poet and critic Apollon Grigoryev, immediately saw that Dostoyevsky had found his true vein at last, and urged him to continue working it. Dostoyevsky needed no persuasion: his next novel was *Crime and Punishment*, and *Notes from Underground* can now be seen as a sort of prelude to the second part of his creative career, the succession of 'great' novels, the novels of ideas.

Like *The Double*, it is essentially a study of a single character. The hero, or rather anti-hero, as Dostoyevsky calls him, is a man turned in upon himself, a man of heightened awareness and self-consciousness, whose sensitivity to slights drives him alternately to retreat into his corner, his underground, and to revenge himself for his humiliations by humiliating others. Dostoyevsky declared in his notebooks that he prided himself on having been the first to portray this 'real man *of the Russian* majority' and lay bare his ugly and tragic aspect.

The tragedy lies in his consciousness of his own deformity. . . . I am the only one to have depicted the tragedy of the underground, made up of suffering, self-torture, the consciousness of what is best and the impossibility of attaining it, and above all the firm belief of these unhappy creatures that everybody else is the same and that consequently it is not worth while trying to reform.

The isolation of this self-isolated, nameless character is emphasized by the construction of the novel, which was published in two parts in the first two numbers of *The Epoch*, the Dostoyevsky brothers' journal. The whole of the first part takes the form of a long monologue, an exposition of the 'philosophy' of the anti-hero, which is to a considerable extent a direct statement of Dostoyevsky's own beliefs. It is a passionate, bitter, jeering, sharp-tongued attack on all those ideals of Utopian socialism to which he once owed allegiance, and it forms, thinks Grossman, one of his

most utterly naked pages. . . . Never afterwards was he so fully and openly to reveal the inmost recesses, unmeant for display, of his heart. . . . It is as if he was trying to pay back the spiritual leaders of his youth for the terrible ordeals of his years as a convict.

The immediate occasion of the outburst was the publication in 1863 of Chernyshevsky's novel *What is to be Done?* which postulates the attainment by mankind of perfect virtue and happiness by the pursuit of enlightened self-interest.

A man does evil only because he does not know his real interests, and if he is enlightened and his eyes are opened to his own best . . . interests, man will cease to do evil and at once become virtuous and noble, because when he . . . understands what will really benefit him he will see his own best interest in virtue, and . . . it is well known that no man can knowingly act against his best interests.

Against such reasoning, such 'mathematical certainties', such 'laws of nature', the man from underground declares that

all these beautiful systems, these theories of explaining his best interests to man . . . are nothing but sophistry. Isn't there something that is dearer to almost every man than his own very best interests, some best good which is more important and higher than any other good, and for the sake of which man is prepared, if necessary, to go against all the laws – that is against reason, honour, peace and quiet, prosperity – only to attain that primary, best good which is dearer to him than all else?

And he answers his own question: that something, the factor that had been omitted from all the calculations and that makes nonsense of 'twice two is four' does indeed exist; it is the perverse insistence of human beings on their right, if they choose, to act against all their own best interests.

One's own free and unfettered volition, one's own caprice, however wild, one's own fancy, inflamed sometimes to the point of madness – that is the one best and greatest good, which is never taken into consideration because it will not fit into any classification, and the omission of which always sends all systems and theories to the devil. Where did all the sages get the idea that a man's desires must be normal and virtuous? Why do they imagine that he must inevitably will what is reasonable and profitable? What a man needs is simply and solely *independent* volition, whatever that independence may cost and wherever it may lead.

The 'story of the falling sleet', constituting the second part of *Notes from Underground*, is a powerful, original, and characteristic production of the mature Dostoyevsky. It appears to have originally been planned as two chapters, and the present single chapter falls naturally into two parts. ... During the months when Dostoyevsky was writing *Notes from Underground* he was living with his dying consumptive wife in Moscow, his mind filled with anxiety for his adolescent stepson Pasha, left behind in St Petersburg, and for his brother Michael struggling to bring out the first numbers of *The Epoch* to take the place of *Time*, suppressed by the censorship. Perhaps it was in search of relief from the sad and painful circumstances of his life during that time that his mind went back to the distant years of his own adolescence and early manhood; the second and third sections of Chapter Two are full of memories of the places, people and events of his lonely days in the School of Military Engineering and in his first employment. These scenes are lively enough, and occasionally, as in the whole episode of the farewell dinner in a restaurant,

highly entertaining, but their colouring is sombre, and they lead
to some of the cruellest and darkest pages in all Dostoyevsky, the
terrible encounter of the man from underground with the prosti-
tute Liza, on whom he takes his revenge for his frustration, his
humiliation, the careless contempt of his old schoolfellows, who
reject his proffered friendship, ignore his attempts to force a
quarrel on them, and fail to recognize the superiority of which
he is so conscious.

The 'fallen woman', seen almost in the abstract as a victim of
society who could and should be rescued and regenerated, was to a
certain extent a stock figure of nineteenth-century literature and
theory, and not only in Russia. A poem of Nekrasov's, quoted
more than once in *Notes from Underground*, paints the picture of
a repentant Magdalen, dissolved in tears, stirred and shaken by
the 'burning words' of her latest lover, 'wringing her hands,
ashamed, dismayed, a fallen spirit on the rack of conscience and of
memory'; finally, purged and purified, she is invited to

> Enter now, then, bold and free;
> Be mistress of my house and me.

The high-flown romantic language of the poem makes it particularly unlikely to engage our present-day sympathies, but that
is not the only reason why this fallen woman seems unreal, a wax
dummy draped in the sentimental and self-regarding rhetoric of
her lover. Dostoyevsky's Liza, though, belongs to real life; she is
human, a human being, a young woman made of flesh and blood,
whose everyday existence began before and will continue after the
part of her history that is told in the story of the falling sleet. Her
reality and truth reveal the hollowness of the underground man
and the falsity of his ideas; when she walks steadily and un-
dramatically away and vanishes in the thickly falling snow, there
is nothing left for him but to go back to 'decaying morally in a
corner'. He cannot escape, he does not even want to try. It is Liza
who goes on: the novel without a hero has acquired a heroine, and
its end is her vindication, almost her triumph.

January 1971.   J.C.

Notes from Underground

The author of these Notes, and the Notes themselves, are both, of course, imaginary. All the same, if we take into consideration the conditions that have shaped our society, people like the writer not only may, but must, exist in that society. I have tried to present to the public in a more striking form than is usual a character belonging to the very recent past, a representative figure from a generation still surviving. In the chapter entitled 'The Underground' this personage introduces himself and his outlook on life, and tries, as it were, to elucidate the causes that brought about, inevitably brought about, his appearance in our midst. In the second section we follow this personage's memoirs of some of the happenings in his life.

FYODOR DOSTOYEVSKY

Chapter One

THE UNDERGROUND

I AM a sick man. . . . I am an angry man. I am an unattractive man. I think there is something wrong with my liver. But I don't understand the least thing about my illness, and I don't know for certain what part of me is affected. I am not having any treatment for it, and never have had, although I have a great respect for medicine and for doctors. I am besides extremely superstitious, if only in having such respect for medicine. (I am well educated enough not to be superstitious, but superstitious I am.) No, I refuse treatment out of spite. That is something you will probably not understand. Well, I understand it. I can't of course explain who my spite is directed against in this matter; I know perfectly well that I can't 'score off' the doctors in any way by not consulting them; I know better than anybody that I am harming nobody but myself. All the same, if I don't have treatment, it is out of spite. Is my liver out of order? – let it get worse!

I have been living like this for a long time now – about twenty years. I am forty. I once used to work in the government service but I don't now. I was a bad civil servant. I was rude, and I enjoyed being rude. After all, I didn't take bribes, so I had to have some compensation. (A poor witticism; but I won't cross it out. When I wrote it down, I thought it would seem very pointed: now, when I see that I was simply trying to be clever and cynical, I shall leave it in on purpose.) When people used to come to the desk where I sat, asking for information, I snarled at them, and was hugely delighted when I succeeded in hurting somebody's feelings. I almost always did succeed. They were mostly timid people – you know what people looking for favours are like. But among the swaggerers there was one officer I simply couldn't stand. He absolutely refused to be intimidated, and he made a disgusting clatter with his sword. I carried on a campaign against him for eighteen months over that sword. I won in the end. He stopped making a clatter with it. This, however, was when I was still young. But do you know what was the real point of my bad temper? The main point, and the supreme nastiness, lay in the fact that even at my moments of greatest spleen, I was constantly and shamefully aware that not only was I not seething with fury, I was not even angry; I was simply scaring sparrows for my own amusement. I might be foaming at the mouth, but bring me some sort of toy to play with, or a nice sweet cup of tea, and I would calm down and even be stirred to the depths, although I would probably turn on myself afterwards, and suffer from insomnia for months. That was always my way.

I was lying when I said just now that I was a bad civil servant. I was lying out of spite. I was simply playing a game with the officer and my other callers; in reality I never could make myself malevolent. I was always conscious of many elements showing the directly opposite tendency. I felt them positively swarming inside me, these elements. I knew they had swarmed there all my life, asking to be let out, but I wouldn't let them out, I wouldn't, I wouldn't. They tormented me shamefully; they drove me into convulsions and – in the end they bored me, oh, how they bored me! You think that now I'm making some sort of confession to you, asking your forgiveness, don't you? . . . I'm sure you do . . . But I assure you it's all the same to me if you do think so.

Not only couldn't I make myself malevolent, I couldn't make myself anything: neither good nor bad, neither a scoundrel nor an honest man, neither a hero nor an insect. Now I go on living in my corner and irritating myself with the spiteful and worthless consolation that a wise man can't seriously make himself anything, only a fool makes himself anything. Yes, a man of the nineteenth century ought, indeed is morally bound, to be essentially without character; a man of character, a man who acts, is essentially limited. Such is my forty-year-old conviction. I am forty now, and forty years is a lifetime; it is extreme old age. To go on living after forty is unseemly, disgusting, immoral! Who goes on living after forty? give me a sincere and honest answer! I'll tell you: fools and rogues. I'll tell all the old men that to their faces, all those venerable elders, those silver-haired, fragrant old men. I'll tell the whole world! I have the right to talk like this, because I'm going to live to be sixty. Seventy! Eighty! ... Stop, let me get my breath back ... !

You probably think I'm trying to amuse you. You're wrong there too. I'm not such a cheerful fellow as you think, or as you perhaps think; if, however, annoyed by all this chatter (and I can feel you are annoyed), you ask me positively who I am – I answer, I am a Collegiate Assessor. I joined the civil service in order to earn my bread (and for no other reason), and when last year a distant relative left me six thousand roubles in his will, I retired immediately and settled down in my little corner. I lived in this same corner even before that, but now I've settled down in it. My room is mean and shabby, on the outskirts of the town. My servant is a peasant woman, old, crabbed, and stupid, and what's more, she always smells bad. I am told that the climate of St Petersburg is bad for me, and that, with my insignificant means, it costs too much to live here. I know all that, a lot better than all my extremely wise and experienced advisers and head-shakers. But I shall stay here; I will not leave St Petersburg! I won't go away because. . . . Oh, after all, it doesn't matter in the least whether I go away or I don't.

However: what can a decent, respectable man talk about with the greatest pleasure?

Answer: himself.

Well, so I too will talk about myself.

2

I should like to tell you now, whether you want to hear it or not, why I couldn't even make an insect of myself. I tell you solemnly that I have wanted to make an insect of myself many times. But I couldn't succeed even in that. I swear to you that to think too much is a disease, a real, actual disease. For ordinary human life it would be more than sufficient to possess ordinary human intellectual activity, that is to say, half or a quarter as much as falls to the lot of an educated man in our unhappy nineteenth century, and especially one having the misfortune to live in St Petersburg, the most abstract and intentional city in the whole round world.

(Towns can be either intentional or unintentional.) It would be quite enough, for example, to have the consciousness of all our so-called men of action and public figures. I am prepared to let you think that in writing all this I am simply striking attitudes and scoring off men of action, and in the worst of taste, too; I am rattling my sword, like that officer. But who can be vain of his disease, still less swagger with it?

Why do I say that, though? Everybody does it – we all show off with our diseases, and I, perhaps, more than anybody. Don't let's argue; I expressed myself clumsily. But all the same I'm firmly convinced that not only a great deal, but every kind, of intellectual activity is a disease. I hold to that. Let us leave it for the moment. Tell me this: why is it that it always had to happen, as if on purpose, that in those moments, yes, in those very same moments, when I was most capable of recognizing all the subtle beauties of 'the highest and the best', as we used to say, I could not only fail to recognize them, but could actually do such ugly, repulsive things as ... well, such things, in short, as perhaps everybody does, but which always happened to me, as if on purpose, when I was most conscious that I ought not to do them? The more aware I was of beauty and of 'the highest and the best', the deeper I sank into my slime, and the more capable I became of immersing myself completely in it. But the chief feature of all this was that it was not accidental, but as if it had to be so. It was as if this was my normal condition, not a disease or a festering sore in me, so that finally I lost even the desire to struggle against the spell. I ended by almost believing (or perhaps fully believing) that this was really my normal state. But before that, in the beginning, how much I suffered in the struggle! I didn't believe the same thing could happen to other people, and so I have kept the secret to myself my whole life. I was ashamed (perhaps I am ashamed even now); I got to the point where I felt an abnormal, mean, secret stirring of pleasure in going back home to my corner from some debauched St Petersburg night, conscious in the highest degree that I had once again done something vile and that what was done could never be undone. And secretly, in my heart, I would gnaw and nibble and probe and suck away at myself until the bitter taste turned at last into a kind of shameful, devilish sweetness and, finally, downright definite pleasure. Yes, pleasure, pleasure! I stand by that. The reason I have spoken of it is that I want to know for certain whether other people feel that kind of pleasure. Let me explain: the pleasure came precisely from being too clearly aware of your own degradation; from the feeling of having gone to the uttermost limits; that it was vile, but it could not have been otherwise; that you could not escape, you could never make yourself into a different person; that even if enough faith and time remained for you to make yourself into something different, you probably wouldn't want to change yourself; and even if you did want to, you wouldn't do anything because, after all, perhaps it wasn't worth while to change. But finally, and chiefly, all this proceeded from the normal basic laws of intellectual activity and the inertia directly resulting from these laws, and consequently not only wouldn't you change yourself, you wouldn't even do anything at all. For example, it turns out in consequence of intensified awareness that it seems to be some kind of consolation to a scoundrel to feel fully conscious that he really is a scoundrel. But that's enough. ... Ach, I've talked a lot, but what have I explained? How can this pleasure be accounted for? But I will explain myself. I'll go on to the end. That's why I took up my pen ...

For example, I'm very touchy. I'm sensitive and quick to take offence, like a hunchback or a dwarf, but there have been times when if somebody had given me a slap in the face I might even have been glad of it. I am speaking seriously: I should certainly have known how to find pleasure in it, the pleasure, of course, of despair, but despair can hold the most intense sorts of pleasure when one is strongly conscious of the hopelessness of one's position. And here, with the slap in the face, it is forced in upon you what filth you are smeared with. The main thing is that, however you look at it, it always turns out that you are chiefly to blame for everything, and what hurts most of all, innocently to blame, by the laws of nature, as it were. I am to blame because, first of all, I am cleverer than anybody else around me. (I have always thought myself cleverer than anybody I knew, and sometimes, if you will believe me, I have felt quite ashamed of it. In any case, I have always turned my eyes away and never been able to look anybody straight in the face.) And, finally, I am to blame because even if I had had any generosity of spirit in me, it would only have been a greater torment to me to realize its complete uselessness. After all, I should probably have been unable to do anything with my generosity of soul; neither forgive, because the person who offended me might have been following the laws of nature, and you can't forgive the laws of nature; nor forget, because even if it was according to the laws of nature, it was still an affront. Finally, even if I refused to show any generosity of spirit, but wanted to be revenged for the insult, I couldn't even take my revenge on anybody for anything, because I should probably find it impossible to make up my mind to take any steps, even if I could. Why not? I should like to say a word or two about that in particular.

3

Those people, for example, who can avenge their wrongs and generally stand up for themselves – how do they do it? They seem to be so possessed by the desire for, say, revenge that for the time there is nothing left in their whole being but that emotion. A man like that goes straight for his goal like a mad bull charging with his horns down, and is to be stopped, if at all, only by a stone wall. (By the way, men like that, men of action, doers, quite genuinely give up when faced with a wall; to them a wall is not a challenge, as it is to us, for example, men who think and therefore don't do anything; nor is it an excuse for turning aside, an excuse that people like us are always glad of, even if we don't usually even believe in it ourselves. No, they give up in all sincerity. A wall is for them something calming, morally decisive and final, perhaps even something mystical. . . . But I'll come back to the wall later.) Well, that sort of spontaneous man is the real man, as Nature his tender mother, lovingly bringing him to birth upon the earth, would wish to see him. I am green with envy of such men. They are stupid, I won't deny that, but perhaps a normal man ought to be stupid, how can you tell? Perhaps it is even a very fine thing to be. I am even more convinced that this suspicion, so to speak, of mine is true by the fact that if one takes the antithesis of the normal man, for example, the man of heightened awareness, who has of course emerged not from the womb of Nature but from a test-tube (this is almost mysticism, but that is a thing I distrust too) – the test-tube man will sometimes give up so completely when confronted by his antithesis that he will honestly look upon himself, with all his sharpened consciousness, as a mouse, not a man. A highly conscious mouse, but all the same a mouse, while the other is a man, and consequently ... and so on. And the point is that he looks on himself as a mouse of his own accord; nobody asks him to do so; that is the important thing. Let us now look at this mouse in action. Suppose, for example, that it too has been insulted (and it will almost always be subjected to slights) and desires revenge. Perhaps even more fury will accumulate inside it than inside l'homme de la nature et de la vérité. The nasty mean little desire to pay back the offender in his own coin may gnaw more viciously inside it than inside l'homme de la nature et de la vérité because l'homme de la nature et de la vérité, with his innate stupidity, considers his revenge to be no more than justice, while the mouse, with its heightened awareness, denies that there is any justice about it. At last comes the act itself, the revenge. The wretched mouse has by this time accumulated, in addition to the original nastiness, so many other nastinesses in the shape of questions and doubts, and so many other unresolved problems in addition to the original problem, that it has involuntarily collected round itself a fatal morass, a stinking bog, consisting of its own doubts and agitation, and finally of the spittle rained on it by all the spontaneous men of action standing portentously round as judges and referees, and howling with laughter. Of course, nothing remains for it to do but shrug the whole thing off and creep shamefacedly into its hole with a smile of pretended contempt in which it doesn't even believe itself. There in its nasty stinking cellar our offended, browbeaten and derided mouse sinks at once into cold, venomous, and above all undying resentment. It will sit there for forty years together remembering the insult in the minutest and most shameful detail and constantly adding even more shameful details of its own invention, maliciously tormenting and fretting itself with its own imagination. It will be ashamed of its fantasies, but all the same it will always be remembering them and turning them over in its mind, inventing things that never happened because they might have done so, and forgiving nothing. Perhaps it will even begin to take its revenge, but somehow in little bits, in snatches, furtively, anonymously, not believing either in its right to revenge itself or in its success in doing so, and knowing in advance that it will suffer a hundred times more painfully from every one of its attempts at revenge than the victims of them, who will perhaps never even notice them. On its deathbed it will recall the whole thing over again, with compound interest, and. . . . But it is precisely this cold, sickening half-despair, half-hope, this deliberately burying oneself in a cellar for forty years out of spite, this well-established and yet somehow unconvincing powerlessness to escape from the situation, all this poisonous accumulation of unsatisfied wishes in the breast, all these feverish vacillations, all these resolutions firmly taken for all time and repented of again after a few minutes, that give rise to and nourish that strange pleasure I was speaking of. It is so subtle, and sometimes so little subject to the conscious mind, that slightly limited people, or sometimes simply those whose nervous systems are stable, will not understand the least thing about it. 'Perhaps,' you will put in with a grin, 'nobody who hasn't had a slap in the face will be able to understand either', thus politely hinting that perhaps I myself have suffered a slap in the face at some time in my life, and therefore speak from experience. I'm prepared to bet that is what you think. But don't worry, I haven't experienced any slaps, though it makes absolutely no difference to me what you think on the subject. Perhaps I am even a little sorry that I have dealt out so few slaps myself. But that's enough; not another word on this subject you find so extraordinarily interesting.

I will go quietly on about the people with strong nerves, who don't understand certain refinements of pleasure. These gentlemen, although they roar full-throatedly like bulls, and I suppose it does them the greatest credit, will on some occasions, as I have already said, calm down at once when they are faced with an impossibility. Impossibility is a stone wall. What do I mean by a stone wall? Well, of course, the laws of nature or the conclusions of the natural sciences or of mathematics. When it is proved, for example, that you are descended from an ape, it's no use scowling about it – accept it as a fact. Or if it is demonstrated that half an ounce of your own fat ought essentially to be dearer to you than a hundred thousand of your fellow-creatures, and that this demonstration finally disposes of all so-called good deeds, duties, and other lunacies and prejudices, simply accept it; there's nothing to be done about it, because twice two is mathematics. Just try to argue!

'Excuse me,' they cry, 'you can't fight it; twice two is four! Nature doesn't ask you about it; she's not concerned with your wishes or with whether you like her laws or not. You must take her as she is, and consequently all her results as well. I mean to say, a wall is a wall,' etc., etc. But good God! what have the laws of nature and arithmetic to do with me, when for some reason I don't like those laws or twice two? Naturally I shan't break through the wall with my head, if I'm really not strong enough, but I won't be reconciled to it simply because it's a stone wall and I haven't enough strength to break it down.

As if a stone wall really was a soothing influence and really did carry a message of peace, simply because it is twice two! That's utterly absurd! The point is to understand everything, to realize everything, every impossibility, every stone wall; not to reconcile yourself to a single one of the impossibilities and stone walls if the thought of reconciliation sickens you; to arrive by way of the strictest logical syllogisms at the most repulsive conclusions on the eternal theme of how you are somehow to blame for the stone wall itself, even though once again it is abundantly clear that you are not to blame at all, and in consequence of all this to sink voluptuously into inertia, silently and impotently gnashing your teeth and reflecting that there isn't even anybody for you to be angry with, that an object for your anger can't even be found, and perhaps never will be, that this is all a fake, a conjuring trick, a piece of sharp practice, and there is nothing there but a morass;

nobody knows what, nobody knows who, but in spite of all the mysteries and illusions, you ache with it all, and the more mysterious it is, the more you ache.

4

'Ha, ha, ha! After that, you will be looking for pleasure even in toothache!' you will exclaim, laughing.

'Why not? There is pleasure even in toothache,' I shall reply. I once had toothache for a whole month, so I know what I'm talking about. People don't suffer *that* in silence, of course, they groan; but the groans aren't straightforward and honest, they are spiteful and the spite is the whole point of them. Those groans are an expression of the sufferer's pleasure; if he didn't enjoy them he would stop groaning. This is a good example, and I will develop it. The groans are an expression, to begin with, of all the pointlessness, which the conscious mind finds so humiliating, of your pain; it's a law of nature, for which, of course, you feel the utmost contempt, but from which you nevertheless suffer, while she doesn't. They express your awareness of the fact that nobody has inflicted the pain on you and yet you feel it, your awareness that in spite of all the Wagenheims you are utterly at the mercy of your teeth; that if something wills it, they will stop aching, and if it doesn't, they will go on aching for another three months; and finally, that even if you still object and try to protest, your only satisfaction will be lashing your own back or running your head even more painfully against your stone wall, and that's absolutely all! Well, it is from these bloody wrongs, these practical jokes of an unidentifiable jester, that pleasure finally arises, pleasure that sometimes attains the utmost rapture. I ask you to listen some time to the groaning of a cultured man of the nineteenth century who has been suffering from toothache for two or three days, and whose groans are beginning to be different from those of the first day; that is, he is not groaning simply because his teeth ache, nor like a coarse peasant, but like a man touched by enlightenment and European civilization, like a man who has 'cut himself off from the soil and his roots among the people', as they say nowadays. His groans have become something vicious and maliciously nasty, and they go on all day and all night. And yet he knows perfectly well that his groans won't do the slightest good, he knows better than anybody else that he is harrowing and irritating himself and everybody else for nothing; he realizes that even the audience for which he is performing, even his own family, are sick of listening to him, they don't believe a word of it, and they know in their hearts that he could very well groan in another, simpler fashion, without roulades and flourishes, and is merely indulging himself out of spite and ill humour. Well, the pleasure lies in all this conscious shamefulness. 'I'm disturbing you,' he seems to say, 'I'm lacerating your feelings and preventing everybody in the house from sleeping. Well, don't sleep, then; you ought to be feeling my toothache all the time. I'm not a hero to you any longer, as I used to try to seem, but only a worthless good-for-nothing. All right, then! I'm very glad you've seen through me. You don't like to hear my mean-spirited moans, do you? Dislike them then; now I'll treat you to an even more harrowing performance. . . .' Do you understand yet, gentlemen? Yes, evidently one must be highly developed and deeply conscious of oneself to understand all the devious ins and outs of that voluptuous delight. . . . Are you laughing? I'm very glad. My jokes are in bad taste, of course, gentlemen, uneven, confused, full of self-distrust. But that, you know, comes from having no respect for myself. Can a thinking man have any self-respect whatever?

5

No, a man can't have a trace of self-respect, can he, who has attempted to find his pleasure in the consciousness of his own degradation?

I'm not saying this out of some sort of pretended repentance. I never could bear, anyhow, to say, 'Forgive me, Daddy dear, I won't do it again,' not because I was incapable of saying the words, but on the contrary, perhaps because I was too capable of saying them, and on what occasions? As sure as fate, I used to come out with them when I was absolutely innocent. That was the most degraded aspect of it. In such circumstances, I would be deeply moved, filled with remorse, and shedding tears, and, of course, I was deceiving myself, although I wasn't consciously pretending. My heart seemed to purge itself of its own accord. . . . For this I couldn't even blame the laws of nature, although I have always resented the laws of nature more than anything else all my life. It is degrading to remember all this, and it was degrading at the time, too. Of course, after a few minutes I would be reflecting that the whole thing was a lie, a disgusting lie, an unnatural lie – all that remorse, I mean, all those emotions, all those promises of regeneration. Do you ask why I tortured and tormented myself? The answer is that it was too boring to sit and do nothing, and so I indulged my fancy. That really is true. Watch yourselves as closely as you can, gentlemen, and you will see that it's true. I imagined happenings, I invented a life, so that I should at any rate *live*. How many times have I – well – taken offence, for example, just like that, deliberately, for no reason at all? And, you know, one always knew that one was taking offence at nothing at all, putting on an act, but one went to such lengths that at last one really and truly felt affronted. I've had a tendency all my life to play that kind of trick, so much so that, in the end, I really lost all control over myself. There was one time, or even two, when I simply longed to fall in love. I really suffered, gentlemen, I assure you. At the bottom of my heart I can't believe in my own suffering, I feel a stirring of derision, but all the same I do suffer, and in a real, definite fashion; I am jealous, I fly into rages. . . . And all out of boredom, gentlemen, all out of boredom; I am crushed with tedium. After all, the direct, immediate, legitimate fruit of heightened consciousness is inertia, that is, the deliberate refusal to do anything. I have mentioned this before. I repeat, and repeat emphatically: all spontaneous people, men of action, are active *because* they are stupid and limited. How is this to be explained? Like this: in consequence of their limitations they take immediate, but secondary, causes for primary ones, and thus they are more quickly and easily convinced than other people that they have found indisputable grounds for their action, and they are easy in their minds; and this, you know, is the main thing. After

all, in order to act, one must be absolutely sure of oneself, no
doubts must remain anywhere. But how am I, for example, to be
sure of myself? Where are the primary causes on which I can take
my stand, where are my foundations? Where am I to take them
from? I practise thinking, and consequently each of my primary
causes pulls along another, even more primary, in its wake, and so
on *ad infinitum*. That is really the essence of all thinking and self-
awareness. Perhaps this, once again, is a law of nature. And what,
finally, is the result? The same thing over again. Do you remember
that I was talking just now about revenge? (You probably didn't
understand me.) I said a man takes his revenge because he finds
justice in it. That means he has found his primary reason, his
foundation, namely justice. Thus he is easy on all counts, and
consequently takes his revenge calmly and successfully, being convinced that he is performing a just and honourable action. But
really I can't find any justice, or any kind of virtue, in it, and
consequently, if I take my revenge, it is purely out of resentment.
Resentment, of course, might overcome all my doubts and hesi-
tations, and might therefore serve quite successfully instead of a
primary cause, precisely because it isn't a cause. But what can I do
if I don't even feel resentment? (This was my starting-point of a
short time ago.) My anger, in consequence of the damned laws of
consciousness, is subject to chemical decomposition. As you look,
its object vanishes into thin air, its reasons evaporate, the offender
is nowhere to be found, the affront ceases to be an offence and
becomes destiny, something like toothache, for which nobody is to
blame, and consequently there remains only the same outcome,
which is banging one's head as hard as one can against the stone
wall. Well, you shrug it off, because you haven't found a primary
cause. But try letting yourself be carried along blindly by your
feelings, banish your reason if only for the moment; hate, or love,
anything rather than do nothing. The day after tomorrow, at the
very latest, you will begin to despise yourself for your conscious
self-deception. The result is a soap-bubble, and inertia. Oh, gentlemen, perhaps the only reason I consider myself a clever man is
that I have never in all my life been able to either begin or finish
anything. A windbag I may be, an ineffective, irritating windbag,

like all of us. But what can one do, if the only straightforward
task of every intelligent man is pointless chattering, the deliberate
pouring out of emptiness?

6

Oh, if only it was only out of laziness that I do nothing! Lord,
how much I should respect myself then! I should respect myself
because I had something inside me, even if it was only laziness; I
should have at any rate one positive quality of which I could be
sure. Question: what is he? Answer: a lazy man; and it really
would be very pleasant to hear that said of me. It would mean
being positively defined, it would mean that there was something
that *could* be said of me. 'A lazy man!' – that is a name, a calling,
it's positively a career! Don't laugh, it's true. Then I should be by
right a member of the very best club, and have no other occupation than nursing my self-esteem. I once knew a gentleman who
prided himself all his life on being a connoisseur of Chateau Lafite.
He considered that to be his positive merit, and never doubted
himself. He died not so much with a quiet as with a triumphant
conscience, and he was quite right. And I should choose for myself
a career: I should be a lazy man and a glutton, but not a simple
one, rather one who, for example, was in sympathy with all that
is 'best and highest'. How do you like that idea? It has often
crossed my mind. That 'best and highest' is an absolute headache
to me now at forty; but that is now that I am forty; then – oh,
then would have been different! I should have found a suitable
sphere of action for myself at once, namely drinking to the 'best
and highest'. I would have seized every opportunity of first dropping a tear into my glass and then draining it in honour of the
best and highest; I would have sought out the best and highest in
the nastiest, most unmistakable filth. I should have been as tearful
as a wet sponge. For example, an artist has painted a picture of
tortured naturalism. I immediately drink the health of the painter
of this ugly picture because I am a lover of the best and highest.
An author has written an 'As You Like It'; at once I drink the
health of those who do 'like it' because I love all that is best and

highest. I demand general respect in return, and woe betide anybody who does not give me it. I live peacefully and die triumphantly – charming, you know, absolutely charming! And I should grow such a massive corporation and such a multitude of chins, and acquire by my activities such an imperially crimson nose, that everybody seeing me would exclaim, 'Now *he's* somebody! That's a man who positively has something!' And say what you like, gentlemen, in our negative age such exclamations are pleasant to hear!

7

But all these are golden daydreams. Tell me, who was it who first declared, proclaiming it to the whole world, that a man does evil only because he does not know his real interests, and if he is enlightened and has his eyes opened to his own best and normal interests, man will cease to do evil and at once become virtuous and noble, because when he is enlightened and understands what will really benefit him he will see his own best interest in virtue, and since it is well known that no man can knowingly act against his best interests, consequently he will inevitably, so to speak, begin to do good. Oh, what a baby! Oh, what a pure innocent child! To begin with, when in all these thousands of years have men acted solely in their own interests? What about all those millions of incidents testifying to the fact that men have *knowingly*, that is in full understanding of their own best interests, put them in the background and taken a perilous and uncertain course not because anybody or anything drove them to it, but simply and solely because they did not choose to follow the appointed road, as it were, but wilfully and obstinately preferred to pursue a perverse and difficult path, almost lost in the darkness? This shows that obstinacy and self-will meant more to them than any kind of advantage. ... Advantage! What is advantage? Besides, can you undertake to define exactly where a man's advantage lies? What if it sometimes so happens that a man's advantage not only may but must consist in desiring in certain cases not what is good but what is bad for him? And if so, if such cases are even possible, the whole rule is utterly destroyed. Do you think such cases occur? You laugh; laugh, then, gentlemen, but answer me this: can man's interests be correctly calculated? Are there not some which not only have not been classified, but are incapable of classification? After all, gentlemen, as far as I know you deduce the whole range of human satisfactions as averages from statistical figures and scientifico-economic formulas. You recognize things like wealth, freedom, comfort, prosperity, and so on as good, so that a man who deliberately and openly went against that tabulation would in your opinion, and of course in mine also, be an obscurantist or else completely mad, wouldn't he? But there is one very puzzling thing: how does it come about that all the statisticians and experts and lovers of humanity, when they enumerate the good things of life, always omit one particular one? They don't even take it into account as they ought, and the whole calculation depends on it. After all, it would not do much harm to accept this as a good and add it to the list. But the snag lies in this; that this strange benefit won't suit any classification or fit neatly into any list. For example, I have a friend. ... Oh but, gentlemen, he's a friend of yours too; indeed, who is there who doesn't have him among his friends? When he proposes to do something, this gentleman will immediately expound to you, lucidly and polysyllabically, exactly how he must proceed, by the laws of truth and logic. Moreover, he speaks with passion and enthusiasm of the true natural interests of mankind; he condemns with a sneer those short-sighted fools who understand neither their own interests nor the real meaning of virtue, and then, a quarter of an hour afterwards, without any sudden intervention from outside but at the prompting of something inside himself that is stronger than all his self-interest, he will shoot off on a new tack, acting, that is to say, in a way that is obviously the opposite of all he has been saying: contrary to all the laws of reason, and all his own best interests and in short, everything. ... I must warn you that this friend is a generalization, and that consequently it is somewhat difficult to blame only him. ... The point, gentlemen, is this: doesn't there, in fact, exist something that is dearer to almost every man than his own very best interests, or – not to violate logic – some best good (the one that is always omitted from the lists, of which we were speaking just now) which is more important and higher than any other good, and for the sake of which man is prepared if necessary to go against all the laws, against, that is, reason, honour, peace and quiet, prosperity – in short against all those fine and advantageous things – only to attain that primary, best good which is dearer to him than all else?

'Well, but then it is still a good,' you interrupt. By your leave, we will explain further, and the point is not in a play on words, but in the fact that this good is distinguished precisely by upsetting all our classifications and always destroying the systems established by lovers of humanity for the happiness of mankind. In short, it interferes with everything. But before I name this good, I want to compromise myself personally, and so I roundly declare that all these beautiful systems – these theories of explaining his best interests to man with the idea that in his inevitable striving to attain those interests he will immediately become virtuous and noble – are, in my opinion, nothing but sophistry! Really, to maintain the theory of the regeneration of the whole of mankind by means of a tabulation of his own best interests is in my opinion the same as ... well, as to affirm with Buckle that civilization renders man milder and so less bloodthirsty and addicted to warfare. Logically, it appears that that ought to be the result. But man is so partial to systems and abstract deduction that in order to justify his logic he is prepared to distort the truth intentionally. This is why I take this example, because it is an extremely striking one. Look round you: everywhere blood flows in torrents, and what's more, as merrily as if it was champagne. There's our nineteenth century – and it was Buckle's century too. There's your Napoleon – both the great Napoleon and the present-day one. There's your North America – the everlasting Union. There is finally your grotesque Schleswig-Holstein. ... And what softening effect has civilization had on us? Civilization develops in man only a many-sided sensitivity to sensations, and ... definitely nothing more. And through the development of that many-sidedness man may perhaps progress to the point where he finds pleasure in blood. In fact, it has already happened. Have you

noticed that the most refined shedders of blood have been almost
always the most highly civilized gentlemen, to whom all the
various Attilas and Stenka Razins could not have held a candle?
– and if they are not so outstanding as Attila and Stenka Razin, it
is because they are too often met with, too ordinary, too familiar.
At least, if civilization has not made man more bloodthirsty, it has
certainly made him viler in his thirst for blood than he was before.
Before, he saw justice in bloodshed and massacred, if he had to,
with a quiet conscience; now, although we consider bloodshed an
abomination, we engage in it more than ever. Which is worse?
Decide for yourselves. They say that Cleopatra (excuse my taking
an example from Roman history) liked to stick golden pins into
the breasts of her slaves, and took pleasure in their screams and
writhings. You will say that that was in barbarous times, comparatively speaking; that even today the times are barbarous because (again speaking comparatively) pins are still being thrust
into people; and that even now man, although he has learnt to see
more clearly than in the days of barbarism, is still far from having
grown accustomed to acting as reason and science direct. But all
the same you are quite sure that he will inevitably acquire the
habit, when certain bad old habits have altogether passed away,
and common sense and science have completely re-educated and
normally direct human nature. You are convinced that then men
will of their own accord cease to make mistakes and refuse, in spite
of themselves, as it were, to make a difference between their volition and their normal interests. Furthermore, you say, science
will teach men (although in my opinion this is a superfluity) that
they have not, in fact, and never have had, either will or fancy,
and are no more than a sort of piano keyboard or barrel-organ
cylinder; and that the laws of nature still exist on the earth, so
that whatever man does he does not of his own volition but, as
really goes without saying, by the laws of nature. Consequently,
these laws of nature have only to be discovered, and man will no
longer be responsible for his actions, and it will become extremely
easy for him to live his life. All human actions, of course, will
then have to be worked out by those laws, mathematically, like a
table of logarithms, and entered in the almanac; or better still,

there will appear orthodox publications, something like our encyc-lopaedic dictionaries, in which everything will be so accurately calculated and plotted that there will no longer be any individual deeds or adventures left in the world.

'Then,' (this is all of you speaking), 'a new political economy will come into existence, all complete, and also calculated with mathematical accuracy, so that all problems will vanish in the twinkling of an eye, simply because all possible answers to them will have been supplied. Then the Palace of Crystal will arise. Then. ...' Well, in short, the golden age will come again. Of course it is quite impossible (here I am speaking myself) to guaran-tee that it won't be terribly boring then (because what can one do if everything has been plotted out and tabulated?), but on the other hand everything will be eminently sensible. Of course, bore-dom leads to every possible kind of ingenuity. After all, it is out of boredom that golden pins get stuck into people, but all this would not matter. What is bad (again this is me speaking) is that for all I know people may then find pleasure even in golden pins. Man, after all, is stupid, phenomenally stupid. That is to say, although he is not in the least stupid, he is so ungrateful that it is useless to expect anything else from him. Really I shall not be in the least surprised if, for example, in the midst of the future universal good sense, some gentleman with an ignoble, or rather a derisive and reactionary air, springs up suddenly out of nowhere, puts his arms akimbo and says to all of us, 'Come on, gentlemen, why shouldn't we get rid of all this calm reasonableness with one kick, just so as to send all these logarithms to the devil and be able to live our own lives at our own sweet will?' That wouldn't matter either, but what is really mortifying is that he would certainly find fol-lowers: that's the way men are made. And all this for the most frivolous of reasons, hardly worth mentioning, one would think: namely that a man, whoever he is, always and everywhere likes to act as he chooses, and not at all according to the dictates of reason and self-interest; it is indeed possible, and sometimes *positively imperative* (in my view), to act directly contrary to one's own best interests. One's own free and unfettered volition, one's own caprice, however wild, one's own fancy, inflamed sometimes to the point of madness – that is the one best and greatest good, which is never taken into consideration because it will not fit into any classification, and the omission of which always sends all systems and theories to the devil. Where did all the sages get the idea that a man's desires must be normal and virtuous? Why did they imagine that he must inevitably will what is reasonable and profitable? What a man needs is simply and solely *independent* volition, whatever that independence may cost and wherever it may lead. Well, but the devil only knows what volition ...

8

'Ha, ha, ha! But, you know, as a matter of fact volition doesn't exist!' you interrupt me with a laugh. 'Science has already got so far in its anatomization of man that we know that so-called free will is nothing more than ...'

Just a minute, gentlemen, that's how I was going to begin. I confess I shirked it. I was just about to exclaim that the devil only knows what volition depends on, and perhaps it's just as well, but I remembered about science and ... stopped short. And you came in at that point. As a matter of fact, though, if the formula for all our desires and whims is some day discovered – I mean what they depend on, what laws they result from, how they are disseminated, what sort of good they aspire to in a particular instance, and so on – a real mathematical formula, that is, then it is possible that man will at once cease to want anything, indeed I suppose it is possible that he will cease to exist. Well, what's the point of wishing by numbers? Furthermore, he will at once turn from a man into a barrel-organ sprig or something of the sort; for what is man without desires, without will, without volition, but a sprig on the cylinder of a barrel-organ? What do you think? Let us consider the probabilities – could this happen or not?

'H'm,' you decide, 'our desires are for the most part mistaken because of our erroneous view of our own interests. The reason why we sometimes want purely nonsensical things is that in our stupidity we see in those nonsensical things the easiest way to the attainment of some already proposed advantage. Well, but when it has all been worked out and tabulated on paper (which is quite possible, because it is wicked and silly to believe in advance that there are some laws of nature that man will never discover), then of course there will no longer be any so-called volition. If ever volition becomes completely identified with common sense, we shall of course reason, not want, purely because it is impossible to *want* what has no sense, flying in the face of reason and desiring what will do one harm, and still preserve one's common sense. ... And since all volition and all reasoning really may be tabulated, because the laws of our so-called free will may indeed be discovered, it follows, quite seriously, that some sort of table may be drawn up and that we shall exercise our wills in conformity with that table. If, for example, it can one day be worked out and proved to me that I have on some occasion cocked a snook at somebody simply because I could not help it, and that I was obliged to make the gesture in that particular way, then what *freedom* remains to me, especially if I am learned and have taken a science course somewhere? After all, in that case I can calculate my life for thirty years in advance; in short, if things turn out in this way, there won't be anything left for us to do; all the same, we shall need to understand. But in general we ought always to be telling ourselves that, inevitably, at certain times and in certain circumstances nature will not consult us; that we must take her as she is and not as we fancy her to be, and if we really are progressing at great speed towards the tables and almanacs and ... even the test-tube, there's no help for it, we must accept even the test-tube! Or else it will be accepted for us ...'

Yes, but that's just where the snag is for me! Gentlemen, please excuse me for carrying my philosophizing to such absurd lengths – forty years underground, after all! Let me give my fancy free rein. You see, gentlemen, reason is a good thing, that can't be disputed, but reason is only reason and satisfies only man's intellectual faculties, while volition is a manifestation of the whole of life, I mean of the whole of human life *including* both reason and speculation. And although in this manifestation life frequently turns out to be rubbishy, all the same it is life and not merely the extraction of a square root. After all, I, for example,

quite naturally want to live so as to fulfil my whole capacity for
living, and not so as to satisfy simply and solely my intellectual
capacity, which is only one-twentieth of my whole capacity for
living. What does reason know? Reason knows only what it has
succeeded in finding out (and perhaps there are some things it will
never find out; there may be no consolation in this idea, but why
not express it?), but man's nature acts as one whole, with everything that is in it, conscious or unconscious, and although it is
nonsensical, yet it lives. I suspect, gentlemen, that you are sorry
for me; you keep telling me that an enlightened and fully developed human being, in short one like the human being of the
future, cannot knowingly will something that is bad for him, and
that this is mathematics. I quite agree, it really is a mathematical
certainty. But I repeat for the hundredth time that there is one
case, and only one, when a man can consciously and purposely
desire for himself what is positively harmful and stupid, even the
very height of stupidity, and that is when he claims the right to
desire even the height of stupidity and not be bound by the obligation of wanting only what is sensible. After all, this height of
stupidity, this whim, may be for us, gentlemen, the greatest
benefit on earth, especially in some cases. And in particular it may
be the greatest of all benefits even when it does us obvious harm
and contradicts our reason's soundest conclusions on the subject
of what is beneficial – because it does at any rate preserve what is
dear and extremely important to us, that is our personality and
our individuality. Some would assert that it is indeed what is
dearest of all to man; volition can of course coincide with reason,
if it likes, especially if it doesn't abuse reason but uses it in mod-
eration; this is wholesome and sometimes even laudable. But very
often, perhaps more often than not, volition clashes directly and
obstinately with reason, and ... and ... and, do you know, this
too is wholesome and sometimes even laudable. Gentlemen, let us
assume that man is not stupid. (Really, you know, it is quite
impossible to say that he is, if only because after all, if he is stupid
who can be clever?) But if he isn't stupid, he is monstrously ungrateful, all the same. He is phenomenally ungrateful. I even
think that the best definition of man is: a creature that has two

legs and no sense of gratitude. But that isn't all; it isn't even his
greatest defect; his greatest defect is his constant misbehaviour,
constant from the time of the Flood to the Schleswig-Holstein
period of human destiny. Misbehaviour, and hence misreasoning;
for it has long been well known that misreasoning arises from
nothing but misbehaviour. Test it; cast a glance over the history of
mankind: what do you see? Sublimity? Well, perhaps even sublimity; how much value the Colossus of Rhodes alone has, for
example! It is not for nothing that Mr Anaevsky testifies that
while some say it is the work of human hands, others assert that it
was created by Nature herself. Variety? Perhaps variety too; study
only the full-dress uniforms, military and civilian, of all nations in
all ages – and what that alone amounts to! as for undress uniforms, they are uncountable: not a single historian could cope
with them. Monotony? Well, perhaps monotony also: fighting,
fighting, all the time; there was always fighting going on, and it
had gone on before, and it went on afterwards – one must agree
that it was monotonous to excess. In short, anything can be said
of world history, anything conceivable even by the most disordered imagination. There is only one thing that you can't say –
that it had anything to do with reason. The very first word would
choke you. And here is something that is always cropping up:
people are always appearing who are terribly sensible and moral,
terribly sage, terrible lovers of the human race, who really set
themselves, as the goal of their whole lives, to conduct themselves
in the noblest and most rational manner and let their light shine
before their neighbours, simply in order to prove to them that it is
possible to live one's life in this world both virtuously and ration-
ally. And what then? It is notorious that sooner or later many of
these philanthropists have towards the end of their life changed
their nature and furnished material for an anecdote, sometimes of
the most scandalous kind. Now I ask you, what can one expect of
man, as a creature endowed with such strange qualities? Shower
him with all earthly blessings, plunge him so deep into happiness
that nothing is visible but the bubbles rising to the surface of his
happiness, as if it were water; give him such economic prosperity
that he will have nothing left to do but sleep, eat gingerbread, and

worry about the continuance of world history – and he, I mean man, even then, out of mere ingratitude, out of sheer devilment, will commit some abomination. He will jeopardize his very gingerbread and deliberately will the most pernicious rubbish, the most uneconomic nonsense, simply and solely in order to alloy all this positive rationality with the element of his own pernicious fancy. It is precisely his most fantastic daydreams, his vulgarest foolishness, that he wants to cling to, just so that he can assert (as if it were absolutely essential) that people are still people and not piano-keys, as which they would be exposed to the threat of being so played on, even if it was by the laws of nature with their own hands, that they could not so much as want anything that was not tabulated in the almanacs. More than that: if men really turned out to be piano-keys, and if it was proved to them by science and mathematics, even then they would not see reason, but on the contrary would deliberately do something out of sheer ingratitude in order, in fact, to have their own way. And if they had not the means to do this, they would contrive to create destruction and chaos, invent various sufferings, and so still have their own way! They would launch curses upon the world, and since man alone can utter curses (it is his privilege and the thing that chiefly distinguishes him from the other animals), perhaps through cursing alone he would attain his end, to convince himself that he was a man and not a piano-key! If you say that all this, the chaos and darkness and cursing, could also be reduced to tables, so that the mere possibility of taking it into account beforehand would put a stop to it, and reason would still hold sway – in that case men would deliberately go mad, so as not to possess reason, and thus still get their own way! I believe this, I am prepared to answer for it, because it seems to me that the whole business of humanity consists solely in this – that a man should constantly prove to himself that he is a man and not a sprig in a barrel-organ! To prove it even at the expense of his own skin; to prove it even by becoming a troglodyte. And after that, how can I not offend against the rules, or refrain from expressing my satisfaction that all this hasn't happened yet, and meanwhile the devil alone knows what the will is or what it depends on?

You will exclaim (if you still deign to address any exclamations to me) that after all nobody is trying to deprive me of my will; that all anybody is trying to do is to arrange that my volition will of its own accord fall in with my normal interests, the laws of nature, and arithmetic.

Ah, gentlemen, what will have become of our wills when everything is graphs and arithmetic, and nothing is valid but two and two make four? Two and two will make four without any will of mine! Is that what one's own will means?

9

Gentlemen, of course I'm joking, and I know I am not doing it very successfully, but you know you mustn't take everything I say for a joke. I may be joking with clenched teeth. Gentlemen, there are some questions that torment me; answer them for me. For example, here you are wanting to wean man from his old habits and correct his will to make it conform to the demands of science and common sense. But how do you know that you not only can, but ought to remake man like that? What makes you conclude that it is absolutely *necessary* to correct man's volition in that way? In short, how do you know that such a correction will be good for man? And, to sum the whole thing up, why are you so *certain* that not flying in the face of his real, normal interests, certified by the deductions of reason and arithmetic, is really always for his good and must be a law for all mankind? After all, for the time being it is only your supposition. Even if we assume it as a rule of logic, it may not be a law for all mankind at all. Perhaps you think I'm mad, gentlemen? Let me make a reservation. I agree that man is an animal predominantly constructive, foredoomed to conscious striving towards a goal, and applying himself to the art of engineering, that is to the everlasting and unceasing construction of a road – *no matter where it leads*, and that the main point is not *where* it goes, but that it should go somewhere, and that a well-conducted child, even if he despises the engineering profession, should not surrender to that disastrous sloth which, as is well known, is the mother of all vices. Man loves construction and the laying out of roads, that is indisputable. But how is it that he is so passionately disposed to destruction and chaos? Tell me that! But on this subject I should like to put in two words of my own. Doesn't his passionate love for destruction and chaos (and nobody can deny that he is sometimes devoted to them; that is a fact), arise from his instinctive fear of attaining his goal and completing the building he is erecting? For all you know, perhaps it is only from a distance that he likes the building, and from close to he doesn't like it at all; perhaps he only likes building it, not living in it, and leaves it afterwards *aux animaux domestiques*, such as ants, sheep, etc. Ants' likes and dislikes are quite different. They have remarkable buildings of the same sort, that remain eternally undestroyed – ant-hills.

All respectable ants begin with the ant-hill, and they will probably end with it too, which does great credit to their constancy and their positive character. But man is a fickle and disreputable creature and perhaps, like a chess-player, is interested in the process of attaining his goal rather than the goal itself. And who knows, (nobody can say with certainty), perhaps man's sole purpose in this world consists in this uninterrupted process of attainment, or in other words in living, and not specifically in the goal, which of course must be something like twice two is four, that is, a formula; but after all, twice two is four is not life, gentlemen, but the beginning of death. At least, man has always feared this $2 \times 2 = 4$ formula, and I still fear it. We may suppose a man may do nothing but search for such equations, crossing the oceans and dedicating his life to the quest; but succeeding, really finding them – I swear he will be afraid of that. Really, he will feel that if he finds them, he will have nothing left to search for. When workmen have finished work, they at least receive their money, they go and spend it in the pub, they get hauled off to the police-station – that's enough to occupy them for a week. But where can mankind go? To say the least, something uncomfortable is to be noticed in man on the achievement of similar goals. He likes progress towards the goal, but he does not altogether care for the achievement of it, and that, of course, is ridiculous. In short, mankind is comically constructed; all this plainly amounts to a joke. But $2 \times 2 = 4$ is nevertheless an intolerable thing. Twice two is four is, in my opinion, nothing but impudence. 'Two and two make four' is like a cocky young devil standing across your path with arms akimbo and a defiant air. I agree that two and two make four is an excellent thing; but to give everything its due, two and two make five is also a very fine thing.

And why are you so firmly and triumphantly certain that only what is normal and positive – in short, only well-being – is good for man? Is reason mistaken about what is good? After all, perhaps prosperity isn't the only thing that pleases mankind, perhaps he is just as attracted to suffering. Perhaps suffering is just as good for him as prosperity. Sometimes a man is intensely, even passionately, attached to suffering – that is a fact. About this there is no need to consult universal history: ask yourself, if you are a man and have ever lived even in some degree. As for my own personal opinion, I find it somehow unseemly to love only well-being. Whether it's a good thing or a bad thing, smashing things is also sometimes very pleasant. I am not here standing up for suffering, or for well-being either. I am standing out for my own caprices and for having them guaranteed when necessary. There is no place for suffering in farces, for example, I know that. It is quite inconceivable in a millennium: suffering is doubt, negation, and what sort of millennium would it be of which one could have any doubts? All the same, I am certain that man will never deny himself destruction and chaos. Suffering – after all, that is the sole cause of consciousness. Although I declared to begin with that in my opinion consciousness is man's supreme misfortune, I know that man loves it and would not change it for any gratification. Consciousness is infinitely greater than, for example, two and two make four. After twice two is achieved there will of course be nothing left to do, much less to learn. All that will then be possible will be to shut off one's five senses and immerse oneself in meditation. But with consciousness, even if it has the same result, I mean that there will be nothing to do, at least one could sometimes resort to self-flagellation, and that stimulates, at any rate. It may be retrograde, but all the same it's better than nothing.

You believe in the Palace of Crystal, eternally inviolable, that is in something at which one couldn't furtively put out one's tongue or make concealed gestures of derision. But perhaps I fear this edifice just because it is made of crystal and eternally inviolable, and it will not be possible even to put out one's tongue at it in secret.

It's like this, you see: if instead of a palace it was a hen-house, and it began to rain, I might creep into the hen-house so as not to get wet, but I shouldn't take the hen-house for a palace out of gratitude because it had protected me from the rain. You laugh; you even say that in that case it doesn't matter whether it's a hen-house or a mansion. No, I answer, if not getting wet was all one had to live for.

But what if I have taken it into my head that that isn't the sole object of living, and if I have to live, let it be in a mansion? That is my will and my desire. You can drive it out of me only by changing my desire. Well, change it then; attract me by something else, give me a different ideal. Meanwhile, I still refuse to take a hen-house for a palace. Let us grant that a building of crystal is a castle in the air, that by the laws of nature it is a sheer impossibility, and that I have invented it out of nothing but my own stupidity and certain antiquated irrational habits of my generation. But what does it matter to me if it is an impossibility? What difference does it make to me, so long as it exists in my desires, or rather, exists while my desires last? Perhaps you are laughing again. Laugh if you like: I will accept all your ridicule, but all the same I won't say I've had enough to eat when I'm hungry, I won't be satisfied with compromise, with the constantly recurring decimal, merely because it exists by the laws of nature and exists *in reality*. I will not accept as my crowning wish a block of flats for poor tenants on thousand-year leases and, in any case, with 'Wagenheim, Dental Surgeon' as the signboard. Destroy my desire, blot out my ideals, show me something better, and I will follow you. Perhaps you will say it is not worth while to get involved; but in that case I can make the same answer to you. We are discussing seriously;

and if you don't choose to honour me with your attention, I'm not going to plead with you.

Meanwhile, I am still living and still wanting – and may my hand wither if I bring one brick to the building of that block of flats! Don't pay any attention to the fact that just now I rejected the palace of crystal for the sole reason that one won't be able to stick one's tongue out at it. . . . I didn't say that because I am so given to sticking out my tongue. Perhaps I was angry simply because no edifice at which it is impossible to stick out one's tongue is yet to be found among all your constructions. On the other hand, I would let my tongue be cut right out in mere gratitude if only things were so arranged that I never wanted to put it out again. What does it matter to me that that kind of building is impossible, and that one must content oneself with blocks of flats? Why was I made with such desires? Can I have been made for only one thing, to come at last to the conclusion that my whole make-up is nothing but a cheat? Is that the whole aim? I don't believe it.

Do you know one thing, though? I am certain that underground people like me must be kept in check. Though we may be capable of sitting underground for forty years without saying a word, if we do come out into the world and burst out, we will talk and talk and talk . . .

11

Last of all, gentlemen: it is best to do nothing! The best thing is conscious inertia! So long live the underground! Although I have said that I am green with envy of the normal man, I wouldn't like to be him in the circumstances in which I see him (even though I shall not cease to envy him, all the same). No, no, the underground is better, in any case. There one can at least. . . . Ach! The fact is I'm lying even now! I'm lying, because I know, as sure as two and two make four, that it isn't the underground that is better, but something different, entirely different, which I am eager for, but which I shall never find. Devil take the underground!

It would be better if I believed even a small part of everything I have written here. I swear, gentlemen, I don't believe a word, not one single little word, of all I have scribbled down! That is, I do perhaps believe it, but at the same time, I don't know why, I feel or I suspect, that I'm lying like a trooper.

'Then why have you written all this?' you ask me.

'Look, suppose I had put you somewhere for about forty years with nothing at all to do, and came to see you after forty years, in your underground, to find out what had become of you? Can a man really be left alone without occupation for forty years?'

'But that is no disgrace, it is not humiliating!' you may tell me, scornfully shaking your heads. 'You thirst for life, and you try to solve life's problems with muddled logic. And how troublesome and impudent your tricks are, and yet at the same time how terrified you are! You talk nonsense, and are satisfied with it; you are rude, but at the same time you are afraid of the consequences and beg our pardon. You assure us that you are afraid of nothing, and yet you try to coax us to be on your side. You try to convince us that your teeth are clenched, and yet at the same time you crack jokes to make us laugh. You know your witticisms are not very clever, but you are obviously quite satisfied with their literary merit. Perhaps you really have had to suffer sometimes, but you have no respect for your own sufferings. There is truth in you, but no virtue; out of the pettiest vanity you carry your truth to market to be exposed to scorn and shame. ... You really do want to say something, but you keep your last word hidden, because you haven't the resolution to speak it, only cowardly impudence. You pride yourself on your intellectual power, but you do nothing but vacillate, because although your brain works, your heart is clouded with depravity, and without a pure heart there can be no full, correct understanding. And you are so importunate, so thrusting, so full of airs and graces! Lies, lies, all lies!'

Of course, I have just this minute invented all these words of yours. They also come from under the ground. I have been listening to these words of yours through a chink for forty years. I made them up myself, I have nothing else to think about. It is not to be wondered at if they were got by heart and have acquired a literary form.

But you can't really and truly be so credulous as to imagine that I'm going to print all this and give it you to read, can you? And here is the problem that puzzles me: why, in fact, do I address you as 'gentlemen', and speak to you just as if I was genuinely speaking to readers? Confessions of the kind I intend to begin setting forth do not get printed or offered to others to read. At least, I don't possess enough strength of mind for that, and I don't consider it necessary to possess it. But, you see, a fancy has come into my head, and cost what it may I want to translate it into reality. This is the point:

In every man's remembrances there are things he will not reveal to everybody, but only to his friends. There are other things he will not reveal even to his friends, but only to himself, and then only under a pledge of secrecy. Finally, there are some things that a man is afraid to reveal even to himself, and any honest man accumulates a pretty fair number of such things. That is to say, the more respectable a man is, the more of them he has. At least, only a little time ago, I made up my mind to recall some of my former adventures, but up till now I have only skirted round them, with, indeed, some uneasiness. But now, when I am not only remembering, but have decided to write them down, now I want to test whether it is possible to be completely open with oneself and not be afraid of the whole truth. I may remark, by the way, that Heine states that trustworthy autobiographies are almost an impossibility, and that a man will probably never tell the truth about himself. According to him Rousseau, for example, lied about himself in his *Confessions*, even deliberately, out of vanity. I am sure Heine was right; I can understand very well how vanity can make one accuse oneself of downright crimes, and I can even see what kind of vanity is responsible. But Heine was talking of men making public confessions. I, however, am writing for myself alone, and let me declare once and for all that if I write as if I were addressing an audience, it is only for show and because it makes it easier for me to write. It is a form, nothing else; I shall never have any readers. I have already made that clear . . .

Well, but here, perhaps, it is possible to cavil, and to ask me, 'If you really are not counting on having readers, why do you make these compacts with yourself, and in writing too; that is, that you will not observe order and system, that you will put down whatever you remember, and so on and so forth? Who are you explaining to? Who are you making excuses to?'

Wait a minute, I answer.

There is a whole psychology involved in this. Perhaps it is simply that I am a coward. Or perhaps I am imagining an audience in front of me on purpose so that I shall conduct myself becomingly when the times comes for me to write. There may be thousands of reasons.

But there is another question: precisely why, for what purpose, do I want to write? If it isn't for readers, surely I could just remember everything without putting it down on paper?

Exactly; but on paper it will be somehow more impressive. There is something awe-inspiring about it, one sits more severely in judgement on oneself, one's style is enhanced. Besides, perhaps I really shall get relief from writing it down. Now, for example, I am particularly oppressed by one ancient memory. It sprang clearly into my mind the other day, and since then has remained with me like a tiresome tune that keeps on nagging at one. And yet one must get rid of it. I have hundreds of memories like it; but from time to time one out of the hundreds becomes prominent and oppresses me. For some reason I believe that if I write it down I shall get rid of it. Why not try?

Finally, I'm bored, and I never have anything to do. Writing is really something like work. They say work makes a man honest and good. Well, it's a chance, at least.

It is snowing just now, in wet, dingy, swirling flakes. It was snowing yesterday too, and the day before as well. I think it was the sleet that reminded me of this incident that now refuses to leave me alone. So let this be a story apropos of the falling sleet.

Chapter Two

A STORY OF THE FALLING SLEET

AT that time I was no more than twenty-four years old. Even then my life was gloomy, untidy, and barbarously solitary. I had no friends, and even avoided speaking to people, retreating further and further into my corner. At work, in the office, I even tried not to look at anybody, and I saw very clearly that my colleagues not only considered me a queer fish, but – or so it always seemed to me – even almost loathed me. I used to wonder how it was that nobody else but me seemed to think he was regarded with loathing. One of the clerks in our office had a repulsive, pimply face and even looked almost criminal. With such a horrible face I don't think I would have dared to look straight at anybody. Another had a uniform he had been wearing for so long that his neighbourhood positively stank. Yet neither of these gentlemen was embarrassed, whether on account of his clothes, or his face, or on moral grounds. Neither the one nor the other imagined that he was regarded with loathing; or if they did, it didn't matter to them so long as their superiors hadn't that attitude. Now it is quite clear to me that, because of my infinite vanity and the consequent demands I made on myself, I very often looked at myself with frantic dislike, sometimes amounting to disgust, and therefore attributed the same attitude to everybody else. For example, I hated my face, I thought it was a scoundrelly face, and I even suspected there was something servile about it, and so every time I went to the office, I made agonizing efforts to seem as independent as possible, so that I should not be suspected of subservience, and to give my face the most well-bred expression I could manage. 'All right, my face is plain,' I thought, 'but on the other hand I will see to it that it looks noble, expressive, and above all, extremely clever.' But I was utterly and painfully aware that my face would never express any of these perfections. What was the most awful of all was that I thought it was definitely stupid. And I would have been content with cleverness by itself. I would even have been content with a servile expression if only my face could have seemed terribly clever at the same time.

Needless to say, I hated all the members of my department from the first to the last, and despised them, and yet somehow feared them as well. At times I would even rate them above myself. This quite often happened to me at that time; at one moment I despised them, at the next I felt they were superior to me. A decent and intelligent man cannot be vain without making inordinate demands on himself and at times despising himself to the point of hatred. But whether I despised them or rated them above myself, I dropped my eyes before almost everybody I came across. I even tried experiments: 'Shall I be able to bear so-and-so's eyes upon me?' – and I was always the first to lower my eyes. This drove me to frenzy. I was also morbidly afraid of being ridiculous and therefore slavishly observed the ordinary conventions in every outward appearance; I enthusiastically followed the common rut and was terrified of developing any eccentricity. But how was I to keep it up? I was painfully advanced, as a man of our time should be. But they were dullards, as like one another as a flock of sheep. Perhaps I was the only one in the whole office who always seemed to myself a slave and a coward precisely because I also seemed (to myself) civilized. But I not only seemed, I really was a coward and a slave. I say this without shame. Every decent man in this age is, and must be, a coward and a slave. That is his normal condition. I am profoundly certain of this. That is how he is made and what he was made for. And not only at the present time, because of what may be accidental circumstances, but at all times, a decent man must be a coward and a slave. This is a law of the nature of all decent people on the earth. Even if one of them puts on a show of bravery before somebody else, he ought not to take comfort from that or let himself be carried away by it: he is only showing off to the other person. This is the only and the eternal solution. Only donkeys and mules make a show of bravery, and they only to a limited extent. It is not worth while paying any attention to them, because they count for exactly nothing.

There was one other circumstance that tormented me at that time, namely that nobody else was like me and I wasn't like anybody else. 'I am one person, and they are everybody', I would think, falling into a brown study.

It is evident from this that I was still only a boy.

Sometimes contradictory things happened. There were times when it became disgusting to go to the office; things reached such a pitch that I returned home physically ill. But then suddenly, for no reason at all, a streak of indifference and scepticism would reveal itself (everything went in streaks for me), and I would laugh at my own impatience and squeamishness, and reproach myself with *romanticism*. Now I would refuse to speak to anybody, and now again I would not only get into conversation, I would even make up my mind to make friends with them. All my fastidiousness would suddenly disappear, without reason. Who knows, perhaps it had never been real, perhaps it was something affected, made up out of books. I haven't settled that question to this day. Once I went so far as to become really intimate with them; I began visiting their homes, playing whist, drinking vodka, talking about promotion.... But now allow me to digress.

We Russians, generally speaking, have never been stupid transcendental romantics of the German, or especially the French, kind, who are not affected by anything; the earth may crack under their feet, all France may perish on the barricades, but they remain the same, they won't make the slightest change even for the sake of decency, but still go on singing their transcendental hymns right up, one might say, to the grave, because they are fools. But here, on Russian soil, there are no fools, as everybody knows: that is what distinguishes us from all the other, Germanic, countries. Consequently, transcendental souls are not found among us in their pure form. It was all our positivistic journalists and critics of that time, hunting out the Kostanzhogols and Uncle Peter Ivanoviches, and foolishly taking them for our ideal, who invented all that about our romantics being as visionary as in Germany or France. On the contrary, the characteristics of our romantics are the complete and direct opposite of those of the European transcendental, and no European yard-stick fits them. (Allow me to use that word 'romantic' – it is an old word, respected, much-used and familiar to everybody.) What is characteristic of our romantic is understanding everything, seeing everything and seeing it incomparably more clearly than the most practical intellects; never tolerating anybody or anything, and yet never shrinking from anything in disgust; always sidestepping difficulties and always prudently ready to knuckle under; never losing sight of his practical and profitable goals (such as official quarters, nice little pensions, titles and decorations), keeping them in view through all his enthusiasms and slim volumes of lyric verse, while at the same time preserving the 'highest and best' inviolate within himself to the end of his days, and incidentally preserving himself, wrapped like a precious piece of jewellery in cotton-wool, if only for the benefit of that same 'highest and best'. Our romantic is a man of the widest sympathies, and our supreme scoundrel, I can assure you of that – and from experience. Of course, this is all if the romantic is clever. But what am I saying? The romantic is always clever; I merely wished to say that although we have had romantic fools among us, it doesn't count, and was only because in the prime of life they degenerated finally into Germans and, the better to preserve their precious jewel, settled somewhere over there, mostly in Weimar or the Black Forest. For example, I sincerely despised the activities of my department, and it was sheer necessity that kept me from expressing my disgust, because I sat there and received money for those activities. The result was – note this – that I kept my mouth shut. Our romantic will sooner go mad (though this happens only rarely), than express his disgust if he has no other post in view, and he will never be sacked with ignominy, although it is just possible he might be carted off to a madhouse because he thinks he's the king of Spain, but only if he's gone very mad indeed. It's only the wishy-washy and the anaemic who go mad here. There are countless numbers of romantics, though – and they subsequently reach very high ranks in the service. Extraordinary versatility! And what capacity for the most contradictory sensations! Even then I comforted myself with these ideas, as I do still. That's why we have so many generous spirits who even in the last degradation never lose their ideals; and although they won't lift a finger for their ideals, although they are declared thieves and gangsters, they are still tearfully devoted to

their original ideals and extraordinarily pure of heart. Yes, it is
only among us that the most accomplished scoundrel can be utterly, even exaltedly, pure of heart without in the least ceasing to
be a scoundrel. I repeat, very often such finished rogues ('rogues' is
a word I like using) emerge from among our romantics displaying
such a feeling for reality and such knowledge of what is practical
that the astounded authorities and public can only click their
tongues in amazement.

The versatility is indeed astounding, and God knows what it
will turn into or how it will elaborate itself in the circumstances
of the immediate future, and what more distant promises it will
dangle before us. And the material's not bad! I do not say this out
of any kind of ludicrous or jingoistic patriotism. I am sure, however, that you think I am being funny again. But perhaps the
opposite is true, and you believe this is what I really think. In any
case, gentlemen, I shall regard either opinion from you as an
honour and a particular pleasure. And now please forgive this
digression.

I did not, of course, keep up my friendships with my colleagues,
but soon washed my hands of them; indeed, in my still youthful
inexperience I even stopped speaking to them, as though I had cut
them off. This, however, only happened to me once. Generally
speaking, I was always alone.

At home, to begin with, I did a lot of reading. I wanted to stifle
all that was smouldering inside me with external impressions and
reading was for me the only possible source of external impressions. Reading, of course, helped me a great deal – it excited,
delighted and tormented me. But at times it bored me to death. I
wanted to be active, and I would suddenly plunge into dark, sub-
terranean, nasty – not so much vices as vicelets. My measly little
passions were keen and fiery from my constant morbid irritability.
I used to have hysterical outbursts accompanied with tears and
convulsions. I had no resort but reading – I mean that there was
nothing in my environment at that time that I could respect and
feel attracted to. Moreover, an anguish of longing would boil up
inside me; a hysterical thirst for contradictions and contrasts
would appear, and I would embark on dissipations. If I have said

so much, it was not in order to justify myself in the least. ... But no! that was a lie! To justify myself was exactly what I wanted to do. That observation is made for my own benefit, gentlemen. I won't lie. I have given my word ...

My debauches were solitary, nocturnal, secret, frightened, dirty, and full of a shame that did not leave me at the most abandoned moments, and indeed at those moments reached such a pitch that I called down curses on my own head. Even then I already carried the underground in my soul. I was terribly afraid I should be met or seen and recognized. My paths took me through various extremely murky places. One night, walking past a tavern, I saw through a window some gentlemen round a billiard-table using their cues as weapons, and throwing one of their number through a window. At another time I should have been revolted; but this happened to be at a moment when I envied the gentleman who had been flung out so much that I even entered the tavern and went into the billiard-room: 'Perhaps I shall get into a fight too,' I thought, 'and be thrown out of the window.'

I wasn't drunk, but what would you have? – dejection was driving me hysterical. But nothing happened. I turned out to be incapable of even jumping out of a window, and I was going away without having fought.

I was prevented from taking the first step by an officer.

I had been standing by the table and unknowingly blocking the way; he wanted to get past, and he took me by the shoulders and silently – with no warning or explanation – moved me from the place where I stood to another; then he walked past as if he hadn't even seen me. I could have forgiven him for striking me, but I couldn't forgive that moving me from place to place without even seeing me.

The devil only knows what I would have given just then for a real, regular quarrel, more decent, more, so to say, literary! I had been treated like an insect. The officer was a six-footer; I was short and skinny. All the same, I had a quarrel on my hands; I had only to protest and I would certainly have been forced out of the window. But I thought better of it and preferred ... to stay resentfully sulking in the background.

I left the tavern agitated and disturbed, went straight home, and next day went on with my petty debaucheries more timidly, spiritlessly, and sadly than ever, with tears in my eyes, as it were – but all the same, I went on. Don't imagine that I had slunk away from that officer because of cowardice, though; I was never a coward at heart, although I constantly acted like one, but – don't laugh yet, I can explain it; I can explain everything, you may be sure.

Oh, if only that officer had been the sort who would consent to fight a duel! But no, he was one of those gentlemen (long vanished, alas), who preferred to act with billiard cues or, like Gogol's Lieutenant Pirogov, through the authorities. They never fought duels and would have considered a duel with *our* sort, mere penpushers, infra dig. in any case; indeed, they looked upon duels in general as something inconceivable, free-thinking, and French, but they themselves were always ready to give offence, especially if they were six feet tall.

It was not cowardice that made me shrink, but infinite vanity. I was not afraid of the height of six feet, or the fact that I should be painfully beaten and thrown out of the window; I really had no lack of physical courage, but I had not enough moral courage. I was afraid that everybody present – from the impudent lout of a marker to the least of the greasy-collared low-grade clerks hanging about, covered with pimples and rotten with disease – would fail to understand, and laugh at me when I made my protest speaking in a bookish style. Because it is impossible to this day to discuss a point of honour – I don't mean honour, but a point of honour (*point d'honneur*) – in anything but literary language. In ordinary speech one can't even mention a 'point of honour'. I was quite sure (the instinct for realism, in spite of all my romantic attitudes!) that they would all simply laugh till they cried, and the officer would not simply, that is inoffensively, thrash me, but would certainly bump me with his knee all round the billiardtable, and only after that have mercy on me and let me escape through the window. Of course this pitiful story was not allowed to end there, as far as I was concerned. I often met the officer in the street after that, and I took particular notice of him. The only thing I don't know is whether he recognized me or not. Probably not, as I concluded from certain indications. But I, I looked at him with hatred and rage, and this went on ... for several years. My anger even grew and deepened with the years. I began by trying to find out all about this officer. This was difficult for me, because I didn't know anybody. But once somebody in the street hailed him by his name as I followed him at a short distance as though he had me on a lead, and so I learnt his surname. Another time I followed him all the way home, and for ten copecks found out from the porter which was his staircase, on which floor he lived, whether he was living alone, and so on–everything, in short, that could be learnt from a porter. One morning the idea suddenly occurred to me of writing a description of the officer in condemnatory terms – as a caricature, in a kind of story, although I never engaged in literary activities. I enjoyed writing the story. I was censorious, even libellous; at first I disguised the name so slightly that it could be recognized at once, but later, on riper reflection, I changed it completely, and then I sent the story to *Annals of the Fatherland*. But satire was not then in fashion and my story was not published. I was bitterly disappointed. – Sometimes my rage positively choked me. Finally I made up my mind to challenge my enemy to a duel. I composed a really beautiful and charming letter to him, begging him to apologize; I hinted pretty plainly at a duel if he refused. The letter was couched in such terms that if the officer had the slightest understanding of 'the highest and the best' he would come running to me at once, fall on my neck and offer me his friendship. And how splendid that would be. We should begin a new life, and what a life! 'He could protect me with his influential position, and I could develop his better qualities with my culture and ... well, my ideas, and all sorts of things could happen!' You must realize that two years had passed since he insulted me, and my challenge was no more than an outrageous anachronism, in spite of all the cleverness of my letter in explaining and covering up that untimeliness. But thank God (I still thank the Almighty for it with tears in my eyes), I didn't send my letter. It makes my blood run cold to remember what might have happened if I had sent it. And then suddenly ... suddenly I got my revenge in the simplest fashion, and by a stroke of sheer genius! I was struck all at once by a brilliant idea. Sometimes, on holidays, I would go to the Nevsky Prospect in the afternoon and enjoy a walk along the sunny side. That is, I didn't actually enjoy my walk at all: I experienced an endless series of torments, crushing humiliations and attacks of spleen; but probably that was necessary to me. I darted like a minnow through the passers-by, in a most ungraceful fashion, constantly giving way to generals, officers of the Horse Guards and the Hussars, and fine ladies; at those moments I felt a spasmodic pain in my heart and hot flushes down my spine at the thought of the wretched inadequacy of my costume and the mean vulgarity of my small figure darting about. It was an agonizing torment, a never-ending unbearable humiliation, caused by the suspicion, constantly growing into clear-cut certainty, that compared to them I was a fly, a nasty obscene fly – cleverer, better educated, nobler than any of them, that goes without saying – but a fly, always getting out of everybody's way, humiliated and slighted by everybody. Why I courted this torment, why I went to the Nevsky Prospect, I don't know. But I felt *drawn* there on every possible occasion.

I had already begun to experience surges of those pleasures I spoke of in my first chapter. After the incident with the officer, I was even more strongly drawn to the Nevsky Prospect; it was there that I met him most often, there that I feasted my eyes on him. He also went there chiefly on holidays. Although he too moved aside for generals and important personages, and wriggled past them like an eel, he simply trampled over nobodies of my sort, or even rather better than my sort; he bore straight down on them as though there was a clear space in front of him, and never in any circumstances gave way. Observing him fed the fires of my resentment, and ... resentfully, I moved out of his way every time. It was torture to me that even in the street I could not manage to be his equal. 'Why are you invariably the first to give way?' I nagged at myself sometimes, hysterical with rage, when I woke up at three o'clock in the morning. 'Why is it always you, not him? There's no law about it, is there? nothing on the statute-books? Well, then, let's share and share alike, as usually happens when people of any delicacy meet: he partly gives way, and you give way an equal amount, and you pass one another in mutual respect.' But it never happened like that: I was the one who stepped aside, and he never even noticed that I did so – and then I was struck by the most marvellous idea. 'What,' I thought, 'if I were to meet him and ... not step aside? Deliberately refuse to step aside, even if it meant running into him? What about that, eh?' This audacious notion took possession of me bit by bit, to such an extent that it gave me no peace. I dreamed of it, ceaselessly and vividly, and on purpose went oftener to the Nevsky Prospect, so that I could more clearly picture to myself how I would act when the time came. I was full of enthusiasm. More and more my intended action began to seem both likely and possible. 'Of course, I shan't exactly jostle him,' I thought, already mollified in advance by my enjoyment of the idea, 'but just ... not get out of his way, brush against him, not painfully, but just shoulder to shoulder, exactly as much as is laid down by the conventions; so that I shall collide with him as much as he collides with me.' At last my mind was completely made up. But the preparations took a great deal of time. The first thing was that when I carried out my plan I must look more respectable and take pains with my clothes. 'In any case, if there is, for example, a scene in public (and there is enough public and to spare there: a countess walks there, and Prince D., and the whole literary world), I must be well dressed; it makes a good impression, and puts us at once on an equal footing, in a way, in the eyes of good society.' To this end I drew my salary in advance and bought black gloves and a decent hat from Churkin's. Black gloves seemed to me both more respectable and more *bon ton* than the yellow ones that tempted me at first. 'The colour is too glaring, looks too much as if a man is trying to be conspicuous,' and I did not take the yellow gloves. I had had a good shirt, with white bone studs, ready for some time, but the question of an overcoat delayed me for a long time. My overcoat was not bad in itself, it kept me warm; but it was lined with wadding, and had a raccoon collar, which constituted the essence of flunkeydom. I must at whatever cost change the collar and buy instead a beaver one such as officers wore. For this purpose I began to frequent the arcades, and after a few attempts fixed my sights on a cheap imitation beaver. Although these imitation beavers very soon show signs of wear and begin to seem shabby, they look very nice at first, when they are new; and after all, I only needed it for one occasion. I asked the price: it was dear, all the same. After profound deliberation I decided to sell my raccoon collar. The remaining amount, a very considerable one, I decided I would try to borrow from my immediate superior, Anton Antonovich Setochkin, an unassuming but solid and worthy man who never lent money to anybody, but to whom I had been specially recommended when I entered the government service by the important personage who had procured the post for me. I was terribly worried. Asking Anton Antonovich for money seemed to me a monstrous and shameful thing. For two or three nights it even prevented me from sleeping, and indeed at that time I did not ever sleep much; I was in a turmoil, and my heartbeats now seemed to sink and die away, now became a heavy thumping and throbbing. ... Anton Antonovich was taken aback at first, then he frowned on my request, then he thought better of it and made the loan in return for a receipt giving him the right to be repaid the sum he had lent me out of my salary in two weeks' time. Thus at last everything was ready; the beautiful beaver collar reigned in the place of the vile raccoon, and I began a gradual approach to the deed itself. After all, I couldn't just decide on the spur of the moment and at the first opportunity; this affair must be managed skilfully and by degrees. But I confess that after many vain efforts I was almost reduced to despair: we never should come into collision, that was flat! Once, when I wasn't ready and had no plans made, it looked all at once as if we were on the point of colliding – and again I stood aside and he went past without even seeing me. I began putting up prayers every time I approached him that God would strengthen my resolution. Once, when I had definitely made my mind up, I ended by simply falling under his feet, because my courage failed in the very last second, when I was only about two inches away from him. He advanced calmly upon me and I rolled aside like a ball. That night I was again feverish and delirious. But suddenly everything ended in the best possible fashion. On the previous night I had definitely decided not to pursue an enterprise foredoomed to failure but to leave it unfulfilled, and with this in mind I went out to walk along the Nevsky Prospect for the last time, so as to see how it was I came to be leaving my purpose unfulfilled. Suddenly, three paces away from my adversary, I unexpectedly made up my mind, scowled fiercely, and ... our shoulders came squarely into collision! I did not yield an inch, but walked past on an exactly equal footing! He did not even glance round, and pretended he had not noticed; but he was only pretending, I am certain of that. I am certain of it to this day! Of course I was the greatest sufferer, since he was the stronger; but that was not the point. The point was that I had attained my object, upheld my dignity, not yielded an inch, and publicly placed myself on an equal social footing with him. I returned home completely vindicated. I was delighted. I sang triumphant arias from the Italian operas. Of course I shall not describe what happened to me a couple of days later; if you have read my first chapter, 'The Underground', you will be able to guess for yourselves. – The officer was later transferred elsewhere; it is fourteen years since I last saw him. Where is he now, my darling officer? Whom is he trampling down now?

2

But my period of dissipation was coming to an end and I was becoming sickened. I began to feel remorse, but I drove it away: it was sickening too. Little by little, however, I got used to that. I got used to everything, that is not exactly got used, but consented to put up with it. But I had one resource that reconciled all these contradictions – escaping into 'all that is best and highest', in my dreams, of course. I dreamed endlessly. I dreamed for three months, crouching in my corner, and you may rest assured that during those moments I was not in the least like that humble and chicken-hearted gentleman who sewed an imitation beaver collar on his overcoat. I had turned into a hero. My six-foot lieutenant wouldn't even have been allowed to call on me. I couldn't even remember what he looked like. What my dreams were and how I could content myself with them is difficult to say now, but they contented me then. Particularly sweet and powerful were the dreams that came to me after a bout of dissipation, accompanied by repentance and tears, curses and raptures. There were moments of such positive ecstasy, such happiness, that I swear I felt not the slighest stirring of derision deep inside me. There was faith, and hope, and love. The fact is that at that time I blindly believed that by some miracle, through some outside influence, all *this* would suddenly be drawn aside like a curtain, and a wide horizon would open out before me, a field of suitable activity, philanthropic, noble and above all ready-made (I never knew exactly what, but the great point is that it was all ready for me), and I would emerge into God's sunlight, practically riding a white horse and crowned with laurel. I couldn't even conceive of playing a secondary part, and that is why in actuality I quite contentedly filled the last of all. Either a hero, or dirt, there was nothing in between. That was my undoing, because in the mire I comforted myself with the idea that the rest of the time I was a hero, it was the hero who was wallowing in the dirt: for an ordinary man, I felt, it is shameful to roll in filth, but a hero is above really becoming filthy, and so I can let myself experience the dirt. It is worth noticing that these waves of 'all that is best and highest' swept over me even in the heat of debauchery, coming in distinct pulsations as though to make their presence felt, but their coming did not destroy the passions; on the contrary, it seemed to enhance them by contrast, and the waves were just frequent enough to add spice to the dish. The spice was made up of defiance, suffering, and tortured interior analysis, and all these torments and pinpricks imparted a certain piquancy, and even a meaning, to my debauchery – in short, they fully performed the function of a good sauce. All this even had its elements of profundity. Indeed, could I have consented to lend myself to the simple, vulgar, immediate and petty dirtiness of ignorant little clerks and submit to all that filth?! What would have remained in it to attract me and tempt me out into the streets at night? No, sir, I have a high-minded slant on everything . . .

But how much love, oh lord, how much love I used to experience in those dreams of mine, those escapes into 'all that is best and highest', although it was mere fantasy, that love, not applied in reality to any actual human object; but there was so much abundance of it that later I never really felt the need of any object to project it on to: that would have been a superfluous luxury. Everything always ended happily, however, with a lazy and entrancing transition to art; that is, to beautiful ready-made images of life, forcibly wrenched from poets and novelists and adapted to every possible kind of service and requirement. For example, I triumphed over everybody; everybody else was routed and compelled to recognize my supremacy voluntarily, and I forgave them all. I, a famous poet and a courtier, fell in love; I received countless millions, and immediately bestowed them on the whole human race, at the same time confessing all my shameful deeds to all the world, deeds which of course were not simply shameful, but had in them an extremely large admixture of the 'best and highest', a touch of Manfred. Everybody wept and embraced me (how unfeeling they would have shown themselves otherwise), and I went out, barefooted and hungry, to preach new ideas and rout the forces of reaction at Austerlitz. Then a march was played, there was an amnesty, the Pope agreed to leave Rome and go to Brazil; then there was a great ball for all Italy at the Villa Borghese, which is on Lake Como, but Lake Como had been transferred to Rome on purpose for the occasion; then a theatrical performance in the open air, and so on and so forth – as if you didn't know! You will say that it is base and vulgar to make a parade of all this now, after confessing to so many raptures and tears. But why is it base? You don't think, do you, that I am ashamed of all this, or that all this was sillier than anything in your own lives, gentlemen? Besides, I assure you that some of it was not at all badly staged. ... Not everything took place on Lake Como. You are right, however; it really is both base and vulgar. And basest of all is that I have now begun to make excuses for myself to you. And worse still, that I am now making this remark. But enough; otherwise there will be no end to it; everything will be baser than everything else.

But I was not in a position to dream for more than three months at a time, and I began to feel an irresistible urge to plunge into

society. To plunge into society meant for me to pay visits to the
head of my section, Anton Antonovich Setochkin. In all my life
he was the only person with whom I was on continuously
friendly terms, and even I now find this surprising. But I went to
see him only at such periods, when my dreams were so happy that
I absolutely must embrace somebody, indeed all mankind; and for
this I must have available at least one real living person. I had to
go to Anton Antonovich's, however, on Tuesdays (his day for
receiving visitors), and consequently I must always postpone the
necessity of embracing mankind until a Tuesday. Anton Antonovich lived up three flights of stairs at Five Corners, in four
tiny low-ceilinged rooms, economically furnished and jaundiced-
looking. He had two daughters, and their aunt poured out tea for
him. The daughters – one was thirteen and the other fourteen, and
both had snub noses – always made me feel shy, because they were
always whispering to one another and giggling. The host usually
sat in his study, on a leather sofa in front of the table, with one of
his elderly guests, an official from our Ministry or even from one
of the others. I never saw more than two or three visitors there,
and those always the same ones. The talk was about excise duties,
arguments in the Senate, salaries, promotion, His Excellency the
Minister and how to get on the right side of him, and so on. I had
enough patience to sit beside these people like a dummy for about
four hours, listening to them and not daring, indeed not able, to
say a word to them myself. I would sit there dumb, almost para-
lysed, and sometimes breaking into a sweat; but it did me good.
Returning home, I was able to lay aside for a time my desire to
embrace all mankind.

I had another acquaintance as well, however; Simonov, an old
schoolfellow of mine. There were probably a good many of my
former schoolfellows in St Petersburg, but I had nothing to do
with them and had even stopped speaking to them in the street. I
had perhaps even changed to a different Ministry so as not to be
with them, and to make a complete break with my hateful boy-
hood. Curses on that school and those dreadful days in the prison-
house. In short, I parted from my schoolfellows as soon as I regained my freedom. There remained only one or two with whom I

exchanged greetings when we met. One of them was the placid and equable Simonov, who had not stood out in any way at school, but in whom I had discerned a certain independence and integrity of character. I don't think that he was even particularly limited. At one time I had spent some rather pleasant moments with him, but they had not lasted long and seemed to have suddenly clouded over. He evidently found the remembrance of them burdensome, and always seemed afraid that I would lapse into the old tone again. I suspected that he found me extremely repellent, but all the same I went on going to see him, because I was not absolutely certain of this.

So it was that one Thursday, unable to endure my solitude, and knowing that Anton Antonovich's door was not open on Thursdays, I remembered Simonov. As I climbed up to his rooms on the fourth floor, I was thinking that the gentleman found me tiresome and there was no use going to see him. But as considerations of this kind always ended by further encouraging me to get into ambiguous situations, I went in. It was almost a year since the last time I had seen Simonov.

3

I found two more of my old schoolfellows with him. They were evidently discussing something important. They paid hardly any attention to my arrival, which was strange, since it was years since we had met. Evidently they looked on me as something in the nature of a very ordinary fly. I was not treated in that way even in school, although everybody hated me there. I understood, of course, that they must now despise me for my unsuccessful career in the service, for having let myself go, wearing shabby clothes, and so on – things which in their eyes proclaimed my incompetence and unimportance. All the same, I was not expecting such contemptuous treatment. Simonov seemed astonished that I had come. All this took me aback; I sat down, somewhat depressed, and began to listen to their discussion.

It was a serious and even heated conversation on the subject of a farewell dinner which these gentlemen meant to organize the

following day for their friend Zverkov, an officer in the army, who
was being sent to a distant Province. Monsieur Zverkov had been
at school with me during all my time there. I began to detest him
in the upper forms. In the lower forms he had been merely a lively
pretty boy whom everybody liked. I, however, disliked him even
in the lower forms, precisely because he was good-looking and
lively. He did uniformly badly at lessons, and the longer he stayed
the worse he did: but he succeeded in passing his final exam-
inations because he had influential friends. In his last year at
school he inherited an estate of two hundred souls, and since
almost all of us were poor, he began to put on airs even with us.
He was a complete and utter vulgarian, but a decent chap even
when he was showing off hardest. Among us, in spite of our
merely external, fantastic and stilted formulas of the *point
d'honneur*, everybody with few exceptions paid court to Zverkov,
and the more subserviently as he put on more airs. And this was
not for any gain to themselves, but simply because he was a
person endowed with the gifts of nature. Besides, it had somehow
become the accepted opinion among us that Zverkov was an
expert in social dexterity and good manners. This last particularly
infuriated me. I hated the harshly self-confident sound of his voice,
his excessive admiration of his own witticisms, which were extremely stupid, although he was sharp-tongued; I hated his handsome silly face (for which, however, I would gladly have
exchanged my *clever* one) and his careless, lordly manner of an
officer of the forties. I hated the way he talked of his future successes with women (he had decided not to try his luck with them
before he had acquired his epaulets, and was therefore impatient
for these) and of how he would be perpetually fighting duels. I
remember how I, always the silent listener, once suddenly went
for Zverkov when he was talking to his friends in a free period
about these coming delights, positively frolicking like a young
puppy in the sunlight, and all at once declared that not one of the
wenches on his estate would escape his attentions, he would exercise his *droit de seigneur*, and if the moujiks dared to protest, he
would have them all flogged and double the dues he exacted from
the bearded ruffians. Our cads were applauding him and I attacked

him, not because I felt the slightest sympathy for his peasant girls and their fathers, but simply because an insect like that was getting such applause. I won the day, but Zverkov, although stupid, was also cheerful and impudent, and laughed it off so successfully that I was not completely victorious: the laugh remained on his side. Later he several times got the better of me, but smilingly, without malice, in a casual and jesting way. I was too angry and contemptuous to answer him. After we left school he made some effort to keep in touch with me, and I did not resist, because I was flattered by it; but, naturally enough, our ways soon parted. Then I used to hear about his successes as a lieutenant in barracks and his dissipations. Later there were other reports, of how well he was doing in his army career. He no longer acknowledged me in the street, and I suspected that he was afraid of compromising himself by having anything to do with such an insignificant personage. On one occasion I saw him at the theatre, in the third circle, already wearing the aiguillettes of a staff officer. He was dancing attendance on the daughters of an old general and paying court to them. After about three years he was running terribly to seed, although he was still handsome and agile; he seemed somehow puffy and had begun to put on weight; it was plain that by about thirty he would be both fat and flabby. It was this Zverkov, now leaving the capital, that my companions were designing to entertain at dinner. They had been constantly in his company all through the three years, although I am sure that in their own hearts they did not consider themselves his equals.

One of Simonov's two visitors was Ferfichkin, a Russo-German – a small man with a monkey-like face, a stupid fool who poked fun at everybody, and my bitterest enemy ever since we were in the lowest form, a nasty insolent little braggart, posing as a man of extremely touchy sense of honour, although he was of course an abject little coward. He was one of those admirers of Zverkov who played up to him from interested motives and frequently borrowed money from him. Simonov's other visitor, Trudolyubov, was an ordinary sort of person, a military type, tall, with a chilly air, quite honourable, but kowtowing to every kind of success and incapable of discussing anything but promotion. He was some sort of distant connection of Zverkov's and this, stupidly enough, gave him some importance among us. He always considered me a nobody, but treated me tolerably well, if not altogether courteously.

'Well, at seven roubles each,' said Trudolyubov, 'with the three of us, twenty-one roubles – we can dine pretty well. Zverkov won't pay, of course.'

'Well, of course not, if we're inviting him,' answered Simonov decisively.

'Do you really think,' put in Ferfichkin, with the presumptuous zeal of an impudent valet boasting of the decorations of his master the general, 'do you really think Zverkov will allow us to bear the whole cost? He'll accept out of delicacy, but on the other hand he'll stand us half a dozen bottles of the best.'

'Why, what do four of us want with half a dozen bottles?' asked Trudolyubov, with no attention for anything but the half dozen.

'So three of us, with Zverkov four, twenty-one roubles, at the Hotel de Paris, tomorrow at five o'clock,' Simonov, who had been chosen to make the arrangements, finally summed things up.

'Why twenty-one?' I asked, with some agitation, making it plain that I was offended; 'if you count me in it will be twenty-eight roubles, not twenty-one.'

It seemed to me that to propose myself so suddenly and unexpectedly was quite a splendid gesture, and they would all be conquered and regard me with respect.

'You don't really want to come, do you?' asked Simonov, annoyed, and avoiding my eyes. He knew me by heart.

I was furious that he should know me through and through.

'Why not? I was at school with him too, I think, and I confess I am hurt at being left out,' I began to storm.

'Where were we supposed to look for you?' put in Ferfichkin rudely. 'You were always on bad terms with Zverkov,' added Trudolyubov, frowning. But I had seized on the idea and would not let go.

'I don't think anybody has the right to pass judgement on that,' I replied, with a tremor in my voice, as if God knows what had happened. 'Perhaps it is precisely because we weren't on good terms that I want to join in now.'

'Well, how is anybody to understand you? ... all these high-flown notions,' Trudolyubov sneered.

'We'll put your name down,' Simonov decided, turning to me. 'Tomorrow at five o'clock, at the Hotel de Paris; don't make any mistake.'

'The money!' Ferfichkin began in a low voice to Simonov, gesturing towards me, but broke off, because even Simonov looked disconcerted at this.

'All right!' said Trudolyubov, getting up. 'If he's so anxious to come, let him.'

'But we're having our own little circle, all friends,' Ferfichkin, also reaching for his hat, grumbled angrily. 'It isn't an official gathering. Perhaps we don't want you at all ...'

They went off; Ferfichkin didn't even bow to me as he left, and Trudolyubov nodded slightly without looking at me. Simonov, with whom I was left alone, seemed puzzled and disturbed, and looked at me strangely. He did not sit down or invite me to do so.

'H'm ... yes ... tomorrow, then. Are you giving me the money now? I'm asking so that I can be sure ...' he muttered, embarrassed.

I flared up, but as I did so I remembered that I had owed Simonov fifteen roubles for a very long time, and although I never forgot them, I never paid them back either.

'You must see, Simonov, that I couldn't have known, when I came here ... and I'm very sorry that I've been forgetting ...'

'All right, all right, it doesn't matter. Pay me at the dinner tomorrow. I only wanted to know.... Please don't ...'

He broke off and began pacing about the room, even more annoyed, coming down on his heels at each step and stamping noisily.

'I'm not keeping you, am I?' I asked, after a minute or two's silence.

'Oh, not at all,' he answered with a start; 'that is ... well, to tell you the truth, yes. You see, I ought to look in somewhere else. . . .

It's not far away,' he added apologetically and somewhat shame-facedly.

'Good God! Why didn't you tell me?' I shrieked, seizing my cap, though with a surprisingly disengaged manner – God knows where I got *that* from.

'Really, it's quite near. ... Two steps from here ...' Simonov repeated, seeing me to the door with a bustling look that was not at all becoming. 'Tomorrow, then at five o'clock sharp!' he called down the stairs after me; he was very pleased that I was leaving.

'What on earth possessed me to burst out like that?' I growled angrily as I walked home. 'And for that nasty little swine Zverkov. Of course I needn't go; of course I don't give a damn: I'm under no obligation, am I? Tomorrow I'll send Simonov a message ...'

But what made me furious was that I knew perfectly well that I should go; I would go on purpose; and the more tactless, the more unsuitable it was for me to go, the more I should go.

There was even one positive obstacle to my going: I hadn't the money. Nine roubles was absolutely everything I had. But out of that I had to pay a month's wages to my servant Apollon, who lived with me and found his own keep for seven roubles a month.

Given Apollon's character, it was impossible not to pay him. But I will talk about this rascal, this plague, some other time.

I knew, however, that I wouldn't pay him, all the same, and that I would certainly go.

That night I dreamed the most terrible dreams. It is not to be wondered at: all the evening I had been oppressed by memories of the wretched bondage of my schooldays, and I was unable to shake them off. I had been thrust into that school by distant relatives on whom I was dependent and with whom I have since completely lost touch. I was an orphan, already browbeaten by them, introspective, silently and ferociously shy. My schoolfellows greeted me with cruel and ill-natured sneers because I was not in the least like any of them. I could not bear the sneers; I could not get on with my schoolfellows as lightly as they did with one another. I hated them from the first, and shut myself away from them in shy, wounded and exorbitant pride. Their crudeness revolted me. They jeered at my looks and my clumsy figure; and yet how stupid their own faces were! In our school everybody's face seemed to acquire gradually a peculiarly stupid and degenerate expression. How many boys came to us handsome! In the course of a few years they had become revolting to look at. Even at sixteen I was morosely amazed at the triviality of their ideas and the stupidity of their pursuits, their games, and their talk. They had so little understanding of the most essential things, so little interest in the most inspiring subjects, that I could not help looking on them as my inferiors. It was not wounded vanity that made me do so, and for God's sake don't come down on me with such sickeningly familiar retorts as that I was only a dreamer and they already understood real life. They understood nothing at all of real life and that, I swear, is what I found most revolting in them. On the contrary, indeed, their reception of the most obvious and self-evident reality was fantastically stupid, and even by that time they had grown used to worshipping nothing but success. Everything honourable, but humble and downtrodden, they greeted with disgraceful and unfeeling laughter. They thought rank was intellect; at sixteen they were already discussing snug little berths. Of course there was a good deal of stupidity in all this, as well as of the bad examples that always surrounded their childhood and adolescence. They were monstrously lewd. Even in this, of course, there was mostly outward show and obviously artificial cynicism; youth and a certain freshness gleamed even through the vice; but even their freshness was unattractive, taking the form of a sort of childish naughtiness. I abominated them, although I was perhaps worse than they were. They repaid me in my own coin, and made no secret of their loathing for me. But I no longer wanted them to like me; on the contrary, I was always longing to see them humiliated. To escape their derision I deliberately began working as hard as I could, and soon forced my way to a place among the top boys in the school. This impressed them. Besides, they were all gradually beginning to realize that I was already reading books they could not read, and knew about things (not entering into our specialized course of studies) they had never even heard of. They regarded this fact with savage derision, but morally they accepted defeat, especially since in this respect I attracted the attention even of some of the masters. The sneers ceased, but the hostility remained, and our relations were established on a cold footing. Towards the end I myself weakened; with the years I developed a need for company and friendship. I tried to get closer to some of them; but somehow the intimacy was always unnatural, and so came to an end of its own accord. I did once make a friend. But I was a tyrant at heart; I wanted unlimited power over his heart and mind, I wanted to implant contempt for his surroundings in him; I required of him a haughty and final break with them. I frightened him with my passion of friendship; I reduced him to tears and nervous convulsions; he was a simple-hearted and submissive soul, but when he became wholly devoted to me I immediately took a dislike to him and repulsed him – just as though I had needed him only to get the upper hand of him, only for his submission. But I could not conquer all of them; my friend was no more like any of the rest than I was, and he made a very rare exception. My first action on leaving school was to leave the special branch of the service I had been destined for, breaking all links, consigning the past to perdition and scattering its ashes to the winds. ... And after that, God only knows why I hung about that Simonov! ...

Early in the morning I leapt out of bed with as much agitation as though everything was going to begin happening on the spot. But I was sure that some radical break in my life was coming, and would inevitably happen that very day. Perhaps because I was not used to them, whenever I was faced by any external event, however trivial, it always seemed to me that a radical break in my life was about to happen at once. However, I went to work as usual, although I slipped away two hours early to get ready. The main thing, I thought, is not to be first to arrive, or else they'll think I'm overjoyed. But there were thousands of other things that were most important, and the sum of them reduced me to a state of frantic helplessness. I cleaned my shoes again myself; nothing would have induced Apollon to clean them twice in one day: it wouldn't have been seemly. But I purloined the brushes from the

hall so that he should not find out what I had done and despise me
for it. Then I carefully inspected my clothes, and discovered that
they were all old and worn and shabby. I had grown very slov-
enly. My office-uniform coat was fairly decent, but I wasn't going
to go out to dinner in my office coat. But the main thing was that
there was a huge discoloured patch on my trousers, right on the
knee. I foresaw that that mark alone would rob me of nine-tenths
of my self-respect. I knew it was low of me to think so. 'But this is
not the time for thinking: now is the time for reality,' I thought,
with a sinking heart. I knew also, even then, that I was monstrously exaggerating all these things, but I couldn't help it: I had
lost control of myself and shook as though with fever. Des-
pairingly, I pictured to myself the cold condescension with which
that 'scoundrel' Zverkov would greet me; the invincible stupid
contempt of the dull-witted Trudolyubov; the nasty impudent
sniggers at my expense of that blowfly of a Ferfichkin, trying to
curry favour with Zverkov; how well Simonov would understand
all this and despise my petty vanity and meanness of spirit; and
worst of all, how squalid, commonplace, and *unliterary* the whole
thing would be. Obviously the best thing would be not to go at
all. But that was utterly impossible: as soon as ever I got an idea
into my head I was utterly committed to it. I would have taunted
myself all my life afterwards: 'You funked it, you were scared of
reality, you panicked!' I passionately wanted to show all these
'nobodies' that, on the contrary, I was not nearly so much of a
poltroon as I imagined. Moreover in the very worst paroxysms of
my fever of cowardice I still dreamed of coming out on top, win-
ning them over, making them like me, if only for my 'elevated
ideas and undeniable wit'. They would desert Zverkov; he would
sit in a corner, silent and shamefaced, and I would annihilate him.
Then, perhaps I would be reconciled with him and drink to our
intimate friendship, but the worst and most shameful thing was
that even then I knew, knew very well, knew for certain, that in
reality none of this was what I wanted, in reality I had absolutely
no wish to either subjugate or captivate them, and that I wouldn't
give a farthing for such a result even if I did attain it. Oh, how I
prayed for the day to pass quickly! In indescribable anguish I

went again and again to the window, opened the hinged pane and gazed out at the swirling dimness of the wet, thickly falling snow . . .

At long last the cheap clock on the wall wheezed out five o'clock. I seized my hat and, trying not to look at Apollon, who had been waiting for me to pay him his wages ever since the morning, but was pig-headedly determined not to mention the matter first, slipped past him to the door and drove to the Hotel de Paris like a lord, in a cab I hired for my last fifty copecks.

4

I had known ever since the previous evening that I should be the first to arrive. But the order of our arrival no longer had any importance.

Not only was none of them there, but it was hardly possible to find our room. The table was not yet properly laid. What did this mean? After many inquiries I managed to discover from the servants that the dinner had been ordered for six o'clock, not five. The waiters in the bar confirmed this. I felt ashamed at having to ask. It was still only twenty-five minutes to six. If they had changed the time, they cught at least to have let me know – that was what the post was for, wasn't it? – and not subjected me to this indignity in my own eyes and other people's, even if it was only the servants'. I sat down; a servant began to lay the table; somehow his presence made me feel even more humiliated. At six o'clock candles were brought in, in addition to the lamps which were already lit. It had not occurred to the man to bring them in as soon as I arrived. In the next room, two of the hotel guests, gloomy, angry-looking, silent, were dining at separate tables. There was a great deal of noise in one of the other rooms, further away; some shouting, even, the noisy laughter of a whole mob of people, and some nasty French-sounding screams; 'ladies' were being entertained. In short, everything was sickening. I have seldom lived through worse moments, and so when the others arrived in a body at exactly six o'clock, they seemed like rescuers and I was so delighted to see them that at first I almost forgot to look offended.

Zverkov, evidently playing the leader, came in at the head of them. He and all the others were laughing, but when he saw me Zverkov assumed a dignified air and came towards me, without hurrying, and, rather self-consciously leaning forward from the waist, gave me his hand in a friendly but not effusive fashion, almost with the careful courtesy of a very distinguished personage, as if he were protecting himself from something by offering me his hand. I, on the other hand, had been expecting him to begin laughing his old thin tinkling laugh and cracking his flat-footed jokes and witticisms as soon as he came in. I had been preparing myself for them ever since the day before and was not in the least expecting such lofty and condescending politeness. So he already considered himself so immeasurably my superior in every respect? It wouldn't have mattered, I thought, if he had simply intended his condescension to be offensive; somehow or other I would have shrugged it off. But what if in fact, without any desire to be obnoxious, he had in all seriousness got it into his stupid mutton-head that he was immeasurably above me and could not see me in any other light than as the object of patronage? The very supposition made me breathless with indignation.

'I was surprised to hear you wanted to join us,' he began, lisping affectedly and drawling as he never used to before. 'We never seem to meet, somehow. You fight shy of us. There's no need. We aren't nearly as frightening as you think. Well, in any case, I'm ... glad ... to ... re ... new ...'

And he turned away carelessly to put down his hat on the window-sill.

'Have you been waiting long?' asked Trudolyubov.

'I arrived at exactly five o'clock, the time I was given yesterday,' I answered loudly and with suppressed rage that foretold a coming explosion.

'Didn't you tell him we had changed the time?' Trudolyubov asked Simonov.

'No, I forgot,' the latter answered, quite unrepentantly, and without even apologizing to me went off to see about the *za-kuski*.

'So you've been here an hour, poor thing!' laughed Zverkov, because by his standards this was something terribly funny. The cad Ferfichkin copied him in loud yelps of laughter that sounded like a small dog yapping. My situation seemed awkward and comical to him also.

'It's not in the least funny,' I shouted at Ferfichkin, growing more and more angry. 'It's not my fault, it's other people's. Nobody bothered to tell me. It's ... it's ... it's simply uncouth.'

'It's not only uncouth, it's more than that,' grumbled Trudolyubov, naïvely backing me up. 'You're too mild. It's downright uncivil. Not deliberate, of course. How Simonov could. ... H'm!'

'If anybody had treated me like that,' remarked Ferfichkin, 'I'd have ...'

'You'd have ordered yourself something,' interrupted Zverkov, 'or simply had your dinner without waiting.'

'You must agree that I didn't need anybody's permission to do just that,' I retorted. 'If I waited, it was because ...'

'Come, sit down, gentlemen,' cried Simonov, coming back. 'Everything's ready, and I'll answer for it that the champagne's well iced. ... After all, I didn't know your address, how was I to find you?' he went on, addressing me, but again seeming to avoid my eyes. It was plain he was holding something against me. Evidently it was something he had thought of since the previous day.

Everybody sat down; so did I. The table was a round one. I had Trudolyubov on my left and Simonov on my right. Zverkov sat opposite, with Ferfichkin between him and Trudolyubov.

'Tell me, are you ... employed ... in a Mi-ni-stry?' Zverkov went on, still taking an interest in me. Seeing that I was upset, he seriously imagined that I must be treated with kindness and, so to speak, encouraged. 'What, is he trying to make me shy a bottle at him?' I thought angrily. From lack of social experience, my fury was growing with unnatural speed.

I blurted out the name of my Ministry abruptly, with my eyes on my plate.

'Well! . . . and are you all right there? Tell me, what in-du-u-uced you to leave your former post?'

'What in-du-u-uced me to leave was that I wanted to,' I drawled out, three times as slowly, hardly able to control myself. Ferfichkin snorted. Simonov threw me an ironical glance; Trudolyubov stopped eating and stared at me curiously.

This jarred on Zverkov, but he refused to notice it.

'We-ell, and what about monetary matters?'

'What monetary matters?'

'I mean, your salary.'

'Why all this cross-examination?'

I named the amount of my salary, however, turning bright red.

'It's not much,' remarked Zverkov, full of self-importance.

'No, one can't dine in decent restaurants on that!' added Ferfichkin insolently.

'I think it's absolutely beggarly,' Trudolyubov said seriously. .

'And how thin you've grown, how much you've changed . . . since those days,' added Zverkov, not without venom, eyeing me and my clothes with a sort of impertinent pity.

'Do stop embarrassing him,' said Ferfichkin with a titter.

'My dear sir, let me tell you I am not embarrassed,' I exploded at last; 'do you hear me? I am dining here, in a "decent restaurant" at my own expense, my own and not somebody else's, take note, Monsieur Ferfichkin!'

'What do you mean? Which of us isn't dining at his own expense? You seem to . . .'

'Oh, all right,' I answered, feeling that I had gone rather far, 'and I suggest it would be better if we chose a slightly more intelligent topic.'

'I suppose you intend to show us how witty you are!'

'Don't worry, that would be quite wasted here.'

'But what are you cack-cack-cackling on about, my dear sir? Are your wits crazed already, with living in your *apart-ment*?'

'Enough of that, gentlemen, drop it!' exclaimed Zverkov commandingly.

'This is all so stupid,' grumbled Simonov.

'Really stupid! we've all come here as friends to say good-bye to an old school-friend who is going away, and you are counting the cost,' said Trudolyubov, rudely addressing himself exclusively to me. 'You invited yourself yesterday, so don't disturb the general harmony ...'

'That's enough, that's enough,' Zverkov exclaimed. 'Stop it, gentlemen; this won't do. You'd do better to let me tell you about how I nearly got married the day before yesterday ...'

And the gentleman embarked on the long and scandalous story of how he had barely avoided getting married a couple of days earlier. However, marriage wasn't even mentioned, but his story was full of generals and colonels and even gentlemen-in-waiting, with Zverkov figuring as practically the first and foremost among them. There was a burst of approving laughter; Ferfichkin positively squealed.

I sat there neglected, crushed and humiliated.

'Oh Lord, these aren't my sort of people!' I thought. 'And what a fool I've made of myself in front of them! All the same, I let Ferfichkin go rather far. The idiots think they've done me a favour by giving me a seat at their table; they don't understand that it's I who am doing them the favour, not the other way round! "You've got thin! Your clothes!" – Oh, those damned trousers! Zverkov noticed the stain on my knee just now. ... But what's the use? I ought to get up now, this very minute, pick up my hat and simply go, without a word. ... Out of contempt! Even if it means a duel tomorrow! The swine! It isn't as if I can spare seven roubles. Perhaps they'll think. ... Oh hell! I don't grudge seven roubles! I'll leave this minute!'

But of course I stayed.

I drowned my sorrows in great bumpers of claret and sherry. I was so unused to it that I got drunk very quickly, and my anger increased with my intoxication. Suddenly I wanted to be outrageously rude to every one of them, and then go. To find the right moment and show them who I was: make them say, 'He may be ridiculous, but he's damned clever ...' and ... and ... in short, to hell with them!

I looked them over insolently, if with slightly glazed eyes. But they seemed to have forgotten all about me. *They* were noisy and cheerful and amused. Zverkov was doing all the talking. I began to listen. Zverkov was telling them about some fine lady whom he had finally brought to the point of confessing her feelings for him (of course he was lying like a trooper), and about how much he had been helped in the matter by his bosom friend, some Prince Kolya of the Hussars, who owned an estate of three thousand souls.

'This Kolya, who owns three thousand souls, isn't here to say good-bye to you, though,' I said suddenly, breaking into the conversation. For a moment nobody said anything.

'You're drunk already,' Trudolyubov condescended to remark at last, with a contemptuous glance in my direction. Zverkov was silently staring at me as if I was some crawling insect. I looked down. Simonov hastily began pouring out champagne.

Trudolyubov raised his glass, and everybody but me followed his example.

'Your health, and a prosperous journey,' he cried; 'let us drink to the old days, gentlemen, and to our future. Hurrah!'

The others drained their glasses and got up to embrace Zverkov. I did not move; my full glass stood untouched in front of me.

'Surely you're not going to refuse to drink the toast?' Trudolyubov howled menacingly, completely out of patience.

'I'm going to make my own speech, personally ... then I'll drink, Mr Trudolyubov.'

'Nasty bad-tempered little brute!' grumbled Simonov.

I sat up straight in my chair and feverishly clutched my glass, getting ready to say something out of the ordinary, but not having the least idea what it would be.

'*Silence!*' yelled Ferfichkin in French. 'This is going to be really clever!' Zverkov, understanding what it was all about, waited with great gravity.

'Lieutenant Zverkov,' I began, 'I must tell you that I detest empty phrases and phrase-mongers, and also tight-laced formality – that is my first point. My second follows.'

There was a slight general stir.

'My second point is that I hate dirty stories and people who tell them. Especially people who tell them!'

'My third point: I love truth, sincerity and honesty,' I went on almost mechanically, because I was growing numb with horror at myself, unable to understand how I could say such things. . . . 'I love ideas, *Monsieur* Zverkov. May you make a conquest of all the little Circassian beauties, shoot down the enemies of your fatherland, and . . . and. . . . Your health, *Monsieur* Zverkov!'

Zverkov stood up, bowed to me and said, 'I am very much obliged to you.'

He was terribly offended; he had even turned white.

'Damn it all!' yelled Trudolyubov, thumping his fist on the table. 'No, he's asking for a punch on the jaw!' squealed Ferfichkin.

'Throw him out!' Simonov grumbled.

'Say nothing, do nothing, gentlemen!' said Zverkov loudly and solemnly. 'Thank you all, but I am quite capable of showing him what value I put on his words.'

'Mr Ferfichkin, tomorrow you will give me satisfaction for what you said just now,' I cried importantly.

'You mean a duel? Very well, sir,' he answered, but I suppose it was so funny for me to be issuing a challenge, and went so badly with the figure I cut, that everybody, even Ferfichkin at last, simply rocked with laughter.

'Yes, of course, leave him alone! He's drunk already!' said Trudolyubov disgustedly.

'I shall never forgive myself for counting him in!' Simonov grumbled.

'I'd like to sling a bottle at the lot of them this minute,' I thought, taking up a bottle and – pouring myself a full glass.

'No, I'd better sit it out to the end,' I went on to myself. 'You'd be glad if I went, gentlemen. Nothing will make me. I shall sit here and drink to the very end, on purpose to show you I don't attach the slightest importance to you. I shall sit and drink, because this is a public house and I've paid to come in. I shall sit and drink, because I think of you as pawns, without real existence. I will sit and drink . . . and sing, if I want to, yes, sing, because I have a right . . . to sing. . . . H'm.'

But I didn't sing. I merely tried not to look at any of them; I put on the most independent air I could manage and waited impartially for them to speak to me *first*. But unfortunately, they didn't do so. And how much I would have given at that moment to make my peace with them! It struck eight o'clock and finally nine. They left the table for more comfortable seats. Zverkov sprawled on a sofa, resting one leg on a little round table. The wine was carried over there as well. Zverkov had indeed contributed three bottles of his own. I was naturally not invited to share them. They were all clustered round him on the sofa, listening to him almost deferentially. It was plain that they were attached to him. 'Why, why?' I wondered to myself. From time to time, in drunken transports, they even embraced him. They talked about the Caucasus, about the nature of true passion, about baccarat, about the most advantageous postings; about how much income the hussar Podkharchevsky (whom none of them knew personally) had, and how glad they were that it was so enormous; about the extraordinary beauty and grace of Princess D. (whom none of them had ever set eyes on); and finally they came to the conclusion that Shakespeare is immortal.

Smiling scornfully, I paced backwards and forwards on the side of the room opposite the sofa, along the wall from the table to the stove and back. I was trying with all my might to show that I could do without them; meanwhile I purposely made a clatter with my boots, coming down hard on the heels. But it was all in vain; they didn't even notice. I had the patience to walk about straight in front of them in this fashion from eight o'clock till eleven, always in the same track, from the table to the stove and from the stove back again to the table: 'I am walking to please myself and nobody can stop me.' The servant, coming into the room, several times stopped to stare at me; my head was dizzy from the frequent turns; there were times when I thought I was delirious. In those three hours I three times burst into a sweat and dried out again. At times the idea pierced into my heart with the most agonizing pain that ten years might pass, twenty years, forty years, and still, after forty years, I should remember with loathing and humiliation those hours, the nastiest, most comical, and most terrible of my whole life. To humiliate oneself more shamelessly and wilfully was impossible, and this I fully, all too fully, understood, yet all the same I continued to pace from the table to the stove and back. 'Oh, if only you know what thoughts and emotions I am capable of, and how enlightened I am!' I thought sometimes, turning in imagination to the sofa where my enemies sat. But my enemies acted as though I wasn't even in the room. Once, and only once, they turned towards me, and that was when Zverkov began to talk about Shakespeare and I let out a sudden contemptuous laugh. It was such a vilely artificial snort that they all ceased talking at once and silently watched me for about two minutes, attentively and seriously, as I walked along the wall from the table to the stove, *without paying them the slightest attention*. But nothing happened: they did not speak to me and after two minutes they ignored me again. Eleven o'clock struck.

'Gentlemen,' cried Zverkov, rising from the sofa, 'Now we'll all go *there*.'

'Of course, of course,' said the others.

I turned sharply towards Zverkov. I felt so exhausted, so shattered, that I had to end it if it killed me. I was in a fever; my hair, soaked with sweat, had stuck to my forehead and temples as it dried.

'Zverkov! I ask your pardon!' I said firmly and harshly; 'and yours too, Ferfichkin, and everybody's, everybody's. I was offensive to you all!'

'Aha! So you're not the man for a duel!' Ferfichkin spat out venomously.

It cut me to the quick.

'You're wrong, Ferfichkin, I'm not afraid of a duel! I'm ready to fight you tomorrow, even after a reconciliation. I insist on it, and you can't refuse me. I mean to show you I'm not afraid of a duel. You shall fire first and I will fire into the air.'

'He's just trying to cut a good figure,' remarked Simonov.

'He's simply cracked!' retorted Trudolyubov.

'Be good enough to stand aside; why are you standing in our way? . . . What do you want?' Zverkov answered contemptuously.

They were all red in the face, and their eyes glittered; they had had a lot to drink.

'I am asking you to be friends, Zverkov. I offended you, but . . .'

'Offended me? You? Offended *me*? Let me tell you, my dear sir, that you could never in any circumstances offend *me*!'

'That's enough from you. Clear out!' Trudolyubov closed the argument. 'We're off.'

'Olympia is mine, gentlemen, that's the bargain!' cried Zverkov.

'We don't dispute it,' they answered laughing.

I had been snubbed. The whole mob went noisily out, Trudolyubov drawling some stupid song. Simonov stayed behind for a fraction of a second to give the waiters a tip. I went up to him suddenly.

'Simonov, lend me six roubles!' I said firmly but desperately.

He gazed at me with the utmost amazement in his bleary eyes. He too was drunk.

'You're not going *there* with us, are you?'

'Yes.'

'I haven't any money,' he snapped, with a contemptuous grin, and started out of the room.

I caught at his overcoat. It was like a nightmare.

'Simonov! I saw you with money; why do you refuse me? I'm not a scoundrel, am I? Beware of refusing me: if you knew, oh, if only you knew, what I want it for! Everything hangs on it, my whole future, all my plans . . .'

Simonov took out some money and almost flung it at me.

'Take it, if you have so little shame!' he said cruelly, and hurried away to catch up with them.

I remained for a few moments alone. Disorder, scraps of food, a broken glass on the floor, spilt wine, cigarette ends, intoxication and drunken babble in my mind and, finally, the waiter who had seen and heard everything and was staring curiously into my face.

'I'll go *there*,' I shrieked. 'Either they shall all kneel before me, embracing my knees and begging for my friendship, or . . . or I'll give Zverkov a slap in the face!'

5

'So here it is, it has come at last, my encounter with reality,' I muttered, rushing down the stairs. 'This isn't a case of the Pope leaving Rome and travelling to Brazil; this is no ball on Lake Como!'

'You're a scoundrel,' the thought passed through my mind, 'if you laugh at this now!'

'Who cares?' I yelled at myself in reply. 'It's all up now, anyhow!'

The scent was cold; but that didn't matter: I knew where they had gone.

By the steps stood a solitary 'night-driver', his coarse homespun greatcoat powdered all over with the snow, which was still falling in wet and one might almost say warm flakes. The air seemed steamy and suffocating. His shaggy little skewbald horse was also powdered with snow, and coughing, as I clearly remember. I rushed to the sledge, but I had scarcely raised my foot to step in when the recollection of the way Simonov had flung me the six roubles turned my knees to water, and I tumbled into it like a sack.

'No, I shall have to do a lot to redeem my position!' I shouted, 'but I will redeem it, or perish on the spot this very night. – Drive on!'

We moved off. There was a positive maelstrom in my head.

'They are not going to kneel before me begging for my friendship. That's a mirage, a vulgar illusion, disgusting, romantic, and fanciful. Lake Como again. And that's why I *must* give Zverkov a slap in the face! I'm obliged to. So it's settled. I'm in a tearing hurry to slap his face. – Faster!'

The cabby jerked at the reins.

'I'll do it as soon as I go in. Need I say a few words before the slap, by way of a preface? No. I'll simply walk in and deliver the slap. They'll all be sitting in the big drawing-room and he'll be on the sofa with Olympia. That damned Olympia! She's the one that refused me that time because she thought I had a funny face. I shall drag Olympia away by the hair, and pull Zverkov by the ears. No; better by one ear, and I'll parade him all round the room, pulling him by the ear. Perhaps they will all sit on me and throw me out. In fact, they're certain to. Let them! I shall still have delivered the first blow; the initiative will have been mine, and by the laws of honour that is everything: he will be branded and no amount of fisticuffs will wash out that slap in the face, nothing but a duel. He will have to fight me. And let them all rain blows on me now. Let them, like the ungrateful wretches they are! Trudolyubov will strike specially hard: he is so strong; Ferfichkin will hang on to me on one side, by the hair, most likely. But let them, let them! That's what I'm going for. Their addled pates will be forced to realize to the full the whole tragedy of the situation! When they drag me to the door, I will yell that they aren't worth my little finger. Get on, cabby, get on!' I shouted to my driver. Startled, he flourished his whip. My shout must have sounded extremely wild.

'We shall fight at dawn, that's settled. I've finished with the Ministry. But where shall I get pistols? Rubbish! I'll take my salary in advance and buy them. And what about powder and bullets? That's the second's business. But how shall I find time for everything before dawn? And where shall I look for a second? I don't know anybody. ... Rubbish!' I cried, my thoughts whirling faster than ever, 'rubbish! The first passer-by I ask is obliged to be my second, just as he would be to pull a drowning man out of the water. The most exceptional cases must be allowed for. And if I were to ask the head of the Ministry himself to be my second, even he would have to consent, out of mere chivalry, and to keep my secret! – Anton Antonovich ...'

The fact was that at that moment the whole revolting absurdity of my speculations, the reverse of the medal, had presented itself to me more clearly and distinctly than it could to anybody else in the whole wide world, but:

'Get on, cabby, get on, get on, you wretch!'

'Oh lord, sir!' groaned the son of the soil.

Cold suddenly seized me.

'But hadn't I better ... hadn't I better ... go straight home? Oh my God! Why, why did I have to invite myself to this dinner yesterday? But no, it's impossible! What about that three hours promenading between the table and the stove? No, they, they and nobody else, must make up to me for that promenade. They must wipe out that dishonour! Faster!

'What if they give me into custody? They wouldn't dare! They are afraid of scandal. What if Zverkov refuses to fight me out of contempt? That's even very likely; but in that case I'll show them. ... I'll rush to the posting-station when he's leaving tomorrow, and grab him by the leg and drag off his overcoat as he climbs into the coach. I'll fix my teeth in his hand, I'll bite him. "Look, everybody, see to what lengths a desperate man can be driven." Let him beat me about the head, and the rest attack me from behind. I'll shout out to everybody there, "Look at this young puppy going off to captivate the beautiful Circassians with my spittle on his cheek!" I shall be seized and tried, driven out of the service, put in prison, sent to Siberia, to a penal settlement. It doesn't matter. In fifteen years' time I shall drag myself in search of him, destitute, in rags, when I am let out of prison. I shall find him somewhere in a provincial capital. He will be married, and happy. He will have a grown-up daughter. ... I shall say, "Look, monster, look at my wasted cheeks, and at my rags and tatters! I have lost everything – career, happiness, art, science, a *loved woman*, and all because of you. Look at these pistols. I have come to discharge my pistol, and ... and I forgive you." Then I shall fire into the air, and nothing more will ever be heard of me ...'

I was on the point of tears, although at the same time I quite definitely knew that all this came out of *Silvio* and Lermontov's *Masquerade*. And suddenly I felt terribly ashamed, so ashamed that I stopped the horse, climbed out of the sledge and stood in the snow in the middle of the street. The cabby stared at me in amazement and sighed.

What was I to do? I couldn't go *there* – it was becoming nonsensical, and I couldn't leave things as they were, because that would prove. . . . Oh lord! How could I drop it? And after such insults! 'No!' I shrieked, flinging myself into the sledge again, 'it is predestined – it is fate! Drive on, drive on, *there*!'

And in my impatience I thumped the cabby on the back of the neck.

'What's that for, why are you knocking me about?' cried my wretched peasant, but he whipped up his miserable nag, so that it began to lash out with its hoofs.

The snow was still falling in great damp flakes, but I flung open my coat; I had no attention to spare for the snow. I had forgotten everything else because I had finally determined to deliver the slap and felt that now it must *inevitably* happen, that *no power on earth could stop it now*. The isolated street-lamps glimmered sadly through the haze of snow like torches at a funeral. The snow packed itself thickly under my greatcoat, inside my frock-coat, and under my cravat, and melted there; I did not cover myself up: after all, everything was lost anyhow! At last we arrived. I sprang out, hardly conscious of what I was doing, ran up the steps and began beating at the door with fists and feet. My legs, especially, were growing very weak about the knees. The door was quickly opened, as though they knew I was coming. (Indeed, Simonov had forewarned them that there might be one more, this being a place where it was necessary to give forewarnings and generally take precautions. It was one of the 'fashion shops' of those days, which the police long ago swept out of existence. By day it really was a shop; but in the evening suitably recommended visitors were received there.) I hurried through the dark shop and into the familiar salon, lit only by a single candle, and stopped in bewilderment: there was nobody there.

'Where are they?' I asked.

But of course they had already separated . . .

In front of me, with an idiotic simper, stood the mistress of the house herself, who knew me slightly. A minute later the door opened and another person entered.

Taking no notice of anybody, I paced about the room, I think talking aloud to myself. It was as if I had been saved from death and my whole being rejoiced: I would have delivered that slap, certainly, certainly, I would have delivered it! But now they were not here and . . . it had all vanished, everything was changed! . . . I looked round. I still could not realize what had happened. Mechanically I glanced at the girl who had come in: before me gleamed a fresh, young, rather pale face, with dark level eyebrows and a serious and, as it were, slightly wondering expression. I instantly liked this; I should have hated her if she had been smiling. I began to look at her more attentively, with a kind of effort: I had not yet completely collected my thoughts. There was something kind and simple-hearted in that face, but also something so serious as to be strange. I am certain that it was to her disadvantage in that place, and that none of those fools had even noticed her. She could not, however, have been called a beauty, although she was tall, strong, and well-built. She was extremely simply dressed. Something foul seemed to sting me; I went straight to her . . .

I caught sight of myself in a mirror. My agitated face seemed to me repulsive in the extreme: pale, vicious, mean, with tangled hair. 'All right, I'm glad of it,' I thought; 'I'm glad to seem repulsive to her; I like that . . .'

6

Somewhere on the other side of the wall a clock wheezed, sounding as though it was being crushed or strangled. An unnaturally long spell of wheezing was followed by an unpleasant, thin and somehow unexpectedly rapid double beat – as if somebody had suddenly jumped forward. It was two o'clock. I roused myself, although I had not been asleep, only lying in a half-trance.

In the cramped narrow low-ceilinged room, crowded with an enormous wardrobe, scattered cardboard boxes, a litter of clothes and odds-and-ends, it was almost completely dark. The candle-end on the table at the far end of the room was almost burnt out, and only flared up feebly from time to time. In a few minutes more the darkness would be complete.

I was not long in coming to full consciousness; everything came back to me at once, without effort, in an instant, as if it had been lying in wait for me, ready to pounce again. Indeed, even while I dozed there had remained a kind of fixed point in my mind, never wholly forgotten, round which my sleepy imaginings revolved heavily. But strangely enough everything that had taken place during the day seemed to me now, when I woke up, to have happened long long ago, as though I had lived through it in the distant past.

My head was full of fumes. Something seemed to be hovering over me, nagging at me, rousing and disturbing me. Anger and misery seethed up in me again, seeking an outlet. Suddenly, beside me, I saw two eyes, open, regarding me with curiosity and fixed attention. Their look was coldly indifferent, sullen, like something utterly alien; it irked me.

A resentful feeling arose in my mind and swept through my body with something like the unpleasant sensation of going into a damp and musty cellar. It seemed somehow unnatural that it was only at this moment that those two eyes had decided to examine me. I remembered, too, that for two whole hours I had not spoken a single word to this being, or considered there was any need to do so; until a few moments before I had even felt pleased about it. But now, absurd and disgusting, like a spider, there rose before me suddenly and vividly the image of lust, which lovelessly, crudely, shamelessly, begins where true love finds its crown. We lay there for a long time looking at one another, but she did not lower her eyes or change her expression, and at last I was filled with an ... eerie feeling.

'What's your name?' I asked abruptly, to bring it to an end as quickly as possible.

'Liza,' she answered almost in a whisper, but somehow ungraciously, turning away her eyes.

I was silent for a short time.

'The weather today ... the snow ... filthy!' I said almost to myself, folding my hands behind my head and staring up at the ceiling, bored.

She did not answer. The whole situation was tiresome.

'Do you belong to St Petersburg?' I asked a moment later, almost angrily, turning my head slightly towards her.

'No.'

'Where are you from?'

'Riga,' she said reluctantly.

'Are you German?'

'No, Russian.'

'Have you been here long?'

'Where?'

'In this house.'

'Two weeks.' She was speaking more and more abruptly. The candle had guttered right out; I could no longer make out her face.

'Are your parents alive?'

'Yes ... no ... yes, they are.'

'Where are they?'

'There ... in Riga.'

'Who are they?'

'People ...'

'What do you mean? Who are they, what do they do?'

'Shop-keepers.'

'Have you always lived with them?'

'Yes.'

'How old are you?'

'Twenty.'

'Why did you leave them?'

'Because.'

That *because* meant, 'Leave me alone. I'm sick of this.'

God knows why I didn't go away. I was getting steadily more disgusted and depressed. Pictures of all the day's happenings had begun crowding higgledy-piggledy through my head of their own accord, without my volition. Suddenly I remembered something I had seen in the street in the morning, when I was anxiously trotting along to the office.

'They were carrying a coffin out this morning and very nearly dropped it,' I burst out suddenly. I had had no intention of starting a conversation; it had simply slipped out.

'A coffin?'

'Yes, in the Haymarket; it was being carried out of a cellar.'

'A cellar?'

'Not a cellar, a basement ... well, you know ... downstairs ... it was a bad house. ... Everything was so filthy. ... Eggshells, dust ... smells; thoroughly nasty.'

Silence.

'It's a nasty day for a funeral!' I began again, for something to say.

'Why?'

'The snow, the damp . . .' (I yawned.)

'It makes no difference,' she said suddenly, after a minute.

'Yes it does; it's nasty. . . .' (I yawned again.) 'The gravediggers probably cursed because they were wet with the snow. And there was probably water in the grave.'

'Why should there be water in the grave?' she asked with some curiosity, but speaking more gruffly and shortly than ever. All at once something seemed to be egging me on.

'Why of course, water in the bottom, a foot or so. Here, in Volkovo, it's impossible to dig a dry grave.'

'Why?'

'Why? Because it's such a wet place. There's marsh everywhere here. So they just plant them in the water. I've seen it myself . . . lots of times . . .'

(I had never seen it, indeed had never been to Volkovo Cemetery – I had only heard people talking about it.)

'Does it really make no difference to you, dying?'

'Why should I die?'

'Some day you will, and you'll die exactly like that woman I saw. She was a girl like you. . . . She died of consumption.'

'A tart would have died in hospital.' (She knows it all already, I thought, and she said 'tart', not girl!)

'She was in debt to the madam,' I retorted, feeling that I was being pushed further and further by the discussion, 'and she worked for her right up to the end, in spite of the consumption. The cabmen round about, and the soldiers, were talking about it all. Probably they knew her. They were holding a wake for her in the pub.' (There was a good deal of this that wasn't exactly true either.)

Silence, utter silence. She did not even move a muscle.

'Do you mean it's better to die in hospital?'

'Does it make any difference? . . . And why should I be going to die?' she asked irritably.

'If not now, later on.'

'Well, later on . . .'

'Not a chance! . . . You're young now, pretty, and fresh – you're worth a certain amount to them. But a year of this life and you won't be the same, you'll have lost your bloom.'

'In one year?'

'At any rate, your value will be less in a year's time,' I went on sadistically. 'You'll leave here for somewhere more degraded, another house. A year more and you'll go into yet another, and so on, always getting lower and lower, and in about seven years you'll come to a cellar in the Haymarket. But that's not the worst. What would be disastrous would be if you contracted some illness – a weakness of the chest, for example – or simply caught a cold. Illness clears up very slowly when you're leading that kind of life. It will settle and perhaps you'll never be able to get rid of it. So then you'll die.'

'Well then, I'll die,' she answered, now quite angry, with a quick movement.

'But really, I'm sorry.'

'Who for?'

'For the life you lead.'

A silence.

'Had you a young man, eh?'

'What's it got to do with you?'

'I'm not trying to find out about you. It doesn't matter to me. Why are you annoyed? Of course you may have your troubles. What is it to me? I'm just sorry.'

'Who for?'

'I'm sorry for you.'

'There's no need to be,' she whispered, almost inaudibly, again stirring restlessly.

This made me definitely angry at once. What, I had been so gentle with her, and she . . .

'Why, what do you think? That your feet are on the right road, eh?'

'I don't think anything.'

'That's a bad thing, too, not thinking. Wake up while there's still time. And there is time. You are still young, you are pretty; you could fall in love and get married and be happy . . .'

'Not every married woman is happy,' she said sharply, in her former gruff gabble.

'Not every one, of course – but all the same it's much better than this. It's incomparably better. And when there is love, you can live even without happiness. Life is good even in sorrow; it is good to live in the world, however you live. But what is there here, except . . . a stink? Pah!'

I turned away, sickened. I was no longer coldly reasonable. I was beginning to feel what I said, and growing heated over it. I was desperately anxious to expound those cherished little ideas, the fruits of my withdrawn existence in my corner. Something had caught fire within me, a purpose had revealed itself.

'Don't take any notice of my being here; I'm not an example to follow. Perhaps I'm even worse than you. However, I was drunk when I came here,' I added, in a hurry to find excuses for myself, all the same. 'Besides, a man is no sort of example for a woman. They're different; I may wallow in filth, but I'm nobody's slave; I can come and go, and that's all there is to it. I shake it all off, and become a different person. But you have to admit that you've been a slave from the start. Yes, a slave! You give yourself and your own will up completely. And afterwards, if you want to break those chains, it will be too late; the shackles will get stronger and stronger. Those damnable chains. I know them. I say nothing about other things; perhaps you wouldn't even understand, but tell me this: you're probably in debt to the madam, aren't you? There, you see!' I went on, although she did not answer, only listened silently, with her whole being; 'there's a chain for you! You'll never get it paid off! That's how it will happen. Just like selling your soul to the devil . . .

'And besides, I . . . how do you know I'm not just such another miserable wretch, how would you know? – and I've crept into the muck on purpose, because I'm miserable. After all, people drink because they're unhappy; well, I'm here because I'm unhappy. Well, tell me, what's good about this? after all, you and I . . . came together . . . just now, and we didn't speak a word to one another the whole time, and afterwards you began to stare at me like a wild thing; and so did I at you. Is that love? Is that the way two human beings ought to come into contact? It's ugly, that's what it is!'

'Yes!' she agreed sharply and quickly. I was astonished by the swiftness of that *yes*. . . . So the same thought had perhaps been running through her head too, a short time before, when she was watching me? So even she was capable of some ideas? . . . 'Damn it, how very interesting that we should be *akin*!' I thought, almost rubbing my hands. But how with a young heart like this could she fail to understand?

What chiefly attracted me was the game itself.

She had turned so that her head was nearer to me, and, it appeared to me in the darkness, was propped up on her elbow. Perhaps she was watching me. How I regretted that I could not make out her eyes. I heard her deep breathing.

'Why did you come here?' I began again, now somewhat masterfully.

'Because.'

'But really, how good it is to live in the home of your childhood! Warmth, freedom; your own nest!'

'And if it is not like that at all?'

The thought came into my mind that I must hit on the right tone; sentimentality was not likely to have much success.

It was, however, only a passing thought. I swear she genuinely interested me. Besides I was feeling somehow slack and in the mood. Knavery so easily goes with sentiment.

'Who can tell?' I hastened to answer; 'everything is possible. I'm sure, you know, that somebody wronged you, and you were more sinned against than sinning. I know nothing of your history, but a girl like you doesn't come here of her own choice . . .'

'What sort of girl am I?' she whispered almost inaudibly, but I heard her.

Damn it, I was flattering her. This was horrible. Or perhaps it was a good thing. . . . She was silent.

'Look, Liza – I'll tell you about myself. If I had grown up in a family, I shouldn't have been what I am now. I often think that.

After all, however bad a family is – they're always your own
father and mother, not enemies, not strangers. And even if it's
only once a year, they show they love you. You know, all the
same, that you are at home. Now I grew up without a family;
that's probably why I've turned out like this – unfeeling.'

I waited again.

'Perhaps she doesn't understand,' I thought; 'and besides, it's
ridiculous, this moralizing.'

'If I was a father, and had a daughter, I really think I should
love my daughter more than my sons,' I began again, from
another angle, to amuse her. I blushed, I own.

'Why?' she asked.

Aha, so she was listening!

'I just would; I don't know why, Liza. Listen: I knew a father
who was a stern grim man, but he spent his whole life on his
knees before his daughter, kissing her hands and her feet, lost in
wonder and admiration. If she danced in the evening, he would
stand in the same spot for five hours on end, never taking his eyes
off her. He was mad about her: I can understand that. At night
when she was tired and fell asleep, he would wake up and go to
kiss and bless her sleepy head. He wore a dirty old frock-coat, he
was tight-fisted with everybody else, but he would spend his last
farthing on her; he gave her expensive presents, and it was sheer
joy to him if his gift pleased her. A father always loves his daughters better than their mother does. Home is a happy place for some
girls! I don't think I should ever let my daughter get married.'

'But why not?' she asked, with the faintest whisper of a
laugh.

'I should be jealous, honestly. Why, how could she kiss another
man? Would she love a stranger better than her father? It is painful even to imagine it. Of course that's all nonsense; of course
everybody sees reason in the end. But I think before I let her
get married I would take endless pains over one thing: sorting out
all her suitors. But all the same, I should end by marrying her to
the man she loves. You know, the man his daughter falls in love
with always seems worse than the others to a father. That's a

fact. It causes a lot of trouble in families.'

'Some people are glad to sell their daughters instead of giving them in marriage honestly,' she said suddenly.

Ah! So that's it!

'That's in those accursed families where there is neither God nor love, Liza,' I said hotly, 'and where there is no love, there is no reason either. There are such families, certainly, but I am not talking about them. It is clear you never knew kindness in your family, if you say things like that. You are truly unfortunate. H'm. ... It is mostly poverty that does that.'

'Is it any better among gentlefolk then? And decent people lead good lives even if they are poor.'

'H'm ... yes. Perhaps. There's another thing, Liza: people only like to count their sorrows, they don't count their happinesses. But if they reckoned as they ought to, they would see that everybody gets his share of everything. Well, but suppose everything goes well with your family, God is good to you, your husband proves to be a good man who loves you and cherishes you and doesn't leave you! It would be happy in a family like that. Sometimes, even, it's happy with half joy and half sorrow; and besides there's *some* sorrow everywhere. Perhaps you'll get married, and then *you'll find out for yourself.* On the other hand, take the early days of being married to a man you love: what utter happiness that can be! And it is renewed again and again. To begin with, even quarrels with a husband end happily. Sometimes the more a woman loves her husband, the more quarrels she starts with him. It's true; I knew one like that: "It's like this: I love you very much," she'd say, "and I torment you out of love, and I want you to feel that." Do you know that you can deliberately torment somebody out of love? Especially women can. And they think to themselves, "Afterwards I'll be so loving and tender that it's not wrong to make him suffer now." – And at home everybody is glad of you, there is goodness and merriment and peace and decency. ... And there are others who are jealous. I knew one – if her husband was out she couldn't rest, even in the middle of the night she'd get up and go poking and prying to see if he was *there,* in that house, with that woman. That's really bad. And she knew it was bad, and her heart would be heavy, and she would reproach herself, but it was because she loved him, you know; all for love. And how good it is to make it up after a quarrel, and ask his forgiveness and forgive him! And both of them are so happy, everything suddenly becomes wonderful – as if they had just met for the first time, or got married, or fallen in love. And nobody, nobody at all, ought to know what goes on between man and wife, if they love each other. And whatever sort of quarrels they have – they mustn't even call their own mothers in as judges, with one telling tales about the other. They are their own judges. Love is a sacred secret, and ought to be kept hidden from all other eyes, whatever happens. It is holier that way, and better. They respect one another more, and respect is the foundation of many things. And if there was once love, if they married for love, why should love ever come to an end? Is it really impossible to keep it up? It very rarely happens that it can't be kept going. Why, if a husband is a good and honest man, and gets on in life, how can love pass away? The first wedded love passes, true, but then comes an even better love. Then the two come together in soul and have all things in common; they have no secrets from one another. And when children come, even the most difficult of times will seem happiness; one need only love and have courage. Then work itself is cheerful, and even if you have to deny yourself food for the children, that is cheerful too. They will love you for it afterwards, it really means laying up a store for yourselves: when the children are growing you feel you must be an example and a support for them; and that even if you die, they will carry your feelings and thoughts in themselves all their lives, since they have received them from you and will bear your image and likeness. This then is a great duty. How can it fail to draw father and mother even closer together? Is it supposed to be a heavy burden to have children? Who says so? It is heavenly bliss! Do you like little children, Liza? I do, terribly. You know – a rosy little baby sucking at your breast, and any husband's heart will turn towards his wife when he sees her sitting with his baby in her arms! A rosy, chubby little child, stretching and sunning itself; plump little legs and arms, transparent little nails, so tiny that you laugh to see them, and little eyes that seem to understand everything already. And it sucks, its tiny hand pinching and playing with your breast. The father comes near; it tears itself away from the breast, bends over backwards and looks at its father, laughs – as if something was terribly funny – and then applies itself to sucking again. Or else all of a sudden, if its little teeth are coming through, it bites its mother's breast, looking slyly out of the corners of its little eyes as if to say, "Look, I bit it!" And isn't that the whole of happiness, when the three, husband, wife, and child are together? Much can be forgiven for those moments. Yes, indeed, Liza, you have to learn how to live yourself, and after that you can criticize people!'

'Pictures, you have to go on painting that sort of pretty pictures!' I thought to myself, although I swear I had spoken with real feeling; and then suddenly I blushed. 'What if she bursts out laughing, what shall I do with myself then?' The idea made me furious. By the end of my speech I had grown really warm, and now my vanity had somehow been wounded. The silence lengthened. I felt like nudging her.

'Somehow, you . . .' she began, and then stopped.

But I had understood: a different note had quavered in her voice, not the old harsh, brutal, defiant tone, but something gentle and shy, so shy that somehow I felt ashamed and guilty.

'What?' I asked, with indulgent curiosity.

'Well, you . . .'

'What?'

'Somehow you . . . it sounds just like a book,' she said, and again there was a note of mockery in her voice.

The remark stung me painfully. That was not what I had expected.

I didn't understand that the mockery was deliberately assumed, like a mask; it was the last subterfuge of the kind usual with shy and pure-minded people, whose hearts are subjected to coarse and insistent probing, whose pride will not let them yield until the last minute, and who are afraid to express their feelings. The very timidity with which she ventured on her mockery, the several

attempts before she succeeded at last in making herself express it,
ought to have enabled me to guess. But I did not guess, and my
heart brimmed over with spite.

'Just you wait!' I thought.

7

'Oh, stop it, Liza; if I'm disgusted, it's on your behalf and has
nothing to do with books. And not only on your behalf. I've just
wakened up to all this myself.... You must be revolted by all this,
aren't you? No, evidently habit counts for a lot! The devil only
knows what habit can do to a man. But surely you can't seriously
think you'll never get old and will always stay pretty, or that
they'll keep you here for ever? I don't even mention the fact that it
is pretty nasty even here. ... However, I'll say this about it –
about this place you are living in: even though you are young and
attractive and pretty now, with feelings and sensitivity; well, do
you know, as soon as I woke just now, I was revolted to find
myself here with you! You have to be drunk to come here. But if
you were in a different kind of place, living as decent people live,
then perhaps I would not only hang round you, but absolutely
fall in love with you, and be glad of a look, let alone a word, from
you; I'd lie in wait for you at your gate, I'd always be on my knees
to you, I'd look on you as my future wife, and think myself
honoured. I wouldn't dare have any impure thoughts about you.
But here I know I've only to whistle and you'll come to me, like it
or not, and you'll be at my beck and call, not me at yours. The
lowest little peasant can hire himself out to work, but all the same
he won't be altogether a slave, and besides he knows it won't last
for ever. But when will you be free? And think what it is you are
giving up here! What are you selling into slavery? Your soul as
well as your body, the soul you have no right to enslave! You let
your love be profaned by any and every drunken sot! Your love! –
And that is everything, you know, it is a diamond; love is every
young girl's treasure! To earn that love, some men are ready to
give up their lives, their very souls. But what is your love worth
now? You have been bought, the whole of you, and why should

anybody try to win love when he can have everything without it?
And for a girl there's no worse crime than that, do you understand? – I've been told they try to keep you silly creatures happy –
they allow you to have your own lovers. But that's just pam-
pering you, they're fooling you, laughing at you, and you believe
them! Does he really love you, that lover? I don't believe it. How
can he, if he knows you might be called away at any moment to
somebody else? That makes him no better than filthy scum! Will
he have the slightest respect for you? What have you in common
with him? He'll laugh at you and steal from you – that's the
extent of his love! You'll be lucky if he doesn't beat you! But
perhaps he will. Ask him, if you have somebody like that, whether
he'll marry you. He'll laugh in your face, if he doesn't spit on you
or knock you down – and yet perhaps he's not worth a brass
farthing himself. And what do you think you've ruined your life
for? To be given coffee to drink and plenty to eat? And what do
they feed you for? A decent woman wouldn't let that food touch
her lips, because she knows what its purpose is. – You're in debt
here and you'll go on being in debt, you'll be in debt to the very
end, till the time when the customers begin to be disgusted with
you. And that time will soon come; don't rely on your youth. In
this place all that sort of thing is gone like the wind. You'll be
turned out ... and not simply turned out; long before that you'll
begin to be bullied and blamed and sworn at – just as if you hadn't
thrown away your health and youth and soul for her profit, but
instead had ruined *her*, robbed her and reduced her to beggary.
And don't expect any support: the others, your pals, will attack
you as well, to keep on the right side of her, because everybody
here is a slave, and long ago lost all conscience and pity. They are
steeped in filth, and there is nothing on earth as nasty, dirty, and
offensive as their abuse. And you will have given up everything,
everything, whole-heartedly – health, youth, beauty, hope – and
at twenty-two you'll look like thirty-five, and you'll be lucky if
you are not a sick woman – pray God you won't be! I suppose you
think now that you don't have to work, it's all one long holiday!
But there is no harder and more back-breaking toil on earth, and
never has been. I should think anybody would eat her heart out. –

And you won't dare utter a word, not a syllable, when you are
turned out of here; you'll go as if it was all your fault. You'll
transfer yourself to another place, and then to a third, and somewhere else after that, and in the end you'll come to the Haymarket. And there you'll be beaten up as a matter of course; that's
one of their charming habits; they don't know how to show a
guest he's welcome except by beating him up. Don't you believe
it's so horrible there? Go and have a look some time, and perhaps
you'll see for yourself. Once I saw a woman, on New Year's day,
outside a door. Her own people had thrown her out, with ill-
natured laughter, to cool off a bit, because she was making too
much noise, and locked the door behind her. At nine o'clock in the
morning she was already quite drunk, tousled, half-naked, and
covered with bruises. Her face was as white as chalk, but it was
black round the eyes; blood was flowing from her nose; some
cabby had just been using his fists on her. She sat down on the
stone step, holding a dry salt fish in her hand; she was howling
and bewailing her "fate", and battering the fish against the steps.
The cabbies and drunken soldiers crowding round the doorway
mocked at her. You don't believe that you'll ever be like that, do
you? And I should like not to believe it, but how do you know?
perhaps two years ago, or eight, that same woman with the salt
fish arrived here from somewhere, fresh and innocent and pure,
like a little cherub, ignorant of evil and blushing at every word.
Perhaps she was just the same kind as you: proud, sensitive, not
like the others, she looked like a queen, and she knew that perfect
happiness was waiting for the man who would love her and whom
she would love. You see how it ended, don't you? And what if at
that moment when, drunken and dishevelled, she beat that fish
against the dirty steps, what if at that moment all her clean early
life in her father's house came back to her, the years when she was
still going to school, and the neighbour's son waited for her on the
way there, and told her he would love her all his life, and put his
destiny in her hands, and they promised to love one another for
ever, and get married as soon as they grew big? No, Liza, it will be
good luck, good luck for you, if you die soon of consumption
somewhere in a corner, in a cellar, like that girl I told you about

just now. In hospital, do you say? Good – they'll take you there – but if the madam still needs you? Consumption is a special kind of illness; it's not a fever. With it, a person can hope till the last minute, and say she's well. She can reassure herself. And it's to the madam's benefit. Don't worry, it's true; it means you've sold your soul, and besides you owe money, and so you daren't say a word. And when you die, they'll all abandon you, all turn away from you – because what good will you be to them then? What's more, you'll be reproached for uselessly taking up room and not dying quickly enough. You'll beg in vain for a drink of water, and be given it with a curse; "When will you kick the bucket, you slut?" they'll say; "you won't let us sleep, you keep on groaning, you make the customers sick." This is quite true; I have overheard things like it myself. When you're really dying, you'll be pushed into a stinking corner of the cellar, in the darkness and the damp; what will you think about then, lying there alone? When you die, you'll be carted off in a hurry, by strangers, grumbling and impatient – nobody will say a prayer for you, nobody will sigh over you – they'll simply want to get you out of sight as quickly as they can. They'll buy a box and carry you out as they did that poor girl today, and hold your wake in the pub. There'll be wet snow, and slush and slime in the grave, and they're not likely to stand on ceremony with the likes of you. "Let her down, Vanya; well, there's a fine thing! – even here she has to have her legs in the air – that's the sort she is. Shorten those ropes, don't fool about." "It's all right as it is." "What do you mean all right? It's lying on its side, isn't it? After all, she's a human being. Oh well, all right, fill it in." They won't waste much time even arguing about you. They'll shovel in the dark-blue clay and go off to the pub. ... That'll be the end of your memory on the earth; other women have children to come to their graveside, and fathers and husbands – but there'll be no tears or sighs or prayers for you, and nobody, nobody at all in the whole world will ever come to your grave: your name will vanish from the face of the earth – just as if you had never existed, never been born! All in the mud and marsh, you can knock as much as you like on the coffin lid at night, when the dead awaken: "Let me out, good people, to live in the world. When I was alive I saw nothing of life; my life ran away down the drain; I drank it away in a pub in the Haymarket; let me live on earth again, good people!" '

I had let myself be carried away to such an extent that a lump was rising in my own throat, and ... I stopped suddenly, raised myself in a fright on my elbow, bent my head fearfully and began to listen with a beating heart. I had good cause to be disturbed.

For some time I had been feeling that I must have harrowed her soul and crushed her heart, and the more convinced I grew of it, the more I wanted to attain my end as quickly and powerfully as possible. It was the game that carried me along, the game itself, but not only the game ...

I knew that what I said was constrained and artificial, even bookish; in short, the only way I could talk was 'like a book', but that wasn't what disturbed me; I knew I should be understood and felt that my very bookishness might well be a help. But now that I had made my effort my nerve failed all at once. No, never, never had I witnessed such despair! She was lying face downwards, with her head buried in the pillow and her arms strained tightly round it. Her heart was bursting. Her whole young body shook as if she had a fever. Stifling sobs crowded into her breast until they forced their way out as wails and cries; at those moments she would press her face deeper into the pillow, for fear that any living soul in that place should know of her tears and agony. She bit the pillow, bit her hands until the blood came (as I saw later) or, desperately clutching the tangled braids of her hair, grew rigid with effort, holding her breath and clenching her teeth. I tried to say something, to beg her to be calm, but soon realized that I simply dared not, and, trembling violently and almost terrified, began hurriedly groping about for my things, to get away somehow as quickly as possible. It was pitch dark, and try as I might I could not finish quickly. All at once my hand found a box of matches and a candlestick, with a whole new candle. As soon as the light filled the room Liza started up and sat gazing at me almost vacantly, with a half-crazy smile on her distorted face. I sat down beside her and took her hands; she came to her senses and flung herself towards me as if to put her arms round me, but she dared not, and could only hang her head in silence.

'Liza, my dear, I didn't mean ... forgive me,' I began, but she pressed my hand in hers with such force that I realized I was saying the wrong thing.

'Here is my address, Liza; come to me.'

'Yes, I will,' she whispered decidedly, but without raising her head.

'And now I am going; good-bye ... au revoir.'

I stood up and so did she; then she started, blushing violently, seized the shawl lying on a chair and flung it round her shoulders, covering herself to the chin. My heart ached; I was in a hurry to leave, to get right away.

'Wait,' she said suddenly, when we were already in the passage and close to the door, halted me with a hand on the sleeve of my overcoat, hastily set down the candle, and hurried away – she had evidently remembered something, or wanted to bring something to show me. As she ran off, her face was full of colour, her eyes sparkled, there was a smile on her lips – what could it mean? Involuntarily I waited; she returned in a minute, with a glance that seemed to be pleading for forgiveness for something. This was not at all the same face or the same look as just now – sullen, mistrustful and stubborn. Her look now was beseeching, gentle, and at the same time trustful, tender, and humble. It was like the look of children when they are asking for something from somebody they love. Hers were hazel eyes, full of life and capable of reflecting both love and sullen hatred.

Without any explanation – as if I was some higher kind of creature who knew everything without being told, she held out towards me a piece of paper. Her whole face was absolutely glowing with the most naïve, almost childish, delight. I unfolded the paper. It was a letter from a young medical student, or something of the sort, a very stilted and flowery but extremely respectful declaration of love. I can't remember the phrases now, but I remember very well that through the high-flown style there shone a sincerity of feeling impossible to feign. When I had finished it, I met her ardent, curious, and childishly eager gaze fixed on my face as she waited impatiently to hear what I would say. In a few rapid, but joyful and almost boastful words she explained that she had been at a party, with dancing, in the home of some very, very nice people, *family people*, who didn't know *anything, anything at all* – because she was only new here, and she wasn't really ... she hadn't made up her mind at all yet and she would certainly leave as soon as she had paid off her debt. ... Well, this student had been there, and he had danced with her and talked to her all the evening, and it turned out that he had known her in Riga when they were children, they had played together, but it was a long time ago, and he knew her parents, but he didn't know anything, or even suspect anything, *about this!* And the very next day (the day before yesterday), he had sent this letter by the friend who had taken her to the party ... and ... well, that was all.

When she had finished her story she dropped her shining eyes almost shyly.

The poor little creature was preserving the student's letter as a treasure, and it was this treasure she had gone running to fetch, not wanting me to leave without knowing that she was loved, honourably and sincerely, and that people spoke to her with respect. The letter was almost certainly destined to remain put away, without consequences. But that didn't matter; I am sure she would treasure it all her life, as her pride and justification, and now, at a moment like this, she had remembered it and brought it to me, as a way of naïvely showing off and re-establishing herself in my eyes, so that I should see and value her too. Without saying anything I pressed her hand and went out. I couldn't wait to get away. ... I walked the whole way, although the snow was still falling in great wet flakes. I felt tired out, crushed, uncertain. But the truth already gleamed through the uncertainty. The filthy truth!

8

It was a long time, however, before I consented to recognize that truth. I awoke in the morning, after some hours of leaden sleep, to an immediate realization of the whole of the previous day's happenings, and was astounded by my *sentimentality* with Liza and

all yesterday's 'horrors and miseries'. 'Pah! A fine state of woman-
ish nerves one gets into!' I thought. 'And what possessed me to
give her my address? What if she comes? However, let her come;
perhaps it doesn't matter. . . .' But *obviously*, the chief and most
urgent matter now was something different: I must make haste, at
whatever cost and as soon as possible, to save my reputation in the
eyes of Zverkov and Simonov. That was the main thing now. And
in my fever of activity that morning I even forgot all about Liza.
First of all, it was necessary to repay yesterday's debt to Simonov
without delay. I resolved on a desperate measure: borrowing the
whole fifteen roubles from Anton Antonovich. It so happened
that he was in an excellent humour that morning and gave it me
at once, as soon as I asked. I was so pleased at this that as I signed
the IOU with a somewhat dashing air I *carelessly* mentioned that
the day before 'some friends and I had been going the pace at the
Hotel de Paris; we were seeing off an old pal, one might even say a
childhood friend, and, you know, he's a bit of a lad, a spoilt darling – well, of course, of good family, pretty well off, a brilliant
career, a wit, an awfully nice chap, carries on intrigues with certain ladies . . . you understand what I mean; well, we drank the
extra half dozen and . . .' And nothing: it had all been said with
great lightness, ease, and smugness.

When I got home I immediately wrote to Simonov.

To this day, remembering the gentlemanly sincerity, the frank
and good-hearted tone of my letter, I am filled with admiration.
Skilfully, nobly, and above all without wasting words, I took the
blame for everything. I used as my excuse, 'if I may still be permitted to make excuses for myself', the fact that since I was completely unused to drinking, the very first glass, supposedly drunk
before their arrival, while I was waiting for them in the Hotel de
Paris from five until six o'clock, had made me drunk. I begged
Simonov's pardon in particular, and asked him to convey my
apologies to all the others, especially Zverkov, whom I seemed to
have a 'hazy recollection' of having insulted. I added that I would
have called on each of them, but my head ached and, most of all, I
was ashamed of myself. I was especially pleased with the kind of
'lightness of touch', almost amounting to the casual, with which

my pen was suddenly endowed, and which gave them to understand, better than any arguments, that I took a rather detached
view of all yesterday's swinishness; I was not, absolutely not, I
implied, killed on the spot, so to speak, as you probably imagine,
gentlemen, but regarded it, on the contrary, as a serenely self-regarding gentleman ought. 'The affair did no discredit to a young
man of spirit,' I quoted.

'Is there perhaps even a touch of aristocratic playfulness?' I
thought admiringly, reading over my note. 'And all because I am
an intelligent and educated man! Other men in my place would
not know how to extricate themselves from an awkward situation,
but I've disentangled myself and can carry on as before, and all
because I am "a mature and educated man of our time" – and
perhaps everything that happened yesterday really was because of
the drink. H'm ... well no, it wasn't because of the drink. I didn't
touch any vodka at all between five o'clock and six, while I was
waiting for them! I told Simonov a lie, a shameless lie, and I still
am not ashamed ...'

'Oh, to hell with it!' What mattered most was that I had got
myself out of it.

I put six roubles in the letter, sealed it, and asked Apollon to
take it to Simonov. When he knew that there was money in the
letter, Apollon became more respectful and agreed to go. Towards
evening I went out for a walk. My head was still aching and dizzy
from the previous night. But the later it grew, and the thicker
became the dusk, the more my feelings, and with them my
thoughts, became changed and muddled. There was something
within me, in the depths of my heart and conscience, that had not
died, that refused to die, and that manifested itself in burning
anguish. For the most part I wandered in the busiest shopping
streets – the Meshchansky, the Sadovaya, and near the Yusupov
Gardens. I had always been especially fond of strolling through
those streets at dusk, just when the passing crowds of craftsmen
and factory-workers going home from their day's work, their faces
bad-tempered with worry, were at their thickest. This anxious
preoccupation with farthings, this undisguised prose, was what
particularly appealed to me. This time the jostling crush in the

streets only inflamed my nerves still more. I simply couldn't get myself straightened out. Something was working and seething in my soul, incessantly and painfully. I returned home utterly shattered. It was as though I had a crime on my conscience.

The thought that Liza might come never ceased to torment me. It was strange that of all the memories of the previous day that of Liza was especially, almost separately, oppressive. By the evening I had succeeded in forgetting all the rest, I had shrugged my shoulders over them, and I remained completely satisfied with my letter to Simonov. But this was something I could no longer be complacent about. The thought of Liza still nagged at me. 'What if she comes?' I never stopped thinking. 'Well, suppose she does, it makes no difference; let her come. H'm. But the mere fact that she will, for example, see how I live is bad. Yesterday I made myself out such ... a hero ... to her ... and now, h'm. It's a great pity I've let things go so much. My flat is positively beggarly. And yesterday I had the nerve to go out to dinner in such clothes! And my oilcloth sofa with the stuffing coming out! And my dressing-gown, that you can't even cover yourself decently with! Rags and tatters. ... And she will see it all; and what's more, she'll see Apollon. That oaf will certainly insult her. He'll be rude to her to get his own back on me. And as usual I'll play the coward, of course. I'll put on airs, wrap the skirts of my dressing-gown round me, and start smiling and trying to pretend. Pah, disgusting! And that's not the worst. There's something more important, nastier, and still lower. Yes, lower! And I shall put on that dishonest lying mask again, again ...!'

But when I reached this point in my thoughts, I burst out: 'Why dishonest? What is there dishonest about it? What I said yesterday was quite sincere. I remember feeling genuinely moved. I really wanted to arouse her noblest emotions. ... If I made her cry, that was a good thing, I was producing a wholesome effect ...'

But all the same I could not make my mind easy.

All that evening, even after I had got home, even after nine o'clock, when it was plain that Liza could not possibly come, the thought of her still kept running in my head and, most important, always in one and the same condition. I mean that one moment out of all those I had lived through the day before kept presenting itself to me with especial clarity; that was the moment when I struck a match and saw her pale distorted face with its expression of martyrdom. How pitiful, how unnatural, how twisted her smile had been at that instant! I did not know then that even after fifteen years I should still go on seeing Liza in my imagination with the same pitiful, twisted, useless smile on her lips as she had worn at that moment.

The next day I was again prepared to see all this as rubbish, the result of frayed nerves and, above all, exaggeration. I have always recognized this as my weak point, and sometimes feared it greatly: 'I always exaggerate, that's my weakness,' I constantly repeated to myself. Nevertheless, 'Liza may still come, all the same,' was the refrain that at that time always brought those internal discussions of mine to a close. I was so worried that at times I became almost frantic: 'She'll come, she's sure to come,' I exclaimed, scurrying about the room, 'tomorrow if not today, and she'll find me! That's what comes of the damned romanticism of all these "pure hearts"! Oh, the vileness, the stupidity, the narrowness of these "sentimental pagan souls"! Well, how could she fail to understand? Surely she must have understood that . . . ?' But here I would pull myself up, in the greatest confusion.

'And how little need,' I thought in passing, 'how little need there was of the idyllic (and moreover, idylls are so artificial, bookish, invented) to change a whole human life to suit one's own ideas! That's your innocence for you! that's your inexperience!'

Sometimes I had the idea of going to see Liza myself, 'telling her everything,' and begging her not to come. But at the thought such rage boiled up in me that I think I would have crushed that 'damned' Liza if she had suddenly appeared at my side; I should have insulted her, abused her, driven her away, even struck her!

One day passed, however, and a second, and a third – she did not come and I began to grow calmer. I became particularly cheerful and light-hearted after nine o'clock, and even began to indulge in soothing dreams; for example: 'I save Liza by the mere fact that she comes to me and I talk to her. . . . I develop her, educate her.

... Finally I notice that she loves me, loves me passionately. I pretend not to understand. (I don't know, though, why I pretend, I just do – probably as an ornamental touch.) Finally, covered with confusion, beautiful, trembling and sobbing, she throws herself at my feet and declares that I am her saviour and she loves me better than anything else in the world. I am amazed, but. ... "Liza," I say, "do you really think I haven't noticed your love? I saw everything, I guessed it all, but I did not dare trespass on your heart the first, because I have influence over you, and I was afraid you would deliberately make yourself respond to my love out of gratitude, trying to produce by force an emotion that perhaps does not exist, and I didn't want that, because that is ... despotism. ... It is indelicate." ' (In short, here I would indulge in a lot of European, George-Sandish, ineffably noble and subtle nonsense.) ' "But now, now you are mine, my creation, beautiful and pure, you are – my lovely wife.

> Enter now then, bold and free,
> Be mistress of my house and me!" '

Then we should begin living happily ever after, travelling abroad, etc., etc. In short the whole dream would get extremely low and common, and I would end by jeering at myself.

'Besides, they won't let her come, a "fallen woman",' I thought. 'I don't think they let them go out much, least of all in the evening.' (For some reason I was absolutely convinced that she would come in the evening, at exactly seven o'clock.) 'On the other hand she said she wasn't completely committed, she still kept a certain independence; so ... h'm! Damn it all, she'll come, she'll certainly come!'

It was a good thing that Apollon's boorishness distracted my attention during that time. He completely exhausted my patience! He was my executioner, my cross, the scourge inflicted on me by Providence. For several years he and I had been constantly skirmishing, and I hated him. My God, how I hated him! I think I have never in my life hated anybody as much, especially at certain times. He was a pompous elderly man who also did a little tailoring. For some reason he held me in boundless contempt and treated me with intolerable condescension. But then he was condescending with everybody. You had only to look at that smooth flaxen poll and the heavily oiled quiff poking up above his forehead, or at that prim mouth always pursed into a V-shape, to feel that you were in the presence of a man who had never doubted himself in his life. He was consummately pedantic, the greatest pedant I have ever met, and his self-esteem would have been hardly becoming in Alexander of Macedon. He was besotted with himself, he doted on every one of his buttons, every one of his finger-nails: that was his essence! He tyrannized over me completely, spoke to me extremely seldom, and if he cast me an occasional glance, it was with a royally self-assured and perpetually derisive look that sometimes drove me wild. He carried out his duties as though he was doing me the greatest of favours. He did practically nothing for me, however, and did not even consider himself obliged to do anything. There could be no doubt that he considered me the greatest fool on earth, and if he 'kept me in his service' it was solely because he could get his wages from me every month. He consented to *do nothing* for me for seven roubles a month. I shall be forgiven much for his sake. My hatred grew to such proportions that his very way of walking sometimes made me shudder. But what I loathed most was his lisping speech. His tongue was a little too long for him, or something, and this gave him a perpetual lisp and hiss, of which he appeared to be very proud, imagining that it conferred extraordinary distinction on him. He spoke in quiet, measured tones, with his hands behind his back and his eyes on the ground. I found it particularly infuriating when he used to begin reading the psalter aloud in his room. I fought many battles over that reading. But he was terribly fond of reading the psalter in the evening in his quiet, monotonous voice, as though he was reading over a corpse. It is interesting that that is what he ended by doing; now he reads the psalter over the dead, as well as exterminating rats and making blacking. But at that time I found I could no more dismiss him than if his being had been chemically combined with mine. Besides, he wouldn't have consented to leave on any account. I couldn't live in a furnished room; my flat was my private possession, my shell, my sheath, in which I hid from all mankind, and Apollon, God knows why, seemed to belong to that flat, and for the whole seven years I found it impossible to turn him out.

To keep back his wages for even two or three days was equally impossible. He would have made such an issue of it that I shouldn't have known what to do with myself. But at this period I was so furious with everybody that I made up my mind to punish Apollon for some fault or other by withholding his wages for two weeks. I had been intending to do this for a long time, about two years, simply to show him he could not give himself such airs with me, and that if I chose I could always refuse to give him his wages. I proposed not to mention the matter to him, keeping quiet in order to conquer his pride and force him to be the first to speak about it. Then I would take the seven roubles out of the drawer and show them to him, so that he could see that I had them put away on purpose, but I wouldn't, I wouldn't, I simply wouldn't give him his wages; I wouldn't because I wouldn't, because that was my decision as his master, because he was disrespectful, because he was an oaf; but if he would ask politely I would perhaps relent and pay him; if not, he could wait another two weeks, or three, or a month ...

But angry though I was, he won. I didn't even hold out for four days. He began as he always did in such cases (because there had been such cases before, it had all been tried before and, let me remark, I knew it all beforehand, I knew his sneaking tactics by heart); that is to say he began by gazing at me sternly for several minutes together, especially when we met face to face or when he was showing me out. If I contained myself and pretended I did not notice these looks, he proceeded, still without saying anything, to further tortures. Suddenly, for no reason at all, he would glide silently into my room when I was moving about or reading, stop close to the door, put one hand behind his back, and stand 'at ease', his eyes fixed on me with an expression no longer so much stern as contemptuous. If I asked him what he wanted, he would make no reply, but continue to gaze steadily at me for a few more seconds, then slowly turn about and, with tightly compressed lips and a highly significant air, slowly retreat into his room. Two hours later he would suddenly emerge again and make another appearance before me. It sometimes happened that I was too angry to ask him what he wanted, but sharply raised my head and gazed steadily and masterfully at him. We would stare at each other like this for about two minutes; finally, slowly and pompously, he would turn away and disappear for a further two hours.

If even this failed to make me see reason and I remained mutinous, he would begin to sigh as he looked at me, sigh long and deeply, with a sigh that seemed to measure the full depth of my infamy, and of course in the end he always triumphed; I raged and shouted, but all the same I was compelled to concede the point in dispute.

This time, the usual manoeuvre of 'stern looks' had hardly begun before I completely lost control of myself and attacked him furiously. I had too many other things to annoy me.

'Stop!' I shouted frantically as, slowly and silently, with one hand behind his back, he turned to go away into his own room, 'stop! Come back, I tell you, come back!' And I must have yelled so unnaturally that he turned back again and examined me with some amazement. He remained mute, however, and this drove me into a frenzy.

'How dare you come in here without permission and stare at me like that? Answer me!'

But after gazing at me calmly for half a minute he again began to turn away.

'Stop!' I howled, rushing up to him; 'stay where you are! That's it! Now answer me: why did you come in to stare at me?'

'If you have any orders for me just now, it is my business to carry them out,' he replied after another silence, in his hushed, measured, hissing tones, raising his eyebrows and quietly changing the inclination of his head from left to right.

'That's not what I'm asking you about, torturer!' I shrieked, trembling with fury. 'I'll tell you what you came for: you can see I'm not giving you your money, and you're too stiff-necked to submit and ask for it, and that's why you come in here with your stupid stares, to punish me, and you haven't the least idea, torturer, how stupid, stupid, stupid, stupid, stupid, it is!'

He was again beginning to turn away without speaking, but I seized him.

'Listen!' I shouted. 'Here's the money, you see, here it is!' (I took it out of the table-drawer), 'all seven roubles, but you won't get it, you wo-o-on't get it, until such time as you come, respectfully and repentantly, to ask my forgiveness. You hear what I say!'

'That can never be!' he answered with unnatural self-assurance.

'It will!' I shouted. 'On my word of honour, it will!'

'And there is nothing for me to ask your pardon for,' he went on, as if he hadn't noticed my shouts, 'because you called me "torturer" just now, and I can always claim against you for slander at the police-station.'

'Go there then! Make your claim!' I howled. 'Go now, this minute, this second! But all the same you're a torturer. Torturer! Torturer!' But he only looked at me, then turned round and, without heeding my shouted commands or looking back, glided away to his own room.

'None of this would have happened if it wasn't for Liza!' I said to myself. Then, after standing there for a moment, I followed him, stalking in a solemn and dignified way, but with a heart that beat slowly and heavily, round the screen to his quarters.

'Apollon!' I said, with the utmost calm and deliberation, although I was choking with rage, 'go at once, without a moment's delay, for the police-sergeant!'

He had already sat down at his table, put on his spectacles, and taken up a piece of sewing. But when he heard my order, he snorted with laughter.

'Go at once, go this instant! – Go, or you can't even begin to imagine what will happen!'

'Seriously, you must be out of your mind!' he lisped slowly, continuing to thread his needle without even looking up. 'Whoever heard of a man going to fetch the police to himself? And, as for frightening me, it's no use your straining yourself, because nothing will come of it.'

'Go on!' I shrieked, seizing him by the shoulder. I felt I was on the point of striking him.

But I had not noticed the outer door opening slowly and quietly at that very moment, and now a figure entered, stopped, and stared at us in bewilderment. I looked round and, transfixed with shame, immediately dashed into my own room. There, clutching my hair with both hands, I leaned my head against the wall and remained rigid in that position.

About two minutes I heard Apollon's slow tread.

'A *person* is asking for you,' he said, looking at me extremely severely, and then he stood aside and admitted Liza. He did not go away again, but watched us derisively.

'Get out! Get out!' I ordered, flustered. At that moment my clock gathered up its strength, wheezed, and struck seven.

9

Enter now then, bold and free,
Be mistress of my house and me.

I stood before her, crushed, discredited, foully covered with confusion, smiling, I think, and straining the skirts of my ragged wadded dressing-gown round me – in fact exactly as I had pictured myself in my depression a little earlier. Apollon went out after he had stood over us for a couple of minutes, but I felt no relief. The worst of it was that she was suddenly overcome with confusion to a most unexpected degree. It was of course the result of seeing the state I was in.

'Sit down,' I said mechanically, moving a chair to the table for her and myself taking a seat on the sofa. All eyes, she obediently sat down, evidently expecting something from me at once. This naïve expectation drove me into a rage, but I contained myself.

If I could only try not to notice anything, as if everything was as usual, but she. . . . And I was vaguely aware that I should make her pay dearly for all this.

'You find me in a strange situation, Liza,' I began, stammering and knowing that this was just how *not* to deal with it.

'No, no, don't mistake me!' I cried, seeing that she had suddenly coloured up, 'I am not ashamed of my poverty. . . . On the contrary, I am proud of it. I am poor but high-minded. . . . One can be poor and high-minded,' I muttered. 'However ... would you like some tea?'

'No ...' she was beginning.

'Wait a moment!' I jumped up and ran out to Apollon. I had to find some excuse for disappearing from sight.

'Apollon,' I babbled in a feverish whisper, throwing down the seven roubles, which I had been holding in my hand the whole time, 'here's your wages! You see, I'm giving you them, but in return you must come to my rescue: bring me some tea and ten rusks from the pub. If you refuse, you'll make me most unhappy! You don't know what sort of woman that is.... That's the whole point! Perhaps you imagine something. ... But you don't know what that woman is ...!'

Apollon, who had already sat down to his work again, and put on his spectacles, squinted at the money first of all, without putting down his needle; then he went on fussing with the thread, still trying to get it into the needle, without paying me the slightest attention or saying a word. I waited for about three minutes, standing before him with my arms folded in a Napoleonic pose. My temples were damp with sweat and I could feel that I was pale. But thank God, he probably felt sorry just to look at me. Finishing with his thread he slowly stood up, slowly moved away from the table, slowly counted the money and at length slowly left the room, throwing at me over his shoulder the question: 'Do you want me to bring a complete order?' On the way back to Liza, the thought crossed my mind of simply running away, come what might, following my nose and just as I was, in my dressing-gown.

I sat down again. She looked at me anxiously. Neither of us spoke for a few minutes.

'I'll kill him!' I yelled suddenly, banging my fist on the table so violently that the ink splashed out of the ink-well.

'Oh, what are you saying?' she cried, starting.

'I'll kill him, I'll kill him,' I yelled again, thumping the table in an utter frenzy, and at the same time realizing what extreme stupidity it was to be in such a frenzy.

'You don't know, Liza, what that executioner is to me. He stretches me on the rack! ... He's gone for rusks now; he ...'

And all at once I burst into tears. It was a real fit of hysteria. I was hot with shame, but I could not restrain my sobs.

She was frightened. 'What's the matter? Whatever is the matter?' she cried, hovering round me.

'Water, give me some water – over there!' I muttered feebly, conscious, however, that I could quite well do without water, or feeble mutterings either. I was *putting on an act*, as they call it, to preserve the decencies, even though my hysteria was genuine enough.

She gave me the water, looking at me forlornly. At that moment Apollon carried in the tea. This ordinary prosaic tea suddenly seemed to me so wretched and unsuitable after all that had happened that I blushed for it. Liza looked at Apollon in fright. He went out without glancing at us.

'Liza, do you despise me?' I said, looking hard at her and trembling with impatience to find out what she was thinking.

She became flustered and could not answer.

'Drink your tea,' I said angrily. I was angry with myself, but of course it was she who had to suffer for it. A terrible rage against her boiled up suddenly in my heart; I think I could have killed her. To be revenged on her, I swore I would not say a word to her all the time she was there. 'She is the cause of it all,' I thought.

Our silence had already lasted some five minutes. The tea stood on the table; we did not touch it: I had reached the stage where I refused to drink mine, on purpose to make it harder for her; and for her to begin first seemed awkward. Sometimes she looked at me in sad perplexity. I remained stubbornly silent. I was of course the greatest sufferer myself, because I was fully conscious of the sickening baseness of my stupid rage, and at the same time unable to restrain myself.

'I want to ... leave ... that place altogether,' she began, to break the silence somehow, but, poor thing! that was just the wrong subject to broach in a situation that was stupid enough already. Even my heart ached with pity for her clumsiness and needless honesty. But something inside me instantly choked all pity, and even egged me on still further; let the sky fall! Five minutes more passed.

'Am I disturbing you?' she began, timidly and almost inaudibly, beginning to get up.

But the moment I saw this first flash of offended dignity I began to shake with rage and immediately burst out furiously.

'Why did you come here? Tell me that, if you please!' I began, choking with anger and not even trying to preserve the logical order of my words. I wanted to get it all out in one volley; I didn't even bother about where to begin.

'Why did you come? Answer me, answer me!' I shouted, almost beside myself. 'I'll tell you why you came, my dear. You came because I spoke to you with pity and sympathy. Well, now you've gone soft, and you want *sympathetic words* again. Let me tell you that I was laughing at you. And I'm laughing at you now. What are you trembling for? Yes, I was laughing at you. I had been insulted earlier, at dinner, by those fellows who arrived before me. I came to your place intending to thrash a certain officer who was one of them; but I didn't succeed, he wasn't there. So I had to be revenged on somebody for the insult and get my own back; you turned up and so I vented my fury on you, and had a good laugh. I had been humiliated, so I wanted to humiliate somebody else; I had been treated like dirt, so I wanted to show my power. ... That's what happened, and you thought I'd come on purpose to rescue you, didn't you? Didn't you? Didn't you?'

I knew that she might be getting confused and would not understand all I was saying, but I knew also that she would understand the essence of it perfectly well. And so she did.

She went as white as a sheet and tried, with painfully distorted lips, to say something, but only dropped back on her chair as though she had been felled with an axe. And all the time afterwards she listened to me with gaping mouth and staring eyes, trembling with terror. She was crushed, crushed by my cynicism ...

'Save you!' I went on, jumping up from my chair and almost running backwards and forwards in front of her. 'Save you from what? But I am perhaps worse than you. Why didn't you fling the question in my face when I began preaching at you: "What did *you* come here for then? To teach us morality, I suppose?" It was power, power, I wanted then, the fascination of the game; I wanted to get your tears, your humiliation, your hysterics – that's what I wanted then! It's true that I couldn't go through with it, because I'm trash, and I got scared and, God knows why, was fool enough to give you my address. Afterwards, even before I got home, I was already cursing you for all I was worth because of that address. I really hated you then, because I had lied to you. Because I only want to amuse myself a bit with words, to have a few dreams in my head, but in real life do you know what I want? for you to vanish, that's what! I want to be left in peace. Just left undisturbed, I'd sell the whole world this minute for a copeck. For the whole world to vanish into thin air, or for me not to drink my tea? I say, let the world perish, if I can always drink my tea. Did you know that or not? Well, I know this: I'm a blackguard, a scoundrel, an egotist, a sluggard. For the last three days I've been shaking with fear that you would come. And do you know what worried me particularly all those three days? That I'd made myself out to be such a hero to you and now all at once you would see me in this ragged dressing-gown, poverty-stricken, repulsive. I said just now that I was not ashamed of being poor; let me tell you that I *am* ashamed of it, more ashamed than of anything else, I fear it more than anything else, more than being a thief, because I am so vain that it's as if my skin had been flayed off and the very air was painful to me. Surely you must have guessed by now that I shall never forgive you for having found me in this disgraceful dressing-gown at a time when I was going for Apollon like a bad-tempered little cur. The saviour, the hero, flying at his servant like a mangy, neglected mongrel, while the servant laughs at him! And the tears that I could no more hold back just now than some old woman who's been put to shame, I will never forgive you those! And I shall never forgive you for what I am confessing now, at this moment. Yes, you and you alone will have to answer for everything, because you turned up, because I am a cad, because I am the nastiest, most ridiculous, pettiest, stupidest, most envious of all the worms on this earth, who are none of them any better than me, but who, the devil only knows why, are never put out of countenance; but all my life any nit will be able to give me

a fillip on the nose, and that's my distinguishing feature! And
what business is it of mine that you don't understand a word of
this? And what on earth has it to do with me whether you are
perishing in that place or not? Do you understand how much I
shall hate you for being here and hearing me tell you all this?
After all, a man doesn't talk like this more than once in a lifetime,
and then only if he's hysterical! ... What more do you want?
Why are you still here, tormenting me, after all that, why don't
you go?'

But at this point something exceedingly strange happened.

I was so used to thinking and imagining everything like a book,
and seeing everything in the guise in which I had previously created it in my dreams, that at first I didn't even understand this
strange circumstance. But this is what happened: Liza, whom I
had so abused and humiliated, understood a great deal more than I
imagined. She understood that part of it that a woman always
understands first, if she sincerely loves, and that was that I myself
was unhappy. The terrified and outraged feeling in her face
changed first of all into sorrowful bewilderment. But when I
began to call myself a cad and a scoundrel, and my tears began to
flow again (I uttered the whole tirade to the accompaniment of
tears), her whole face underwent a kind of convulsion. She tried to
rise to her feet, and to stop me somehow; when I finished, however, she paid no attention to my cries of 'Why are you here?
Why don't you go away?', but only to the fact that it must be
very difficult for me to say all this. And she was so cowed, poor
thing; she considered herself so infinitely beneath me; why should
she be resentful or offended? On some sort of irresistible impulse
she sprang up from her chair, and straining towards me but still
timid and not daring to move from the spot, held out her arms to
me. ... Now my heart too turned over. Then she rushed towards
me, flung her arms round my neck, and burst into tears. I
also was unable to control myself, and sobbed as I never had
before ...

'They give me no. ... I'm incapable of being ... good!' I cried,
hardly able to get the words out, then I went over to the sofa, fell
face downwards on it and sobbed for a quarter of an hour in real

hysterics. She pressed herself against me, embraced me, and remained motionless.

But all the same, the hysterics could not go on for ever. And now (I am telling the sickening truth), as I lay face down on the sofa, flat, with my face buried in my cheap leather cushion, I began little by little, as if from afar, unwillingly but uncontrollably to feel that it would be awkward to raise my head and look Liza in the eyes. What was I ashamed of? I don't know, but I was ashamed. The idea came also into my overwrought mind that our roles had definitely been reversed, she was the heroine and I was just such another crushed and degraded creature as she had been that night – four days before. ... And all this came into my head while I still lay face downwards on the sofa.

My God, surely I didn't envy her even then, did I?

I don't know, I still can't make up my mind, but then, of course I was still less able to understand it than I am now. Without power and tyranny over somebody I can't live. ... But ... but after all, discussion won't explain anything, and consequently there's no point in discussing it.

However, I overcame my reluctance and lifted my head slightly; after all, I had to raise it some time. ... And then, purely because, as I am convinced to this day, I was ashamed to look at her, a different feeling was kindled in my heart and flared up all at once ... a feeling of mastery and ownership. My eyes glittered with passion and I squeezed her hands hard. How I hated her and how strongly I was attracted to her at that moment! One feeling reinforced the other. It was almost like revenge ...! At first her face expressed what might have been perplexity, or perhaps even fear, but only for one instant. Rapturously, ardently, she embraced me.

10

A quarter of an hour later I was scurrying round the room in frantic impatience, at every other moment rushing up to the screens and peering through the crack between them at Liza. She was sitting on the floor, leaning her head against the bed and probably crying. But she was not going, and that was what annoyed me. This time she knew everything. I had insulted her finally, but ... there is no point in telling *that* story. She had divined that my fit of passion was in fact vengeance, a fresh indignity for her, and that to my recent almost aimless hatred had been added a personal, envious hatred of her. ... I do not maintain, however, that she understood it all distinctly; but on the other hand she fully understood that I was a vile creature and, most important, not in a condition to love her.

I know I shall be told this is incredible – incredible to be as ill-natured and stupid as I am; perhaps it will be added that it was incredible not to fall in love with her, or at least not to value her love. But why is it incredible? To begin with, I could no longer fall in love, because, I repeat, with me to love meant to tyrannize and hold the upper hand morally. All my life I have been unable to conceive of any other love, and I have reached the stage when I sometimes think now that the whole of love consists in the right, freely given to the lover, to tyrannize over the beloved. Even in my underground dreams I did not picture love otherwise than as a struggle, always beginning with hatred and ending with moral subjugation, and after that could not even imagine what to do with the conquered victim. And indeed, what *is* incredible here is that I had already become so morally depraved and so unaccustomed to 'real life' that just now I had taken it into my head to reproach and decry her for coming to me to hear 'sympathetic words'; and I didn't even guess that to hear sympathetic words was not what she had come for at all, but to love me, because for a woman love comprises all resurrection, all salvation from whatever sort of ruin, and all regeneration, and cannot be manifested in any other way. I no longer hated her so much, however, as I scuttled about the room, peering through the cracks in the screens. It simply was intolerably burdensome to me that she was there. I wanted her to disappear. I wanted 'to be left in peace', alone in my underground. I had grown so unused to 'real life' that I could hardly breathe for the oppressiveness of it.

But several minutes more passed, and still, oblivious of everything round her, she did not get up. I was shameless enough to knock gently on the screen to recall her to herself. ... She roused herself abruptly, started from her place, and began hurriedly groping for her shawl, her hat, her coat, as if she was running away from me. ... Two minutes later she came slowly out from behind the screen and rested her eyes, with painful effort, on me. I gave her a forced and angry smile, *for the sake of decency*, and turned away from her look.

'Good-bye,' she said as she went towards the door.

I rushed after her, seized her hand, opened it, put ... something into it, and closed it again. Then I at once turned away and darted into the furthest corner of the room, so that at least I should not see.

I wish I could lie now and write that I had done it without premeditation, without thinking, absent-mindedly, out of stupidity. But I won't lie, and so I say straight out that I had unclenched her hand and put something in it ... with malice aforethought. The idea had come to me while I was scurrying about the room and she was sitting behind the screens. But what I can say for myself with certainty is that although I committed this cruelty deliberately, it came from my wicked head, not from my heart. It was so artificial, so intellectual, so contrived, so *bookish* that I could not sustain it even for a minute – first I fled into the corner, so that I should not see, and then, full of shame and despair, dashed headlong after Liza. I opened the outer door and listened intently.

'Liza! Liza!' I called towards the stairs, but timidly, only half-aloud.

There was no answer, but I thought I heard her steps on the lowest stairs.

'Liza!' I called, more loudly.

No answer. But at that moment I heard the close-fitting glazed street-door dragged open and slammed shut. The noise echoed up the stairway.

She had gone. I went back irresolutely into the room. I felt utterly wretched.

I stood near the table, by the chair in which she had sat, and stared mindlessly in front of me. After about a minute, I started

violently: straight before me on the table I saw ... in a word, I saw
a crumpled blue five-rouble note, the one I had thrust into her
hand a few moments ago. It was the same note: there wasn't
another in the house. She must have managed to throw it on the
table just as I was rushing into the corner.

What then? It was what I might have expected. Might have?
No. I was so egotistical, I had so little respect for other people, that
it never entered my head that she would do such a thing. This was
too much. A split second later I had flung on my clothes in frantic
haste and was rushing headlong after her. She had not had time to
go even two hundred yards when I ran out into the street.

It was quiet, and the snow fell thickly, almost perpendicularly,
spreading a soft white sheet over the pavement and the empty
road. There were no passers-by; there was not a sound. The street-
lamps gleamed sadly and uselessly. I ran a couple of hundred yards
to the next crossing and halted. – Which way had she gone? And
why was I running after her?

Why? To fall in front of her, burst into repentant sobs, kiss her
feet and beg her forgiveness. That was what I wanted; my heart
was torn, and never, never, can I remember that moment with
indifference. But – to what end? I thought. Should I not begin to
hate her, the very next day, perhaps, precisely because I had kissed
her feet today? Could I possibly give her happiness? Had I not
recognized my own true value today, for the hundredth time?
Could I avoid torturing her?

I stood in the falling snow, gazing into the hazy darkness, and
thought about it.

'And isn't it better,' I wondered later on, at home, when I was
already trying to dull the sharp pain in my heart with fanciful
imaginings, 'isn't it better if she carries away with her now an
everlasting wound to her pride? Humiliation, after all, is
purification; it is the acutest and most vivid consciousness!
Tomorrow I should have polluted her mind and wearied her heart
by my presence. But now the insult will never die within her, and
however revolting the filth in store for her, her humiliation will
elevate and purify her ... through hate and ... h'm, perhaps ...
forgiveness also. But will all this make things easier for her?'

And in fact: here, for my own benefit, I posed an empty question: which is better, a cheap happiness or lofty suffering? Tell me then, which is better?

So things appeared to me as I sat at home that evening, more than half dead with mental pain. – I have never experienced such pain and penitence; but could there have been the slightest doubt, when I went running out of my room, that I would turn back half-way and go home? I never saw Liza again, or heard what had become of her. I will add that for a long time I remained pleased with my *phrase* about the benefits of insult and hatred, in spite of the fact that I almost fell ill from anguish at that time.

Even now, after so many years, all this comes back to me as very nasty. There are many things that I remember as bad, but ... ought I not to end my 'Notes' here? I think I made a mistake in beginning to write them at all. At least, I have felt ashamed all the time I have been writing this *Story of the Falling Sleet*: therefore it is no longer literature, but penal correction. After all, to tell a long story about how I missed life through decaying morally in a corner, not having sufficient means, losing the habit of living, and carefully cultivating my anger underground – really is not interesting; a novel needs a hero, but here all the features of an anti-hero have *purposely* been collected, and most of all, the whole thing produces a bad impression, because we have all got out of the habit of living, we are all in a greater or less degree crippled. We are so unused to living that we often feel something like loathing for 'real life' and so cannot bear to be reminded of it. We have really gone so far as to think of 'real life' as toil, almost as servitude, and we are all agreed, for our part, that it is better in books. And what is it we sometimes scratch about for, what do we cry for, what do we beg for? We don't know ourselves. And it would be worse for us if our stupid whims were indulged. Just try giving us, for example, as much independence as possible, untie the hands of any one of us, loosen our bonds, and we. ... I assure you we should all immediately beg to go back under discipline. I know that you may be angry with me for saying this, you will cry out against me and stamp your foot: 'You are talking only about yourself and your underground miseries, don't dare speak of "all

of us!" ' Excuse me, gentlemen, I am not trying to excuse myself
with that *allness*. As for what concerns me personally, after all I
have only carried to a logical conclusion in my life what you
yourselves didn't dare take more than half-way; and you supposed
your cowardice was common sense, and comforted yourselves with
the self-deception. So perhaps I turn out to be more alive than
you. Look harder! After all, we don't even know where 'real life'
is lived nowadays, or what it is, what name it goes by. Leave us
to ourselves, without our books, and at once we get into a muddle
and lose our way – we don't know whose side to be on or where
to give our allegiance, what to love and what to hate, what to
respect and what to despise. We even find it difficult to be human
beings, men with real flesh and blood *of our own*; we are ashamed
of it, we think it a disgrace, and are always striving to be some
unprecedented kind of generalized human being. We are born
dead, and moreover we have long ceased to be the sons of living
fathers; and we become more and more contented with our condition. We are acquiring the taste for it. Soon we shall invent a
method of being born from an idea. But that's enough; I shall
write no more from the underground . . .'

*

This is not the end, however, of the 'Notes' of this paradoxical
writer. He could not help going on. But to us too it seems that this
will be a good place to stop.
1864.

The Double

A Poem of St Petersburg

Chapter One

IT was a little before eight o'clock in the morning when Titular Councillor Yakov Petrovich Golyadkin woke from a long sleep, yawned, stretched, and finally opened his eyes completely. He lay motionless in bed, however, for a couple of minutes more, like a man who is not yet quite sure whether he is awake or still asleep, and whether what is happening around him is real and actual or only the continuation of his disordered dreams. Soon, however, Mr Golyadkin's senses began to receive more clearly and distinctly their usual ordinary impressions. The dingy-green, smoke-begrimed, dusty walls of his little room, his mahogany chest-of-drawers, the imitation mahogany chairs, the red-painted table, the Turkish divan covered in reddish oil-cloth with a pattern of little green flowers, and finally the clothes hastily removed the day before and flung down in a heap on the sofa, all looked familiarly back at him. Finally, the dull, dirty, grey autumn day peered into the room at him through the cloudy window-panes with a grimace so sour and bad-tempered that Mr Golyadkin could no longer have the slightest doubt: he was not in some far-distant realm but in the capital, in the town of St Petersburg, in his own flat on the fourth floor of a large and imposing building in Shestilavochny Street. Having made this important discovery, Mr Golyadkin convulsively closed his eyes, as though regretting his recent awakening and wishing to bring his sleep back for a minute. But a moment later he leapt from his bed with one bound, probably because he had at last stumbled upon the idea round which his scattered thoughts, not yet reduced to order, had been revolving. As soon as he had sprung out of bed he ran to the small round mirror standing on his chest-of-drawers. Although the sleepy, short-sighted, rather bald figure reflected in the glass was of such an insignificant character that nobody at all would have found it in the least remarkable at first glance, its owner was evidently quite satisfied with all he saw there. 'It would be a fine thing,' said Mr Golyadkin half aloud, 'it would be a fine thing if something was wrong with me today, if a pimple had suddenly appeared out of the blue, for example, or something else disastrous had hap-

pened; however, for the moment, it's all right; for the moment
everything is going well.' Very pleased that everything was going
well, Mr Golyadkin put back the mirror where it had been before
and, disregarding the fact that he was bare-footed and still wore
the costume in which he was accustomed to retire to bed, he ran to
the window and with great concern began searching with his eyes
for something in the courtyard on which the windows of his
apartment looked out. Whatever he was looking for in the courtyard was evidently also completely satisfactory; his face lighted
up with a complacent smile. Then, but not before glancing behind
the partition into the cubby-hole where his servant Petrushka
slept, to make sure that Petrushka was not there, he tip-toed to the
table, opened a drawer in it, rummaged in the very back of the
drawer and finally drew out a shabby green wallet from under
some yellowed old papers and odd scraps of rubbish, opened it
carefully and peered with cautious enjoyment into its innermost
hidden pocket. The packet of green, grey, blue, red and rainbow-
coloured paper inside it seemed to look back at Mr Golyadkin in a
friendly and approving fashion; with a beaming countenance he
laid the open wallet in front of him on the table and briskly
rubbed his hands together in token of extreme delight. Finally he
took it out, his comforting packet of bank-notes, and began for the
hundredth time since the previous day to count them over, carefully rubbing each piece of paper between his thumb and
forefinger. 'Seven hundred and fifty roubles,' he concluded at last
in a low voice. 'Seven hundred and fifty roubles ... an impressive
sum! It's a nice amount,' he went on, in a voice trembling and
somewhat faint with satisfaction, pressing the packet between his
hands and smiling significantly, 'a very nice amount! Anybody at
all would think so! I'd like to see the man for whom it was a trifle!
That amount could take a man a long way ...'

'But what is going on?' thought Mr Golyadkin; 'where is Petrushka?' Still in the same costume, he looked behind the partition
for the second time. Again Petrushka was not there, there was
nothing there but the samovar that was now raging and hissing
fiercely, almost beside itself with anger and threatening to boil
over any minute, gabbling away in its strange gibberish, lisping

and babbling to Mr Golyadkin, probably, something like, 'Come along, good people, here I am, use me, I'm quite ready and waiting.'

'Devil take him!' thought Mr Golyadkin. 'That lazy good-for-nothing could finally drive a man past all bearing; where can he be hanging about?' Full of righteous indignation, he went out into the hall, which consisted of a narrow corridor with a door at one end leading to the back entrance, and saw his man surrounded by a fair-sized crowd of domestic servants and chance riffraff. Petrushka was talking while the rest listened. Mr Golyadkin plainly liked neither the subject of the talk nor the talk itself. He shouted to Petrushka and returned to his room quite displeased and even upset. 'The scoundrel's ready to give anybody away for nothing, much more his master,' he thought to himself; 'and he's done it, he must have done it. I'm willing to bet he's sold me for nothing. . . . Well?'

'The livery's come, sir.'

'Put it on and come here immediately.'

Having put on the livery, Petrushka came into his master's room with a silly smile on his face. His costume was inconceivably odd. He was wearing a man-servant's livery with tarnished gold lace, acquired at fifth or sixth hand and evidently made for somebody a foot taller than Petrushka. In his hand he held a hat, also gold-laced, and trimmed with green feathers, and by his side hung a lackey's sword in a leather scabbard.

Finally, to complete the picture, Petrushka, in accordance with his favourite habit of going about incompletely dressed, was barefooted even now. Mr Golyadkin inspected Petrushka on all sides and was evidently satisfied. The livery had obviously been hired for some great occasion. It was noticeable that during the inspection Petrushka watched his master with a strange kind of expectancy and followed his every movement with extraordinary curiosity, a circumstance which Mr Golyadkin found extremely embarrassing.

'Now what about the carriage?'

'The carriage has come too.'

'For the whole day?'

'Yes, sir. Twenty-five roubles.'

'And have the shoes come?'

'Yes, the shoes have come as well.'

'Blockhead! Why can't you say the shoes have come, sir? Give them here.' Having expressed his satisfaction at finding that the shoes fitted satisfactorily, Mr Golyadkin demanded tea and the means to wash and shave. He shaved very carefully, washed in the same manner, hastily swallowed his tea and proceeded to the final and most important stage of his dressing: he drew on a pair of almost new trousers, then a shirt-front with brass buttons and a flowered waistcoat in bright and agreeable colours; he tied a broad silk cravat round his neck and finally put on a formal tail-coat, also nearly new and carefully brushed. From time to time as he dressed he glanced enthusiastically at his shoes, lifting now one foot and now the other, admiring their style and whispering something all the time under his breath, occasionally emphasizing his thoughts with a grimace. But this morning Mr Golyadkin must have been extremely preoccupied, because he hardly noticed the half-smiles and grimaces which Petrushka indulged in at his expense as he helped him to dress. At last, when everything was adjusted as it should be and he was fully dressed, Mr Golyadkin put his wallet in his pocket, bestowed a last admiring look on Petrushka, who had now put on his boots and was thus also fully ready, and, seeing that everything was done and there was nothing more to wait for, ran down the stairs with bustling haste and some small trepidation. A blue hackney-carriage adorned with some kind of heraldic device rattled up to the foot of the outer steps. Petrushka, exchanging winks with the driver and a few idle bystanders, settled his master in the carriage; in an unaccustomed voice, and hardly able to contain his idiotic giggles, he shouted, 'Right away!' and jumped up behind, and the whole equipage rolled with a rattle and a clatter, jingling and creaking, out towards the Nevsky Prospect. As soon as the blue carriage had passed through the gates, Mr Golyadkin rubbed his hands feverishly together and dissolved into inaudible laughter, like a wag of a fellow who has brought off a fabulous joke with which he is as pleased as Punch. Immediately after this access of mirth, however, the laughter in Mr Golyadkin's face changed into a strangely anxious expression. In spite of the fact that the day was damp and overcast he let down both windows and began carefully scrutinizing the passers-by to right and left, assuming a sedate and decorous air as soon as he noticed anybody looking at him. At the corner of the Nevsky Prospect and Liteiny Street, he started at a most unpleasant sensation, like a poor wretch with a corn somebody has just accidentally trodden on, and hastily, even fearfully, flattened himself into the darkest corner of the carriage. The fact was that they had met two of his colleagues, two young clerks in the same Government department in which he worked himself. The clerks for their part seemed to Mr Golyadkin to be extremely perplexed at encountering their colleague in this fashion, and one of them even pointed his finger at Mr Golyadkin. Mr Golyadkin fancied he heard the other call loudly to him by name, a proceeding which was, of course, quite improper in the street. Our hero remained in concealment and did not respond.

'Young cubs!' he began, discussing the matter with himself. 'What's so strange about this? A man in a carriage; a man needs a carriage, so he has hired a carriage. They're just trash! I know them, they're nothing but schoolboys still in need of flogging. They ought to stick to playing pitch-and-toss with their salaries, and gadding about everywhere, that's all they're concerned with. I'd have something to say to the lot of them, only. . . .' Mr Golyadkin did not finish what he was saying, and his heart sank. A pair of dashing Kazan horses, very well known to Mr Golyadkin, harnessed to a smart droshky, were rapidly overtaking his carriage on the right. The gentleman sitting in the droshky, who had accidentally caught sight of Mr Golyadkin's face when he rather carelessly thrust his head out of the window, was plainly also extremely perplexed at the unexpected encounter and, leaning as far forward as he could, gazed with the greatest curiosity and interest into the corner of the carriage where our hero had hurriedly tried to conceal himself. The gentleman in the droshky was Andrey Philippovich, head of the section in the Department where Mr Golyadkin was also a member of the staff, in the capacity of assistant to the head of his subsection. Mr Golyadkin, seeing that Andrey Philippovich had recognized him beyond doubt and was staring with all his might, so that he could not hope to remain concealed, blushed to the roots of his hair. 'Ought I to bow? Should I speak to him or not? Ought I to acknowledge our acquaintance?' our hero wondered in indescribable anguish. 'Or shall I pretend it's not me but somebody else strikingly like me, and look as if nothing's the matter?' said Mr Golyadkin, lifting his hat to Andrey Philippovich and not taking his eyes off him. 'I. . . . It's all right,' he whispered, hardly able to speak, 'It's quite all right; this is not me at all, Andrey Philippovich, it's not me at all, not me, and that's all about it.' Soon, however, the droshky had passed the carriage and the magnetic power of the eyes of authority ceased to be felt. But he was still blushing, smiling, and muttering something to himself. . . . 'I was a fool not to speak to him,' he thought at last; 'I ought simply to have taken the bull by the horns and said, frankly, but with good breeding, "Well, that's how it is, Andrey Philippovich, I've been invited to dinner too, that's all!" ' Then, remembering what a hash he had made of things, our hero turned as red as fire, frowned, and directed a terrible challenging stare at the opposite corner of the carriage, a stare calculated to reduce all his enemies to dust. Finally, on a sudden impulse, he tugged at the cord attached to the coachman's elbow, stopped the carriage and ordered him to turn back into Liteiny Street. The fact was that Mr Golyadkin felt an immediate need, probably for the sake of his own peace of mind, to say something very interesting to his doctor, Christian Ivanovich. And although he had been acquainted with Christian Ivanovich for only a very short time, and had in fact paid him only one visit, in consequence of some necessity, and that during the past week, a doctor after all is the same as a confessor, as they say; it would be stupid to try to keep anything from him and it is a doctor's duty to know his patient. 'Will it be all right, though?' went on our hero, stepping out of his carriage at the porch of a five-storey house on Liteiny Street, beside which he had ordered the vehicle to stop; 'will it be all right? Is it a proper thing to do? Will this be the right time? However, does it really matter?' he continued as he mounted the stairs, breathing hard and trying to control the beating of his heart, which always seemed to beat hard on other people's stairs; 'does it matter? I've come about my own business, after all, and there's nothing reprehensible in that. ... It would be stupid to try to keep anything from him. So I'll just make it appear that it's nothing special, I just happened to be driving past. ... He will see that's how it must have been.'

Reasoning thus, Mr Golyadkin reached the first floor and stopped at the door of number five, on which was displayed a handsome brass plate bearing the inscription,

CHRISTIAN IVANOVICH RUTENSPITZ
PHYSICIAN AND SURGEON

Coming to a halt, our hero hastily tried to give his countenance a suitably detached but not unamiable air, and prepared to give a tug at the bell-pull. Having taken hold of the bell-pull, he hastily decided, just in time, that it might be better to wait until the next day, and that meanwhile there was no great urgency. But suddenly hearing footsteps on the stairs, Mr Golyadkin immediately changed his mind again and, while still retaining a look of the most unshakable decision, at once rang Christian Ivanovich's bell.

Chapter Two

DOCTOR Christian Ivanovich Rutenspitz, Physician and Surgeon, a hale and hearty, although now elderly, man endowed with bushy greying eyebrows and whiskers, with an expressive glittering eye which might have seemed enough in itself to drive away any kind of disease, and finally with the ribbon of an important Order, sat this morning alone in his surgery, in his comfortable armchair, drinking coffee brought to him by his wife's own hand, smoking a cigar, and from time to time writing prescriptions for his patients. Having prescribed the last bottle for a little old man with haemorrhoids, and seen him out by the side door, Christian Ivanovich sat down to await his next patient. Mr Golyadkin entered.

Christian Ivanovich had apparently neither in the least expected to see Mr Golyadkin before him, nor wished to do so, because he was for a moment acutely embarrassed and involuntarily revealed a strange and one might almost say displeased expression. Mr Golyadkin for his part, since he somehow seemed almost always to choose the wrong moment and grew flustered whenever he had to approach somebody direct about his own little affairs, and since he had not thought out his opening sentence, always a stumbling-block to him on such occasions, was even more acutely embarrassed, muttered what appeared to be some sort of apology, and not knowing what to do next took a chair and sat down. But remembering that he had done this without being invited, he became conscious of his lack of manners and immediately hastened to correct his ignorance of the world and breach of good form by getting to his feet again. Then recollecting himself and dimly apprehending that he had now committed two solecisms in a row, he instantly decided on a third, that is he embarked on an apology, muttered a few words, smiled, blushed, grew confused, lapsed into eloquent silence, and finally sat down and remained sitting, while protecting himself against all contingencies with the same challenging stare that possessed such exceptional powers of mentally annihilating and reducing to ashes all the enemies of Mr Golyadkin. The stare, moreover, fully conveyed Mr Golyadkin's independence, that is, it stated clearly that Mr Golyadkin didn't care, he was his own master, like anybody else, and his life was his own. Christian Ivanovich coughed, cleared his throat, evidently in token of agreement and approval of all this, and fixed a questioning inspectorial look on Mr Golyadkin.

'I've come to trouble you for a second time, Christian Ivanovich,' began Mr Golyadkin with a smile, 'and to crave your indulgence once again....' Mr Golyadkin was plainly at a loss for words.

'H'm ... yes!' said Christian Ivanovich weightily, letting the smoke escape from his lips and laying his cigar on the table, 'but you must follow my instructions; I explained to you, you know, that the treatment must consist in changing your habits.... Well, relaxation, something to take you out of yourself; well, for instance, visiting friends and acquaintances, and at the same time not being afraid to take a drink; and, likewise, keeping to cheerful company.'

Mr Golyadkin, still smiling, lost no time in remarking that it seemed to him he was like everybody else, that he had his own flat, he had his amusements like anybody else ... that he could, of course, go to the theatre, for he had means, like anybody else, that he was working during the day, but spent his evenings at home, and that it was absolutely all the same to him; he even stated in passing that as far as he was aware he was no worse than other people, he lived at home in his own flat and, to conclude, he had Petrushka. Here Mr Golyadkin paused.

'H'm, no, that kind of arrangement is not what I meant, and not at all what I should like to ask you about. I am interested to learn whether in general you are fond of convivial company and like having a good time. ... Well, are you now leading a melancholy or a cheerful kind of life?'

'Well, Christian Ivanovich, I ...'

'H'm. ... I was saying,' the doctor interrupted, 'that you require a radical transformation of your whole life and, in a certain sense, a change in your character.' (Christian Ivanovich strongly emphasized the word 'change' and paused for a moment with a very significant air.) 'Don't shun the pleasures of life; go to the theatre and the club, and whatever you do, don't be afraid of taking a drink. It's not good to stay at home all the time ... you simply must not sit at home.'

'I like quiet, Christian Ivanovich,' said Mr Golyadkin, casting a significant glance at the doctor, and obviously searching for the words that would most successfully express his meaning, 'and in my flat there's only me and Petrushka. ... I mean my man-servant, Christian Ivanovich. I mean, I go my own way, Christian Ivanovich, my own particular way, Christian Ivanovich. I am a man apart, and as far as I can see, I don't depend on anybody. I want to go out, too, Christian Ivanovich.'

'What? ... Oh, yes! Well, there's no pleasure in going out nowadays; the weather's very bad.'

'Yes, Christian Ivanovich. I'm a quiet man, a mild man, Christian Ivanovich, as I think I've had the honour of explaining to

you before, but I go my own way, Christian Ivanovich. The road
of life is broad. . . . I want. . . . I want to say this, Christian Ivanovich. . . . Excuse me, Christian Ivanovich, I am not a master of
eloquence.'

'H'm . . . you were saying . . .?'

'I was saying you must excuse me, Christian Ivanovich, I am
not a master of eloquence, as far as I am aware,' said Mr Golyadkin, in a half-offended tone of voice, slightly losing the thread and
stumbling a little. 'In this respect, Christian Ivanovich, I am not
like other people,' he added, with a special kind of smile, 'and I
have not the art of talking at length; I never learned to beautify
my phrases. On the other hand, Christian Ivanovich, I act; I act,
on the other hand, Christian Ivanovich!'

'H'm. . . . How do you mean . . . you act?' answered Christian
Ivanovich. There followed a moment's silence. The doctor looked
strangely and mistrustfully at Mr Golyadkin, and Mr Golyadkin
in his turn squinted somewhat mistrustfully at the doctor.

'I, Christian Ivanovich,' resumed Mr Golyadkin, still in the
same slightly irritated tone of perplexity at Christian Ivanovich's
extremely stubborn persistence, 'I, Christian Ivanovich, like peace
and quiet and not fashionable hubbub. There, Christian Ivanovich, in society, I say you must learn how to polish the parquet
with your shoes . . .' (here Mr Golyadkin scraped his foot lightly
over the floor); 'it's expected of you, sir, and you're expected to
make puns, too . . . you have to be able to produce a well-turned
compliment . . . that's what's expected of you. And I've not learnt
to do all that, Christian Ivanovich, I've never studied all those
clever tricks; I had no time. I am a simple, uncomplicated person,
and it isn't in me to shine in society. In that respect, Christian
Ivanovich, I lay down my arms; I lower my sword, speaking in
that sense.' All this Mr Golyadkin uttered, of course, with an air
that said plainly that he was not in the least sorry to lay down his
arms in that sense, or that he had never learnt social tricks, even
quite the contrary. Christian Ivanovich, listening to him with a
very sour grimace, kept his eyes lowered and seemed somewhat
apprehensive. Mr Golyadkin's tirade was followed by a rather
long and significant silence.

'You appear to have digressed slightly from the point,' said Christian Ivanovich at last softly, 'and I confess I couldn't quite follow you.'

'I am not a master of eloquence, Christian Ivanovich; I have already had the honour of informing you, Christian Ivanovich, that I am not a master of eloquence,' said Mr Golyadkin, this time in a positive and cutting tone.

'H'm.'

'Christian Ivanovich,' began Mr Golyadkin again, in a quiet but highly significant voice, dwelling portentously on every point, 'Christian Ivanovich, when I came in here, I began by apologizing. Now I repeat myself, and again beg your indulgence for a moment. I have nothing to hide from you, Christian Ivanovich. I am a little man, you know yourself; but, luckily for me, I am not sorry to be a little man. On the contrary, Christian Ivanovich; to tell you the truth, I am proud to be not a great man but a little man. I am not an intriguer – and I am proud of that, too. I don't do things on the sly, but openly, without guile, and although I might do harm, like other people, and very great harm, and I even know how I might do it, and to whom, I won't sully myself, Christian Ivanovich, and in that sense I wash my hands of it. In that sense, I say, I wash my hands, Christian Ivanovich!' Mr Golyadkin paused impressively for a moment; he had been speaking with modest animation.

'I proceed, Christian Ivanovich,' our hero resumed, 'directly, openly, and without beating about the bush, because I despise deviousness, I leave that to other people. I don't try to belittle those who may be a bit better than you and me ... that is, I mean to say than me, Christian Ivanovich, I didn't mean to say you. I dislike hints; I don't like petty two-faced people; I loathe gossip and scandal-mongering. I only put on a mask at masked balls, I don't wear one in public every day. I will only ask you, Christian Ivanovich, how you would set about revenging yourself on an enemy, your bitterest enemy – somebody you hadn't thought of in that way,' Mr Golyadkin ended, with a challenging glance at Christian Ivanovich.

Although Mr Golyadkin had said all this with the utmost possible distinctness and clarity, confidently, weighing his words and calculating their probable effect, nevertheless it was now with anxiety, with great anxiety, with the utmost anxiety, that he gazed at Christian Ivanovich. Now he had become all eyes, and awaited Christian Ivanovich's answer with sad and melancholy impatience. But to his complete surprise and bewilderment, Christian Ivanovich merely muttered something below his breath; then he moved his chair to the desk and rather drily, although quite politely, declared that his time was precious, that he did not altogether follow, that he was prepared to help in any way and to any extent that lay in his power, but that he would leave aside all the rest, which had nothing to do with him. Here he took up his pen, drew a sheet of paper towards himself, cut from it a piece such as doctors habitually use, and announced that he was ready to write what was required at once.

'No, Christian Ivanovich, it's not required! no, sir, that's not necessary at all!' said Mr Golyadkin, rising from his chair and grasping Christian Ivanovich's right hand; 'there's no need of anything of that sort here, Christian Ivanovich . . .'

But even while he was saying all this, Mr Golyadkin was undergoing a strange transformation. His grey eyes had a curious shine, his lips twitched, every muscle and every feature of his face seemed to be in fluid motion. He was shaking from head to foot. Having followed his first impulse and arrested Christian Ivanovich's hand, Mr Golyadkin now stood still, as if mistrusting himself and waiting for fresh inspiration before taking further steps.

The scene that followed was rather odd.

Slightly confounded, Christian Ivanovich seemed for a moment glued to his chair, and stared helplessly at Mr Golyadkin, who gazed back at him in the same manner. Finally, Christian Ivanovich rose to his feet, with some little assistance from the tails of Mr Golyadkin's frock-coat. They stood like that for a few seconds, without moving or taking their eyes from each other. But then Mr Golyadkin's second action also decided itself in an extraordinarily odd fashion. His lips trembled, his chin quivered, and our hero unexpectedly burst into tears. Sobbing, hanging his head and striking his breast with his right hand, while his left grasped at the lapels of Christian Ivanovich's informal garment, he tried to speak, wishing to make some point clear without delay, but could not utter a word. At last, Christian Ivanovich roused himself from his stupor.

'Come, no more of this, calm yourself, sit down!' he said finally, trying to make Mr Golyadkin sit in his own chair.

'I have enemies, Christian Ivanovich, I have enemies; I have bitter enemies who have sworn to ruin me. ...' Mr Golyadkin answered in a frightened whisper.

'Come, come, why talk of enemies? There's no need to bring enemies into it, that's quite unnecessary! Sit down, sit down,' went on Christian Ivanovich, still trying to get Mr Golyadkin settled in the arm-chair.

Mr Golyadkin sat down at last, without taking his eyes from Christian Ivanovich. Christian Ivanovich, with an extremely dissatisfied look, began pacing from one corner to another of his room. There was a long silence.

'I am grateful to you, Christian Ivanovich, very grateful, and I am deeply conscious of everything you have just done for me. I shall never forget your kindness, Christian Ivanovich,' said Mr Golyadkin at last, rising from the chair with an aggrieved look.

'No more of that! Enough, I tell you, enough!' Christian Ivanovich replied to these capers of Mr Golyadkin's with some severity, once more making him sit down in his place. 'Now, what is the matter with you? Tell me what is troubling you now,' he went on, 'and what enemies you were speaking of. What is it?'

'No, Christian Ivanovich, we'd better leave it now,' Mr Golyadkin answered, looking down at the floor, 'we'd better leave it all aside for now ... until another time, Christian Ivanovich, a more convenient time, when everything is revealed, and the mask has fallen from certain faces, and something is laid bare. But now, for the time being, of course, after what has happened between us ... you will agree yourself, Christian Ivanovich. ... Allow me to wish you good morning, Christian Ivanovich,' said Mr Golyadkin, this time rising resolutely and seriously, and taking up his hat.

'Oh well ... as you please ... h'm. ...' There followed a minute
of silence. 'For my part, anything I can do, you know. ... I
seriously desire your welfare.'

'I understand you, Christian Ivanovich, I understand you; now
I understand you completely. ... In any case, excuse me for troubling you, Christian Ivanovich.'

'H'm. ... No, that is not what I meant to say to you. However,
as you please. Go on with the medicines as before ...'

'Yes, I'll go on with the medicines as you say, Christian Ivanovich, I'll go on taking them, and I'll get them from the same chemist. ... Nowadays, Christian Ivanovich, even a chemist is a
somebody.'

'What? In what sense do you mean?'

'In a perfectly ordinary sense, Christian Ivanovich. I mean
that's the way things are nowadays ...'

'H'm ...'

'And that every young puppy, not only the chemists, turns up
his nose at decent citizens now.'

'H'm. ... What do you understand by that?'

'I am talking about a certain person, Christian Ivanovich, our
mutual friend Vladimir Semyonovich, for instance, Christian
Ivanovich.'

'Ah ...!'

'Yes, Christian Ivanovich; and I know some people, Christian
Ivanovich, who are not such slaves to public opinion that they
can't sometimes speak the truth.'

'Ah ...! How is that?'

'Oh, it just is so; however, that's a side issue; sometimes they
know how to serve an egg with sauce.'

'What? Serve what?'

'An egg with sauce, Christian Ivanovich; that's a Russian proverb. They can sometimes produce congratulations that are very
much to the point, for example; there are people who can, Christian Ivanovich.'

'Congratulations?'

'Yes, congratulations, Christian Ivanovich, as somebody I know
very well did the other day ...'

'Somebody you know very well ... ah! How was that?' said Christian Ivanovich, watching Mr Golyadkin attentively.

'Yes, somebody I know very well congratulated somebody else whom I also know very well, and who is, moreover, a friend, as it is termed, of the object of my affections, on being promoted, receiving the rank of Assessor. This is how he put it. "I feel really glad," he said, "of this opportunity to offer you my congratulations, my *sincerest* congratulations, Vladimir Semyonovich, on your promotion. And I am all the more delighted because nowadays, as all the world knows, a lot of maundering old women have been getting promotion." ' Here Mr Golyadkin nodded his head slyly and looked at Christian Ivanovich with a frown.

'H'm. ... So he said that ...'

'Yes, Christian Ivanovich, that's what he said, looking at the same time at Andrey Philippovich, our darling boy's uncle. And what does it matter to me if he's been made an Assessor, Christian Ivanovich? What has it to do with me? And he wants to get married, with the milk, if I may be permitted the expression, not yet dry on his lips. That's just what I said. "Now, Vladimir Semyonovich," I said, "now I've said everything; please allow me to go." '

'H'm ...'

'Yes, Christian Ivanovich; I said, "please allow me to go now." Then, so as to kill two birds with one stone, when I had taken the young whipper-snapper down a peg or two with my "maundering old women", I turned to Clara Olsufyevna (all this happened the day before yesterday at Olsufi Ivanovich's), who had just been singing a ballad with great feeling, and I said, "You have been kind enough to sing to us very touchingly, only some people have not listened to you with unmixed motives." And that was giving a clear hint, you understand, Christian Ivanovich, that was hinting clearly that somebody was paying court to her not for her own sake but with ulterior motives ...'

'Ah! And what did he say?'

'He'd bitten into a lemon, as the proverb goes, Christian Ivanovich.'

'H'm ...'

'Yes, Christian Ivanovich. I told the old man himself, as well. "I know how much I'm indebted to you, Olsufi Ivanovich," I said. "I fully appreciate all the kindnesses you've heaped on me practically ever since I was a child. But open your eyes, Olsufi Ivanovich," I said. "Take care," I said. "I am acting openly and above board, Olsufi Ivanovich." '

'Ah, indeed!'

'Yes, indeed, Christian Ivanovich, indeed!'

'What did he say?'

'What did he say, Christian Ivanovich? He mumbled something or other; yes ... no ... I know you. ... His Excellency is full of benevolence – and so on and so on. ... But what does it matter? – old age has made him pretty shaky, as they say.'

'Ah, so that's how it is now?'

'Yes, Christian Ivanovich. But of course we're all the same! a little old man! one foot in the grave, as they say, and as soon as some old wives' tales begin going the rounds he listens to them; they'd be impossible without him ...'

'Scandal, you say?'

'Yes, Christian Ivanovich, they've worked up some tittle-tattle. Our Bear is mixed up in it, and so is his nephew, our little treasure; they're in league with the old women, of course, and they've cooked something up. And what is it, do you think? What have they invented to kill a man with?'

'To kill a man with?'

'Yes, Christian Ivanovich, to kill him with, kill him morally. They spread it about. ... I am still talking about this person I know very well ...'

Christian Ivanovich nodded.

'They started a rumour about him. ... I confess, Christian Ivanovich, I'm ashamed even to tell you ...'

'H'm ...'

'They started a rumour that he was already engaged to be married, he was already pledged to another. ... And what do you think, Christian Ivanovich, who was it to?'

'Really?'

'To a disreputable German woman, the keeper of a cookshop

where he takes his dinner; instead of paying his debts he is supposed to have offered her his hand.'

'Is that what they say?'

'Would you believe it, Christian Ivanovich? A German, a nasty low shameless German, Karolina Ivanovna, if you know her . . .'

'I confess, for my part . . .'

'I understand you, Christian Ivanovich, I understand, and for my part I feel . . .'

'Tell me, please, where are you living now? Yes. . . . I should like. . . . I think you were formerly living . . .'

'I was living, Christian Ivanovich, I was living even formerly. I must have been, mustn't I?' answered Mr Golyadkin, accompanying his words with a little laugh, and slightly disconcerting Christian Ivanovich with his reply.

'No, you misunderstood me; for my part, I meant to say . . .'

'I also meant to say, for my part, Christian Ivanovich, I also meant to say,' went on Mr Golyadkin, laughing. 'However, I have quite outstayed my welcome, Christian Ivanovich. I hope you will now permit me . . . to wish you good morning.'

'H'm . . .'

'Yes, Christian Ivanovich, I understand you; I understand you completely now,' said our hero, strutting a little in front of Christian Ivanovich. 'And so allow me to wish you good morning.'

On this our hero made a bow and went out of the room, leaving Christian Ivanovich extremely bewildered. As he went down the doctor's stairs he smiled and rubbed his hands. Outside the front door, breathing the fresh air and conscious of his freedom, he was even quite ready to acknowledge himself the happiest of mortals and make his way straight to the Department – when suddenly he heard his carriage clatter up to the porch; he looked up and remembered everything. Petrushka was already opening the carriage-door. A strange and most unpleasant sensation gripped Mr Golyadkin. He seemed almost to blush for an instant. Something irked him. Almost in the act of raising his foot to the carriage step, he turned round suddenly and looked at Christian Ivanovich's windows. Exactly! Christian Ivanovich was standing at the window, smoothing his beard with his right hand and watching our hero with some curiosity.

'That doctor's a fool,' thought Mr Golyadkin, hiding himself in the carriage, 'a great fool! He may perhaps be good at curing his patients, but all the same, he's as stupid as a donkey.' Mr Golyadkin sat down, Petrushka shouted 'Right away!' and the carriage rolled away again to the Nevsky Prospect.

Chapter Three

ALL Mr Golyadkin's time that morning was full of intense activity. Reaching the Nevsky Prospect, our hero ordered the carriage to stop near the Arcades. He jumped out and hurried into one of the arcades, accompanied by Petrushka; there he went straight to a goldsmith's and silversmith's. It was evident from the very look of him that Mr Golyadkin had his hands full with the enormous number of things he had to do. Having bargained for a complete tea and dinner service for something over fifteen hundred paper roubles, managed to get a cigar-case of elaborate design and a full set of shaving equipment in silver included in the total, and finally priced some other useful and pretty little articles, Mr Golyadkin ended by promising to send for the things without fail next morning, or even that day, made a note of the number of the shop and, after listening attentively to the merchant's anxious request for a deposit, promised a deposit as well in due course. After that he hastily took leave of the bewildered merchant and walked further along the row, pestered by a whole pack of shop-assistants, looking round constantly for Petrushka and carefully searching for another shop. In passing, he darted into a money-changer's to change all his large notes for smaller, and although he lost by the transaction, all the same he changed them, and his wallet became appreciably fatter, which evidently gave him the utmost satisfaction. Finally he stopped in a shop selling all kinds of materials for ladies. Here again, having committed himself to spending a sizable sum of money, Mr Golyadkin promised the proprietress to call without fail for the goods, took the number of the shop and, in answer to a question about a deposit, again stated that there would be a deposit in due course. Then he visited several more shops; in all of them he haggled, priced various articles, and sometimes argued for a long time with the shopkeeper, walking out of the shop and returning to it as many as three times – in short, he displayed extraordinary activity. From the Arcades our hero took his way to a famous furniture-shop, where he chaffered over furniture for six rooms, admired a fashionable and extremely elaborate lady's dressing-table in the latest taste and, assuring the proprietress that he would not fail to send for everything, left the shop in his usual way, with a promise to pay a deposit, and then went on elsewhere and made further purchases. In short, there seemed to be no end to what he had to do. Finally, all this apparently began to be utterly tiresome even to Mr Golyadkin himself. He even began, God knows why, to suffer from the prickings of conscience all of a sudden. He would not now have willingly met, for example, Andrey Philippovich or even Christian Ivanovich. At last the town clocks struck three in the afternoon. When Mr Golyadkin got back into his carriage for the last time, he actually had, out of all the purchases he had made that day, only a pair of gloves and a bottle of scent costing one and a half paper roubles. Since it was still rather early, he ordered his coachman to draw up at a famous restaurant in the Nevsky Prospect, which he had until then known only by reputation, got out of the carriage and went in for something to eat and a rest, and to wait for a certain hour.

Having eaten as a man eats in contemplation of a rich dinner-party, that is having taken a bite 'to stay the pangs of hunger', as they say, and drunk one glass of vodka, Mr Golyadkin sat down in an armchair, glanced modestly about him, and peacefully applied himself to the columns of a thick national newspaper. He read a couple of lines, got up, looked at himself in a mirror, straightened his dress and smoothed himself down; then he walked over to the window and looked to see whether his carriage was there . . . and then sat down and took up the paper again. It was evident that our hero was in an extremely nervous state. Looking at his watch and seeing that it was only a quarter past three and that consequently there was still some time to wait, Mr Golyadkin, finding it awkward to sit there in that fashion, ordered some chocolate, for

which, however, he had no great inclination at the moment.
When he had drunk the chocolate and observed that the time had
progressed a little, he went out to pay his bill. Suddenly somebody
slapped his shoulder.

He turned and saw in front of him two of his colleagues – the
same he had seen in the morning in Liteiny Street – two young
men still very junior in both age and rank. Our hero's relations
with them were neutral, neither of friendship nor of open enmity.
Needless to say, propriety was observed on both sides; but there
was no close intimacy, nor indeed could there be. The encounter at
this particular time was extremely unwelcome to Mr Golyadkin.
He frowned slightly and became for a moment confused.

'Yakov Petrovich, Yakov Petrovich,' twittered the two young
clerks, 'you here? What has . . .?'

'Ah, it's you, gentlemen!' Mr Golyadkin hurriedly interrupted
them, somewhat disconcerted and scandalized by the clerks'
amazement and at the same time by the familiarity of their
address, but involuntarily acting the free-and-easy good fellow all
the same. 'You are deserters, gentlemen, he-he-he!' Here, in order
not to lower himself and yet show indulgence to the young people
in his office, with whom he had always remained within proper
limits, he even tried to pat one of the young men on the shoulder;
but in this instance the popular touch eluded Mr Golyadkin and
something quite different resulted instead of a becomingly friendly
gesture.

'Well, and is our Bear at his post?'

'Who is that, Yakov Petrovich?'

'Why, the Bear; as if you didn't know who is called the Bear!'
Mr Golyadkin laughed and turned to the waiter to take his
change. 'I am talking of Andrey Philippovich, gentlemen,' he
went on, finishing his business with the waiter and turning back
to the young men, this time with a perfectly serious look. The
clerks exchanged significant winks.

'Yes, he's there, and he's been asking for you, Yakov Petrovich,'
one of them answered.

'Still at his post, eh! In that case let him stay there, gentlemen.
And he was asking for me, eh?'

'Yes, Yakov Petrovich. But how do you come to be scented and pomaded like this, and all dressed up . . .?'

'Because I choose, gentlemen! That is enough!' answered Mr Golyadkin, glancing aside with a strained smile. Seeing the smile, the clerks guffawed. Mr Golyadkin was a little annoyed.

'Let me tell you something, in a friendly way,' said our hero after a short silence, as if he had made up his mind ('So be it, then!') to confide something to them. 'You all know me, gentlemen, but up till now you have only known one side of me. Nobody is to blame for that, and I admit it is partly my own fault.'

Mr Golyadkin compressed his lips and looked meaningly at the clerks. The young men again winked at each other.

'Until now you have not known me, gentlemen. It would not be entirely appropriate for me to explain myself here and now. I will only tell you something casually in passing. There are people, gentlemen, who do not like deviousness and who wear a mask only at masked balls. There are people who do not regard acquiring the ability to polish a parquet floor with their shoes as the true purpose of human life. There are people too, gentlemen, who will not say they are happy and living life to the full just because, for example, their trousers are a good fit. Finally, there are people who don't care to caper about and fidget aimlessly and flirt and make advances, or, most of all, thrust their noses in where they are not wanted. I have said almost everything, gentlemen; now permit me to leave you . . .'

Mr Golyadkin stopped. Since the young gentlemen were by now highly amused, they had most impolitely burst into uproarious laughter. Mr Golyadkin flared up.

'Laugh, gentlemen, laugh, for the present! You will live and learn,' he said with a feeling of wounded pride, taking his hat and retreating to the door.

'But I will say more, gentlemen,' he added, turning to the clerks for the last time. 'I will say more – you are here face to face with me. These are my rules, gentlemen: if things go badly, I stand firm; if all goes well, I hold my ground; and in any case, I undermine nobody's position. I am not an intriguer, I am proud to say. I should never have made a diplomat. They say that the bird flies of its own accord to the fowler. Quite true, I am prepared to agree: but which is the fowler here and which is the bird? That's another question, gentlemen!'

Mr Golyadkin lapsed into eloquent silence and with a significant expression, that is with his eyebrows raised as high and his lips compressed as tightly as possible, exchanged bows with the two young gentlemen and went out, leaving them utterly amazed.

'Where to?' Petrushka, who was probably tired of hanging about in the cold, asked rather curtly. 'Where to?' he asked again, as he met the terrible annihilating glance with which our hero had twice already protected himself that morning, and to which he had recourse now for the third time as he came down the steps.

'Izmailovsky Bridge.'

'Izmailovsky Bridge! Right away!'

'Dinner won't begin before four o'clock, or perhaps even not until five,' thought Mr Golyadkin; 'is this too early? However, I can be a little early; besides, it's a family dinner-party. I can behave *sans façon*, as fashionable people say. Why shouldn't I behave *sans façon*? Our Bear said everything would be *sans façon*, so I can also. . . .' Such were Mr Golyadkin's thoughts, but meanwhile his agitation grew steadily greater. It was obvious that he was preparing himself for something very worrying, to say the least, as he whispered to himself, gestured with his right hand, and glanced constantly out of the carriage window, so that really nobody would have said, to look at Mr Golyadkin, that he was getting ready to dine well, without ceremony, and moreover in a family circle – *sans façon*, as the fashionable people say. At last, near Izmailovsky Bridge, Mr Golyadkin pointed out a house; the carriage rattled noisily through the gates and drew up at the doorway in the right-hand façade. Noticing a woman's figure at a first-floor window, Mr Golyadkin blew her a kiss. He hardly knew what he was doing, however, since at that moment he felt decidedly more dead than alive. He emerged from the carriage looking pale and flustered, entered the porch, took off his hat, mechanically straightened his clothes, and with a trembling sensation in his knees mounted the steps.

'Olsufi Ivanovich?' he asked the man who opened the door to him.

'Yes, sir, he's at home, or rather no, sir, he's not at home.'

'What? What do you mean, my man? I ... I've come to dinner, my good fellow. Surely you know me?'

'Of course, sir. My orders is not to admit you, sir.'

'My good fellow, you ... you're making a mistake, I'm sure, my good man. It's me. I have been invited, my good fellow; I've come to dinner,' said Mr Golyadkin, throwing off his overcoat and displaying the evident intention of entering the reception rooms.

'Excuse me, sir, you mustn't, sir. My orders is not to let you in, sir; I was told to refuse you, sir, that's what it is!'

Mr Golyadkin turned pale. At the same moment the door to the inner rooms opened and Gerasimych, Olsufi Ivanovich's old butler, came out.

'The gentleman's here, Emelyan Gerasimych, and he wants to come in, but I ...'

'But you're a fool, Alexeich. Go into the reception room and send that scoundrel Semyonovich out here. I'm sorry, sir,' he said, addressing Mr Golyadkin politely but firmly. 'It's quite impossible, sir. My master asks you to excuse him, sir; he can't receive you, sir.'

'He actually said that, that he couldn't receive me?' asked Mr Golyadkin irresolutely. 'Excuse me, Gerasimych. Why is it quite impossible?'

'It's quite impossible, sir. I was announcing you, sir; he said, "Beg him to excuse me. He can't be received," he said.'

'But why? How is that? How ...?'

'Please, sir, please!'

'But how can that be? You can't do this! Announce me. ... How can it be? I've come to dinner ...'

'Please, sir, please!'

'Well, though, that's a different matter – he asks to be excused; still, excuse me, Gerasimych, how can it be, Gerasimych?'

'Excuse me, sir, excuse me!' returned Gerasimych, determinedly blocking Mr Golyadkin's progress with his right arm and making a broad way for two gentlemen who were just entering the hall. The gentlemen were Andrey Philippovich and his nephew Vladimir Semyonovich. Both gave Mr Golyadkin puzzled looks. Andrey Philippovich was on the point of saying something, but Mr Golyadkin had already made up his mind; he was leaving Olsufi Ivanovich's hall with downcast eyes, blushing and smiling with an expression of extreme embarrassment.

'I will call later, Gerasimych; I will clear the matter up; I hope it will not be long before this whole thing is explained,' he said as he reached the door and began descending the stairs.

'Yakov Petrovich, Yakov Petrovich!' came the voice of Andrey Philippovich, who had followed him out.

Mr Golyadkin was already on the first half-landing. He turned quickly to face Andrey Philippovich.

'What can I do for you, Andrey Philippovich?' he said in a reasonably firm tone.

'What's the matter, Yakov Petrovich? Why did you . . .?'

'It's all right, Andrey Philippovich. I am here on my own account. This is my private life, Andrey Philippovich.'

'What do you mean?'

'I am saying that this is my private life, Andrey Philippovich, and that, as far as I can see, it is impossible to find anything prejudicial here in connection with my official relations.'

'What? In connection with your official. . . . What is the matter with you, my good sir?'

'Nothing, Andrey Philippovich, nothing at all; a mischievous young lady, that's all . . .'

'What? . . . what?' Andrey Philippovich was flustered and completely bewildered. Mr Golyadkin, who until then, talking to Andrey Philippovich from half-way down the stairs, had looked ready to jump straight down his throat, now seeing that the head of his section was a little disconcerted almost unconsciously took a step forward. Andrey Philippovich fell back. Mr Golyadkin mounted first one stair and then another. Andrey Philippovich looked anxiously about him. Suddenly Mr Golyadkin bounded swiftly up the stairs. Even more swiftly Andrey Philippovich leapt into the

room and slammed the door behind him. Mr Golyadkin was left
alone. Everything went dark before his eyes. He felt utterly
crushed, and now stood in a kind of stupid abstraction, as though
recalling some circumstance, also extremely stupid, that had come
about very recently. 'Oh dear!' he whispered, smiling with an
effort. Meanwhile the sound of voices and footsteps on the stairs,
probably belonging to more guests invited by Olsufi Ivanovich,
reached him from below. Mr Golyadkin regained partial consciousness of his surroundings, hastily turned up the raccoon
collar of his coat, hiding as much of his face in it as possible, and
began to descend the stairs with clumsy haste, tottering and stumbling. He felt somehow weak and numb inside. His confusion was
so great that when he came out on the porch he did not even wait
for his carriage, but himself went straight out to it across the
muddy courtyard. As he came to it and prepared to take his place,
Mr Golyadkin found himself mentally entertaining the desire to
sink through the ground or hide himself, together with his carriage, in a mouse-hole. It seemed to him that everything whatever
in Olsufi Ivanovich's house was staring at him through the
windows. He knew that if he turned round he would die on the
spot.

'What are you laughing at, blockhead?' he rapped out at Petrushka, who was preparing to hand him into the carriage.

'What have I got to laugh at? I wasn't laughing at anything.
Where to now?'

'Home, and quick about it!'

'Home!' shouted Petrushka, taking his place on the step at the
back.

'He croaks like a raven!' thought Mr Golyadkin. Meanwhile
the carriage had already travelled some distance beyond Izmailovsky Bridge. Suddenly our hero pulled the cord with all his
might and shouted to the coachman to turn back immediately.
The coachman turned his horses and two minutes later drove into
Olsufi Ivanovich's courtyard once more. 'Not here, fool, not here;
back!' shouted Mr Golyadkin – and the coachman seemed almost
to have been expecting the order; without a word of protest and
without stopping at the porch he swept right round the courtyard
and out again into the street.

Mr Golyadkin did not go home, but when they had passed Semyonovsky Bridge ordered the carriage to turn into a side street and stop at a tavern of rather modest exterior. When he got out of the carriage our hero paid off the coachman and, having thus finally got rid of his equipage, told Petrushka to go home and wait for his return, went into the tavern, hired a private room and ordered dinner. He felt very unwell, and his head seemed to be all chaotic disorder. For a long time he walked in agitation about the room; then at last he sat down on a chair, propped his forehead in his hands and began trying with all his might to come to a decision about something relating to his present situation.

Chapter Four

THE day on which was celebrated the festival of the birth of Clara Olsufyevna, only daughter of State Councillor Berendeyev, at one time Mr Golyadkin's patron – the day, marked by a magnificent and splendid formal dinner-party, a dinner-party such as had not been seen for a long time within the walls of any of the flats near Izmailovsky Bridge and round about, occupied by high-ranking officials – a dinner, more like some Belshazzar's feast than a dinner, which called to mind something Babylonian with its brilliance, luxury, and tastefulness, its Veuve Clicquot, its oysters and its fruits from Eliseyev's and Kilyutin's, all its well-fed little ladies and representatives of the higher grades of the Government service – this red-letter day, distinguished by so festive a dinner, ended with a brilliant ball, a small family ball, but brilliant all the same in respect of taste, culture, and good breeding. Balls like this do take place, of course, I entirely agree, but they are rare. Balls like this, more like family rejoicings than balls, can only be given in houses like that, for example, of State Councillor Berendeyev. I will go further: I doubt whether even all State Councillors could give balls like it. Oh, if only I were a poet! – I mean, of course, one of at least the quality of Homer or Pushkin (with less talent than that one can't thrust one's oar in) – I would certainly have painted the whole of these highly festive celebrations for you, Reader, with glowing colours and a broad brush. Nay, more: I should have begun my poem with the dinner, and applied myself with special diligence to that solemn and yet joyful moment when the first wine-cup was raised in honour of the queen of the festivities. I should have depicted for you first the guests, plunged in silence and expectancy, more like Demosthenian eloquence than silence. Then I should have portrayed Andrey Philippovich, the oldest of the guests and indeed one with some claim to the first place among them, adorned with grey hairs and with the Orders befitting those grey hairs, rising to his feet and raising higher than his head a goblet of sparkling wine – wine specially brought from a distant kingdom for drinking on such occasions, a wine more like the nectar of the gods than a mere wine. I should have pictured for you the guests and the fortunate parents of the queen of the festi vities, following the example of Andrey Philippovich in raising their glasses, and turning on him eyes full of anticipation. I should have pictured for you how the Andrey Philippovich so frequently referred to let a tear fall into his glass before he expressed his felicitations and good wishes, then proposed the toast, and drank it. . . . But I confess, humbly confess, I could never have described all the majesty of that moment when the queen of the festivities herself, Clara Olsufyevna, glowing like a fresh-picked rose with a blush of modesty and happiness, fell, overcome by her feelings, into the embrace of her tender mother, how the tender mother dissolved in tears and how upon this the father himself burst into sobs – the venerable old man and State Councillor, Olsufi Ivanovich, who had been deprived of the use of his legs by his long service and been rewarded by the fates for his zeal and diligence with a nice little sum of money, and a house, and a country estate, and a beauty for a daughter, sobbed like a child and proclaimed through his tears that His Excellency was a man of the greatest benevolence. I could not, no, I really could not, depict for you the universal stirrings of emotion inevitably following on that moment – stirrings that found their expression in the conduct of one young registry clerk (who was at that moment more like a State Councillor than a Registrar) who, listening to Andrey Philippovich, even shed a few tears himself. In his turn

Andrey Philippovich did not in the least resemble in that solemn moment a Collegiate Councillor and the head of a department – no, he seemed more like something else. . . . I am not sure exactly what, but not a Collegiate Councillor. He was something higher. Finally . . . oh, why do I not possess the secret of the lofty style, a powerful, ceremonial style, for the portrayal of all those beautiful and edifying moments of human life, which might have been designed to demonstrate that there are occasions when the virtuous triumph over disloyalty, free-thinking, vice, and envy? I will say nothing, but – what will be better than any kind of oratory – silently point out to you that fortunate stripling, entering upon his twenty-sixth year, Vladimir Semyonovich, Andrey Philippovich's nephew, who has risen in his turn from his seat and is in his turn proposing a toast, and on whom are directed the tearful eyes of the parents of the queen of the festivities, the proud eyes of Andrey Philippovich, the shy eyes of the queen of the festivities herself, the enthusiastic eyes of the guests, and even the suitably envious eyes of several of the brilliant stripling's young colleagues. I will say nothing, although I cannot refrain from remarking that everything in that youth, more like an old man than a stripling – speaking in a sense favourable to him – everything, from his blooming cheeks to the very rank of Assessor that he bore, everything in that festive moment all but proclaimed aloud in so many words the heights to which good behaviour could raise a man! I will not describe how, finally, Anton Antonovich Setochkin, the head of a subsection, a colleague of Andrey Philippovich's and formerly of Olsufi Ivanovich's, and in addition an old friend of the family's and Clara Olsufyevna's godfather – a small gentleman hoary with age, proposing a toast in his turn, crowed like a cock and recited amusing doggerel; or how, with such decorous obliviousness to decorum, if I may so express myself, he made the whole company laugh till they cried, and Clara Olsufyevna, at her parents' behest, gave him a kiss for being so entertaining and so nice. I will only say that at length the guests, who after such a dinner naturally felt towards one another as friends and brothers, rose from the table; the old gentlemen and solid citizens then, after a short time spent in friendly con-

versation and even some outspoken remarks, expressed of course
very amiably and decorously, passed sedately into the next room
and, without losing a golden moment, arranged themselves in
groups of four and sat down, full of self-satisfaction, at tables
covered with green baize; that the ladies, seating themselves in the
drawing-room, all became suddenly very friendly and began discussing various dress-materials; that finally the highly esteemed
host himself, who had lost the use of his legs in true and loyal
service and been rewarded in all the ways mentioned above, began
moving about on crutches among his guests, supported by Vladimir Semyonovich and Clara Olsufyevna, and that, having also
developed a sudden amiability, he decided to improvise a small and
modest ball, in spite of the expense; that to this end an efficient
young man (the same who at dinner had seemed more like a State
Councillor than a stripling) was sent out for musicians; that subsequently a band of no less than eleven instrumentalists arrived,
and that finally, at exactly half-past eight, the inviting strains of a
French quadrille and various other dances began to be heard. ... I
need hardly say that my pen is too feeble, languid, and dull for the
proper description of the ball improvised with such extreme amiability by the hoary-headed host. Besides, how, I ask, how can I,
the humble reporter of Mr Golyadkin's adventures, curious
enough in their own way though they may be – how can I depict
that uncommon and seemly compound of beauty, brilliance, decorum, extraordinary gaiety, amiable solidity and solid amiability,
playfulness, joy, and all the gambols and laughter of all the high
official ladies, more like fairies than ladies – speaking in a sense
favourable to them – with their lily-white shoulders, their rosy-
pink faces, their airily slender waists, their playfully twinkling,
homeopathically (speaking in the high style) tiny feet? Finally,
how shall I depict for you those splendid partners of high official
standing, cheerful and sedate, youthful and staid, joyful and becomingly melancholy, smoking a pipe in the intervals between
dances in a small, remote, green room, or not smoking between
dances – partners every one from the first to the last bearing a
distinguished name and a high rank in the service – partners
deeply imbued with a sense of elegance and a feeling of proper

pride, partners for the most part speaking French to the ladies or, if Russian, Russian full of expressions of the very highest tone, compliments, and profound sentiments – partners who only in the smoking-room might perhaps permit themselves some affable lapses from language of the highest tone, certain sentences of friendly and good-humoured familiarity, such as 'You old so-and-so, Petka, you were kicking up your heels famously in the polka,' or, 'You dog, you, Vasya, you gave your partner a fine time of it, didn't you?' For all this, as I had the honour of explaining to you above, Reader, my pen is inadequate, and therefore I am silent. Let us rather turn to Mr Golyadkin, the real and sole hero of our highly veracious story.

The fact is that he is now in a position that is, to say the least, extremely strange. He is here too, ladies and gentlemen, that is to say not at the ball, but almost at the ball; he is all right, ladies and gentlemen; although he goes his own way, yet at this moment he stands upon a path that is not altogether straight; he stands now – it is strange even to say it – he stands now in the passage from the back entrance of Olsufi Ivanovich's flat. But that he is standing there means nothing; he is all right. He is standing, though, ladies and gentlemen, in a corner, lurking in a much darker, if no warmer, place, half concealed by an enormous cupboard and an old screen, among every kind of dusty rubbish, trash, and lumber, hiding until the proper time and meanwhile only watching the progress of the general business in the capacity of casual looker-on. He is only watching now, ladies and gentlemen; but, you know, he may also go in, ladies and gentlemen ... why not? He has only to take a step, and he is in, and in very neatly. Only just now – after standing, however, three hours in the cold among every kind of dusty rubbish, trash, and lumber – he was citing in his own justification a phrase from the French minister Villèle, of blessed memory, to the effect that 'everything comes in due course, if you only wait long enough'. Mr Golyadkin had come across this sentence at some time in some quite casual reading, but now recalled it to mind very appropriately. In the first place, it suited his present position extremely well, and secondly, what doesn't come into the head of a man who has been waiting for a fortunate

resolution of his position for almost three solid hours by the clock
in the back entrance, in the dark and cold? Having very aptly
quoted the late French minister Villèle's phrase, as we have
already stated, Mr Golyadkin immediately, I don't know why,
remembered the former Turkish vizier Montsemiris and the
beautiful Margravine Louise, whose story he had also read in some
book at some time or other. Then it came into his mind that the
Jesuits even made it a rule to count all means justified if only the
end could be attained. Having fortified himself a little by a histori-
cal point like this, Mr Golyadkin proceeded to ask himself what
the Jesuits were. The Jesuits were all, to the last man, utter fools,
and he would surpass the lot of them; and if only the room where
the refreshments were (whose door opened directly into the back-
stairs passage where Mr Golyadkin now found himself) would
remain empty for a single moment, he would simply walk straight
through, bidding defiance to all Jesuits, first from the refreshment
room into the one where tea was served, then into the room where
they were playing cards, and then straight into the room where
they were now dancing the polka. And he would get through, he
would certainly get through, looking neither to right nor to left,
he would slip through, that was all, and nobody would notice; and
when he got there, he knew what to do. That is the situation,
ladies and gentlemen, in which we now find the hero of our utterly veracious story, although it is difficult to explain what
exactly has been happening to him. The fact of the matter is that
he had been able to get to the entrance and the back stairs because,
as he said to himself, 'Why not? anybody can get there'; but he
had not dared, simply not dared, to go further ... not because
there was anything he dared not do, but just because he didn't
choose to, because he would rather do things quietly. So there he
is now, ladies and gentlemen, waiting for the chance to do things
quietly, and he has been waiting for exactly two and a half hours.
Why not wait? Villèle himself used to wait. 'But what's Villèle
got to do with this?' thought Mr Golyadkin. 'Who's Villèle, anyhow? And what if I were to ... just go through ...? Oh you,
dummy that you are,' said Mr Golyadkin, pinching his frozen
cheek with his frozen fingers, 'what a stupid fool you are. An

empty-headed fool! You . . . you – Golyadkin! (What a name!)' However, these flattering remarks addressed to himself at this moment did not mean anything, they were merely said in passing, without any real purpose. But now he thrust himself away from his corner and took a step forward; the time had come; the refreshment room had emptied, there was nobody left in it; Mr Golyadkin had seen all this through the hatch; in two strides he was at the door and had begun to open it. 'Shall I go in or not? Well, shall I or shan't I? I will . . . why shouldn't I? Where there's a will there's a way.' Encouraging himself thus, our hero suddenly and quite unexpectedly retreated behind the screen. 'No,' he thought, 'what if somebody comes in? There you are, somebody *has* come in; why did I shilly-shally when there was nobody there? I ought to have just barged straight in! . . . No, what's the use of going in, with a character like mine? What a mean-spirited creature! I ran like a rabbit. Cowardice is my speciality! Base behaviour is always my speciality, no question about it. Well, then, go on standing here like a dummy, that's all! If I could just be drinking a cup of tea at home this minute! . . . It would be very nice to have a quiet cup of tea. If I'm any later than this, Petrushka will sulk, perhaps. Hadn't I better go home? To the devil with all this! I'll go home, and that's all about it!' Having thus settled the situation, Mr Golyadkin stepped briskly forward, as if somebody had touched a spring inside him; in two strides he was in the refreshment room, where he threw off his overcoat, removed his hat, hastily thrust everything into the corner, straightened his coat and looked round; then . . . then he moved on into the room where tea was served, whisked into the next room, and slipped almost unnoticed between the card-players engrossed in their game; then . . . then . . . here Mr Golyadkin, forgetting for a moment everything that was going on, stepped like a bolt from the blue straight into the drawing-room.

As luck would have it, they were not dancing. The ladies were strolling about the room in elegant groups. The men clustered together or darted about, engaging their partners. Mr Golyadkin noticed none of this. He saw only Clara Olsufyevna, with Andrey Philippovich beside her, then Vladimir Semyonovich and two or

three officers as well, and in addition two or three other young
men, also very prepossessing, who showed promise or had even, as
could be seen at first glance, fulfilled it. ... He also saw another
person. Or no; he no longer saw anybody or looked at anybody ...
but, propelled by the same spring that had projected him unin-
vited into somebody else's ball, he was moving forward, and forward again, and still further forward; he stumbled into some high
official on the way and trod on his foot, stepped on the dress of a
respectable old lady and tore it slightly, bumped into a man with a
tray, bumped into somebody else besides and, without noticing
any of this, or rather noticing it but only in passing, without
looking at anybody, pushed his way further and further forward,
until suddenly he found himself directly in front of Clara Olsufyevna. There is not the slightest doubt he could most gladly have
sunk through the floor at that moment without so much as blinking; but what's done can't be undone ... no, indeed it can't. What
was he to do? 'If things go wrong, stand your ground, if all goes
well, stand firm.' Mr Golyadkin, of course, was 'not an intriguer,
nor was he good at polishing the parquet with his shoes. . . .' Well,
now the worst had happened. And besides, the Jesuits were mixed
up in it somehow. ... However, Mr Golyadkin had no time for
them now! The whole walking, talking, laughing, noisy throng
fell silent as if by magic and little by little crowded round Mr
Golyadkin. Mr Golyadkin, however, seemed to hear nothing, see
nothing, he could not look ... nothing could have made him look;
he cast his eyes down and simply stood there – although, by the
way, he had already promised himself that he would blow his
brains out before the night was over. Having promised himself
this, Mr Golyadkin thought to himself, 'Here goes!' and, to his
own immense surprise, quite unexpectedly began to talk.

   Mr Golyadkin began with congratulations and good wishes.
The congratulations went well, but over the good wishes our hero
stumbled. He had been feeling that if he stumbled everything
would immediately be lost. And so it happened – he stumbled and
got stuck; got stuck and blushed crimson; blushed crimson and
became flustered; became flustered and raised his eyes; raised them
and looked around; looked around and – and was struck dumb

with horror. . . . Everything was stillness and silence and expectancy; a little further away someone whispered, a little nearer, someone tittered. Mr Golyadkin cast a humble, desperate look at Andrey Philippovich. Andrey Philippovich answered him with a glance which, if our hero had not been quite, quite dead already, would certainly have killed him again, if that were possible. The silence continued.

'This has more to do with my home circumstances and my private life, Andrey Philippovich,' said Mr Golyadkin, more dead than alive, in a barely audible voice; 'this is not anything official, Andrey Philippovich . . .'

'For shame, sir, for shame!' said Andrey Philippovich in a half-whisper, with an air of irrepressible indignation – and as he spoke, he took Clara Olsufyevna's arm and turned his back on Mr Golyadkin.

'I have nothing to be ashamed of, Andrey Philippovich,' answered Mr Golyadkin in the same half-whisper, casting his forlorn glances all around, hopelessly striving at all costs to find a centre and a social status among the bewildered crowd.

'Well, it doesn't matter, it's nothing at all, ladies and gentlemen! Well, what does it amount to? why, it might happen to anybody,' whispered Mr Golyadkin, shifting his position and trying to find his way out of the surrounding crowd. They stood back for him. Somehow or other our hero made his way between two rows of curious and bewildered onlookers. Fate was carrying him on. Mr Golyadkin himself felt that it was fate that carried him on. He would, of course, have given a great deal for the chance of finding himself, without any breach of etiquette, at his former station once more, in the passage by the back stairs; but since that was definitely impossible, he began trying to slip away somewhere into a corner where he could simply stand apart quietly, modestly, discreetly, disturbing nobody, not drawing any attention to himself, and yet earning the favourable opinions of the guests and his host. But Mr Golyadkin felt as if he was being undermined, as it were, as if he was tottering and on the point of falling. Finally he managed to reach a corner and took up his position in it, like a casual, rather unconcerned onlooker, resting his hands on the backs of two chairs, thus taking possession of them, while he tried his utmost to look cheerfully at those of Olsufi Ivanovich's guests who were grouped near him. Nearest of all was an officer, a tall and handsome youth before whom Mr Golyadkin felt an utter insect.

'These two chairs are engaged, Lieutenant, one for Clara Olsu-fyevna and the other for Princess Chevchekhanova, who is dancing close to here; I am keeping them for them, Lieutenant,' said Mr Golyadkin breathlessly, turning an imploring glance on the young officer. The lieutenant silently turned away, with a devastating smile. Having missed fire in one direction, our hero decided to try his luck in another, and turned straight to an important-looking State Councillor, with a resplendent Order hanging round his neck. But the Councillor eyed him with a look so cold that Mr Golyadkin had a distinct sensation of having been drenched with a whole bucket of icy water. Mr Golyadkin held his peace. He made up his mind that it was better to keep quiet and not begin talking, so as to show that he was quite at home, that he was no different from anybody else, and that as far as he could see his position also was at least tolerably comfortable. With this object he stared fixedly at the cuffs of his dress-coat, then raised his eyes and rested them on a highly respectable-looking gentleman. 'That gentleman is wearing a wig,' thought Mr Golyadkin, 'and if the wig were removed he would have an absolutely bald head, as bare as the palm of my hand.' Having made this important discovery, Mr Golyadkin remembered those Turkish emirs who, if they remove from their heads the green turban they wear in token of their kinship with the prophet Mohammed, are also left with bald completely naked heads. Then, probably because of all the conflicting ideas about Turks in his mind, Mr Golyadkin progressed to the subject of Turkish slippers, and was reminded by it that Andrey Philippovich wore shoes that were more like slippers than shoes. It was noticeable that Mr Golyadkin was now to some extent in command of the situation. An idea floated through his head: 'If that chandelier there were to fall from its place and crash down on the dancers, I would rush forward immediately to save Clara Olsufyevna. "Don't worry," I should say as I did so, "It is

nothing, and I am here to rescue you." Then. . . .' Here Mr Golyadkin glanced round, looking for Clara Olsufyevna, and saw Gerasimych, Olsufi Ivanovich's old butler. With a most concerned
and solemnly official air, Gerasimych was making his way straight
towards him. Mr Golyadkin started and frowned with an unaccountable but highly unpleasant feeling. He glanced round mechanically: it occurred to him to try to sidle stealthily out of the
way, to efface himself instantly, that is to behave as if it had
nothing to do with him, as if he wasn't the person concerned at
all. But before our hero had had time to decide on anything, Gerasimych was already standing before him.

'Look, Gerasimych,' said our hero, turning to Gerasimych with a
little smile, 'you must give orders at once; look there, that candle
in the chandelier there, Gerasimych – it's just about to fall; so, you
know, go and give orders for it to be straightened; it really is going
to fall, Gerasimych.'

'The candle, sir? No, sir, the candle is standing quite straight,
sir; but there's somebody asking for you, sir.'

'Why, who can be asking for me here, Gerasimych?'

'To tell you the truth, I don't know exactly who it is, sir. Some
sort of person, sir. They said, "Is Yakov Petrovich Golyadkin here?
Well, call him out," they said, "he's wanted on very special urgent
business . . ." – that's what they said, sir.'

'No, Gerasimych, you're mistaken; you're mistaken there, Gerasimych.'

'Undoubtless, sir . . .'

'No, Gerasimych, it's not undoubtless; there is nothing un-
doubtless about it, Gerasimych. Nobody is asking for me,
Gerasimych; nobody has any need to ask for me, Gerasimych, and
I'm at home here, I mean I'm in my rightful place, Gerasimych.'

Mr Golyadkin paused for breath and looked round. It was just
as he supposed! Everybody in the room was straining his eyes and
ears in a sort of solemn expectation. The men were crowding as
close as they could and listening hard. A little further away the
ladies were whispering to one another. The host himself had appeared only a very short distance away from Mr Golyadkin, and
although it was impossible to tell from his looks that he was di-

rectly and immediately concerned with Mr Golyadkin's position, because everything was being kept on the most delicate footing, nevertheless everything gave the hero of our story plainly to understand that the decisive moment had arrived. Mr Golyadkin realized clearly that the time for a bold stroke, the time for putting his enemies to shame, had come. Mr Golyadkin was excited. Mr Golyadkin felt somehow inspired and in a solemn, trembling voice began again, addressing the waiting Gerasimych.

'No, my friend, nobody was asking for me. You are mistaken. I will go further: you were mistaken this afternoon when you assured me ... when you had the temerity to assure me, I say,' (Mr Golyadkin raised his voice), 'that Olsufi Ivanovich, who has been so kind to me from time immemorial, who has in a certain sense taken the place of a father to me, had forbidden me his doors at this moment of solemn family rejoicing for his paternal heart.' (Mr Golyadkin looked round, complacently but with profound feeling. Tears glittered on his eye-lashes.) 'I repeat, my friend,' our hero concluded, 'you were mistaken, cruelly and unforgivably mistaken ...'

It was a solemn moment. Mr Golyadkin felt that he had produced an effect of the truest sincerity. Mr Golyadkin stood with modestly downcast eyes, waiting for Olsufi Ivanovich to clasp him in his arms. The guests were visibly touched and wondering; even the terrible and unshakable Gerasimych hiccoughed as he began, 'Undoubtless, sir ...' when the band, for no discernible reason, suddenly and heartlessly struck up a noisy polka. All was lost, everything had gone with the wind. Mr Golyadkin jumped, Gerasimych started back, the whole room sprang into motion like the sea, and Vladimir Semyonovich had already carried Clara Olsufyevna to the position of the leading pair, followed by the handsome lieutenant and Princess Chevchekhanova. Onlookers crowded round to watch the dancers – the polka was a new, interesting, fashionable dance that had turned everybody's head. For a time Mr Golyadkin was forgotten. But then suddenly all was excitement, confusion, fluster; the music stopped ... something strange had happened. Tired with dancing and almost out of breath with her exertions, Clara Olsufyevna, with flaming cheeks and wildly heaving bosom, had at last fallen exhausted into a chair. All hearts went out to the fascinating charmer, everybody hastened towards her, vying with each other in complimenting her and thanking her for the pleasure she had given them – when suddenly Mr Golyadkin appeared in front of her. Mr Golyadkin was pale and extremely disturbed; he also seemed somehow exhausted and hardly able to move. He was smiling for some reason, and he invitingly held out his hand. Clara Olsufyevna was too surprised to have time to draw back her hand, and mechanically rose at Mr Golyadkin's invitation. Mr Golyadkin swayed forwards, once, then again, then he raised one leg and executed a kind of shuffle, then a kind of stamp, then stumbled ... he also wanted to dance with Clara Olsufyevna. Clara Olsufyevna screamed; everybody rushed forward to free her hands from Mr Golyadkin's clasp, and our hero found himself immediately pushed away by the press to a distance of almost twenty feet. A little crowd gathered round him also. Cries and shrieks arose from two old ladies whom Mr Golyadkin had almost knocked down in his retreat. There was a terrible commotion; the room was full of questions and cries and arguments. The band stopped playing. Our hero revolved in his little circle, mechanically muttering to himself with a half-smile, 'Well, why not? The polka, at least as far as I am aware, is a new dance and highly interesting, created for the delectation of the ladies ... but if that's how things stand, I am perhaps ready to consent to. ...' But nobody, it seemed, was even asking for Mr Golyadkin's consent. Our hero felt somebody's hand fall suddenly on his shoulder, while another pushed lightly against his back, and he found he was being steered with particular solicitude in a certain direction. Finally he realized that he was going straight towards the door. Mr Golyadkin tried to do something, say something. ... But no, he no longer wanted to do anything. He simply laughed it all off mechanically. Finally he felt his overcoat being put on him and his hat pulled down over his eyes; then he felt himself in the passage, in the dark and the cold, and lastly on the stairs. At length he stumbled and felt himself falling into an abyss; he wanted to scream – and suddenly found himself in the courtyard. The fresh air blew on him and he

paused for a moment; in the same instant there reached his ears
the sound of the orchestra striking up again. All at once, Mr
Golyadkin remembered everything; all his failing powers seemed
to return to him again. He tore himself away from the place where
he had been standing as if rooted to the spot, and dashed headlong
away, anywhere, into the fresh air and the open spaces, straight in
front of him . . .

Chapter Five

IT had just struck midnight from all the St Petersburg clock-
towers that displayed or chimed the hour when Mr Golyadkin ran
out, beside himself, on to the Fontanka embankment near Izmailovsky Bridge, escaping from his enemies, from persecution,
from the hail of slights that had descended on him, the shrieks of
alarmed old women, the gasps and exclamations of the ladies, and
Andrey Philippovich's annihilating stare. Mr Golyadkin was
crushed – utterly crushed, in the full sense of the word, and if he
still retained the capacity to run at that moment, it was by a
miracle, a miracle which he himself, of course, refused to believe
in. It was a terrible night, a November night, damp, foggy, rainy,
snowy, fraught with agues, catarrhs, colds, quinsies, fevers of
every possible species and variety, in short with all the blessings of
a St Petersburg November. The wind howled in the empty streets,
whipping the black water of the Fontanka higher than the moor-
ing-rings and mischievously snatching at the flickering embankment lights, which in their turn echoed its wailing with the
thin piercing squeak that makes up the endless whining, creaking
concert so familiar to every inhabitant of St Petersburg. It was
snowing and raining both together. Jets of rainwater, broken off
by the wind, spouted all but horizontally as if from firehoses,
pricking and cutting the wretched Mr Golyadkin's face like thousands of pins and needles. In the nocturnal quiet, broken only by
the distant rumble of coaches, the howl of the wind and the
squeaking of the swinging street-lamps, the splash and murmur of
the water running from every roof, porch, gutter, and cornice on

to the granite flags of the pavement had a dismal sound. There was not a soul to be seen far or near, and it seemed there could be nobody about at that hour and in that weather. Thus only Mr Golyadkin, alone with his despair, trotted with his small quick steps along the pavement of the Fontanka, hurrying to reach as quickly as possible his Shestilavochny Street, his fourth floor, and his own flat.

Although the snow, rain, and all the conditions for which there is not even a name, which prevail when blizzard and tempest rage under the November sky of St Petersburg, had assailed Mr Golyadkin, already crushed by his misfortunes, suddenly and all at once, showing him not the slightest mercy, giving him not a moment's respite, piercing him to the marrow, plastering up his eyes, blowing right through him from every direction, driving him off his course and out of his last remaining wits, although all this together had crashed down on Mr Golyadkin, as though purposely joining in league and concert with all his enemies to bring the ruin of his day, his evening, and his night to a triumphant completeness – in spite of it all, Mr Golyadkin remained almost insensitive to this last evidence of the malignancy of fate, he had been so shaken and over-whelmed by all that had happened a few minutes earlier in State Councillor Berendeyev's house. If some casual and un-involved passer-by had chanced to give an indifferent side-glance at Mr Golyadkin's melancholy flight, even he would immediately have been stirred to the depths by all the dire horror of his disastrous plight, and would infallibly have said that Mr Golyadkin looked as if he was trying to hide from himself, as if he wanted to run away from himself. Yes, it really was so! We will say more: Mr Golyadkin wanted not only to run away from himself but even to annihilate himself, to cease to be, to return to the dust. At the present moment he was not taking in his sur-roundings, understood nothing of what was going on around him, and looked as though in truth none of the discomforts of the wintry night, not the long journey, nor the rain, the snow, the wind or any other ingredient of the bad weather, existed for him. The galosh that fell off Mr Golyadkin's right foot remained where it was in the mud and slush on the Fontanka pavement, and Mr Golyadkin did not think of going back for it, did not indeed even notice its loss. He was so bemused that several times, completely preoccupied in spite of his surroundings with the idea of his recent terrible disgrace, he stopped dead in the middle of the pavement and stood there motionless as though turned to stone; in those moments he died and disappeared off the face of the earth; then suddenly he would tear himself away from the spot like a madman and run, run without a backward glance, as though trying to escape from some pursuit or an even more terrible disaster. . . . His situation really was one of horror. . . . At last, drained of all strength, Mr Golyadkin stopped, leaned his arms on the parapet of the embankment in the attitude of a man whose nose has suddenly and unexpectedly begun to bleed, and gazed fixedly into the seething black waters of the Fontanka. I don't know exactly how long he spent in this occupation. I only know that at that juncture Mr Golyadkin had reached such a state of despair, was so harassed and weary, had so drained and exhausted the already feeble remnants of his spirit, that he forgot for a short time all about everything, Izmailovsky Bridge, Shestilavochny Street, his present. . . . His present what, in fact? After all, it was all the same to him: the thing was done, finished with, the verdict signed and sealed; what did it matter to him? Suddenly . . . suddenly his whole body quivered, and involuntarily he leapt to one side. He began to look around him with inexplicable anxiety; but there was nobody, nothing particular had happened, and yet . . . and yet it seemed to him that just now, this very moment, somebody had been standing there, close to him, by his side, also leaning on the parapet and – an extraordinary thing! – had even said something to him, something hurried and abrupt, not altogether understandable, but about a matter touching him nearly, something that concerned him. 'Why, have I been imagining things?' said Mr Golyadkin, again gazing all round him. 'But where am I? . . . Dear, dear!' he concluded, shaking his head, and yet meanwhile staring with dismayed and uneasy feelings, even fearfully, into the damp, cloudy distance, straining his sight and striving with all his power to pierce with his near-sighted eyes the featureless haziness stretching before him. But there was nothing new, nothing particular met Mr Golyadkin's eyes. Everything seemed to be in order, as it ought to be; that is to say the snow was falling still heavier and thicker, in bigger flakes; not a thing could be seen at a distance of fifteen yards; the street lights creaked even more stridently than before, and the wind seemed to wail its long-drawn-out lament still more dolefully and drearily, like an importunate beggar whining for a copper coin to buy food. 'Dear, dear, what on earth is the matter with me?' Mr Golyadkin repeated once more, setting out on his way again and still occasionally glancing round. Meanwhile a new kind of feeling began to make itself evident in all Mr Golyadkin's being: not exactly depression, nor exactly fear . . . a feverish shiver ran through his veins. It was unbearably unpleasant. 'Well, it doesn't matter,' he said to give himself heart, 'well, it doesn't matter; perhaps it's nothing at all, no stain on anybody's honour. Perhaps it had to happen,' he went on, himself not understanding what he was saying; 'perhaps it will all turn out for the best in its own good time, and there will be no recriminations and nobody will be put in the wrong.' Talking in this way, trying with the words to lighten his mood, Mr Golyadkin gave himself a slight shake and brushed off the snowflakes with which his hat, his collar, his coat, his cravat, his shoes, and everything else about him were thickly encrusted, – but he still could not succeed in shaking off or freeing himself of the strange feeling, his terrible black depression. The sound of a cannon echoed from somewhere far away. 'This terrible weather!' thought our hero; 'Listen! isn't that a flood warning? – Evidently the water is rising very fast.' No sooner had Mr Golyadkin said, or thought, this, than he caught sight of a figure coming towards him, probably some belated wanderer like himself. On the face of it, it seemed a trivial chance encounter, but for some unknown reason Mr Golyadkin was troubled and even afraid, and felt at a loss. It was not that he feared this might be some bad character, he was simply afraid. 'And besides, who knows?' – the thought came unbidden into Mr Golyadkin's mind – 'perhaps this passer-by is – *he*, himself, perhaps he is here and, what matters most, he is not here for nothing, he has a purpose, he is crossing my path, he will

brush against me.' Perhaps, indeed, Mr Golyadkin did not think
all this, but merely felt for a moment something resembling it and
extremely unpleasant. There was, however, no time now for
thinking or even for feeling; the passer-by was already within a
yard of him. At once Mr Golyadkin, in his usual way, put on a
very special air, an air clearly expressing that he, Golyadkin, went
his own way, that he was all right, that the road was wide enough
for everybody and that he, Golyadkin, would not interfere with
anybody. Suddenly he stopped as if rooted to the spot, as if he had
been struck by lightning, and then turned sharply about after the
stranger, who had only that moment passed him – turned about as
though he had been twitched from behind, or as though the wind
had whirled him round like a weathercock. The stranger was
rapidly disappearing in the snowstorm. He also was walking
swiftly, he also, like Mr Golyadkin, was bundled up in clothes
from head to foot and, again like him, trotted and pranced along
the pavement with small pattering steps and a slight hop in his
gait. 'What is this, what is it?' whispered Mr Golyadkin incredu-
lously – and he was shaking all over. A shiver ran down his spine.
Meanwhile the passer-by had completely disappeared, his steps
were not even audible, but Mr Golyadkin still stood looking after
him. Little by little, however, he recovered his composure. 'What
on earth is the matter with me?' he thought with vexation; 'why
am I behaving like this, have I gone out of my mind in good
earnest?' He turned back and pursued his way, quickening his
steps, hurrying faster and faster and trying to avoid thinking of
anything at all. Finally, with this object, he even closed his eyes.
Suddenly, through the wailing of the wind and all the noises of
the storm, the sound of footsteps very close to him again reached
his ears. He started and opened his eyes. In front of him, about
fifteen yards away, the small black figure of a man hastening
towards him was again visible. The man was hurrying, scurrying,
almost running; the distance between them rapidly decreased. Mr
Golyadkin was even able to examine the new belated passer-by
closely – and when he did so, he exclaimed aloud in horrified
bewilderment; his knees shook. It was the same pedestrian, the
one already known to him, the one he had made way for ten

minutes earlier, who had now suddenly and startlingly appeared in front of him again. But it was not this miracle alone that had startled Mr Golyadkin – and Mr Golyadkin was so startled that he stopped dead, almost shrieked aloud, tried to say something – and started in pursuit of the stranger, even calling out to him, probably with the intention of making him stop as quickly as possible. The unknown did stop, some ten paces from Mr Golyadkin, in such a position that the light from a near-by street-lamp fell full on his face – stopped, turned, and waited with a look of pre-occupied impatience to hear what Mr Golyadkin had to say. 'Excuse me, I seem to have made a mistake,' said our hero in a shaking voice. The stranger turned away in annoyed silence and went swiftly on his way, as if hurrying to make up the two seconds he had wasted on Mr Golyadkin. As for Mr Golyadkin himself, he trembled in every muscle, his knees, too weak to support him, buckled under him, and he collapsed with a groan on a bollard on the pavement. There was, indeed, good reason for him to be so upset. The fact was that the unknown now seemed to him to be somehow familiar. This would not have mattered. But he had now recognized this man, almost completely recognized him. He had seen him often, this man, had even seen him on some very recent occasion; but where was it? and was it only the previous day? Once again, however, what mattered most was not that Mr Golyadkin had often seen him; there was, indeed, nothing special about the man, there was nothing about him to make anybody take particular notice of him at first glance. The man was like everybody else, respectable, of course, like all respectable people, and perhaps even possessing some special and even fairly important merits of his own – in short, he was an ordinary man. Mr Golyadkin felt neither dislike nor enmity, indeed no kind of hostility to this man – even, it would seem, the opposite – and yet not for the greatest treasure in the world would he willingly have met him, especially as he had just done. I will say more: Mr Golyadkin knew this man thoroughly well; he even knew what he was called, knew his name; and yet, I repeat, not for anything, not for the greatest treasure in the world, would he have been willing to name him, or consented to declare that his Christian name was

such-and-such, his patronymic and surname such-and-such.
Whether it was a long or a short time that Mr Golyadkin's irreso-
lution lasted, or whether he remained for long on his bollard on the
pavement, I cannot say, only that at length, having come to himself a little, he suddenly set off at a run, without a backward
glance and with all the strength that remained to him; his mind
was working; twice he stumbled and nearly fell – and this caused
the orphaning of his other shoe, when its galosh too abandoned it.
At length Mr Golyadkin slackened his pace a little to get his
breath back, looked hurriedly round him and saw that without
noticing it he had already run all the way along the Fontanka,
crossed Anichkov Bridge, gone some way along the Nevsky
Prospect, and was now at the corner of Liteiny Street. Mr Golyadkin turned the corner into Liteiny Steet. His situation at that
moment was like that of a man standing above a terrible chasm
when the ground has begun to break away, is already rocking and
sliding, sways for the last time and falls, carrying him into the
abyss, while the poor wretch has neither the strength nor the
willpower to spring backwards or to turn his eyes away from the
yawning gulf; the abyss draws him and at last he leaps into it of
his own accord, himself hastening his own doom. Mr Golyadkin
knew and felt, was indeed quite sure, that some other evil thing
would inevitably happen to him on the way, something else unpleasant would burst upon him; for instance, he might meet the
stranger again; but, horrible to tell, he even wanted the meeting,
felt it was unavoidable and only asked for the whole thing to be
over and done with as quickly as possible, and his situation
settled, in whatever way, so long as it was soon. Meanwhile he
ran on and on, and it was as though he was kept in motion by
some outside force, for he felt a kind of growing weakness and
numbness throughout his whole being; he could not keep his
mind on anything, although his thoughts clutched at everything
like brambles. A miserable lost dog, wet through and shivering,
attached itself to Mr Golyadkin and hurried along beside him,
running sideways, with tail and ears drooping, and from time to
time looking hastily and timidly up at him. Some far-off long-
forgotten idea, the remembrance of some long-past happening,

now came into his head, knocked like a little hammer in his brain, pestered him, would not leave him alone. 'Oh, this wretched mongrel!' whispered Mr Golyadkin, not understanding his own words. Finally he saw his stranger at the corner of Italiansky Street. Only now the stranger was not coming towards him but going in the same direction as himself, and he too was running, a few steps in front of him. At last they came into Shestilavochny Street. Mr Golyadkin could hardly breathe. The stranger stopped directly in front of the house in which was Mr Golyadkin's flat. The sound of a bell was almost immediately followed by the squeaking of an iron bolt. The gate opened, the stranger stooped, hurried through, and vanished. Almost at the same moment Mr Golyadkin hurried up and sped like an arrow through the gateway. Heedless of the grumbling porter he ran breathlessly into the courtyard and immediately caught sight of his interesting fellow-traveller, who had for an instant been lost to him. The stranger appeared momentarily at the entrance of the staircase which led to Mr Golyadkin's flat. Mr Golyadkin hurried after him. The staircase was dark, damp, and dirty. Every landing was heaped with all sorts of tenants' rubbish, so that a stranger unused to the place, coming to this staircase in the dark, was obliged to spend half an hour climbing up it, at the risk of breaking a leg, while he cursed both the stairs and the friends who were so inconveniently housed. But Mr Golyadkin's fellow-traveller seemed to be at home there; he ran lightly up, without difficulty and with complete knowledge of the place. Mr Golyadkin almost managed to catch up with him; two or three times the tail of the stranger's overcoat even struck him on the nose. His heart sank. The mysterious personage stopped just outside Mr Golyadkin's own flat and knocked, and (what would at any other time have astonished Mr Golyadkin), Petrushka opened the door immediately, as though he had not gone to bed but been waiting, and followed the newcomer in with a candle in his hand. Beside himself, the hero of our story flew into his flat; without waiting to take off his coat and hat he ran along the short passage and stopped thunderstruck at the door of his room. All Mr Golyadkin's forebodings had come true. Everything he had feared and foreseen had now become cold reality. It took his breath away and made his head whirl. The unknown, also still in hat and overcoat, was sitting before him, on his own bed, with a slight smile on his lips; narrowing his eyes a little, he gave him a friendly nod. Mr Golyadkin wanted to cry out but could not, to make some sort of protest but his strength failed him. His hair stood on end and he collapsed into a chair, insensible with horror. Mr Golyadkin had recognized his nocturnal acquaintance. Mr Golyadkin's nocturnal acquaintance was none other than himself, Mr Golyadkin himself, another Mr Golyadkin, but exactly the same as himself – in short, in every respect what is called his double ...

Chapter Six

THE next morning, at exactly eight o'clock, Mr Golyadkin came back to consciousness in his own bed. Immediately the unusual events of the previous day and the whole wild night with its almost incredible happenings, returned suddenly and all at once, in all their horrible completeness, to his memory and his mind. So much bitter hellish spite on the part of his enemies, and especially the last manifestation of that spite, froze Mr Golyadkin's heart. But at the same time it was all so impossible, that it was really difficult to believe a word of it; even Mr Golyadkin himself would have been ready to admit that the whole thing was a fantastic delusion, a temporary aberration of the mind, an overclouding of the intellect, if he had not, fortunately for him, known by hard practical experience to what lengths malevolence can sometimes drive a man and to what heights the embitterment of an enemy seeking revenge for his frustrated pride and ambition can sometimes mount. Besides, Mr Golyadkin's exhausted limbs, his fumy head, his aching back, the pernicious cold in his head, were powerful testimony to uphold the reality of the previous day's nocturnal excursion on foot, and to some degree of everything else that had happened in the course of that walk. And finally, Mr Golyadkin had known for a very long time that something was being prepared, that there was *somebody else* in reserve. But – what then?

When he had thought it over carefully, Mr Golyadkin decided to say nothing, to submit, to raise no objections in the matter for the time being. 'Perhaps they have only taken it into their heads to try to scare me, and when they see that I'm not affected, make no protest, am perfectly patient and bear it all submissively, they will retreat, they will retreat of their own accord, they will be the first to draw back.'

These were the thoughts that were in Mr Golyadkin's mind as, stretching himself in his bed and straightening his tired limbs, he waited, this time, for Petrushka's usual appearance in his room. He had been waiting for about a quarter of an hour already; he could hear the lazy Petrushka occupying himself with the samovar on the other side of the partition, and yet he simply could not make up his mind to call him. We will go further: Mr Golyadkin was even a little afraid now of a confrontation with Petrushka. 'God only knows,' he thought, 'God only knows what that scoundrel's attitude will be to all this. He keeps quiet and says nothing, but he's crafty.' At last the door creaked and Petrushka appeared with a tray in his hands. Mr Golyadkin cast him a timid sidelong look, waiting impatiently for what would come next and expecting that something would at last be said about a certain circumstance. But Petrushka did not utter a word; on the contrary, indeed, he seemed more uncommunicative, grim, and ill-humoured than usual, and his sidelong glances were sullen; altogether it was evident that he was extremely discontented about something. He would not look even once at his master – a fact, by the way, that rather piqued Mr Golyadkin; he put down on the table everything he had brought, turned round and silently retreated behind the partition. 'He knows, he knows, that idle rogue knows everything!' muttered Mr Golyadkin, applying himself to the tea. Our hero, however, did not question his man at all, although several times Petrushka came into the room on various errands. Mr Golyadkin was in a very anxious state of mind. It would be terrible going into the office again. He had a strong foreboding that it was precisely there that something was wrong. 'You'll go there,' he thought, 'and then what if you stumble into something? Wouldn't it be better to be patient? Oughtn't I to wait a bit? Let them do as they like; but I'd better wait here today, get my nerve back and recover a bit, think the whole thing over as well as I know how, and then go and take them all by surprise, and behave as though nothing had happened.' Pondering in this way, Mr Golyadkin smoked pipe after pipe; the time flew, it was almost half-past nine already. 'Why, it's half-past nine,' thought Mr Golyadkin, 'and too late to put in an appearance now. And besides I'm ill, of course I'm ill, certainly I'm ill; who's going to say I'm not? What is it to me? Let them send to inquire, let the timekeeper come; what difference does it make to me, after all? My back aches, I've got a cough and a cold in the head; and really, after all, I simply can't go, I can't go out in this weather; I could fall ill and even die, perhaps; the deathrate's very high, especially just now. . . .' With this kind of reasoning Mr Golyadkin succeeded at last in calming his conscience and excusing himself beforehand in his own eyes in anticipation of the expected carpeting from Andrey Philippovich for remissness in the performance of his duties. In all such circumstances our hero was in general extremely inclined to justify himself in his own eyes by irrefutable arguments, and making his conscience completely easy. And so, having now made his conscience completely easy, he applied himself to his pipe, filled it, and as soon as he had lighted it, sprang up from the sofa, threw down the pipe, quickly washed, shaved, and smoothed his hair, put on his frock-coat, snatched up some papers, and hurried to the office.

Mr Golyadkin entered the office timidly, in quivering anticipation of something very tiresome – an instinctive and obscure anticipation, but nevertheless unpleasant; timidly he sat down in his usual place beside his immediate superior, Anton Antonovich Setochkin. Without a glance at anybody, without allowing himself to be distracted by anything, he began investigating the contents of the papers lying in front of him. He had resolved, and made himself a promise, to avoid as far as he could every kind of challenge and anything that might seriously compromise him, like indiscreet questions and certain persons' jokes and unseemly remarks about the events of the previous evening; he had even decided to shun the usual polite exchanges with his colleagues, inquiries about their health, that is, and so on. But it was quite plain that it was impossible to keep it up – it simply couldn't be done. Anxiety about and ignorance of anything that threatened to touch him closely always caused him more torment than the thing itself. That was why, in spite of having given himself his word not to enter into all that, whatever happened, but to refrain from absolutely everything, Mr Golyadkin stealthily and with the most extreme caution raised his head from time to time and secretly stole a glance at the faces of his colleagues to right and to left, trying to decide from them whether there was anything new and special that concerned himself and was being kept from him for some improper reason. He assumed that there was inevitably a connection between his present surroundings and the events of the previous evening. At length, in his boredom and depression, he began to want to get something settled quickly, no matter how, even if it was utterly disastrously, it didn't matter! Here fate seemed to take him at his word: he had hardly formulated his wish before all his doubts were abruptly settled, but in the strangest and most unexpected fashion.

The door into the next room opened with a quiet and timid creak, as though pleading the insignificance of the person entering, and a figure familiar to Mr Golyadkin appeared bashfully in front of the very desk at which our hero was sitting. Our hero did not raise his head – no, he only gave the figure a casual glance of the very shortest kind, but he knew everything already, he understood everything down to the smallest detail. He was burning with shame, and hid his vanquished head in his papers for exactly the same reason as the ostrich pursued by the hunter hides his in the hot sand. The newcomer bowed to Andrey Philippovich, and thereupon the conventionally kind voice in which all senior officials in all government departments speak to newly-entered subordinates made itself heard. 'Sit here,' said Andrey Philippovich, pointing to Anton Antonovich's section, 'here opposite Mr Golyadkin, and we'll find you something to do at once.' Andrey Philippovich ended by making the newcomer a gesture of suitable admonition, and then immediately became engrossed in the contents of some of the papers which lay in a pile before him.

Mr Golyadkin now at last raised his eyes, and if he did not swoon away it was only because he had already foreseen the whole thing and, having divined the identity of the newcomer, was forewarned. Mr Golyadkin's first move was to cast a quick glance all round for any evidence of whispering or the firing off of some bureaucratic witticism, and to see whether somebody's face was distorted with astonishment, or somebody else was cowering under his desk with fright. But to Mr Golyadkin's great surprise nobody showed any sign of anything of the sort. The behaviour of Mr Golyadkin's acquaintances and fellow-workers astounded him. It seemed contrary to all common sense. Mr Golyadkin even found the unaccustomed silence frightening. The reality of the situation spoke for itself: it was a strange, scandalous, outrageous affair. There was good reason to be disturbed. He himself was on tenterhooks. And indeed he had cause to be. The man now sitting opposite Mr Golyadkin was Mr Golyadkin's horror, he was Mr Golyadkin's shame, he was Mr Golyadkin's nightmare of the previous day; in short, he was Mr Golyadkin himself – not the Mr Golyadkin who now sat in his chair with his mouth gaping and the pen frozen in his grasp; not the one who liked to keep in the background and bury himself in the crowd; not, finally, the one whose demeanour said so clearly, 'Leave me alone and I'll leave you alone,' or, 'Leave me alone; I'm not interfering with you, am I?' – no, this was another Mr Golyadkin, a completely different one, and yet at the same time very like the other – of the same height and build, dressed in the same way and with the same bald patch – in short, nothing, absolutely nothing, was lacking to complete the resemblance, so that if they were taken and placed side by side nobody, absolutely nobody, would have taken it on himself to say which was the old and which the new, which was the original and which the copy.

Our hero was now, if the comparison is allowable, in the position of a man on whom some joker has amused himself by focusing a burning-glass. 'What is this, a dream?' he wondered. 'Is it real, or just a continuation of yesterday? But why? what right has all this to happen? Who gave permission for the appointment of this employee, who authorized this? Am I asleep, am I dreaming awake?' Mr Golyadkin tried to pinch himself, he even tried to make up his mind to pinch someone else. ... No, it wasn't a dream, that was flat. Mr Golyadkin felt the sweat pouring off him in streams, and he was conscious that what was happening to him was something unprecedented, hitherto unheard-of, and, crowning misfortune, made by that very fact disgraceful, for Mr Golyadkin felt all the disadvantage of being the first to be involved in such a scandalous farce. He even began at last to doubt his own identity, and although he had been prepared for anything to begin with, and eager for something, anything, to happen to resolve his perplexities, the very essence of the circumstances of course consisted in their unexpectedness. His anguish crushed and tormented him. At times he seemed bereft of reason and memory. Coming back to himself after one such moment, he noticed that he was mechanically and unconsciously moving his pen over the paper. Not trusting himself, he began to check all he had written – and could not understand a word of it. At length the other Mr Golyadkin, who had been sitting staidly and peacefully all this time, got up and disappeared through the door of another section on some errand. Mr Golyadkin looked round – there was nothing, all was quiet; there was no sound but the scraping of pens, the rustle of papers being turned over, and a little talking in the corners furthest removed from Andrey Philippovich's seat. Mr Golyadkin looked at Anton Antonovich, and since in all probability our hero's face fully expressed his present situation, harmonized with the implications of the matter, and was in consequence highly remarkable in one sense, the good Anton Antonovich laid aside his pen and with unusual solicitude inquired about Mr Golyadkin's state of health.

'I, thank God, Anton Antonovich,' stammered Mr Golyadkin, 'I am quite well, Anton Antonovich. I am quite all right now, Anton Antonovich,' he added undecidedly, still not altogether trusting the Anton Antonovich whose name he so frequently mentioned.

'Ah! I thought you were unwell; and it wouldn't have been a bit surprising. There's a lot of illness about, especially just now. Do you ...?'

'Yes, Anton Antonovich, I know there's a lot of infection about. ... That is not what I wanted to say, Anton Antonovich,' went on Mr Golyadkin, staring hard at Anton Antonovich. 'The fact is, Anton Antonovich, I don't even know how to make you ... I mean to say, how to tackle the question, Anton Antonovich.'

'What? I advise you ... you know ... I confess I don't quite understand ... You. ... look, explain yourself a bit more fully; what is it you find so difficult here?' said Anton Antonovich, who found it a little difficult himself, seeing that tears had started to Mr Golyadkin's eyes.

'Anton Antonovich, I ... here ... I'm an employee here, Anton – Antonovich ...'

'Well? I still don't understand.'

'I mean, Anton Antonovich, that there's a new employee here.'

'Yes, there is; his name's the same as yours.'

'What?' exclaimed Mr Golyadkin.

'I said his name's the same as yours; he's another Golyadkin. Is he your brother?'

'No, sir. Anton Antonovich, I ...'

'H'm! Then how is it ... and I supposed he must be a close relative of yours. You know, there is some ... what might be called family likeness.'

Mr Golyadkin was dumb with astonishment; for a time he simply could not speak. To treat such a shocking, such an unprecedented subject so lightly, a matter really unique of its kind, a matter that would have astonished even an indifferent bystander, to talk about a family likeness, when there was no more difference between them than if they were two peas in a pod!

'Do you know what my advice to you is, Yakov Petrovich?' went on Anton Antonovich. 'You just go to the doctor and ask him what he thinks. You know, you don't *look* at all well. You know, your eyes are peculiarly ... you know, there's a special sort of expression in them.'

'No, Anton Antonovich, of course I feel ... that is, I wanted to ask you, what is this new man?'

'What, sir?'

'I mean, Anton Antonovich, haven't you noticed something specially – something very striking about him?'

'You mean?'

'I mean, Anton Antonovich, what I meant was some very special likeness to somebody, for example, I mean to me, for example. Just now, Anton Antonovich, you talked of a family likeness, you made a passing reference. ... You know, sometimes there are twins, I mean as like as two peas, so that you can't tell the difference. Well, that was what I meant.'

'Yes,' said Anton Antonovich, after a moment's thought, as if he had been struck by the idea for the first time, 'yes! you're quite right. The resemblance is indeed striking, and you are right, you really could take one of you for the other,' he continued, while his eyes grew rounder and rounder. 'And do you know, Yakov Petrovich, the resemblance is positively miraculous, it's fantastic, as people say; I mean he's exactly like you. ... Have you noticed it, Yakov Petrovich? I was wanting to ask you myself if you could explain it; yes, I own I didn't pay it enough attention at first. Miraculous, really miraculous! And you know, Yakov Petrovich, your family isn't from here, I believe?'

'No.'

'He's not from here, either, you know. Perhaps he's from the same place as you. And really, it's absolutely marvellous,' went on the loquacious Anton Antonovich, for whom the opportunity of a good gossip was a real holiday, 'it really could attract attention; and, you know, how often you can walk past him, or brush against him, or bump into him, and not notice it! However, you mustn't be upset. These things happen. These things, you know – let me tell you about my aunt on my mother's side, the very same thing happened to her; she saw her double, too, just before she died ...'

'No, I – excuse me for interrupting you, Anton Antonovich – I wanted to know what this new man is, Anton Antonovich, I mean, what brings him here?'

'He's in place of Semyon Ivanovich, the one who died, in his vacant post; the post fell vacant, so it has been filled. You know, that poor nice Semyon Ivanovich left three small children, they say, all very young. The widow has been begging his Excellency for assistance, in great distress. However, they say she's hiding something: she has a little bit of money, and she's keeping it dark . . .'

'No, Anton Antonovich, I'm still talking about the same thing.'

'You mean? Oh yes! but why are you so interested in that? I tell you, you mustn't let it upset you. It's all partly a matter of time. What does it matter? – after all, it's nothing to do with you; it was the Lord God who ordained it, it was His will, and to murmur against it is sinful. It reveals His supreme wisdom. But you, Yakov Petrovich, as far as I can understand, are not in the least to blame. There are plenty of miracles in the world! Mother Nature is bounteous; and you will not be called to account for this, you won't have to answer for it. Well, appropriately enough, you know, you have heard, for example, of those – you know what I mean – what the devil do they call them? – oh yes, Siamese twins, with their backs joined together, they have to live and eat and sleep together; I'm told they make a lot of money.'

'Excuse me, Anton Antonovich . . .'

'I understand, I know what you want to say! Yes! – but what does it all amount to? – nothing! I say that to the best of my knowledge there is nothing for you to feel upset about. What of it? he's a civil servant like any other, and he seems an efficient sort of person. He says his name is Golyadkin; he is not from here, he says, and he's a Titular Councillor. He had a personal interview with His Excellency.'

'Well, what happened?'

'Nothing; they say he explained himself sufficiently well, he produced his reasons; "Well, Your Excellency," says he, "it's like this, and so on and so forth, and I've nothing to live on, and I want to enter the service, and especially under your distinguished leadership . . ." and, well, everything that ought to be said, you know, and all neatly expressed. He must be a clever fellow. Well, of course, he turned up with some sort of recommendation; after all, you can't get anywhere without one . . .'

'Well, who from? . . . that is, I mean to say, exactly who had a finger in this shameful business?'

'Yes. A good recommendation, they say; they say His Excellency had a laugh over it with Andrey Philippovich.'

'A laugh with Andrey Philippovich?'

'Yes; well, they just smiled and said that was all right, and perhaps ... and for their part they had no objection, so long as he served loyally ...'

'Well, go on. This reassures me a little, Anton Antonovich; do go on, I beg you.'

'Excuse me, there was something else I. ... Well yes; well, it doesn't matter; it's a simple circumstance; I tell you, you mustn't let yourself be upset or find anything suspicious in it ...'

'No. That is, I should like to ask you, Anton Antonovich, whether His Excellency didn't add anything ... about me, for example?'

'Good heavens! No! Oh, no, nothing; you can be quite easy about that. You know, it is of course self-evident that the circumstance is rather striking, and at first ... but take me, for example at first I hardly even noticed. I don't know, really, why I didn't notice until you reminded me. But, however, you can be quite easy. There was nothing special, they said absolutely nothing,' added the good Anton Antonovich, rising from his chair.

'So I, Anton Antonovich ...'

'Oh, you must excuse me. Here I've been chatting away about trifles, and I've an important piece of business; it's urgent. I must deal with it.'

'Anton Antonovich!' came Andrey Philippovich's politely peremptory voice, 'His Excellency is inquiring.'

'At once, at once, Andrey Philippovich, I'm coming at once.' And Anton Antonovich, taking up a pile of papers, hurried first over to Andrey Philippovich and then into His Excellency's room.

'What is all this?' Mr Golyadkin wondered to himself; 'so that's the sort of game that goes on here! That's the way the wind blows now. ... It's not bad; it comes to this, that things have taken the most favourable possible turn,' said our hero, rubbing his hands together, beside himself with glee. 'So our affair is perfectly ordinary. So the whole thing will just peter out, nothing will get settled. In fact, nobody has done anything, and they haven't a word to say, the scoundrels, they just sit there and go on with their work; fine, fine! I like a good man, I've always liked him, I'm always prepared to respect him. ... But still, when you come to think of it, it's not so good; that Anton Antonovich. ... I'm afraid to trust him: he's far gone in years, and he's pretty shaky. However, the great thing, the colossal thing, is that His Excellency didn't say anything, he simply let it pass: that's splendid, I'm pleased about that! Only why has Andrey Philippovich to come putting his oar in with his little laughs? What's it got to do with him? Old fox! He's always in my way, always trying to cross a man's path like a black cat, always a hindrance to a man and full of spite, always full of spite and a stumbling-block to a man ...'

Mr Golyadkin looked round him again, and again his hopes revived. He also felt, though, that there was some remote idea troubling him, some unpleasant idea. It even occurred to him for a moment to try to get his colleagues on his side, to draw attention to himself, even (as they were leaving after the day's work, perhaps, or going up to them as if on some sort of business) to throw out a hint in the course of conversation, such as, 'Well, gentlemen, it's like this or it's like that ... a striking resemblance ... a strange circumstance ... a curious irony ... that is, to make a joke of the whole thing himself and thus probe the depths of the danger. 'Still waters run deep,' our hero mentally concluded. Mr Golyadkin, however, only thought all this; he changed his mind before it was too late. He realized that it would be going too far. 'That's just like you!' he said to himself, striking his forehead lightly with his hand, 'You go plunging straight in, you're delighted! you guileless creature! No, Yakov Petrovich, better be patient, wait and be patient!' Nevertheless, as we have already said, Mr Golyadkin's hopes had been restored, as though he had come back from the dead. 'It's all right,' he thought. 'I feel as though a ton weight had been lifted from my heart! That's what it is! "There is no trick: you simply lift the lid!" Krylov was right, Krylov was right! ... he's a master, a cunning old fox, that Krylov, and a great writer of fables! As for *him*, let him work here, let him work if he likes, so long as he doesn't interfere with anybody or get in anybody's way; let him work – I agree, I approve!'

Meanwhile the hours sped past, and before he knew it four o'clock had struck. The office closed; Andrey Philippovich went for his hat, and as usual everybody followed his example. Mr Golyadkin lingered a little, just long enough, and purposely went out after the others, last of all, when they had already dispersed in various directions. Reaching the street, he suddenly felt absolutely blissful, so much so that he even experienced a desire to make a detour by way of the Nevsky Prospect. 'Well, life's like that!' said our hero; 'the whole thing has taken an unexpected turn. The weather has cleared up too; a nice frost, and it has brought the sledges out. Frost suits the Russians, Russians and frost get on famously together! I love Russians. And there's the snow, the very first new-fallen snow. As the hunter would say, "Oh, to be out after a hare in the new-fallen snow!" Ah well! Well, everything's all right!'

Thus Mr Golyadkin's delighted mood expressed itself, but all the time something went on nagging away at the back of his mind, a kind of ache, which sometimes so drained his spirits that Mr Golyadkin did not know where to turn for consolation. 'However, we'll wait a day, and then we can be happy. Still, what does it amount to, after all? Well, we'll think about it, and we'll see. Well, let's think it over, my young friend, let's discuss it. Well, he's a man like you, to begin with, exactly the same. Well, what of that? If that's what he is, ought I to weep over it? What's it got to do with me? I'm outside it; I just whistle, that's all! Let him work! Well, it's something strange and queer; just like the Siamese twins, as they call them. . . . Well, why them, the Siamese twins? – all right, they're twins, but even the very greatest people have seemed a bit queer sometimes. Why, even in history, it's well known the famous Suvorov crowed like a cock. . . . Well, but that was all for political reasons; and great generals . . . but why talk about generals? I go my own way, that's all, and I don't want to know anybody, and in my innocence I scorn my enemies. I am no intriguer, and I'm proud to say it. Honest, straightforward, orderly, agreeable, mild . . .'

Suddenly, Mr Golyadkin stopped short, trembling like a leaf; he even closed his eyes for a moment. Hoping, however, that the object of his terror was simply an illusion, he did at last open them again, and glanced timidly to his right. No, it was no illusion! There beside him minced his acquaintance of the morning, smiling, looking into his face, and apparently waiting for an opportunity to begin talking. But no conversation got started. They walked along together like that for about fifty yards. Mr Golyadkin concentrated all his efforts on wrapping himself up as closely as possible, burying himself in his overcoat and pulling his hat down over his eyes as far as it would go. The crowning insult was that even his acquaintance's coat and hat looked exactly as if Mr Golyadkin himself had just taken them off.

'My dear sir,' said our hero at length, trying to speak almost in a whisper and not looking at his companion, 'I think we go different ways. . . . In fact, I am sure of it,' he went on after a short silence. 'And finally, I am sure you completely understand me,' he added rather sternly in conclusion.

'I should like,' Mr Golyadkin's companion said at last, 'I should like . . . you will perhaps be kind enough to excuse me. . . . I don't know who I can turn to here . . . my circumstances – I hope you will excuse my boldness – it even seemed to me that this morning your sympathy prompted you to take an interest in me. . . . For my part, I felt attracted to you at first sight, I. . . .' Here Mr Golyadkin mentally consigned his new colleague to the devil. 'If I dared hope, Yakov Petrovich, that you would be good enough to condescend to hear what I have to say . . .'

'We – here we – we . . . we'd better go to my place,' answered Mr Golyadkin. 'Let us cross the Nevsky Prospect at once, it will be more convenient for us over there, and then by the side-turning . . . we'd better go by the side-street.'

'Very well. Let's go by the side-street, by all means,' said Mr Golyadkin's meek companion humbly, seeming to imply by the very tone of his answer that he had no right to be fussy and that in his position he was prepared to be content even with a side-street. As for Mr Golyadkin, he was utterly unable to understand what was happening to him. He did not trust his own senses. He could not get over his amazement.

Chapter Seven

HE had recovered a little, however, by the time they stood on the stairs at the entrance to his own flat. He was mentally cursing himself: 'Blockhead that I am, where on earth am I taking him? It's putting my head in a noose of my own accord. What on earth will Petrushka think, seeing us together? What will that scoundrel have the nerve to think? he's suspicious. ...' But it was already too late to repent; Mr Golyadkin knocked, the door opened and Petrushka began helping his master and the guest off with their coats. Mr Golyadkin glanced at him, simply throwing him a rapid casual look and trying to read his face and guess his thoughts. But, to his immense astonishment, he saw that it had not even entered his servant's head to be surprised; on the contrary, he even seemed to have been expecting something of the kind. He still, of course, kept his wolfish look, squinting sideways and apparently ready to eat somebody. 'Everybody seems bewitched today,' thought our hero, 'some kind of devil's got into all of them! There must certainly be something special in everybody today. Devil take it, what a torture!' Turning things over in his mind in this way, Mr Golyadkin led his visitor into his room and begged him to take a seat. The visitor evidently felt highly embarrassed and extremely shy; he humbly followed his host's every movement and caught his every look, apparently trying to guess his thoughts from them. All his gestures expressed something meek, downtrodden, and cowed, so that at that moment he was, if the comparison is permissible, like a man who for want of his own clothes is wearing somebody else's; the sleeves have crept half-way up his arms, the waist is almost round his neck, and he is either constantly tugging at the too-short waistcoat, or sliding away somewhere out of the way, or striving to find somewhere to hide, or looking into everybody's eyes and straining to hear whether people are talking about his plight and laughing at him or ashamed of him; and the poor man blushes, he loses his presence of mind, his pride suffers. ... Mr Golyadkin placed his hat on the window-sill with a gesture so careless that it fell to the floor. His visitor rushed to pick it up, brushed off the dust and carefully restored it to the same place, while he put his own hat on the floor beside the chair on the edge of which he had meekly perched. This small incident partly opened Mr Golyadkin's eyes; he realized that the fellow was in dire need and ceased to hesitate over how he should begin to talk to his guest, instead leaving it all to him, as was fitting. The guest, for his part, did not begin either, whether from shyness, or because he felt ashamed, or was waiting for his host out of politeness, it was difficult to decide. Meanwhile Petrushka entered, posted himself in the doorway and stared fixedly in the direction exactly opposite to the position of his master and the visitor.

'Shall I get dinner for two?' he asked huskily and carelessly.

'I ... I don't know ... yes, get it for two.'

Petrushka departed. Mr Golyadkin looked at his guest. The guest blushed up to his eyes. Mr Golyadkin was a kind man, and in the goodness of his heart he immediately formed a hypothesis: 'He's a poor man,' he thought, 'and he's only held his position for one day; he has suffered in his time, no doubt; perhaps he only had enough money for a respectable suit of clothes and has nothing left to feed himself on. Dear me, how dispirited he is! Well, that doesn't matter; in some ways it's better ...'

'Excuse me for ...' began Mr Golyadkin. 'But first, please tell me what to call you.'

'Ya ... Ya ... Yakov Petrovich,' his guest almost whispered, as if sorry and ashamed to be called Yakov Petrovich also, and begging forgiveness for it.

'Yakov Petrovich!' repeated our hero, quite unable to hide his dismay.

'Yes, sir, that's right. ... Your namesake,' Mr Golyadkin's visitor answered meekly, venturing a smile and permitting himself a slightly playful tone. But he settled back again at once with an extremely serious and at the same time somewhat embarrassed expression when he noticed that his host had no time for jests at that moment.

'You ... permit me to ask you to what I owe the honour ...'

'Knowing your generosity and goodness,' interrupted his guest briskly but in a timid tone of voice, half rising from his chair. 'I have ventured to turn to you to ask for your ... friendship and protection ...' he concluded, evidently experiencing difficulty in finding expressions neither so flattering and servile as to compromise his pride, nor so confident as to seem to claim an unsuitable equality. Altogether, Mr Golyadkin's visitor may be said to have conducted himself like a well-bred beggar in a patched frock-coat and with an honourable passport in his pocket, not yet accustomed to holding out his hand in the proper way.

'This is rather embarrassing,' answered Mr Golyadkin, his gaze wandering all round, over himself, the walls of his room, and his guest. 'What can I do ... that is, I mean to say, in exactly what respect can I be of service to you?'

'I felt attracted to you at first sight, Yakov Petrovich, and I ventured, please be good enough to forgive me, to rely on you, Yakov Petrovich ... I ... I am lost here, Yakov Petrovich, I am poor, I have suffered a very great deal, Yakov Petrovich, and I am still new here. When I learnt that you, with all the excellent qualities natural to your noble heart, had the same name as me ...'

Mr Golyadkin frowned.

'Had the same name as me and came from the same district, I made up my mind to address myself to you and explain my difficult situation.'

'Yes, yes; really, I don't know what to say to you,' answered Mr Golyadkin in an embarrassed tone. 'We'll have a talk after dinner ...'

The guest bowed; the dinner arrived. Petrushka laid the table, and host and guest addressed themselves to satisfying their hunger. Dinner did not take long; they were both in a hurry, the host because he was slightly upset and besides he was ashamed that the dinner was bad, ashamed partly because he wanted to give his guest a good meal and partly because he wanted to show that he did not live like a beggar. For his part the guest was in great embarrassment and extreme confusion. Having helped himself to bread and eaten it, he was afraid to stretch out his hand for another piece; he was ashamed to take the best portions; and he constantly asserted that he was not at all hungry, that the dinner was excellent and that for his part he was quite content and would be grateful to his dying day. When the meal was over Mr Golyadkin lit his pipe and offered another, kept for friends, to his visitor; the two settled down facing one another, and the visitor began the story of his adventures.

Mr Golyadkin junior's story lasted for three or four hours. The history of his adventures was, however, made up of the most trivial, the most meagre, if that word is possible, happenings. It was a story of government service somewhere in a court in the provinces, of prosecuting lawyers and chairmen of the Bench, of office intrigues, of the debauchery of a correspondence-clerk, of the inspector, of a sudden change of superiors, of how the second Mr Golyadkin suffered in spite of his complete innocence; of his very old aunt, Pelageya Semyonovna; of how he lost his position through the intrigues of his enemies, and came to St Petersburg on foot; of how he had languished and led a life of misery here in St Petersburg, how his efforts to find a post were for a long time fruitless, how he had run through his money, spending everything on day-to-day expenses, almost lived in the street, eaten dry bread and watered it with his tears, slept on the bare floor, and finally persuaded some kind person to take up his cause, give him a recommendation and generally fix him up with a new position. Mr Golyadkin's guest wept as he told his story, and wiped away the tears with a blue check handkerchief that looked very like oilcloth. He ended by opening his heart completely to Mr Golyadkin and confessing that not only had he not for the time being enough to live on and equip himself respectably with, but not even enough to buy a proper outfit; here he was, he concluded, unable to scrape up enough to buy boots for his feet, and his office frockcoat was one he had borrowed for a short time.

Mr Golyadkin was genuinely moved and touched. Moreover, even in spite of the fact that his guest's story was such empty stuff, every word of it rained down on his heart like manna from heaven. The fact was that Mr Golyadkin had forgotten his last doubts, given his heart permission to feel free and happy, and, finally, bestowed on himself the rank of fool. It was all so natural! Much reason he had had for distressing himself or raising such a

clamour of alarm! Well, there was, indeed, that one ticklish circumstance – but after all, it wasn't disastrous: it could not stain a
man's reputation, damage his self-respect, or ruin his career if a
man was innocent and nature itself had taken a hand in the game.
Besides, his guest was asking for his patronage, his guest was
weeping, his guest laid the blame on fate, and he seemed quite
unassuming, without ill-will or cunning, pitiful and insignificant,
and apparently he himself was ashamed, although perhaps from a
different point of view, of the strange resemblance of his person to
his host's. He had behaved with the greatest possible propriety, his
only aim seemed to be to please his host, and he looked like a man
suffering from pangs of conscience and feeling guilty towards
another man. If, for example, the talk touched on some disputable
point, the visitor hastened to agree with Mr Golyadkin's opinion.
If his opinion happened by mistake to run contrary to Mr Golyadkin's, and he then noticed that he had gone astray, he immediately
corrected what he had said, brought out some explanation, and
made it clear without delay that really he held the same view as
his host, thought in the same way and looked at everything with
exactly the same eyes. In short, the guest strove with all his might
to ingratiate himself with Mr Golyadkin, so that in the end Mr
Golyadkin decided that his visitor must be a most amiable person
in all respects. Meanwhile tea was served; it was eight o'clock. Mr
Golyadkin found himself in an excellent mood; he was cheerful,
cracked a joke or two, relaxed little by little, and finally launched
into a very lively and diverting conversation with his guest.
When he was feeling in a good mood, Mr Golyadkin was rather
fond of passing on interesting information. So now: he told his
guest a good deal about the capital, its beauties and amusements,
its theatres and clubs, and about Brülov's picture of the destruction of Pompeii; about the two Englishmen who travelled all
the way from England to St Petersburg on purpose to see the
wrought-iron railings of the Summer Garden, and then went
straight back home; about the office, and Olsufi Ivanovich and
Andrey Philippovich; about how Russia was hourly making progress towards perfection, and how philology flourished here; about
an anecdote he had recently read in the *Northern Bee*, and about

how there is a snake in India which has an extraordinary power of crushing its prey; and finally about Baron Brambeus, and much more besides. In short, Mr Golyadkin was thoroughly pleased, first of all because he was quite reassured; secondly because not only did he not fear his enemies, but he was even ready to challenge all of them to a decisive combat; thirdly because now he had become a patron and protector in his own right, and finally, he was doing a good deed. In the privacy of his own thoughts, however, he confessed that he was not yet completely happy, that somewhere inside him a tiny worm, the smallest possible worm, was still lurking and gnawing at his heart even now. He was still tormented by the memory of the previous evening at Olsufi Ivanovich's. He would have given a great deal at that moment if no part of the previous evening had ever happened. 'However, after all, it doesn't matter!' our hero at last concluded, and he made a firm resolution to behave perfectly in future and never make such blunders again. Since Mr Golyadkin was now utterly relaxed and had suddenly become almost completely happy, he felt a sudden impulse to enjoy life. Petrushka brought rum and they made a punch. Guest and host each drained a glass, and then another. The guest grew even more amiable than before and, for his part, gave more than one proof of his happy and open-hearted nature, entering energetically into Mr Golyadkin's pleasure, seeming to rejoice in his joy and to look on him as his real and only benefactor. Taking a pen and a piece of paper, he begged Mr Golyadkin not to look at what he was writing and then, when it was finished, showed it to his host. It turned out to be four lines of verse, written with some feeling and in a beautiful style and handwriting, and evidently his own composition. The lines were as follows:

'Even though thou may'st forget me,
I shall e'er remember thee;
So whatever life may bring thee,
Do thou too remember me!'

With tears in his eyes, Mr Golyadkin embraced his guest and, moved at last to the depths of his being, confided to him some of his own secrets in a speech laying great stress on Andrey Philip-

povich and Clara Olsufyevna. 'Well, you know, Yakov Petrovich, you and I are going to get on well together,' said our hero;
'you and I, Yakov Petrovich, will get on like a house on fire, we'll
live together like brothers; the two of us will be very clever, old
chap, very clever we're going to be; we'll be the ones to intrigue
against them ... intrigue against them, that's what we'll do. After
all, I know you, Yakov Petrovich, I understand what you're like;
you blurt out everything straight away, like the honest soul that
you are. You just keep away from all of them, old man.' The guest,
in full agreement, thanked Mr Golyadkin and shed a few tears
himself. 'Do you know what, Yasha?' Mr Golyadkin went on in a
voice faint and tremulous with emotion; 'you come and live here
with me for a bit, Yasha, or even altogether. We'll get on well. It's
all the same to you, old man, eh? And you mustn't be embarrassed
or repine because of this strange circumstance between us: it's a
sin to repine, old man; this is nature! And Mother Nature is
bountiful, that's what, brother Yasha! I say that because I love
you, I love you like a brother. And you and I will be very cunning, Yasha, and we'll do some undermining ourselves, and wipe
their eyes for them.' The punch stretched to three and then to four
glasses each, and then Mr Golyadkin began to experience two
feelings: one that he was uncommonly happy, and two that he
could no longer stand on his feet. The guest was of course invited
to stay the night. A bed was somehow contrived out of two rows
of chairs. Mr Golyadkin junior declared that beneath the roof of
friendship even the bare floor was as good as sleeping in a soft bed,
that he for his part would sleep wherever he had to, humbly and
gratefully, that he was now in paradise, and finally that he had
borne much misfortune and unhappiness in his time, seen everything, endured everything, and perhaps – who can foresee the
future? – would endure it again. Mr Golyadkin senior protested at
this, and proceeded to show that one must put all one's trust in
God. His guest fully concurred, and said that there was of course
nobody like God. Here Mr Golyadkin senior remarked that the
Turks were right, in a sense, to call upon the name of God even in
their sleep. Then, without however agreeing with some scholars in
certain aspersions they cast upon the Turkish prophet Mo-

hammed, and while recognizing that he was in his way a great
political leader, Mr Golyadkin passed on to a highly interesting
description of an Algerian barber's shop, about which he had once
read in some miscellany. Host and guest laughed a great deal over
the simple-mindedness of the Turks; they could not, however,
withhold a well-deserved tribute of admiration from the fan-
aticism aroused in them by opium. . . . At length the visitor began
to undress, and Mr Golyadkin withdrew behind the partition,
partly out of the goodness of his heart, since he thought his guest
might not even possess a decent shirt, and partly to reassure himself as far as possible about Petrushka, test his mood, cheer him up
if he could, and make much of him, so that everybody should be
happy and all unpropitious omens avoided. It must be remarked
that Petrushka was still something of an embarrassment to Mr
Golyadkin.

'You go to bed now, Petrushka,' said Mr Golyadkin meekly, as
he entered his servant's apartment, 'you go to bed now, and wake
me at eight tomorrow morning. Do you understand, Petrushka?'

Mr Golyadkin's speech was unusually gentle and kind. But Petrushka said nothing. He was busy at the moment about his bed
and did not even turn to face his master, as he ought to have done
out of mere respect for him.

'Did you hear me, Petrushka?' went on Mr Golyadkin. 'You go
to bed now, Petrushka, and tomorrow wake me at eight o'clock;
do you understand?'

'Of course I do; what is there to understand?' Petrushka
grumbled to himself.

'Very well then, Petrushka; I am only saying it so that you
shall be easy in your mind and happy. We're all happy now, you
see, so you must be easy and happy too. And now I wish you good
night. Sleep well, Petrushka, sleep well; we all have to work. . . .
You know, my friend, you mustn't think . . .'

Mr Golyadkin was beginning to say something, but stopped.
'Won't that be too much?' he thought; 'aren't I going too far? It's
always the same; I always overdo things.' Our hero left Petrushka's room highly dissatisfied with himself. He felt besides a

little hurt by Petrushka's rudeness and stubbornness. 'People can try to get on well with the wretch, his master goes out of his way to be nice to the wretch, but he doesn't feel it,' thought Mr Golyadkin. 'But that's the sort of nasty tendency all those sort of people show!' Swaying slightly, he returned to his room, and seeing that his guest was already in bed, sat down for a moment on his bed. 'Come, confess, Yasha,' he began in a whisper, wagging his head, 'you're the one that's to blame, you old villain! – after all, namesake mine, you know very well ...' and he went on teasing his guest with some familiarity. Finally, bidding him a friendly good night, Mr Golyadkin betook himself to his own couch. Meanwhile the guest had begun to snore. Mr Golyadkin got into bed in his turn, giggling as he did so and whispering to himself, 'You're drunk today, you know, my dear Yakov Petrovich, you rascal! Why, what reason have you to be happy? Tomorrow you'll be weeping, you know, you snivelling baby; what am I to do with you?' By now a rather strange feeling, something like doubt or repentance, seemed to have taken possession of all Mr Golyadkin's being. 'I've been letting myself go,' he thought; 'and now my head is ringing and I'm drunk; *and* I couldn't keep my mouth shut, gullible fool that I am! and I talked enough nonsense to fill a barrel, and I'm still trying to be clever. Of course, to forgive and forget injuries is a prime virtue, but all the same it's a bad thing, that's what it is!' Here Mr Golyadkin got to his feet, took up the candle, and tiptoed across once more to look at his sleeping guest. For a long time he stood over him in deep deliberation. 'Not a pretty picture! A libellous joke at my expense, that's what it is, and that's all about it!'

At last Mr Golyadkin really settled down to sleep. His head was splitting and full of buzzing and ringing. Little by little he drifted into a doze ... he struggled to think about something, or remember something, of extreme importance, some ticklish sort of affair – but he could not. Slumber descended on his hapless head, and he slept the sleep of a man unused to drinking who has swallowed five glasses of punch one after the other in an evening of friendly festivity.

Chapter Eight

MR GOLYADKIN awoke next morning as usual at eight o'clock, and as soon as he was awake he remembered everything that had happened on the previous evening, remembered it with a frown. 'Oh dear, what a fool I made of myself yesterday!' he thought, raising himself on his pillows and glancing at his visitor's bed. But to his great surprise the room was empty not only of his guest but of the bed on which he had slept as well! What's this?' Mr Golyadkin almost shrieked. 'What on earth can have happened? What can this new turn of things mean?' While he was gaping in bewilderment at the empty space, the door creaked open and Petrushka came in with the tea-tray. 'But where, where?' said our hero in a barely audible voice, pointing to the place vacated by yesterday's guest. At first Petrushka did not answer, but squinted his eyes towards the corner on the right, so that Mr Golyadkin felt constrained to look towards the same corner himself. After a short silence, however, Petrushka answered, in his surly husky tones, that the master wasn't at home.

'You're a fool, Petrushka; I'm your master, aren't I?' said Mr Golyadkin in a broken voice, staring hard at his servant.

Petrushka said nothing, but looked at Mr Golyadkin in such a way that the latter crimsoned up to the eyes; it was a look of such insulting reproach that it was no better than downright abuse. Mr Golyadkin simply gave up, as they say. At length Petrushka declared that *the other one* had left something like an hour earlier, and that he wouldn't wait. The answer was of course probable, and seemed truthful; plainly Petrushka was not lying, and the words *the other one* and the reproachful look were merely the result of the whole distasteful position, but all the same Mr Golyadkin knew, though obscurely, that something was definitely wrong and that fate was preparing another surprise for him, and not a pleasant one. 'Very well, we'll see,' he thought to himself, 'we'll see, we'll get to the heart of the matter in due course. . . . Oh my God!' he groaned in conclusion, in a very different tone of voice, 'what on earth did I invite him here for, what could have been my purpose in doing that? I really and truly am putting my head in the noose, I'm twisting a rope for my own neck. Oh my head, my head! you can't help blabbing everything out, can you, like a schoolboy or an office-boy, like some wretched little junior clerk, a spineless creature, a mouldy dish-rag, you old gossip, you chattering old woman! ... And he wrote verses, the wretch, and told me he liked me. How should I ...? What would be the politest way of showing the scoundrel the door if he comes back? Of course there are many different turns of expression, many ways of doing it. You might say, "Well ... it's this way ... in view of my limited salary. ..." Or perhaps intimidate him somehow, say for example. ... "Taking this and that into account ... I am obliged to express myself in such terms ..." or, "it will have to mean paying half the rent and living expenses, and payment in advance." H'm, no! devil take it, no! That would be a blot on my reputation. It's not exactly delicate! What about, say, putting the idea into Petrushka's head of annoying him somehow, neglecting him in some way, being rude to him, and making the place too uncomfortable for him like that? That would play them off against one another. ... No, devil take it, no! It's dangerous, and besides, if you look at it – well, no, it's not right at all! It's altogether wrong! Well, then, what if he doesn't come? will that be bad too? I blabbed everything out to him last night! ... Oh, it's bad, it's bad! Oh, how very bad the whole business is! Oh, what a head, what a damned head! You'll never learn, will you, you'll never be able to drive any sense into yourself. Well, what if he comes and turns the whole thing down? God grant he may, if he does come. I should be extremely glad if he came; I'd give a lot for him to come. ...' Thus Mr Golyadkin pondered as he swallowed his tea, glancing constantly at the clock on the wall. 'It's a quarter to nine now; it's time I went. But what is going to happen; what will happen next? I wish I knew just exactly what special secret is being hidden – the purpose, the general aim, the various ins and outs. It would be nice to find out exactly what all these people are aiming at, and what their first step will be. ...' Mr Golyadkin could bear it no longer, but abandoned his half-smoked pipe, got dressed, and set off for the office, hoping to take unawares the source of the danger and make everything secure by being present

in person. And danger there was; he knew there was danger.
'Well, now we'll get to the bottom of it,' said Mr Golyadkin,
taking off his overcoat and galoshes in the hall; 'now we'll fathom
the business straight away.' Having made up his mind to do this,
our hero straightened his clothes, assumed an air of formal propriety, and was just about to make his way into the next room
when right in the doorway he almost collided with his acquaintance, friend and companion of the day before. Mr Golyadkin
junior appeared not to notice Mr Golyadkin senior, although he
almost knocked him down. Mr Golyadkin junior seemed to be
very busy and quite out of breath with hurrying somewhere; his
aspect was so business-like and official that anybody could have
told from his face, it seemed, that he had been sent on a special
errand.

'Oh, it's you, Yakov Petrovich,' said our hero, grasping the hand
of his yesterday's visitor.

'Later, later; you must excuse me, tell me later,' cried Mr Golyadkin junior, pressing forward.

'But, excuse me, I think, Yakov Petrovich, you wanted . . .'

'What, sir? Explain yourself quickly.' Here his former guest
stopped as if forced against his will to do so, and thrust his ear
almost into Mr Golyadkin's face.

'I must tell you that I am astonished at this reception, Yakov
Petrovich . . . a reception which is not at all what I have been led
to expect.'

'There is a time and a place for everything, sir. Report yourself
to His Excellency's secretary and then address yourself in the
proper manner to the gentleman in charge of the office. Have you
a petition to present?'

'You, Yakov Petrovich, I don't know! You absolutely astound
me, Yakov Petrovich! you don't recognize me, I suppose, or else
you're just having a joke, in your own high-spirited way.'

'Oh, it's you!' said Mr Golyadkin junior, as if he had only that
moment seen Mr Golyadkin senior, 'so it's you, is it? Well, did
you have a good night?' Here Mr Golyadkin junior, with a slight
smile – a formal and official smile, not at all like what it should
have been (because after all he owed Mr Golyadkin senior at least

thanks) – with, then, a formal and official smile, added that for his part he was extremely glad that Mr Golyadkin senior had slept well; then he bowed slightly, shifted from one foot to the other, looked to the right, then to the left, glanced down at the floor, then fixed his eyes on a side door and hastily whispering that he had been charged with a very special errand, whisked into the next room and was gone in a flash.

'There's a nice thing,' whispered our hero after a moment's petrified pause, 'a nice thing indeed! So that's how things are here now!' At this point, Mr Golyadkin felt a cold shiver run down his spine. 'However,' he went on to himself, as he made his way to his section, 'However, I've been talking of this kind of thing, after all, for a long time now; I had a presentiment long ago that he had a special mission – it was only yesterday that I was saying the man must certainly be being used for a very special mission . . .'

'Have you finished the document you were working on yesterday, Yakov Petrovich?' Anton Antonovich Setochkin asked Mr Golyadkin as he sat down beside him. 'Is it here?'

'Yes,' whispered Mr Golyadkin, looking at his superior with a somewhat forlorn expression.

'Very good. I asked because Andrey Philippovich has inquired about it twice already. His Excellency will be wanting it before you know where you are . . .'

'Yes, sir, it's finished . . .'

'Well then, good.'

'I think, Anton Antonovich, I've always done what was required of me in a satisfactory manner, and I'm very pleased to do anything my superiors wish to entrust me with, and I do it with the utmost zeal . . .'

'Yes. Well, sir, what do you mean by all that?'

'Nothing, Anton Antonovich. I only want to explain, Anton Antonovich, that I . . . I mean, I wanted to convey the idea that sometimes malice and envy spare nobody, in their hunt for their revolting daily nourishment . . .'

'Excuse me, I don't quite understand. I mean, to whom are you referring now?'

'I mean, I only wanted to say, Anton Antonovich, that I go

straight ahead, and I scorn to do anything underhand, and that I am no intriguer and that, if I may say so, I have every right to pride myself on the fact that . . .'

'Yes, that is quite true, and as far as I know I do full justice to your argument; but allow me to remark, Yakov Petrovich, that in good society personal remarks are not entirely permissible; I, for example, can stand them behind my back – because who ever escapes criticism behind his back? – but to my face, my dear sir, by your leave, I don't allow anybody, for example, to take any liberties with me. I have grown grey in the public service, my dear sir, and I am not going to allow anybody to be rude to me in my old age . . .'

'No, Anton Antonovich, you see, Anton Antonovich, you – I think, Anton Antonovich, you haven't quite understood my meaning. For my part, Anton Antonovich, excuse me, I can only take it as an honour . . .'

'And I can only beg you to excuse me as well, sir. I was trained in the old school, sir. And it is too late to try to teach me these new-fangled ways of yours. It seems to me that my understanding has been good enough for the service of my country up to now. As you very well know, my dear sir, I have a decoration for twenty-five years of irreproachable service, sir . . .'

'I feel it, Anton Antonovich, for my part I feel absolutely all that, sir. But I didn't mean that, sir. I was talking about masks, Anton Antonovich . . .'

'Masks, sir?'

'That is . . . again . . . I am afraid you may take my idea in the wrong way, I mean the idea of my speeches, as you say, Anton Antonovich. I am only developing a theme, Anton Antonovich, that is I am putting forward the notion that people wearing masks have ceased to be a rarity, sir, and that it is difficult nowadays to recognize the man under the mask, sir . . .'

'Well, sir, do you know, it's not altogether difficult, sir. Sometimes it's quite easy, sir; sometimes you don't even have to look very hard, sir.'

'No, sir, but you know, Anton Antonovich, I was speaking of myself, sir; for example, I put on a mask only when it is requisite, that is exclusively for carnivals and convivial gatherings, speaking in the ordinary sense, but I do not wear a mask to people every day, speaking in another, more occult sense. That's what I meant, Anton Antonovich.'

'Well, let us leave it at that for now; besides, I have no time,' said Anton Antonovich, getting up from his place and collecting together some papers to lay before His Excellency. 'Your business, I suppose, will be cleared up shortly, in its own good time. You will see for yourself who is at fault and whom you must blame, and I humbly beg you to spare me further personal explanations and gossip prejudicial to the service, sir . . .'

'No, but, Anton Antonovich, I . . .' began Mr Golyadkin, turning a little pale, to Anton Antonovich's retreating back, 'it never even entered my head, sir. What can this mean?' went on our hero, finding himself left alone. 'What is in the wind here, what's the meaning of this new complication?' Even while our forlorn and half-desperate hero was preparing to try unravelling this new knot, a noise arose in the next room, the sounds of purposeful movement became audible, the door opened, and Andrey Philippovich, who had vanished only a moment before into His Excellency's room, appeared in the doorway and called to Mr Golyadkin. Knowing what it was about, and not wishing to keep Andrey Philippovich waiting, Mr Golyadkin sprang up from his chair and, as was fitting, busied himself without delay and with all his might with the final putting together and tidying up of the required documents, and with preparing to follow them and Andrey Philippovich into His Excellency's room. Suddenly, almost under the nose of Andrey Philippovich, who was standing full in the doorway, Mr Golyadkin junior pranced into the room, bustling, breathless, in zealous pursuit of his duties, with a self-important and resolutely official air, and skipped straight up to Mr Golyadkin senior, from whose expectations nothing could have been further than such an attack . . .

'The papers, Yakov Petrovich, the papers. . . . His Excellency wishes to be informed whether you have them ready,' he twittered rapidly, under his breath. 'Andrey Philippovich is waiting for you . . .'

'I don't need you to tell me that,' said Mr Golyadkin, also in a rapid whisper.

'No, Yakov Petrovich, don't take it like that, I didn't mean it like that at all; I am in sympathy with you, Yakov Petrovich, I am moved by heartfelt sympathy.'

'Which I most humbly beg you to spare me. Allow me, sir, allow me . . .'

'You will, of course, put them in a folder, Yakov Petrovich, and use the third page to mark the place; allow me, Yakov Petrovich . . .'

'You allow me, if you don't mind . . .'

'But there's a blot here, Yakov Petrovich, did you notice the blot . . .?'

At this point Andrey Philippovich called to Mr Golyadkin again.

'At once, Andrey Philippovich; I'm only a little . . . just here. . . . My good sir, do you understand plain Russian?'

'The best thing would be to take it out with a penknife, Yakov Petrovich, and you'd better let me do it; you'd better not touch it yourself, Yakov Petrovich, leave it to me – I'll just touch it with a knife here . . .'

For the third time Andrey Philippovich called to Mr Golyadkin.

'For pity's sake, where is there any blot? Come, there's no blot there at all, you know.'

'A huge blot, there it is! allow me, I saw it just here; here, allow me . . . just allow me, Yakov Petrovich, I'll just scrape it a bit here with a knife, out of concern for you, Yakov Petrovich, with a penknife, in all sincerity . . . there, like that, and that will be an end of the matter . . .'

Here Mr Golyadkin junior, suddenly and unexpectedly, without rhyme or reason, totally against Mr Golyadkin senior's will, but overpowering him in the momentary struggle that had arisen between them, gained possession of the document required by his superiors and instead of scraping it in all sincerity with a knife, as he had treacherously assured Mr Golyadkin senior he would – rapidly rolled it up, tucked it under his arm, in two bounds was

beside Andrey Philippovich, who had not noticed any of his
manoeuvres, and hurried with it into His Excellency's room. Mr
Golyadkin senior remained rooted to the spot, holding a penknife
in his hand and apparently preparing to scrape something with
it ...

Our hero did not yet fully understand his new position. He had
not yet recovered his wits. He had felt the blow, but thought that
everything was somehow all right. In terrible, indescribable
anguish he finally tore himself from the spot and rushed straight
to His Excellency's room, praying to heaven as he went, however,
that everything would turn out for the best, and it would all be all
right. ... In the last room before His Excellency's he almost ran
full tilt into Andrey Philippovich and his own namesake. They
were already on their way back: Mr Golyadkin made way for
them. Andrey Philippovich was in a good mood, smiling and talking cheerfully. Mr Golyadkin senior's namesake was also smiling,
fulsomely, mincing along at a respectful distance from Andrey
Philippovich and whispering something with an excited air in his
ear, while Andrey Philippovich nodded his head most graciously.
Our hero at once understood the whole position of affairs. The fact
was that his work (as he afterwards learned) had almost exceeded
His Excellency's highest expectations, and had really come at
exactly the right moment. His Excellency was extremely pleased.
It was even reported that His Excellency had thanked Mr Golyadkin junior, thanked him warmly; he had said he would remember
him if the occasion arose, and in any case would certainly not
forget. ... It goes without saying that Mr Golyadkin's first impulse was to protest, to protest with all his might, as strongly as
he possibly could. Almost beside himself, and as pale as death, he
rushed to Andrey Philippovich. But when Andrey Philippovich
heard that Mr Golyadkin's business was a private matter, he refused to listen, saying decisively that he had not a minute to spare
even for his own concerns.

The dryness of his tone and the abruptness of the refusal stag-
gered Mr Golyadkin. 'But perhaps I had better try a different approach ... it would be best to go to Anton Antonovich.'
Unfortunately for Mr Golyadkin, Anton Antonovich was not

available either: he was otherwise occupied. 'So evidently it was not without deliberate design that he begged to be spared explanations and gossip!' thought our hero. 'That's what he was aiming at, the old trickster! In that case, I shall venture to beg His Excellency to listen to me.'

Still pale, conscious that his head was in an utter muddle, and thoroughly puzzled as to what to decide on, Mr Golyadkin sat down in a chair. 'It would have been much better if things had remained as they were,' he repeated over and over to himself. 'Really, such a fishy business is quite incredible. In the first place it's nonsense, and in the second place it's an impossibility. It was probably some sort of dream, or it somehow seemed different from what really happened; or probably it was me walking along ... and I somehow took myself for someone else ... in short, the whole thing's quite impossible.'

No sooner had Mr Golyadkin decided that the whole thing was quite impossible than Mr Golyadkin junior came flying into the room with both hands full of papers and more under his arm. Having spoken a necessary two or three words to Andrey Philippovich as he passed, exchanged a few more with somebody else, greeted a third politely and yet another with free-and-easy familiarity, Mr Golyadkin junior, evidently having no time to waste, seemed about to leave the room again, but fortunately for Mr Golyadkin senior stopped just at the door and chatted for a moment with two or three clerks who happened to be there. Mr Golyadkin senior hurried straight up to him. As soon as he saw Mr Golyadkin senior's move, Mr Golyadkin junior began glancing uneasily about for some way of slipping out as quickly as possible. But our hero had already grasped his visitor of the previous evening by the sleeve. The young clerks standing round the two Titular Councillors fell back and waited with curiosity to see what would happen. The older Titular Councillor knew very well that popular opinion was not on his side now, and clearly understood that his position was being undermined: it was all the more imperative for him to maintain it. The moment was decisive.

'Well, sir?' asked Mr Golyadkin junior, facing Mr Golyadkin senior with some insolence.

Mr Golyadkin senior could hardly breathe.

'Sir,' he began, 'I do not know how you propose to explain your strange conduct towards me.'

'Well, sir? Go on, sir.' Here Mr Golyadkin junior looked round and winked at the clerks who surrounded them as though giving them to understand that the comedy was just about to begin.

'The impudence and shamelessness of your conduct towards me in the present instance, sir, are even more revealing than ... than any words of mine. Don't count on the success of your game: it's a bad one ...'

'Well, Yakov Petrovich, now do tell me how you slept,' answered Golyadkin junior, gazing straight into Golyadkin senior's face.

'Sir, you forget yourself,' said our Titular Councillor, utterly frustrated and hardly knowing how he kept his feet; 'I hope you will change the tone ...'

'My dear, dear friend,' said Mr Golyadkin junior, pulling a rather unseemly face at Mr Golyadkin senior, and he suddenly and unexpectedly, under the pretence of a friendly gesture, pinched our hero's rather chubby cheek between two of his fingers. Our hero coloured up like fire. ... As soon as Mr Golyadkin senior's dear friend observed that his adversary, shaking in every limb, dumb with rage, as red as a lobster, and finally driven to the utmost limits of his endurance, might even bring himself to make a physical attack on him, he in his turn lost no time in forestalling the move. He tapped his cheeks once or twice more, tickled him a few more times and then, having played with him thus, to the great delight of the youthful audience surrounding them, for a few more seconds as he stood rooted to the spot and mad with fury, Mr Golyadkin junior, with exasperating impudence, gave Mr Golyadkin senior one last fillip on his little round paunch and said, with a smile full of the most venomous and far-reaching implications: 'Oh no, you don't, Yakov Petrovich, my little friend, oh no, you don't. We'll dodge you, Yakov Petrovich, we'll dodge you.' Then, before our hero had had time to recover even a trace of his composure after this last attack, Mr Golyadkin junior suddenly (with no more than a preliminary little smile to the onlookers standing round them) assumed an extremely busy, efficient, and official air, cast down his eyes, seemed to shrink and contract into himself, briskly spat out the words, 'a special errand', kicked up his short little legs and darted into the next room. Our hero could not believe his eyes, and remained unable to collect his thoughts . . .

At length he came to his senses. Realizing instantly that he was lost, that he had in a certain sense destroyed himself, that he had soiled his hands and sullied his reputation, that he had been ridiculed and humiliated in the presence of outsiders, treacherously insulted by the man whom he had thought of only the day before as his foremost and most trustworthy friend, and that he had disgraced himself utterly and for ever – Mr Golyadkin rushed in pursuit of his enemy. At that moment he would not think of the witnesses of his humiliation. 'They're all in league with one another,' he said to himself; 'one backs up the other, one sets another at me.' After he had gone a few steps, however, our hero saw clearly that all pursuit was vain and useless, and therefore turned back. 'You won't get away,' he thought, 'your card will be trumped in due time, the lamb's tears will bring retribution on the wolf.' With cold-blooded fury and the most drastic resolution our hero returned to his chair and sat down on it. 'You won't get away!' he said again. Now it was not a question of any kind of passive defence: now there was an atmosphere of resolve, of aggression, and anybody who saw Mr Golyadkin at that moment when, his colour becoming high and his agitation barely controlled, he plunged his pen into the inkwell and set it racing furiously over the paper, could have prophesied that the matter would not end there or be allowed simply to collapse harmlessly. In his inmost heart he had formed a resolution, and in his inmost heart he swore to carry it out. To be honest, he did not yet know very well what steps to take, or rather he did not know at all; but it did not matter, it was nothing! 'In this day and age, my good sir, success does not come by imposture and impudence. No good will come of imposture and impudence, my good sir, they can only lead to downfall. Grishka Otrepyev deceiving the blind multitude, my good sir, was the only one who succeeded by imposture, and that

not for long.' Notwithstanding this last circumstance, Mr Golyadkin proposed to wait until such time as the mask fell from certain
faces and something came to light. For this it was first necessary
for the office-hours to come to an end as soon as possible, and until
then our hero proposed to undertake nothing. Afterwards, when
the office was closed, he would take a certain step. After taking
the step he would know what to do and how to arrange his whole
campaign in order to crush the serpent and bring low the horn of
pride. Mr Golyadkin could not allow himself to be used as a doormat for people to wipe their dirty boots on. That he could never
consent to, and especially not in the present instance. If it had not
been for that last humiliation our hero might have resolved to
overcome his reluctance to hold his peace and submit without
protesting too stubbornly; thus, he might have argued, made
some claims, proved that he was in the right, and afterwards
might even perhaps have allowed his heart to be touched – and
perhaps, who knows, a new friendship might have been born, a
warm, strong friendship, even more all-embracing than yesterday's, a friendship that might finally have so completely wiped
out the unpleasantness of this rather indecent likeness between
two people that both Titular Councillors would have been highly
delighted and lived happily ever after, and so on. To tell the whole
truth, Mr Golyadkin even began to be a little sorry that he had
stood up for himself and his rights, and run into trouble as a
consequence. 'If he would make some concession,' thought Mr
Golyadkin, 'if he would say it was a joke – I would forgive him, I
would even forgive him more than that, if only he would acknowledge it aloud. But I won't let myself be used as a doormat. I have
never allowed people to wipe their feet on me, and I'm even less
likely to let an infamous wretch try it. I am not a doormat; I am
not, my good sir, a doormat!' In short, our hero had made up his
mind. 'It's your own fault, gentlemen!' He had decided to protest,
and to protest with all his strength, to his last breath. That was
the sort of man he was! He could not at any price consent to allow
himself to be insulted, still less to be used as a doormat, and,
finally, least of all by an utterly infamous wretch. We will not
argue, however, certainly not. Perhaps, if it had occurred to some-

body, if somebody had been seized, for instance, with an irresistible desire to turn Mr Golyadkin into a doormat, he could have
done so, and done so without opposition and with impunity (there
were times when Mr Golyadkin himself recognized this), and the
result would have been a doormat, not a Golyadkin – an ignoble
and dirty doormat, and yet not simply a doormat, but a doormat
with self-respect, a doormat with feelings and a soul, even if the
self-respect and the feelings were dumb, and – though they might
be hidden deep in the filthy recesses of the doormat, yet still with
feelings ...

The hours stretched out to unbelievable lengths, but at last four
o'clock struck. A short time after that, in the wake of the heads of
the department, everybody got up and left for home. Mr Golyadkin mingled with the crowd; his eye was alert and never lost sight
of a certain personage. At last our hero saw his acquaintance
hurry up to the office porters, who were distributing the over-
coats, and fidget round them in his usual nasty fashion while he
waited for his. It was the opportune moment. Somehow Mr Golyadkin elbowed his way through the crowd and, not wishing to be
held up, also began making urgent demands for his overcoat. But
Mr Golyadkin's acquaintance and friend got his first, since even
here he had contrived to worm his way in and curry favour with
his crawling and his whispering in people's ears.

Throwing on his coat, Mr Golyadkin junior glanced ironically
at Mr Golyadkin senior, thus openly and impudently flouting
him, then after gazing all round him with his own peculiar
effrontery, began for the last time mincing about among his colleagues – probably in order to leave behind a favourable impression of himself – spoke a word to one, whispered a moment
with another, slobbered respectfully over a third, smiled at a
fourth, gave his hand to a fifth, and skipped cheerfully down the
steps. Mr Golyadkin senior followed, and to his immense satisfaction overtook him on the bottom step and seized him by the overcoat collar. Mr Golyadkin junior seemed somewhat startled and
looked round with an air of bewilderment.

'How am I to understand this?' he whispered at last in a faint
voice.

'My dear sir, if you have anything of the gentleman in you, I hope you will remember the friendly relations we established yesterday,' said our hero.

'Ah, yes. Well, what then? Did you sleep well?'

Fury deprived Mr Golyadkin senior of his tongue for a moment.

'I slept well enough, sir. . . . But allow me to tell you, sirrah, that you are playing an extremely tortuous game . . .'

'Who says so? It's my enemies who say that,' the man who called himself Mr Golyadkin answered abruptly, and with the word unexpectedly broke free from the real Mr Golyadkin's weak hands. As soon as he was free he rushed away from the steps, looked round to find a cab-driver, ran up to him, got into his droshky and in an instant was lost to Mr Golyadkin senior's sight. Despairing and abandoned, the Titular Councillor looked all over for another cabby, but there wasn't one. He tried to run in pursuit, but his legs failed him. With a frustrated and chapfallen countenance and a mouth gaping in dismay, crushed, shrunken and helpless, he leaned against a lamp-post and remained there in the middle of the pavement for some minutes. It seemed that for Mr Golyadkin all was lost . . .

Chapter Nine

EVERYTHING, even Nature itself, was evidently in arms against Mr Golyadkin; but he was still on his feet and undefeated; he felt that he was undefeated. He was ready to fight. When he recovered from his first consternation, he rubbed his hands together with such feeling and energy that it would have been possible to conclude from the mere sight of him that he would not yield. The danger, however, was evident and imminent; Mr Golyadkin felt that too; and how was it to be tackled, that danger? that was the question. The thought even crossed Mr Golyadkin's mind: 'Suppose I leave it all as it is, simply give up? What then? – why, nothing. I shall stand aside, as though it had nothing to do with me,' thought Mr Golyadkin, 'and let it all go by me; I'm not

concerned, that's all. Just possibly he might step to one side, too;
he'll twist and turn, the scoundrel, and make a fuss, and then he'll
give up. There it is, then! I'll win by submitting. And really
where's the danger in that? Why, what danger? – I'd like someone
to point out to me what danger there is in all this! A trumpery
affair! a very ordinary business!' Here Mr Golyadkin broke off
abruptly. The words died on his tongue; he even cursed himself for
the thought; he convicted himself on the spot of baseness and
cowardice because of the thought; but for all that, he had not
advanced an inch. He felt that to decide on some action at the
present moment was an absolute necessity for him; he even felt he
would have paid anybody handsomely to tell him exactly what
action to decide on. How indeed could he guess right? There was,
moreover, no time for guessing. In any case, so as to lose no time,
he took a cab and hurried home. 'Well, how do you feel now?' he
asked himself. 'Pray how do you feel now, Yakov Petrovich? Are
you going to do something? Will you do something now, you
scoundrel, you rogue? You've reached the end of your tether, and
now you're beginning to snivel and whine!' So Mr Golyadkin
nagged at himself, bouncing along in his cabby's jolting vehicle.
Nagging at himself in this fashion, and so rubbing salt in his
wounds, gave Mr Golyadkin at the present moment a kind of
profound, indeed almost voluptuous satisfaction. 'Well, if some
sort of magician turned up now,' he thought, 'or if it somehow
became an official requirement, so that they said, "Cut off a finger
of your right hand, Golyadkin, and you are quits; there will be no
other Golyadkin, and you can be happy, only without your
finger," I would give up the finger, of course I would, give it up
without a murmur. Oh, the devil take the whole business!' cried
the desperate Titular Councillor, 'why had all this to happen?
Well, it all had to be, just inevitably this, exactly this; it's as if
nothing else could possibly happen! Everything was fine to begin
with, everybody was pleased and happy; but no, this had to
happen! However, you won't get anywhere with words. One must
act.'

So, having almost come to a definite decision, Mr Golyadkin
entered his flat, reached without a moment's delay for his pipe

and, sucking at it with all his might, sending out puffs of smoke to right and left, began scurrying in extraordinary excitement backwards and forwards about his room. Meanwhile Petrushka had begun to lay the table. At last Mr Golyadkin finally made up his mind, abruptly abandoned his pipe, flung on his overcoat, told Petrushka that he would not be dining at home, and dashed out of the flat. Petrushka overtook him on the stairs, out of breath and carrying his forgotten hat. Mr Golyadkin took it and was about to say a casual word or two in the hope of justifying himself a little in Petrushka's eyes, so that he should not give the matter any particular thought – to say, 'certain circumstances have arisen,' and 'dear me, I forgot my hat!' and so on – but as Petrushka would not even look at him and retreated without a word, Mr Golyadkin put on his hat without more ado, ran down the stairs and, endlessly repeating to himself that perhaps it was all for the best, and that everything would somehow come out right, although, all the same, he felt a shiver run right down to his heels, emerged into the street, hired a cab, and went dashing off to Andrey Philippovich's. 'Still, wouldn't tomorrow be better?' Mr Golyadkin wondered as he grasped the bell-pull at the door of Andrey Philippovich's flat. 'Besides, have I anything special to say? There isn't anything special about it. It's such a paltry affair, it's really paltry, a trumpery business, well, almost trumpery ... it's really just – a circumstance, like all of this. ...' Mr Golyadkin tugged suddenly at the bell; the bell tinkled, and somebody's steps could be heard inside. ... At this point Mr Golyadkin really cursed himself, at least for his haste and audacity. The recent unpleasantness, which Mr Golyadkin had all but forgotten in his preoccupation with his own affairs, and his difference with Andrey Philippovich, now returned to his memory. But it was too late to run away: the door had opened. Fortunately for Mr Golyadkin, he was informed that Andrey Philippovich had not returned from the office and would not be dining at home. 'I know where he is dining: at Izmailovsky Bridge,' thought our hero, inexpressibly delighted. To the servant's question about whom to announce, he answered, 'That's all right, my man. It will do later,' and it was even with some cheerfulness that he ran back down the stairs. Coming out into the

street, he decided to let his cab go and paid off the cabby. When
the man asked for something extra, because, 'I waited a long time,
sir,' and 'I didn't spare my horse, along of you was in a hurry,' he
readily gave him an extra five copecks; then he went his way on
foot.

'Really, you know, matters are in such a state,' thought Mr
Golyadkin, 'that they can't be left as they are; and yet, if you
think about it, if you think sensibly, what is there really to make
a fuss about? No, really, I must say it again, what is there for me
to make a fuss about? Why should I toil and moil, rack my brains,
take no end of trouble, wear myself out? To begin with, the
thing's done and it can't be undone ... really it can't! Let's look at
it like this: a man appears, a man reasonably well recommended as
capable, well-conducted, but poor, a man who has had some disagreeable experiences, been in some trouble; well, but poverty is
no crime, you know, and it's nothing to do with me. Well, really,
what sort of nonsense is all this? Well, he comes along and it
turns out – it turns out that Nature itself has made him and
another man as like as two peas, he's a perfect copy of the other
man: well, is that a reason for refusing to take him into the Department? If it's fate and nothing else, if it's mere blind chance
that's to blame – then you can wipe your feet on him, you can
prevent him from working ... but where's the justice in that?
He's a poor man, bewildered and frightened; your heart aches for
him, it tells you to regard him with compassion! Yes! Fine superiors they would have been, I must say, if they had reasoned as I
did, wretch that I am. What an addled head! Sometimes it can
hold dozens of stupid ideas all at the same time! No, no! they did
right, and they ought to be thanked for taking pity on the poor
wretched creature. ... Well, let's assume we really are twins, for
example, we were born twins, we are brothers, that's all – that's it!
Well, what then? Why, nothing! All our colleagues can be got
used to the idea, and no stranger coming into the department
would be likely to find anything unseemly or shocking in the
situation. There is even something touching in it; here's how it is,
we say: divine providence has created two people exactly alike,
and the benevolent authorities, recognizing the hand of provi-

dence, have given asylum to the pair of twins. Of course,' went on
Mr Golyadkin, pausing for breath and lowering his voice, 'of
course, it . . . it would, of course, have been better if this touching
situation had never arisen, if there had been no twins of any sort.
. . . Devil take the whole business! Why had it to happen? What
sort of urgent necessity was there? My God! What a hell-broth the
devil's concocted here! As for him, he's such a base and ignoble
wretch, so mischievous and wanton, so frivolous and sycophantic
and grovelling, such a Golyadkin! He may misconduct himself and
bring disgrace on my name, the scoundrel. So now we must keep
an eye on him and look after him! And what a nuisance that is!
But what of that? – never mind! All right, he's a scoundrel – well,
let him be – other people are honest, to make up for it. Well, then
he'll be a scoundrel and I'll be honest, and people will say, "That
Golyadkin's a scoundrel, pay no attention to him, and don't get
him mixed up with the other; now *he's* honest, virtuous, modest,
gentle, utterly trustworthy at work, and deserving of promotion,"
– that's how it will be! Well, all right . . . but what if . . .? What if
they . . . they *will* get us mixed up! It will all be his fault! Oh lord!
And he'll supplant a man, supplant him – take his place as if he
was nothing but an old rag, and never stop to think that a man's
not an old rag. Oh lord, oh dear! What a misfortune . . .!'

Lamenting and arguing with himself in this fashion, Mr Golyadkin hurried along without noticing the route he followed, and
hardly knowing where he was making for. He came back to earth
in the Nevsky Prospect, and then only because he ran full tilt into
a passerby with such force that the sparks flew. Without looking
up, Mr Golyadkin mumbled an apology and it was only when the
passerby, muttering something uncomplimentary, had got some
distance away that he lifted his head and looked round to see
where he was. Finding himself close to the restaurant where he
had taken a rest while waiting to go to Olsufi Ivanovich's dinner-
party, our hero became conscious of a few pinches and nudges
from his stomach, remembered that he had not dined and could see
no prospect of an invitation to dinner, and ran up the steps into
the restaurant in order to snatch a hurried bite as quickly as possible and with no hanging about, so as not to waste any of his

precious time. And the trifling circumstance that everything in the restaurant was rather dear did not deter Mr Golyadkin; he had no time now to hesitate over such trivialities. In the brightly lighted room a fairly large crowd of customers stood near a counter heaped with an assortment of all the various things consumed by respectable people as *zakuski*. The waiter had hardly time to pour out the drinks, serve and distribute the dishes and take the money. Mr Golyadkin waited his turn and when it came modestly stretched out his hand to a savoury patty. He carried it into a corner and, turning his back on the crowd, ate it with enjoyment, then returned, put his plate down on a table and, knowing the price, took out a silver ten-copeck piece and laid the coin on the counter, catching the waiter's eye as if to say, 'Here's the money, one patty,' and so on.

'Yours comes to one rouble ten copecks,' said the waiter nastily.

Mr Golyadkin was considerably startled.

'Were you speaking to me? . . . I . . . I had one patty, I think.'

'You had eleven,' retorted the waiter confidently.

'You . . . as far as I'm aware . . . I think you are mistaken. Really, I think I had one patty.'

'I counted; you had eleven. And so long as you had them, you must pay for them; nothing's free here.'

Mr Golyadkin was stunned. 'What is this? Have I come under a magic spell?' he wondered. Meanwhile the waiter was waiting for Mr Golyadkin to make up his mind; Mr Golyadkin was surrounded by a crowd; Mr Golyadkin had already put his hand in his pocket to take out a rouble, so as to settle up quickly and get as far from the scene as possible. 'Well, if it was eleven, it was eleven,' he thought, turning as red as a lobster. 'Well, what's wrong with a man eating eleven patties? Let him eat them, and good luck to him. There's nothing surprising in it, and nothing to laugh at. . . .' All at once Mr Golyadkin seemed to feel something like a stab; he raised his eyes and – instantly understood the riddle and realized the nature of the spell; all his difficulties were resolved in a moment. . . . In the doorway of the next room, almost directly behind the waiter and facing Mr Golyadkin (and, by the

way, until then our hero had taken the door for a mirror), a little
man was standing – *he* was standing, Mr Golyadkin himself, not
the hero of our story but the other Mr Golyadkin, the new Mr
Golyadkin. The new Mr Golyadkin was evidently in the highest
spirits. He smiled at the first Mr Golyadkin, nodded to him,
winked his little eyes, shifted his feet and looked as if at a
moment's warning he might efface himself, vanish, slip into the
next room and from there out of the back door, perhaps, and get
clean away ... and all pursuit would be hopeless. In his hand was
the last piece of his tenth patty, which he put into his mouth
under Mr Golyadkin's very eyes, smacking his lips with satisfaction. 'He pretended he was me, the scoundrel!' thought Mr Golyadkin, turning as red as fire with shame, 'He's not ashamed
before all these people! Has anybody seen him? Nobody seems to
be noticing. ...' Mr Golyadkin threw down the silver rouble as
though it had burnt his fingers and, paying no attention to the
waiter's meaningful and impertinent smile, a smile of triumph and
assured power, worked himself free of the crowd and hurried off
without a backward glance. 'There's one thing to be thankful for:
at least a man isn't finally compromised,' thought Mr Golyadkin
senior. 'I must thank the fellow, him and the fates both, that so far
everything has been settled successfully. Only the waiter was rude
to me. Well, what of that? – he had a right to be. He had to have
one rouble ten, so he had every right. Nothing's free here, he said!
He could at least have been a bit more civil, the wretch ...!'

Mr Golyadkin said all this to himself as he ran down the steps
to the porch. As he reached the last step, however, he stopped as
though transfixed and coloured up suddenly in a paroxysm of
wounded pride that even brought the tears to his eyes. For half a
minute he stood there like a stone, then he stamped his foot resolutely, leaped down from the porch to the street in one bound and
set off without a backward look, panting but oblivious of his
weariness, for his flat in Shestilavochny Street. When he reached
home he set himself down on the sofa without even waiting to
remove his outer clothing first, contrary to his habit of comfortable informality at home, or to pick up his pipe, and moving the
inkwell closer to himself, taking up a pen and getting out a sheet

of letter-paper, proceeded to scribble the following missive in a hand shaking with emotion:

My dear sir, Yakov Petrovich,

I should not have taken up my pen if my situation and your own action, my dear sir, had not forced me to do so. Believe me, necessity alone obliges me to enter into this explanation, and therefore I must first of all request you, my dear Sir, to regard this measure not as a deliberate attempt to insult you, but as the inevitable consequence of the circumstances which now link us together.

'That seems all right, I think, suitable and polite, although not without force and firmness. ... I don't think there is anything to take offence at there. Besides, I'm in the right,' thought Mr Golyadkin, reading over what he had written.

Your strange and unlooked-for appearance, my dear sir, on that stormy night, after I had suffered discourteous and unseemly treatment at the hands of enemies of mine, whose names I pass over in silent contempt, sowed the seed of all the misunderstanding between us at the present juncture. Your obstinate desire, my dear sir, to insist on your own way and force yourself into the sphere of my activities and into all the relationships of my practical life, however, oversteps all the boundaries set by common courtesy and simple social intercourse. I consider it unnecessary to refer here, my dear sir, to your theft of my papers and my honourable name in order to win the approbation of your superiors, an approbation you had not merited. Nor is it necessary to refer here to your deliberate and offensive evasions of the explanations necessitated by that occurrence. Finally, so that everything may be said, I will not here refer to your recent strange and, as it may well be called, incomprehensible behaviour to me in the restaurant. I am far from complaining of the useless, as far as I am concerned, expenditure of one silver rouble, but I cannot refrain from expressing my full indignation, my dear sir, at the recollection of your manifest infringement of propriety to the detriment of my honour, and that moreover in the presence of several persons who, although unknown to me, clearly belonged to highly respectable circles ...

'Am I going too far?' thought Mr Golyadkin. 'Will it be too much? Is it too offensive, this allusion to respectable society, for example? ... Well, it doesn't matter. I must show him the

firmness of my character. However, it will be possible, in miti-
gation, to use a bit of flattery and make up to him a little at the
end. And then we'll see.'

But, my dear sir, I should not have wearied you with my letter if I
had not been firmly convinced that the nobility of your sentiments
and the frank straightforwardness of your character would point out
to you the means of repairing all omissions and restoring the status
quo.

I venture, in the fullest confidence, to remain assured that you will
neither take this letter to be in any sense offensive to you nor, at the
same time, refuse to convey to me your explanations, on this particular occasion in writing, through the medium of my man-servant.

In expectation of the same, I have the honour to remain, my dear
sir,

> Your most obedient servant,
> Ya. Golyadkin.

'Well now, that's all right. The thing is done; it has even got as
far as being put into writing. But who is to blame? He is: he has
driven a man to the necessity of demanding explanations in writing. And I'm in the right . . .'

Having read through his letter for the last time, Mr Golyadkin
folded and sealed it and summoned Petrushka. Petrushka made his
appearance with sleepy eyes, as usual, and extremely annoyed
about something.

'Here, my man, take this letter . . . do you hear?'

Petrushka said nothing.

'Take it to the office; find the official on duty, Regional Secretary
Vakhrameyev. Vakhrameyev is on duty today. Do you understand?'

'Yes.'

'Yes! Can't you say yes, sir? Ask for Mr Vakhrameyev and say,
"My master," you must say, "presents his compliments and
desires me to request you most respectfully to look up the address
of the new clerk, Mr Golyadkin, in the office address-book." '

Petrushka remained silent but, as it appeared to Mr Golyadkin,
gave a brief smile.

'Well, so you, Petrushka, will ask for the address and find out where the newly-appointed Mr Golyadkin lives.'

'Yes, sir.'

'You will ask for the address and you will take this letter to that address; do you understand?'

'Yes.'

'If the gentleman there – where you take the letter . . . if the gentleman to whom you give the letter, Mr Golyadkin. . . . What are you laughing at, blockhead?'

'What have I got to laugh at? Why should I laugh? I wasn't doing nothing, sir. The likes of me hasn't got anything to laugh for.'

'Well, so then . . . if that gentleman asks how your master is, or where he is, if he says, "Why has your master . . ." well, if he asks you anything, you are to hold your tongue and tell him, "My master is all right, and he asks for your answer in writing." Do you understand?'

'Yes, sir.'

'Well then, so you say, "My master," you say, "is all right, and he's quite well," you say, "and he is getting ready to go out; and he asks for an answer," you say, "in writing." Do you understand?'

'Yes.'

'Well, be off!'

'Really, what a lot of trouble with that blockhead! He just laughs to himself, and that's all. And what is he laughing at? Oh, I'm in a pretty mess, a pretty mess indeed! However, perhaps it will all turn out for the best. . . . That wretch will probably hang about somewhere for a couple of hours now, he'll get himself lost somehow. You can't send him anywhere. Oh, what a mess! A mess that's too much for me!'

With such feeling meditations on the full disastrousness of his situation, our hero resigned himself for two hours to the passive role of waiting for Petrushka. For about an hour he paced backwards and forwards, smoking, then abandoned his pipe and sat down with a book. then lay down on the sofa, then applied himself to his pipe again, then once more began pacing about the room. He tried to think things over, but was absolutely unable to keep his mind on anything. At length the agonies of this passive state rose to such a pitch that Mr Golyadkin resolved to take a certain step. 'Petrushka won't be here for another hour,' he thought; 'I can leave the key with the porter, and in the meantime I'll ... I'll investigate the matter, I'll make some inquiries on my own behalf.' Losing no time, since he was in a hurry to pursue his investigations, Mr Golyadkin took his hat, walked out of the room, locked his door, looked out the porter, gave him the key and ten copecks – Mr Golyadkin had somehow become very free with his money – and set out on his way. He went on foot, and first to Izmailovsky Bridge. The journey took about half an hour. Reaching his destination, he went straight into the courtyard of the familiar house and looked up at the windows of State Councillor Berendeyev's flat. Except for three hung with red curtains, all the windows were dark. 'Olsufi Ivanovich has no guests today, I suppose,' thought Mr Golyadkin; 'they are probably alone.' After standing for some time in the courtyard our hero tried to come to some decision. But the decision was evidently not destined to be made. Mr Golyadkin changed his mind, gave the idea up and returned to the street. 'No, it wasn't here I needed to come. What can I do here? ... Now I'd better just ... and I'll inquire into it myself.' Having made this decision Mr Golyadkin set off for his office. The way was not short, and moreover it was very dirty, and snow was falling heavily in enormous wet flakes. But for our hero at that moment difficulties apparently did not exist. He got soaked through, certainly, and liberally splashed with dirt, 'but that's how it is, everything's in league against me, but on the other hand my end is attained.' And in fact Mr Golyadkin was already nearing his goal. The dark mass of the enormous government building was already looming up a short distance ahead. 'Stop!' he thought, 'Where am I going, and what can I do here? Suppose I find out where he lives; meanwhile Petrushka has probably returned with the answer already. I'm simply wasting my valuable time. Well, it doesn't matter; I can still make up for it all. Only oughtn't I really to call on Vakhrameyev? No, certainly not! But no, that's my nature. It's the way I'm made; necessary or not, I always tend to run ahead. ... H'm. ... What's the time? probably nine o'clock already. Petrushka may get back and not find me at home. It was sheer stupidity on my part to come out. ... Oh, really, what a mess!'

With this sincere acknowledgement of the sheer stupidity of his behaviour, our hero hurried back home to Shestilavochny Street. He arrived weary and exhausted. From the caretaker he learnt that Petrushka had not condescended to put in an appearance. 'Fine! Just as I foresaw!' thought our hero, 'and meanwhile it's nine o'clock. What a good-for-nothing wretch he is! He's eternally soaking somewhere! Oh lord, what a day this has been for my poor unhappy destiny!' Meditating and lamenting in this way, Mr Golyadkin unlocked his room, made a light, undressed, lit his pipe and sank down, tired, weary, dispirited and hungry, to wait for Petrushka. The candle needed snuffing and burned dimly, the light flickered on the walls. ... Mr Golyadkin lay there with his eyes wide open, thinking and thinking, and at last fell asleep.

It was very late when he woke up. The candle had almost burned right down; it was smoking and on the point of going out. Mr Golyadkin sat up with a start and remembered everything, absolutely everything. Petrushka's heavy snores resounded from behind the partition. Mr Golyadkin rushed to the window – not a light anywhere. He opened the ventilator – all was quiet; the town was sleeping like the dead. So it must be two or three o'clock in the morning; and so it was: the clock behind the partition gathered itself up and struck two. Mr Golyadkin hurried out there.

Somehow or other, not without considerable exertions, he shook Petrushka awake and made him sit up. At that moment the candle went out altogether. Ten minutes went by before Mr Golyadkin succeeded in finding another candle and lighting it. Meanwhile, Petrushka had managed to fall asleep again. 'You scoundrel, you good-for-nothing wretch!' said Mr Golyadkin, shaking him again, 'will you wake up? will you get on your feet?' After a further half-hour of effort, Mr Golyadkin managed to rouse his servant completely and drag him out into the room. It was only then that our hero perceived that Petrushka was, as they say, blind drunk and hardly able to stand on his feet.

'You lazy good-for-nothing!' shouted Mr Golyadkin. 'You miserable wretch! you'll drive me to distraction! Oh lord, where on earth did he get rid of the letter? Oh my lord, how shall I. ... Why did I write it? much need I had to write it! Fool that I was, I let my pride run away with me! My pride drove me to it! That's what pride does for you, that's your proper pride, wretch that you are! ... Well, you, what did you do with the letter, you scoundrel? Who did you give it to ...?'

'I didn't give no letter to nobody; I never even had no letter, straight I didn't!'

Mr Golyadkin wrung his hands in despair.

'Listen, Petrushka ... now listen, you listen to me ...!'

'I *am* listening ...'

'Where did you go? ... answer me ...!'

'Where did I go ...? I went to see some nice people, where else?'

'Oh my God! Where did you go first? did you go to the office ...? Listen, Petrushka; you're drunk, aren't you?'

'Me drunk? If I was to be struck dead this minute, n-not the leasht – I'm not drunk ...'

'No, no, it doesn't matter if you are drunk. ... I was only asking; it's fine for you to be drunk; I didn't mean anything, Petrushka, nothing at all. ... Perhaps you've only forgotten for the moment, and you'll remember soon. Well, now, just try to remember, did you go to Mr Vakhrameyev, or didn't you?'

'No, I didn't, and there wasn't no such person. If I was to be ...'

'No, no, Petrushka! No, Petrushka, really it's all right. Really, you can see I didn't mean. ... Why, what does it amount to? Why, when it's cold outside and it's wet, if a man takes a little drink, why, it doesn't matter. ... I'm not angry. Why, I've had something to drink myself, today. ... Just tell me the truth, try to remember, there's a good chap; did you go to Mr Vakhrameyev?'

'Well, if that's right, that's what happened, well, to tell the truth – I did go, if I was to be ...'

'Well, fine, Petrushka, that's good, you did go. You can see I'm not angry. . . . Well, well,' went on our hero, trying still harder to conciliate his servant, patting him on the shoulder and smiling at him, 'well, you rascal, you took a little drop, eh? . . . about ten copecks' worth, eh? you rogue, you! Well, that's all right; you can see I'm not angry. . . . I'm not angry, my dear fellow, I'm not angry . . .'

'No, excuse me, sir, I'm not a rogue. . . . I just called on some good people, but I'm not a rogue and I've never been one . . .'

'No, of course not, Petrushka, no! Listen, Petrushka: after all, I don't mean anything, I'm not criticizing you when I call you a rogue. I'm saying it to cheer you up, I'm using it in the most honourable sense. After all, Petrushka, another man would be flattered to be told he's an artful dodger, a sly one, he's nobody's fool, and he won't let anybody pull the wool over his eyes. Some people like that. . . . Well, well, it doesn't matter; now tell me frankly, Petrushka, like a friend, without keeping anything back . . . well, so you went to see Mr Vakhrameyev, and he gave you the address?'

'Yes, he gave me the address, he gave me the address as well. He's a good man at his job! And your master, he says, is a good man, a very good man, he says; I, he says, you tell him this, he says – my compliments to your master, he says, thank him and tell him, he says, that I, he says, like him very much – you see how much I respect your master, he says, because, he says, you, your master, he says, is a good man, Petrushka, he says, and you are a good man too, Petrushka, he says – there . . .!'

'Oh my God! But the address, the address, you Judas?' Mr Golyadkin said the last words almost in a whisper.

'The address . . . he gave me the address.'

'Did he? Well then, where does he live, Golyadkin, the clerk Golyadkin, Titular Councillor Golyadkin?'

'Your Golyadkin, he says, will be in Shestilavochny Street, he says, turn right and go upstairs, fourth floor. You'll find Golyadkin is there, he says . . .'

'You scoundrel!' shouted our hero, losing patience at last. 'You miserable wretch, that's me! you're talking about me. But there's another Golyadkin; I mean the other one, you scoundrel!'

'Well, just as you please. What's it to me? You have it your
own way – there ...!'

'But the letter, that letter ...'

'What letter? There wasn't no letter, I never seen no letter!'

'But what did you do with it, you miserable wretch?'

'I handed it over, I gave the letter to him. My compliments, he
says, and thank your master; he's a good master, he says, yours.
My compliments, he says, to your master ...'

'But who said it? Was it Golyadkin?'

Petrushka was silent for a short time, grinning all over his face
and looking straight at his master.

'Look here, you good-for-nothing scoundrel!' began Mr Golyadkin, choking with rage and almost at his wits' end, 'what have
you done to me? Tell me, what have you done to me? You've cut
my throat, you scoundrel! You've cut the head off my shoulders,
you Judas!'

'Well, now you do what you like! What's it to me?' said Petrushka in decided tones, as he retreated behind the partition.

'Come back, do you hear? come back here at once, you scoundrel!'

'No, I won't come there now, I won't come to you at all. Why
should I? I shall go to some good people. ... Good people live
honestly, good people live without any faking, and they never
come double ...'

Mr Golyadkin was taken aback, and his hands and feet seemed
turned to ice.

'Yes, sir,' went on Petrushka, 'they never come in twos, and
they're not an offence to God and honest people ...'

'You idle creature, you're drunk! You can go to sleep now, you
scoundrel! And tomorrow you'll catch it!' added Mr Golyadkin in
a scarcely audible voice. As for Petrushka, he grumbled a few more
words, then he could be heard lying down on the bed, so that it
creaked, then a prolonged yawning and stretching and finally he
was snoring as he slept the sleep of the just, as they say. Mr
Golyadkin was left neither dead nor alive. Petrushka's behaviour,
his hints, extremely strange although so remote that they gave no
excuse for being annoyed, especially as it was a drunken man who

made them, and, finally, the nasty turn the whole affair was taking – all this shook Mr Golyadkin to the core. 'What possessed me to start shouting at him in the middle of the night?' said our hero, shaking all over with a feeling of sickness. 'And what on earth made me try to get anything out of a drunken man? – every word he utters is nonsense! All the same, what was the scoundrel hinting at? Oh my God! Why on earth did I write all those letters, like a suicidal idiot? – a suicidal idiot, that's what I am! I couldn't keep my mouth shut! I had to blab. And really, why? If you are ruined, be a doormat. But no, that won't do for you, you have to bring your pride into it, you say "my honour suffers", you say, "honour must be saved", forsooth! Suicidal, that's what I am!'

Thus Mr Golyadkin, sitting on his sofa and too apprehensive to move. Suddenly his eyes lighted on an object that positively riveted his attention. Fearing that the object that had attracted his notice was an illusion, a trick of the imagination, he stretched out his hand towards it, hopefully, timidly, with indescribable curiosity. . . . No, it was no deception, no illusion! A letter, it really was a letter, it was certainly a letter, and addressed to him. Mr Golyadkin took the letter from the table. His heart was beating heavily. 'I suppose that scoundrel brought it,' he thought, 'and put it down here, and forgot all about it; that's probably just how it happened.' The letter was from Vakhrameyev, a young colleague and once a friend of Mr Golyadkin's. 'However, I foresaw all this,' thought our hero, 'and now I foresee everything I shall find in the letter.'

The letter was as follows:

Dear Sir, Yakov Petrovich,

Your servant is drunk, and there is no getting any sense out of him; for that reason I prefer to answer you in writing. I hasten to inform you that the commission with which you have entrusted me, consisting of the transmission of a letter by my agency to a certain individual, I am prepared to fulfil with the utmost faithfulness and exactitude. The said individual, with whom you are well acquainted, who now occupies the position of a friend of mine, and whose name I here pass over in silence, for the reason that I do not desire to blacken the reputation of a completely innocent person, now lodges with us in Karolina Ivanovna's flat in the room which was formerly occupied, during your residence among us, by an infantry officer temporarily seconded from Tambov. You may always find this individual, however, in the society of people of sincere and honest heart, which cannot be said of some. I intend that my relations with yourself shall cease as of today's date; it is no longer possible for us to remain on a footing of friendship or continue our former harmonious comradeship, and for that reason, my dear sir, I must request you to send me without delay on receipt of this confidential letter the two roubles owing to me for the razors of foreign workmanship which, I am sure you will be good enough to remember, I sold you seven months ago on credit, while you were still living with us in the flat of Karolina Ivanovna, for whom I have the most heartfelt respect. I am acting in this manner because, according to the information I have received from knowledgeable people, you have lost your self-respect and your reputation and become dangerous to morally innocent and uncontaminated people, for certain individuals do not live according to the truth, and, moreover, their words are hypocrisy and their appearance of loyalty suspect. People capable of defending the wronged Karolina Ivanovna, who has always been well-conducted, and moreover an honest woman, and a lady besides, although no longer young, yet bearing a good foreign name – such people can be found always and everywhere, a fact which certain individuals have asked me to mention in passing in my letter and speaking in my own person. In any case you will learn all in due course, if you have not already done so, despite the fact that, on the testimony of knowledgeable people, you have made yourself notorious in every quarter of the capital and, consequently, my dear sir, might well have received appropriate intelligence about yourself in many places. In conclusion, my dear sir, I beg to inform you that a certain individual, whose name, for reasons of good breeding, I do not mention here, is highly esteemed by right-thinking people; moreover, that individual is of a lively and pleasant disposition, is making good progress in his employment as well as among all people of sound judgement, is true to his word and to friendship and does not insult behind their backs those with whom he finds himself on amicable terms to their faces.

> In any case I have the honour to remain,
> Your obedient humble servant,
> N. Vakhrameyev.

P.S. You ought to get rid of your servant: he is a drunkard and will in all probability cause you a great deal of trouble; and take on Eustaphy, who used to be employed in the office and now finds himself without a post. Your present servant is not only a drunkard, he is a thief in addition, for last week he sold Karolina Ivanovna at a reduced price a pound of lump sugar, which in my opinion he could not have done without cunningly filching it from you little by little at different times. I write this as a well-wisher, in spite of the fact that certain individuals can only insult and cheat everybody, especially people who are themselves honest and possessed of a good character; moreover, they revile them behind their backs and represent them as the opposite, purely out of envy and because they themselves are unable to lay claim to the name.

N.V.

After he had read Vakhrameyev's letter, our hero remained for a considerable time sitting motionless on the sofa. A new light was breaking through the cloud of obscurity and mystery that had enveloped him for the past two days. It was partly that our hero was beginning to remember. ... He made one or two attempts to rise from the sofa and take a few turns about the room, to refresh himself and collect his scattered thoughts, focus them on a certain subject and then, having pulled himself together a little, give mature consideration to the situation in which he found himself. But no sooner did he try to get up than he fell feebly and helplessly back in the same place. 'Of course, I foresaw all this before; all the same, how does he write, and what is the true meaning of the words? Well, suppose I know the meaning, but what is it leading up to? If he said straight out: look here, things are thus and so, such and such is required, I'd do it. But the turn the matter has taken is so nasty! Oh, if only tomorrow would come soon, so that I could tackle the business quickly! I know now what to do. I shall say, it's like this, I agree with your arguments, I will not sell my honour, or ... perhaps; but how did he, this certain unpleasant individual, get mixed up in this? and why is it just this he has got mixed up in? Oh, if only tomorrow would come quickly! Till then they'll be taking my good name away, they're intriguing against me, they're working to spite me! The chief thing is, I mustn't lose any time; I could at least write a letter, for example, not letting anything out, only saying things are thus and so and I agree to do this or that. And as soon as it's light tomorrow, send it off to him, before ... and on the other hand, to work against them and forestall them, the darlings. .... They're taking away my good name, that's all about it!'

Mr Golyadkin drew some paper to him, took his pen and wrote the following missive in answer to Provincial Secretary Vakhrameyev's letter:

Dear Sir, Nestor Ignatyevich,

It was with amazement and a sorrowful heart that I read your hurtful letter, for I see clearly that under the description of 'some disreputable individuals' and 'people of suspect loyalty' you mean me. I see with sincere sorrow with what speed and success and how deeply calumny has taken root, to the prejudice of my well-being, my honour and my good name. And it is all the more grievous and insulting because even honourable people with a genuinely noble turn of thought and, above all, endowed with frank and straightforward characters, abandon the interests of high-minded people and cling with the best qualities of their hearts to the pernicious putrefaction which in our troublous and dissolute age has unfortunately bred and multiplied freely and with the most extreme disloyalty. In conclusion, I will say that I shall consider it a sacred duty to return to you intact and in full the whole amount, two silver roubles, of the debt you refer to.

As far as concerns your allusions, my dear sir, on the subject of a certain individual of the female sex, and of the intentions, calculations, and various projects of that individual, I must tell you, my dear sir, that I comprehended all those allusions only vaguely and obscurely. Allow me, my dear sir, to preserve my good name and noble cast of mind unsullied. I am in any case, however, prepared to descend to personal explanations, preferring the trustworthiness of the personal to the written, and I am ready to enter into various peaceable and, naturally, bilateral agreements. With this in view, I beg you to convey to the person in question my readiness to come to a personal understanding, and in addition to ask her to name the time and place of our meeting. It has grieved me, my dear sir, to read your hints that I have insulted you, betrayed our pristine friendship and spoken evil of you. I attribute all these misunderstandings to the vile aspersions, envy, and hostility of those whom I may, without injustice, call my bitterest enemies. But probably they are not aware that innocence is powerful through its very quality of innocence, that

the shamelessness, impudence, and sickening familiarity of some
people will sooner or later earn them the stigma of contempt, and that
these persons will be destroyed by nothing more than their own un-
worthiness and depravity. In conclusion, I earnestly request you, my
dear sir, to convey to those persons that their extraordinary claims
and their ignoble and fantastic attempts to drive others beyond the
bounds occupied by the aforesaid others by the fact of their existence
in this world, and usurp their place, are deserving of amazement,
contempt and, what is more, the lunatic asylum; and, in addition,
such treatment is strictly forbidden by law, which is, in my esti-
mation, quite right, because everybody ought to be satisfied with his
own place. There are limits to everything, and if this is a joke, it is an
unseemly joke, and I will go further: it is completely immoral, for I
can assure you, my dear sir, that my ideas, set forth above, on *knowing one's place*, are entirely moral.

> At all events I have the honour to remain,
> Your Obedient servant,
> Ya. Golyadkin.

Chapter Ten

IT is quite possible to say that the previous day's happenings had
shaken Mr Golyadkin to his foundations. Our hero had passed a
very bad night, that is to say, he simply could not get to sleep
properly for even as much as five minutes: it was as though some
practical joker had scattered itching powder in his bed. He spent
the whole night in a kind of half-sleeping, half-waking state, toss-
ing and turning from side to side, sighing, grunting, dropping off
for a moment and waking up again almost immediately, and all
this to the accompaniment of a strange kind of anguish, obscure
recollections, ugly visions – in short, of everything that could be
called disagreeable. ... Now, in a strange mysterious half-light,
the figure of Andrey Philippovich appeared before him – a spare
figure, an irate figure, with a cold harsh glance and coldly civil
words of reproof. ... And hardly had Mr Golyadkin begun to
approach Andrey Philippovich to justify himself to him in some
way, by hook or by crook, and prove he was not at all the kind of

person his enemies described him as, but was in fact this and that, and even possessed, over and above the ordinary inborn qualities, this and that and the other one; hardly had he done so than just at that point the person distinguished by his mischievous and harmful tendencies appeared and by some outrageous means brought Mr Golyadkin's tentative hopes crashing down, thoroughly blackened his reputation almost to his face, trampled his self-respect in the mud and then at once usurped his place at work and in society. Now it was some little rebuff that rankled in Mr Golyadkin's mind, a rebuff recently administered and taken as degrading, administered either in the presence of others or somewhere else in circumstances that made it difficult to protest against the said rebuff. ... And while Mr Golyadkin was beginning to rack his brains over what exactly it had been that made it difficult to protest against that kind of rebuff, the idea of the rebuff was imperceptibly merging into another form – the form of a certain small, or perhaps not so small, mean trick, seen or heard of or recently performed by himself – perhaps even frequently performed, and not out of nastiness or through vicious impulses, but simply – sometimes, for example, accidentally – out of delicacy; another time because of his own utter defencelessness, or finally because ... because, in short, Mr Golyadkin knew very well why! Here Mr Golyadkin blushed in his sleep and, trying to suppress his blushes, mumbled something like 'here, for example, he might have displayed his firmness of character, in this instance he might have displayed considerable firmness of character' ... concluding with 'but why firmness of character? ... why mention it now?' But what most annoyed and upset Mr Golyadkin was the way in which, summoned or not, a certain person renowned for his ugliness and his satirical propensities now made his appearance, exactly at that minute, and also – in spite of its being well enough known, one would think – also began muttering with an ill-natured grin, 'What's firmness of character got to do with it? what firmness of character can you and I have to show, Yakov Petrovich?' ... Now it seemed to Mr Golyadkin that he was in the midst of a splendid company, all the persons who constituted it being distinguished for their wit and polished manners: that Mr

Golyadkin in his turn distinguished himself in respect of court-
liness and wit, that everybody was charmed with him, and that
even some of his enemies who were there were charmed with him,
which was very pleasing to Mr Golyadkin; everybody yielded him
the first place and finally Mr Golyadkin had the pleasure of over-
hearing his host praising him to one of the guests as he led him
aside . . . and at that very moment there suddenly appeared again
out of the blue a certain person notorious for his disloyalty and
swinish impulses, in the shape of Mr Golyadkin junior, and at
once, on the spot, in the twinkling of an eye, by his mere appearance, Golyadkin junior ruined all Golyadkin senior's triumph
and renown, eclipsed Golyadkin senior, trampled Golyadkin senior
in the mire and, finally, showed clearly that the senior, and also
the genuine, Golyadkin was not genuine at all but a counterfeit,
and that he himself was the real one, that Golyadkin senior was
not at all what he seemed, but this and that, and consequently
ought not, indeed had no right, to belong to a society of people of
decent feeling and good tone. And all this happened so quickly
that before Mr Golyadkin senior had had time to open his mouth
they had all given themselves up, body and soul, to the hideous
fake Mr Golyadkin and repudiated him, the real and blameless Mr
Golyadkin, with the profoundest contempt. There remained not
one whose attitude had not in one instant been transformed in his
own favour by the hideous Mr Golyadkin. There was not one left
whom the empty and spurious Mr Golyadkin had not sucked up
to, in his usual way, in the most honeyed manner, whom he had
not, in his usual way, won over, before whom he had not, in his
usual way, burnt the sweetest and pleasantest incense, so that the
personage, wreathed in smoke, could only sniff and sneeze till the
tears came, in token of the highest satisfaction. But the main
thing was that it had all happened in a flash; the speed of movement of the suspicious and pernicious Mr Golyadkin was aston-
ishing! Hardly had he had time to make up to one person and get
into his good graces, for example, than before you could say knife
he was already talking to another. He would slyly wheedle and
wheedle away, extract a smile of good will, kick up his short,
round, rather vulgar little leg, and be off to a third, playing the

whore and slobbering over him; before you could wink an eye or
have time to feel astonished, he was beside a fourth, and already
on the same terms with him too – it was terrible, sheer witchcraft,
nothing else! And everybody was glad to see him, everybody liked
him, everybody praised him to the skies, everybody proclaimed in
chorus that his amiability and his satirical gifts were infinitely
superior to the amiability and satirical gifts of the real Mr Golyadkin, thus shaming the innocent real Mr Golyadkin, rejecting the
upright Mr Golyadkin, driving the loyal Mr Golyadkin away with
blows, showering insults on the real Mr Golyadkin's well-known
love of his neighbour . . .! In anguish, in horror, in frenzy, the
tormented Mr Golyadkin dashed out into the street and hailed a
cab so that he could rush straight to His Excellency, or if not
there, at least to Andrey Philippovich, but – oh horror! the cabbies
flatly refused to take Mr Golyadkin: 'No sir, your honour, I can't
take two people that are just the same; a good man does his best to
live honestly, your honour, not just higgledy-piggledy, and he's
never double.' In a frenzy of shame the completely honest Mr
Golyadkin looked round and saw for himself, with his own eyes,
that the cabbies and Petrushka, who had somehow merged into
them, were indeed quite right; for the disreputable Mr Golyadkin
really was there, beside him and not very far away, and, in accordance with his usual bad manners, was even here, even at this
critical juncture, undoubtedly preparing to do something quite
shocking, and certainly not showing the least trace of that gentlemanly polish that is usually bestowed by education – a polish on
which the loathsome Mr Golyadkin the second so prided himself
on every possible occasion. Beside himself with shame and desper-
ation, the lost and altogether rightful Mr Golyadkin rushed away,
following his nose, at the mercy of fate, to wherever chance would
lead him; but with every step he took, every time his foot struck
the pavement, there sprang up, as if from under the ground,
another exactly and completely identical Mr Golyadkin, revolting
in his depravity. And all these complete replicas, as soon as they
appeared, began running along one behind the other, stretching
out in a long file like a string of geese and scurrying after Mr
Golyadkin, so that there was no escaping from perfect counter-

parts of himself, so that horror deprived the much-to-be-pitied Mr Golyadkin of breath, so that finally there had sprung up a terrible multitude of perfect replicas, so that at length the whole capital was clogged with perfect replicas and a policeman, seeing such a disturbance of the peace, was obliged to take all the perfect replicas by the collar and put them in a lock-up that happened to be handy. . . . Rigid and frozen with horror, our hero woke up; rigid and frozen with horror, he felt that even awake he could hardly pass the time more cheerfully. . . . It was a cruel and wretched moment. . . . The anguish he experienced was as though the heart was being eaten out of his breast.

At last Mr Golyadkin could bear it no longer. 'This won't do!' he exclaimed, resolutely raising himself from the bed, and with this exclamation he awoke completely.

Dawn had evidently broken long before. The room seemed unusually light; the sun's rays filtered thickly through panes covered with hoar-frost and flooded the room, which surprised Mr Golyadkin not a little for in the normal way the sun did not reach his windows before noon, and such exceptions to the heavenly luminary's usual habits hardly ever happened, at least as far as Mr Golyadkin could remember. Almost before our hero had had time to feel surprised the clock on the other side of the partition whirred and prepared to strike. 'Ah, there we are!' thought Mr Golyadkin, and with dreary expectancy prepared to listen. . . . But to his complete and utter astonishment, his clock gathered itself together and struck – once. 'What nonsense is this?' cried our hero, leaping out of bed. Just as he was, unable to believe his ears, he rushed behind the partition. The clock really did show one o'clock. Mr Golyadkin looked at Petrushka's bed: there wasn't so much as a smell of Petrushka left in the room; his bed had evidently been made long before, his boots were nowhere to be seen – a sure sign that Petrushka really was not at home. Mr Golyadkin rushed to the door: the door was locked. 'Where can Petrushka be?' he went on in a whisper, terribly agitated and conscious of a quite violent trembling in all his limbs. Suddenly an idea darted into his mind. . . . Mr Golyadkin rushed to his table, looked all over it and searched all around – he was right: his yesterday's letter to Vakhrameyev was gone. Petrushka was also gone from behind the partition, it was one by the clock on the wall, and in Vakhrameyev's letter some new points had been introduced, points which had been, however, utterly obscure at first glance but had now become very clear. Finally, Petrushka as well – obviously Petrushka had been bought over! Yes, yes, that was it!

'So that's where the intrigue was being elaborated!' cried Mr Golyadkin, striking himself on the forehead and opening his eyes wider and wider; 'so it's in that stingy German woman's nest that all the devilry is hidden now! So that means she was only creating a strategic diversion by directing my attention to Izmailovsky Bridge – she was distracting me, confusing me, the wicked old hag, and that's how she was undermining my position! Yes, that's right! You have only to look at the matter from that angle and you see that it is inevitably so, and the appearance of that scoundrel is fully accounted for now too: it all adds up. They've had him in reserve for a long time, getting him ready and saving him for a rainy day. So that's how things stand now, that's how it has all turned out! That's what the solution is! Well, it doesn't matter! There's no time lost yet. . . .' Here Mr Golyadkin remembered with horror that it was after one o'clock already. 'What if they have succeeded by now . . .?' A groan broke from him. 'But no, that's nonsense, they haven't had time. Let's see . . .!' He huddled on his clothes, seized paper and pen and scribbled the following missive:

My dear sir, Yakov Petrovich,

Either you or I, one or the other, but both of us together is impossible! And I must therefore inform you that your strange, ludicrous, and altogether impossible desire to seem to be my twin and pass yourself off as the same person will lead to nothing but your utter disgrace and defeat. And therefore I beg you, in your own interest, to stand aside and leave the way clear for genuinely noble people with honourable aims. In the opposite case I am prepared to resolve on the most extreme measures. I lay down my pen and wait. However, I am ready either to be at your service or – for pistols.

Ya. Golyadkin.

When he had finished his note our hero rubbed his hands with satisfaction. Then, pulling on his overcoat and putting on his hat he let himself out with his spare key and set out for the office. He reached it but could not make up his mind to go in; it really was too late; Mr Golyadkin's watch showed half-past two. Suddenly some of his doubts were resolved by a happening of apparently trivial importance: a breathless and red-faced little figure appeared round the corner of the building, darted stealthily up the steps and scurried like a mouse into the hall. It was the copying clerk Ostafyev, a man well known to Mr Golyadkin, a man in somewhat needy circumstances and ready to do anything for ten copecks. Knowing Ostafyev's weak side and realizing that after being forced by the most pressing necessity to be absent, he was probably more avid for ten-copeck pieces than ever, our hero decided to be lavish with them, and immediately darted up the steps and into the hall after Ostafyev, called to him, and with a mysterious air invited him to step aside into a secluded corner behind the huge iron stove. Having led the way there, our hero began asking questions.

'Well, my friend, and how are things – there . . . do you understand?'

'Yes, sir, your honour, I wish your honour well.'

'Good, my friend, good; I thank you, you're a good sort. Well now, my friend, how are they, eh?'

'What did you want to know, sir?' Here Ostafyev covered for a moment with his hand his unexpectedly gaping mouth.

'Well, you see, my friend, I just ... but you mustn't think anything of it. . . . Well, is Andrey Philippovich here?'

'Yes, sir.'

'And the staff, are they here?'

'Yes, the staff are here too, as you'd expect, sir!'

'And His Excellency as well?'

'Yes, sir.' Here the clerk covered his mouth for the second time with his hand and gazed at Mr Golyadkin rather oddly and with some curiosity. At least so it seemed to our hero.

'And nothing special has happened, my friend?'

'No, sir, nothing at all, sir.'

'So there hasn't been anything about me, my friend, nothing . . .

nothing ... or, so to speak, nothing, eh? I'm just asking, my friend, you understand?'

'No, sir, I've not heard nothing up to now, sir.' Here the clerk again held his mouth closed and again gazed at Mr Golyadkin somewhat strangely. The fact was that our hero was now trying to penetrate Ostafyev's expression, to read something into it, to discover if he was hiding something. And there did really seem to be some concealment; the fact was that Ostafyev seemed to be growing less polite, colder, not entering into Mr Golyadkin's interests with the same sympathy as before. 'He's in the right, to a certain extent,' thought Mr Golyadkin; 'what am I to him, after all? Perhaps he's already had something from another source, and so is free of the most pressing needs. And so I'd better. ...' Mr Golyadkin understood that the time had come for ten-copeck pieces.

'Here's a little something for you, my dear friend ...'

'I am deeply obliged to your honour.'

'There will be more to come.'

'At your service, your honour.'

'I'm prepared to give you more at once, and when the matter is disposed of, I'll give you as much again. You understand?'

The clerk said nothing, but stood at attention and fixed his eyes unwinkingly on Mr Golyadkin.

'Well, now tell me: nothing has been said about me?'

'For the time being, sir, I think ... er ... there isn't anything for the time being, sir.' Ostafyev answered in a measured way and he also, like Mr Golyadkin, preserved a slightly secretive air, twitching his eyebrows a little, gazing at the ground, trying to hit upon a fitting tone and, in short, striving with all his might to earn what he had been promised, since he regarded what he had been given as his own and definitely earned already.

'And there is nothing known?'

'Not yet, sir, for the time being.'

'But listen ... er ... it might perhaps become known?'

'Later, of course, sir, it might be known, sir.'

'That's bad,' thought our hero.

'Listen, here's something more for you, my friend.'

'I am deeply obliged to your honour, sir.'

'Was Vakhrameyev here yesterday . . .?'

'Yes, the gentleman was here, sir.'

'And was somebody else here . . .? Try to remember, my good fellow!'

The clerk rummaged among his memories for a few moments and found nothing relevant.

'No, sir, there was nobody else, sir.'

'H'm!' A silence followed.

'Listen, my good fellow, here's a bit more for you; tell me everything, all the ins and outs.'

'Yes, sir.' Ostafyev was now as smooth as silk, just as Mr Golyadkin required.

'Tell me now, my friend, what sort of footing is he on?'

'All right, sir, quite good, sir,' answered the clerk, watching Mr Golyadkin intently.

'How do you mean, good?'

'Just that, sir.' Here Ostafyev twitched his eyebrows significantly. He was, however, becoming decidedly nonplussed, and did not know what more he could say. 'That's bad!' thought Mr Golyadkin.

'Have they anything further going on with Vakhrameyev?'

'Everything's the same as before, sir.'

'Just think a little.'

'Yes, sir, there is, so they say.'

'Well, then, what is it?'

Ostafyev closed his mouth with his hand.

'Isn't there a letter there for me?'

'Mikheyev the watchman went to Vakhrameyev's flat today, to that there German woman of theirs, sir, so I'll go and ask, if you want.'

'Oblige me by doing that, my friend, for God's sake . . .! I'm only asking. . . . Don't think anything of it, my good fellow, I'm just asking. But you ask some questions, my good fellow, find out if some sort of trick is being thought up at my expense there. What is he doing? that's what I want to know; you find that out, my dear fellow, and I shall know how to thank you afterwards, my dear fellow . . .'

'Yes, sir, your honour, and Ivan Semyonovich was sitting in your place today, sir.'

'Ivan Semyonovich? Ah! yes! Really?'

'Andrey Philippovich showed him where to sit, sir.'

'Really? How did that come about? Find that out, my dear chap; find out all about it – and I shall know how to thank you, my dear fellow; that's what I want to know. . . . But you mustn't think anything wrong, my dear chap . . .'

'Yes, sir, certainly sir, I'll go up at once, sir. But aren't you coming in today, sir?'

'No, my friend; I just looked in, I was only doing it. . . . I just came in to have a look, my dear friend, and afterwards I'll show you my gratitude, my dear chap.'

'Yes, sir.' The clerk ran upstairs with zealous speed, and Mr Golyadkin remained alone.

'This is bad,' he thought. 'Oh dear, it's bad, very bad! Oh dear, this little affair of ours. . . . How very bad it is now! What can all this mean? exactly what did certain hints of that drunkard mean, for example, and whose doing was it? Ah, I know now whose doing it was! This is what the trick was. They must have got to know, and so they made him sit. . . . But wait a minute – *they* made him? It was Andrey Philippovich who made him sit there, Ivan Semyonovich; yes, but why did he make him sit there, exactly what purpose was there in that? Probably they got to know. . . . It's Vakhrameyev's work, or rather not Vakhrameyev's, he's as stupid as an oak-log, is Vakhrameyev; but they are all working for him, and they urged that scoundrel to come here for the same purpose; and that one-eyed German woman has been complaining! I always suspected that there was more than met the eye in all this intrigue, and that there must be something behind all this female tittle-tattle and old wives' tales; I said the same thing to Christian Ivanovich, I said some people have sworn to annihilate a man, morally speaking, and they seized on Karolina Ivanovna. No, there are obviously experts at work here. This, my good sir, is the work of an expert hand, not Vakhrameyev's. I've

said before Vakhrameyev is stupid, and this. ... I know now who
is working behind them all: it's that scoundrel, it's the impostor!
He's clinging to that one thing, which all goes to show his successes in the highest society. And I really should like to know
what footing he's on now ... what part is he playing up there?
Only why did they take Ivan Semyonovich? what the devil did
they need Ivan Semyonovich for? It looks as if they couldn't get
anybody else. But whoever it was that was put in my place it
would all amount to the same thing; all I know is that I've been
suspicious of that Ivan Semyonovich for a long time, I noticed
long ago that he was a nasty wicked old man – they say he lends
money and charges interest like a Jew. And it's the Bear who's
contriving it all. The Bear is mixed up in all these happenings.
That's the way it all started. It started there, near Izmailovsky
Bridge; that's how it started. ...' Here Mr Golyadkin grimaced as
though he had bitten into a lemon, probably at the remembrance
of something highly unpleasant. 'Well, it doesn't matter, however,' he thought. 'Only I can't help worrying about my affairs all
the time. But why doesn't Ostafyev come? Perhaps he sat down to
work, or he was detained somehow. It's quite a good thing, really,
that I'm intriguing like this, and doing some undermining from
my side. I only had to give Ostafyev ten copecks, and he set to
work ... and on my side. Only that is the point: is he really on my
side? perhaps they've done the same from their side ... and are
intriguing themselves, in concert with him. After all, he looks like
a criminal, the scoundrel, an absolute criminal! He's keeping something back, the scoundrel! "No, nothing," says he, "and," he says,
"I'm truly grateful to your honour." You scoundrel!'

There was a noise. ... Mr Golyadkin shrank back, and hastily
retreated behind the stove. Somebody came down the stairs and
went out into the street. 'Who could it be, leaving at this time?'
our hero wondered to himself. A moment later he again heard
footsteps. ... Mr Golyadkin could not endure it any longer, and
thrust the tiniest tip of his nose out from behind his breastwork –
thrust it out and immediately jerked it back again, as though
somebody had pricked it with a pin. This time he knew who was
going past, the scoundrel, the intriguer, the villain, going past

with his nasty little pattering steps, mincing along and throwing out his feet as though he was preparing to kick somebody. 'The rascal!' said our hero to himself. Mr Golyadkin could not fail to notice, however, that the rascal was carrying under his arm an enormous green portfolio belonging to His Excellency. 'He's on special business again,' thought Mr Golyadkin, reddening and shrinking still more into himself with vexation. No sooner had Mr Golyadkin junior passed Mr Golyadkin senior, without noticing him, than footsteps became audible for the third time, and this time Mr Golyadkin guessed that they were the copying-clerk's. And indeed an inky little clerk's figure did look round behind the stove at him; the figure, however, was not Ostafyev, but the other copying clerk, whose nickname was Clerkie. This amazed Mr Golyadkin. 'Why has he been letting other people into the secret?' thought our hero. 'These barbarians! nothing is sacred to them!'

'Well, my friend?' he said, addressing Clerkie. 'Who have you come from, my friend?'

'It's like this, sir; about that little business of yours, sir. There's no news from anybody for the time being, sir. If there is, we'll let you know, sir.'

'And what about Ostafyev?'

'He can't come, your honour, not anyhow, sir. His Excellency's walked through the department twice already, and I've got no time now, neither.'

'Thank you, my friend, thank you.... Only tell me ...'

'Honest to God, I haven't got the time, sir.... They keep asking for us all the time, sir.... But if you'll be good enough to stay here a bit longer, sir, then if there is anything about that little matter of yours, sir, we'll let you know, sir.'

'No, but, my friend, tell me ...'

'Excuse me, sir, I haven't the time,' said Clerkie, breaking away from Mr Golyadkin, who was clutching him by the lapels; 'really I can't, sir. You stay here a bit longer, sir, and we'll let you know.'

'In a minute, in a minute, my friend! just one minute, my dear friend! Here, now: here's a letter, my friend; there'll be a little something for you, my friend.'

'Yes, sir.'

'Try to give it to Mr Golyadkin, my friend.'

'Mr Golyadkin?'

'Yes, Mr Golyadkin, my friend.'

'Very good, sir; when I can get away, I'll take it, sir. Meanwhile, you stay here. Nobody will see you here ...'

'No, my friend, I. ... You mustn't think. ... I'm not standing here to keep people from seeing me, you know. I won't be here, my friend. ... I'll be just over there in the side-street. There's a coffeeshop there; so I shall wait there, and if anything happens, you tell me all about it, you understand?'

'Very good, sir. Only let me go; I understand ...'

'I'll make it worth your while, my friend!' Mr Golyadkin called after Clerkie, who had at length managed to free himself. ... 'He's a scoundrel, I think, he got ruder afterwards,' thought our hero, stealthily making his way out from behind the stove. 'There's another snag here, that's clear. ... At first it was neither one thing nor the other. ... However, he really was in a hurry; perhaps they have a lot of work. And His Excellency walked through the office twice. ... What could be the reason for that ...? Ugh! Well, it doesn't matter! perhaps it's nothing, we'll see ...'

Here Mr Golyadkin was about to open the door and go out into the street, but at that very moment His Excellency's carriage clattered up to the door. Before Mr Golyadkin could collect his wits, the carriage door was opened from the inside and the gentleman sitting in it jumped out into the porch. The new arrival was none other than Mr Golyadkin junior, who had gone out about ten minutes earlier. Mr Golyadkin senior remembered that His Excellency's flat was just round the corner. 'He's been on his special errand,' said our hero to himself. Meanwhile Mr Golyadkin junior had reached the bulky green portfolio out of the carriage, then taken out some other papers as well, given an order to the coachman and pushed open the door, almost bumping into Mr Golyadkin senior with it and, deliberately not noticing him, which meant he was only trying to annoy him, set off at a run up the stairs to the department. 'It's bad!' thought Mr Golyadkin; 'oh dear, look what's happening to our little affair now! Oh lord, look at him!'

Our hero stood there for half a minute longer without moving;
then at last he came to a decision. Without further hesitation,
although he felt profound trepidation in his heart and a tremor in
all his limbs, he ran up the stairs after his enemy. 'Well, here
goes! What does it matter to me? it's nothing to do with
me,' he thought, taking off his hat, galoshes and overcoat in
the hall.

When Mr Golyadkin entered his own department it was
already dusk. Neither Andrey Philippovich nor Anton Antonovich was in the room. They were both in the Director's room
with their reports; the Director was rumoured to have hurried
away to His Supreme Excellency. In consequence of these circumstances, and also because the twilight had invaded the rooms and it
was almost closing time, some of the clerks, chiefly the younger
ones, were moving about, drifting together, talking, arguing,
laughing, in a sort of busy idleness, and some of the most junior,
those at the very bottom of the lowest grade, had even set up a
game of pitch-and-toss near a window in the corner, under cover of
the general noise. Knowing the rules of good behaviour, and feeling at that moment a special need to acquire information, Mr
Golyadkin at once went up to some of the colleagues with whom
he got on very well, to wish them good day, and so on. But Mr
Golyadkin's colleagues answered his greetings somewhat
strangely. He was unpleasantly struck by the general coldness,
dryness, and what might even be called severity of his reception.
Nobody shook hands with him. Some merely said, 'Good afternoon' and walked away, others only nodded, one simply turned
away and pretended he had not noticed him, and finally some –
and (what Mr Golyadkin found most offensive of all) they were
some of the most insignificant young whippersnappers who, as Mr
Golyadkin had quite recently remarked, were fit for nothing but
playing pitch-and-toss when they got the chance, or gadding
about – some gradually surrounded Mr Golyadkin, clustering in
groups near him and almost blocking his exit. They were all staring at him with insulting curiosity.

It was a bad sign. Mr Golyadkin felt this, and sensibly prepared
to take no notice, for his part. Suddenly a completely unexpected

circumstance quite finished off, as they say, Mr Golyadkin, and
utterly annihilated him.

Among the crowd of young colleagues surrounding Mr Golyadkin, and, as if on purpose, at the most discouraging moment for
him, Mr Golyadkin junior appeared, as cheerful as ever, wearing
his perpetual little smile, and as restless as ever, skipping about,
mischief-making, ingratiating, guffawing, light of tongue and of
heels, as he always was, as he had been before, exactly as he had
been on the previous day, for example, at a very unpleasant
moment for Mr Golyadkin senior. Grinning, turning and twisting,
mincing along with his little smile that as good as wished everybody a pleasant evening, he wriggled his way through the crowd,
shaking hands with one, clapping another on the shoulder, throwing his arm lightly about a third, explaining to a fourth precisely
what errand His Excellency had employed him on, where he had
gone, what he had done, what he had brought back with him; to
the fifth, probably his best friend, he gave a smacking kiss right on
the lips – everything, in short, happened exactly as it had in Mr
Golyadkin senior's dream. When he had had his fill of prancing
about, dealt with each in his own fashion, won them all round to
his side, whether he needed to or not, and slobbered over all of
them to his heart's content, Mr Golyadkin junior suddenly, and
probably by mistake, not having had time up to then to notice his
oldest friend, held out his hand to Mr Golyadkin senior also. Also
probably by mistake, although he for his part had had plenty of
time to notice the ignoble Mr Golyadkin junior, our hero at once
eagerly seized the hand so unexpectedly proffered and pressed it in
the warmest and most friendly way, pressed it with a kind of
strange and almost completely unlooked-for inner impulse, with
almost tearful emotion. Whether our hero was deceived by the
first movement of his ill-bred enemy, or was simply at a loss, or felt
and realized in his inmost heart the full extent of his own helplessness, it is hard to say. The fact remains that Mr Golyadkin
senior, in his right mind, of his own free will, and in the presence
of witnesses, solemnly shook hands with the man he called his
deadly enemy. But what was Mr Golyadkin senior's consternation, outrage, and fury, what was his shame and horror,

when his adversary and deadly enemy, the despicable Mr Golyadkin junior, realizing the mistake of the persecuted and innocent man he had perfidiously misled, suddenly, without shame, without feeling, without compassion or conscience, snatched away his hand from Mr Golyadkin senior's with unbearable effrontery and discourtesy! Nor was that all: he shook his hand in the air as though he had dirtied it in something extremely nasty; furthermore, he turned and spat, making a most offensive gesture as he did so; furthermore, he took out his handkerchief and with it, in the most outrageous fashion, wiped all the fingers that had rested for a moment in Mr Golyadkin senior's hand. As he did this, Mr Golyadkin junior, in his usual disgusting fashion, deliberately looked all round, making sure that his conduct was visible to everybody, looked everybody in the eye and plainly tried to convey to everybody the most unfavourable idea of Mr Golyadkin senior. The behaviour of the loathsome Mr Golyadkin junior appeared to arouse the universal indignation of the bystanders; even the frivolous young men showed their disapproval. Murmurs and whispers arose on all sides. Mr Golyadkin senior's ears could not fail to distinguish the general sentiment; but suddenly a timely and pointed jest, bursting, I may say, from the lips of Mr Golyadkin junior, shattered and annihilated our hero's last hopes and tipped the scales once more in favour of his deadly and despicable enemy.

This is our Russian Faublas, gentlemen; allow me to present the young Chevalier de Faublas,' squeaked Mr Golyadkin junior, with his own peculiar impudence, mincing and darting among the clerks and indicating the numbed, yet at the same time raging, real Mr Golyadkin. 'Give me a kiss, darling!' he went on with intolerable familiarity, moving near to the man he had treacherously insulted. The worthless Mr Golyadkin junior's witticism seemed to have found an echo in the right quarters, especially as it contained a sly allusion to a circumstance that was clearly already public knowledge. Our hero felt the heavy hand of his enemies on his shoulder. But he had made up his mind what to do. With blazing eyes, a pale face, and a fixed smile he extricated himself somehow from the crowd and made his way with hurried uneven steps straight towards His Excellency's room. In the ante-room he was met by Andrey Philippovich, who had just left His Excellency, and although there were in the room a considerable number of other people who were at that time complete outsiders from Mr Golyadkin's point of view, our hero would not spare even the slightest attention for that circumstance. Directly, decisively, fearlessly, almost surprising himself and inwardly congratulating himself on his courage, he wasted no time but accosted Andrey Philippovich, who was considerably astonished at such an unexpected attack.

'Oh ...! what do you ... what can I do for you?' asked the head of the section, without listening to Mr Golyadkin's stumbling words.

'Andrey Philippovich, I ... may I, Andrey Philippovich, have an interview now, immediately and confidentially, with His Excellency?'

'What? of course not, sir!' Andrey Philippovich's glance measured Mr Golyadkin from head to foot.

'I am saying this, Andrey Philippovich, because I am astounded that nobody here will expose the impostor and scoundrel.'

'Wha-a-at, sir?'

'Scoundrel, Andrey Philippovich.'

'Who is it that you are good enough to regard in that light?'

'A certain person, Andrey Philippovich. I am referring, Andrey Philippovich, to a certain person; I am within my rights. ... I think the authorities ought to encourage such actions, Andrey Philippovich,' added Mr Golyadkin, evidently forgetting who he was; 'Andrey Philippovich ... you can probably see, Andrey Philippovich, that this is a noble action and symbolizes my loyal intention to look on the head of my department as a father, Andrey Philippovich; what it says is that I accept the benevolent authorities as my father, and blindly entrust my fate to them. It says this ... and that ... that's what it is. ...' Here Mr Golyadkin's voice faltered, his face grew flushed, and two tears started from his eyes.

Listening to Mr Golyadkin, Andrey Philippovich was so startled that he involuntarily recoiled a step or two. Then he looked anxiously around. ... It is hard to say how it would all have ended. ... But suddenly the door of His Excellency's room opened and he himself emerged, accompanied by several officials. All those who were in the ante-room trailed along behind. His Excellency beckoned to Andrey Philippovich and walked along beside him, discussing official business. When everybody else had got in motion and disappeared from the room, Mr Golyadkin too recollected himself. Now calm again, he took refuge under the wing of Anton Antonovich Setochkin, who was stumping along in his turn, bringing up the rear with, as it seemed to Mr Golyadkin, a very stern and preoccupied expression. 'I've said too much again, I've made a mess of things again,' he thought to himself; 'well, it doesn't matter.'

'I hope that you at least will consent to listen to me, Anton Antonovich, and try to understand my position,' he said quietly, in a voice still trembling a little with agitation. 'Cast aside by everybody else, I turn to you. I am still puzzled to know what Andrey Philippovich's words meant, Anton Antonovich. Explain them to me, please, if you can ...'

'Everything will be explained in its own good time,' answered Anton Antonovich sternly, in measured tones and, as it seemed to Mr Golyadkin, with an expression that meant it to be clearly understood that Anton Antonovich had no intention of continuing the conversation. 'You will know everything shortly. You will be officially notified in writing today.'

'What is there official about it, Anton Antonovich? why should it be official?' our hero asked diffidently.

'It is not for you and me to question the decision of the authorities, Yakov Petrovich.'

'But why the authorities, Anton Antonovich?' said Mr Golyadkin, still more timidly, 'why the authorities? I don't see any reason to disturb the authorities with this, Anton Antonovich. ... Perhaps you want to say something about what happened yesterday, Anton Antonovich?'

'No not yesterday; there's something else about you that's unsatisfactory.'

'What is, Anton Antonovich? I don't think there's anything about me that is unsatisfactory.'

'And who have you been trying to mislead and delude?' Anton Antonovich sharply interrupted the dumbfounded Mr Golyadkin. Mr Golyadkin started, and turned as white as his handkerchief.

'Of course, Anton Antonovich,' he said in a barely audible tone, 'if you heed the voice of scandal and listen to our enemies, without hearing the justification of the other side, then of course ... of course, Anton Antonovich, then a person can suffer, Anton Antonovich, suffer innocently and without any cause.'

'Very well, sir; then what about your unbecoming conduct to the detriment of a well-born young lady belonging to the benevolent, respectable and well-known family that has been your benefactor?'

'What conduct, Anton Antonovich?'

'Very well, sir. And your laudable conduct in connection with another young lady who, although poor, is nevertheless of honourable foreign extraction, don't you know what that was, either?'

'Excuse me, Anton Antonovich ... be good enough to hear me out, Anton Antonovich ...'

'And your treacherous behaviour, your slander of another person, your accusing somebody else of something you were implicated in yourself? eh? what do you call that?'

'I didn't turn him out, Anton Antonovich,' said our hero, beginning to quake, 'and I didn't tell Petrushka, that's my man, to do anything of the sort either. ... He ate my bread, Anton Antonovich; he took advantage of my hospitality,' he added eloquently and with such deep feeling that his chin quivered slightly and the tears threatened to well up again.

'You only say that he ate your bread,' Anton Antonovich answered, grinning, and with so much sly malice in his voice that Mr Golyadkin's heart seemed to be being raked by some sort of claws.

'May I ask you something else, most humbly, Anton Antonovich? Does His Excellency know about all this?'

'Why ever should he? However, please let me go now. I have no
time for you now, and in this place. . . . You will learn all you
ought to know today.'

'Just another minute, for God's sake, Anton Antonovich. . . .!'

'You can speak to me later.'

'No, Anton Antonovich; you see . . . I . . . if you will only listen
to me, Anton Antonovich. . . . I'm not a free-thinker of any
kind, Anton Antonovich, I shun all kinds of free thought,
for my part I'm quite ready . . . and I forgot to mention the
idea . . .'

'Very well, very well. I've heard it already . . .'

'No, you haven't heard this, Anton Antonovich. This is
different, Anton Antonovich, this is right thinking, really good,
and you will like to hear it. . . . As I said before, Anton Antonovich, I forgot to mention the idea that here God's providence
has created two people exactly alike, and our benevolent authorities, recognizing God's providence, have given shelter to those
twins. That's good, Anton Antonovich. You can see that's very
good, Anton Antonovich, and that I am far from a free-thinker. I
accept the benevolent authorities as a father to me. The benevolent
authorities, it's said, make this or that statement, it's said, and you,
it's said, must . . . a young man must do his duty. . . . Give me your
support, Anton Antonovich, put in a word for me, Anton Antonovich. . . . I don't mean. . . . Anton Antonovich, for God's sake,
just another word. . . . Anton Antonovich . . .'

But Anton Antonovich was already far away from Mr Golyadkin. . . . Our hero didn't know where he stood, what he was
hearing, what was being done with him, or what would yet be
done – he was so confused and shaken by all he had heard and all
that had already happened to him.

With an imploring glance he searched among the crowd of
clerks for Anton Antonovich, in order to make further excuses for
himself and say something extremely Orthodox, very high-flown,
and agreeable about himself. . . . Little by little, however, a new
light began to pierce through Mr Golyadkin's confusion, a new
and terrible light that suddenly illuminated a whole perspective of
hitherto absolutely unknown and totally unexpected circum-

stances. ... At that moment somebody dug our lost and shaken hero in the ribs. He looked round. Clerkie was standing in front of him.

'A letter, your honour.'

'Ah! ... have you been already, my dear friend?'

'No, this was brought here this morning at ten o'clock, sir. Sergey Mikheyev, the watchman, brought it from Provincial Secretary Vakhrameyev's, sir.'

'Good, my friend, good. I shall know how to show my gratitude, my dear friend.'

So saying, Mr Golyadkin hid the letter in the inside pocket of his coat, which he then buttoned all the way up; then he looked round and saw to his astonishment that he was already standing in the hall among a group of employees crowding round the exit, for the hour of closing was past. Not only had Mr Golyadkin failed to notice this last circumstance, he had not even realized, and could not remember how it had come about, that he was wearing his overcoat and galoshes and holding his hat in his hand. All the clerks were standing still and waiting deferentially. The fact was that His Excellency had stopped at the bottom of the stairs to wait for his carriage, which had been delayed for some reason, and was holding a very interesting conversation with two Councillors and Andrey Philippovich. A little removed from Andrey Philippovich and the two Councillors stood Anton Antonovich Setochkin and some of the other clerks, all smiling broadly because they could see that His Excellency was pleased to laugh and joke. The clerks thronging at the head of the stairs smiled too, and waited for His Excellency to laugh again. Only Fedoseich, the pot-bellied hall-porter, who stood at attention holding the door-handle, and impatiently awaiting his daily ration of happiness, the great moment when he flung one-half of the door wide open with a sweep of his arm and then bowed almost double as he respectfully stood aside to allow His Excellency to pass – only he was without a smile. But the person who quite evidently felt the greatest pleasure and happiness of all was Mr Golyadkin's unworthy and ignoble enemy. For the moment he had even forgotten all the other clerks and stopped weaving and prancing among them in his usual disgusting fashion, neglecting even to take advantage of any opportunity to worm his way into somebody's good graces. He had become nothing but eyes and ears; he seemed oddly shrunken into himself, probably in order to hear better, and never took his eyes off His Excellency, while only a barely perceptible convulsive twitch of his hands, feet, and head occasionally betrayed the secret inner workings of his soul.

'He's absolutely bursting with excitement!' thought our hero. The scoundrel looks like the court favourite. I wish I knew how he manages to get on so well in good society. No brains, no character, no education, no feelings; the swine's just born lucky! My God, really, when you come to think of it, how quickly a man can just come along and find his feet! And that man will go a long way, I'm prepared to swear he will, he'll get on, he's a lucky devil. I wish I knew just what he says when he whispers to them all like that. What kind of secrets is he sharing with all these people, what are all the mysterious things they say? What if I was to . . . a word or two with them as well, perhaps . . . I might say, well this, or well that . . . and shall we ask him . . . or, well, say what you like, I'm not going to . . . or perhaps I was wrong, Your Excellency, and a young man has to do something these days; I'm not in the least embarrassed by my ambiguous situation – that's it! Shall I do it that way . . .? Yes, but there's no getting at him, the wretch, no words will make any impression on him; you can't drive any sense into such a creature. . . . However, I'll try. If I happen to hit on the right moment, I'll have a shot . . .'

In his uneasy state of mind, his depression and confusion, feeling that things could not go on in that fashion, that a decisive moment was at hand, and that he must have things out with somebody, our hero was just beginning to move by slow degrees a little nearer to the place where his unworthy and enigmatic friend was standing; but at that very moment His Excellency's long-awaited carriage rolled up to the entrance. Fedoseich snatched open the door, bent himself double, and let His Excellency out. All those who had been waiting surged towards the door and pushed Mr Golyadkin senior away from Mr Golyadkin junior for a moment. 'You won't get away!' said our hero, working his way through the crowd without taking his eyes from the man he was following. The crowd dispersed at last. Our hero found himself free and hurried in pursuit of his enemy.

Chapter Eleven

THE breath laboured in Mr Golyadkin's lungs as he positively flew after his fast-retreating enemy. He felt full of a terrifying energy. In spite, however, of this terrifying energy, Mr Golyadkin was quite convinced that a mere mosquito, if one could have existed in such weather in St Petersburg, could quite easily have knocked him down with one of its wings. He felt, moreover, utterly limp and feeble, being carried along by some extraordinary extraneous power, not by his own legs, which on the contrary were collapsing under him and refusing to obey him. Everything, however, might still turn out for the best. 'Whether it's for the best or the worst,' thought Mr Golyadkin, almost suffocating with the speed of his progress, 'there's not the slightest doubt now that the game's up; I'm done for, that's settled – signed, sealed, and delivered.' Nevertheless, our hero was as if resurrected, like a man who has endured the battle and snatched the victory, when he succeeded in grasping the overcoat of his adversary, who had already raised one foot to the step of the droshky he had summoned. 'My dear sir! my dear sir!' Mr Golyadkin senior cried at last to his captive, the ill-bred Mr Golyadkin junior. 'I hope, my dear sir, that you . . .'

'No, no, pray don't hope, don't hope for anything,' Mr Golyadkin's unfeeling adversary answered evasively, as he stood with one foot on the step of the droshky, trying with all his might to get the other over to the farther side of the carriage, waving it vainly in the air, trying to keep his balance and at the same time struggling to wrench his overcoat from the clutch of Mr Golyadkin senior, who for his part clung to it with all the powers nature had endowed him with.

'Just ten minutes, Yakov Petrovich! . . .'

'Excuse me, I've no time to spare.'

'You must agree, Yakov Petrovich, that. . . . Please, Yakov Petro-

vich! ... For God's sake, Yakov Petrovich! ... It's like this ... a
little talk ... face up to it. ... Just a second, Yakov Petrovich!'

'My dear chap, I've no time,' Mr Golyadkin's enemy replied,
with his false gentility, attempting to conceal his impudent familiarity under a cloak of cordial good nature; 'any other time, believe me, with the greatest good will, and in all sincerity; but just
now – really and truly, I can't.'

'Swine!' thought our hero.

'Yakov Petrovich!' he cried in anguish, 'I have never been an
enemy to you. I've been misrepresented by ill-natured people. ...
For my part, I'm ready to. ... Yakov Petrovich, let's go somewhere
now, you and I, shall we ...? And there, in all sincerity, as you
said just now, in a straightforward fashion, like gentlemen ... this
coffee-house here: then the whole thing will be cleared up – that's
it, Yakov Petrovich! Then it will certainly all come clear of its own
accord ...'

'That coffee-house? all right. I've no objection; let's go into the
coffee-house, but on one condition, my dear old chap, that everything clears itself up there of its own accord. You've talked me
over, my dear boy,' said Mr Golyadkin junior, climbing down
from the cab and shamelessly clapping him on the shoulder,
'you're such a good sort; for you, Yakov Petrovich, I'm willing to
take a side-street (as you so rightly remarked that time, Yakov
Petrovich). You're a sly one, you know, you do whatever you like
with a man,' Mr Golyadkin's false friend went on, fussing and
fidgeting round him with a slight smile on his lips.

The coffee-house into which the two Mr Golyadkins now went,
remote as it was from the busy streets, was at that moment completely empty. A rather fat German woman appeared behind the
counter as soon as the bell sounded. Mr Golyadkin and his unworthy friend went through into the other room, where a puffy-
faced lad with a cropped head was busy at the stove with a bundle
of fire-wood, trying to revive the dead fire. Mr Golyadkin junior
ordered chocolate, and it was served.

'A fine figure of a woman,' said Mr Golyadkin junior, with a sly
wink at Mr Golyadkin senior.

Our hero blushed and said nothing.

'Oh, yes, I was forgetting, excuse me. I know your tastes. We like thin little Germans, my dear sir; you and I are partial, I say, to little German women who, although not entirely without attractions, are thin, my dear good chap; we rent their lodgings, we assail their virtue; we dedicate our hearts to them on account of their beer-soup and their milk-soup, we put various things into writing – that's what we do, you Faublas, you gay deceiver!'

While he was saying all this and making in this fashion his utterly pointless, although maliciously cunning, allusions to a certain person of the female sex, Mr Golyadkin junior was hovering round Mr Golyadkin senior, smiling at him with apparent amiability and a false show of cordiality and pretence of pleasure at their meeting. Noticing, however, that Mr Golyadkin senior was not such a fool or so devoid of education or good breeding as to take him on trust immediately, the ignoble fellow decided to change his tactics and proceed more openly. When he had spoken his infamous words, the spurious Mr Golyadkin ended by slapping the true Mr Golyadkin on the shoulder with revolting familiarity, and not satisfied with that, proceeded to amuse himself with him in a way altogether unacceptable in good society, namely by deliberately, in spite of Mr Golyadkin senior's resistance and slight cries of protest, repeating his former indecent gesture of pinching him on the cheek. In the face of such depravity our hero flew into a rage, but held his peace – although only for a short time.

'That is what my enemies say,' he answered at last in a shaking voice, prudently restraining his anger. At the same time our hero glanced uneasily at the door. The point was that Mr Golyadkin junior was evidently in excellent spirits and capable of launching into various familiarities not permissible in a public place or compatible with the usage of good society, especially in the highest circles.

'Well, in that case, as you please,' said Mr Golyadkin junior seriously, in response to Mr Golyadkin senior's thoughts, setting down on the table the cup he had emptied with unbecoming greediness. 'Well, you and I have nothing that need detain us for long, then. ... Well, how are you getting on now, Yakov Petrovich?'

'I have only one thing to say to you, Yakov Petrovich,' our hero answered coldly and with dignity; 'I have never been an enemy to you.'

'H'm. ... Well, and Petrushka? – is that his name? It is Petrushka, isn't it? – yes, of course! Well, how is he? – all right, eh? – the same as ever?'

'He's the same as before, too, Yakov Petrovich,' answered Mr Golyadkin senior, somewhat bewildered. 'I don't know. Yakov Petrovich ... for my part ... from a gentlemanly point of view, and in all frankness, Yakov Petrovich, you must admit, Yakov Petrovich ...'

'Yes. But you know yourself, Yakov Petrovich,' Mr Golyadkin junior answered in quietly emotional tones, thus falsely representing himself as a man sad, regretful, and full of compassion and decency, 'you know yourself that these are difficult times. ... I leave it to you, Yakov Petrovich, you are wise and will come to the right conclusion,' he went on, basely flattering Mr Golyadkin senior. 'Life is not a plaything, you know that yourself, Yakov Petrovich,' Mr Golyadkin junior concluded, thus laying claim to be a wise and learned man who could judge exalted issues.

'For my part, Yakov Petrovich,' our hero answered with spirit, 'for my part, despising as I do any beating about the bush, speaking boldly and openly in direct and gentlemanly terms, and keeping the whole thing on a well-bred level, I tell you that I can frankly and honourably insist, Yakov Petrovich, that I am absolutely innocent and that, as you well know, Yakov Petrovich, mutual misunderstanding – anything may happen – the world's judgement, the opinions of the slavish mob. ... I tell you frankly, Yakov Petrovich, anything may happen. I will say more, Yakov Petrovich; from that point of view, if the matter is to be looked at from a well-bred and high-minded point of view, I will venture to say without any false shame, Yakov Petrovich, that I would even be glad to admit I was mistaken, it would even be a pleasure to me to make that confession. You know yourself, you are a clever man, and a gentleman besides. I am ready to admit that, without shame, without any false shame,' our hero concluded with dignity and good breeding.

'Fate, destiny, Yakov Petrovich! . . . But let us leave all that,' said Mr Golyadkin junior with a sigh. 'Let us rather use the short minutes we are together in more useful and pleasant conversation, as is proper between colleagues. . . . Honestly, I don't seem to have managed to say two words to you all this time. . . . It hasn't been my fault, Yakov Petrovich . . .'

'Nor mine,' our hero interrupted warmly, 'nor mine! My heart tells me, Yakov Petrovich, that none of this is my fault. We must blame fate for the whole thing, Yakov Petrovich,' added Mr Golyadkin senior in a conciliatory tone. His voice was gradually beginning to tremble and grow faint.

'Well, now, what about your general health?' asked the strayed sheep in honeyed tones.

'I have a bit of a cough,' replied our hero even more sweetly.

'You must be careful. There are so many infections about just now, it's easy to catch tonsillitis, and I admit I'm beginning to wrap up in flannel already.'

'You're right, Yakov Petrovich, it's easy to catch tonsillitis. . . . Yakov Petrovich,' our hero proceeded after a short silence, 'Yakov Petrovich, I see I was mistaken. . . . It touches me to remember those happy moments we spent together under my poor but, I venture to say, hospitable roof . . .'

'That's not what you wrote in your letter, though,' said Mr Golyadkin junior with some reproach, and with the right (only in this respect, however) completely on his side.

'I was mistaken, Yakov Petrovich. . . . I see it clearly now. I was wrong to write that unfortunate letter. I am ashamed to look you in the eye, Yakov Petrovich. Yakov Petrovich, you mustn't believe . . . . Give me the letter so that I can tear it up before your eyes, or if that is quite impossible, I implore you to read it in the opposite sense, — exactly opposite, if you will be so kind, that is, deliberately turning all the words in the letter the other way round. I was mistaken. Forgive me, Yakov Petrovich, I was quite . . . I was grievously mistaken, Yakov Petrovich.'

'You were saying?' asked Mr Golyadkin senior's perfidious friend, rather absently and indifferently.

'I was saying that I was quite mistaken, Yakov Petrovich, and that for my part I am completely without false shame ...'

'Well, then, all right! You were mistaken, good,' answered Mr Golyadkin junior rudely.

'I even had the idea, Yakov Petrovich,' nobly added our frank and open hero, quite blind to his false friend's awful treachery, 'I even had the idea, "Here you have two identical ..."'

'Ah, so that's your idea!'

Here the notoriously worthless Mr Golyadkin junior rose and picked up his hat. Still not conscious of the treachery, Mr Golyadkin senior also stood up, smiling with simple-hearted courtesy at his false friend and innocently trying to create new bonds between them by an encouraging intimacy ...

'Good-bye, Your Excellency!' Mr Golyadkin junior exclaimed abruptly. Our hero started, noticing an almost riotous enjoyment in his enemy's face, and simply in order to get away thrust two of his fingers into the hand that was held out to him; but then ... then Mr Golyadkin junior's impudence passed all bounds. The wretch gripped and squeezed Mr Golyadkin's two fingers hard, then deliberately repeated under his very eyes the offensive gesture of the morning. The stock of human patience was exhausted ...

He was already stuffing the handkerchief with which he had wiped his hands back into his pocket when Mr Golyadkin senior recovered his wits and rushed after him into the next room, to which his irreconcilable enemy had immediately, in his usual nasty fashion, slipped away. He was standing by the counter just as if nothing at all had happened, calmly eating little patties and chatting amiably with the German proprietress, like any virtuous gentleman. 'I can't ... ladies present ...' thought our hero as he too went up to the counter, too agitated to know what he was doing.

'Really not at all a bad-looking little woman! What's your opinion?' Mr Golyadkin junior had embarked again on his indecent sallies, probably relying on Mr Golyadkin senior's inexhaustible patience. As for the fat German, she stared at both her customers with blank pewter-coloured eyes and smiled politely, evidently not understanding Russian. Our hero blushed like fire at the shameless Mr Golyadkin junior's words and, unable to contain himself any longer, sprang at him with the clear intention of tearing him to shreds and so finally finishing him off; but Mr Golyadkin junior, in his usual nasty way, was already out of reach; he had taken to his heels and was now outside the door. Needless to say, when Mr Golyadkin senior recovered his wits after his first natural stupefaction he rushed at full speed after his tormentor, who was already getting into the droshky which had been waiting for him, evidently by previous arrangement with the driver. But at that moment the fat German, seeing her two customers in flight, screamed and rang her little bell as loud as she could. Our hero, almost in mid-air, turned back, flung her some money for himself and the shameless wretch who had not settled his bill, did not wait for change and in spite of the delay succeeded, again almost in mid-air, in overtaking his enemy. Clinging to the mudguard of the droshky with all the strength bestowed on him by nature, our hero was carried some distance along the street as he tried to clamber into the vehicle while Mr Golyadkin junior did his best to fend him off. Meanwhile the cabby, with whip and reins and kicks and shouts, urged on his broken-down nag, which unexpectedly got the bit between its teeth and broke into a gallop, indulging a bad habit it had of kicking up its back legs at every third step. Finally our hero succeeded in getting himself perched up on the droshky, facing his adversary, with his back jammed against the driver's and his knees against the knees of his shameless, depraved, and most implacable enemy, to the shabby fur collar of whose overcoat his right hand was desperately clinging.

The adversaries were carried along for some distance in silence. Our hero could hardly get his breath back; the road was shockingly bad and he bounced at every step, in great danger of breaking his neck. In addition, his obstinate enemy, not yet ready to admit defeat, was still struggling to push him off into the mud. The crowning unpleasantness was the abominable weather. Snow was falling heavily in thick flakes, trying by every means in its power to creep inside the real Mr Golyadkin's overcoat, which had come undone. It was too dark to see anything. It was difficult to distinguish in what direction and through which streets they were moving. ... Mr Golyadkin had the feeling that what was happening was something already familiar. He tried for a moment to remember whether he had not had some presentiment the day before, in a dream, perhaps. ... His anguish was now reaching the last degree of agony. Leaning against his pitiless opponent he was on the point of crying aloud. But the cry died on his lips. ... There was a moment when Mr Golyadkin forgot everything and decided that none of it mattered, that it was just something that was happening in some inexplicable fashion, and that in that case it was vain and useless to protest. ... But suddenly and at almost the same instant as our hero reached this conclusion a careless jolt changed the whole aspect of affairs. Mr Golyadkin toppled from the droshky like a sack of flour and rolled away somewhere, admitting to himself quite rightly, as he fell, that he had allowed himself to lose his temper, and at a most inopportune time. Jumping up at last, he saw that they had arrived somewhere; the droshky was standing in the middle of a courtyard, and our hero recognized at the first glance that it was that of the block of flats where Olsufi Ivanovich lived. At the same time he noticed that his acquaintance was making his way over to the porch, and probably to Olsufi Ivanovich's. In his indescribable agony he was about to rush after and overtake him, but luckily was sensible enough to change his mind in time. Not forgetting to pay the driver first, Mr Golyadkin darted out into the street and hurried away at random as fast as his legs would carry him. The snow was falling as heavily as ever; as before the atmosphere was thick and wet and dark. ... Our hero was not walking but flying, bowling over everybody in the road, men, women, and children, and himself in his turn bouncing off men, women, and children. All round him, and in his wake, there were outbursts of frightened talk, shrieks and screams. ... But Mr Golyadkin seemed to be unconscious of it all and unwilling to pay attention to any of it. ... He did come to his senses, however, but not until he had almost reached Semyonovsky Bridge, and then only because he had managed to bump into and knock down two pedlar women with their wares, and bring himself down into the bargain. 'It doesn't matter,' thought

Mr Golyadkin, 'it may still all turn out for the best,' – and he groped in his pocket for a silver rouble to pay for the scattered gingerbreads, apples, split peas, and other things. Suddenly a new light broke on Mr Golyadkin; he had felt in his pocket the letter the porter had handed to him that morning. Happening to remember that a tavern he knew was not far away, he hurried into it, lost no time in settling down at a little table lighted by a tallow candle and, without paying attention to anything else or listening to the waiter who had come in for orders, broke the seal and began to read the following, which completed his astonishment.

Noble sufferer on my behalf, eternally dear to my heart,

I suffer, I perish, save me! That wicked intriguer, whose evil tendencies are so well known, caught me in his toils, and I was lost! I fell! But he is abhorrent to me, while you ...! We have been kept apart, my letters to you have been intercepted, and it was all the work of that vile man, making use of his only good quality, his likeness to you. One may always be ugly and yet captivate by the force of intellect, feeling, and prepossessing manners. ... I perish! I am to be married against my will, and here the principal plotter is my father and my benefactor, State Councillor Olsufi Ivanovich, who in all probability desires only to secure a place and connections in high society for me. ... But my resolve is taken. I protest with all the means in my power. Be waiting for me in your carriage today at exactly nine o'clock outside Olsufi Ivanovich's flat. We are having another dance, and our handsome young lieutenant will be here. I will come out and we will elope. There are other positions where it is possible to be of use to one's country. In any case, remember, my dear, that innocence is strength simply because it is innocent. Farewell. Wait in your carriage at the door. I will fly to the shelter of your arms at exactly two a.m.

> Yours to the tomb,
> Clara Olsufyevna ...

For some minutes after reading this letter, our hero was too astounded for words. As white as a sheet, he paced backwards and forwards in terrible agitation and distress, with the letter in his hands, not even noticing in the extremity of his disordered state that he was the object of the exclusive attention of everybody in the room. It is likely that his disarray, his uncontrollable agitation, his pacing or rather running about the room, the sweeping gestures of his arms, and perhaps a few random enigmatic words absently spoken aloud – all this, it is likely, produced a very unfavourable impression of Mr Golyadkin in the minds of the other customers; even the waiter began watching him suspiciously. As he came to himself our hero realized he was standing in the middle of the room and staring in an almost boorishly impolite fashion at a most respectable-looking little old man who, having finished his dinner and said grace before the icon, had now sat down again and for his part seemed unable to take his eyes from Mr Golyadkin. Looking vaguely about him, our hero saw that everybody, absolutely everybody, was gazing at him with the most severe and suspicious expression. All at once a retired military man with a red collar loudly demanded the 'Police Gazette'. Mr Golyadkin started and turned red; chancing to let his gaze fall, he had seen that his clothes were in so unseemly a state as to have been impossible even in the privacy of his own home, let alone in company. His boots and trousers and the whole of his left side were covered with mud, the strap on his right trouser-leg had been pulled off, and his coat was torn in many places. In overwhelming distress our hero went back to the table where he had read his letter and saw that the waiter was approaching him with a strangely and impudently insistent expression on his face. Flustered and utterly deflated, our hero began to examine the table at which he was standing. On it lay dirty dishes not yet cleared away after somebody's dinner, a soiled napkin and a recently used knife, spoon and fork. 'Who had dinner here?' our hero wondered. 'Can it have been me? Anything is possible! I've had dinner and never even noticed; what shall I do?' Raising his eyes, Mr Golyadkin again saw the waiter, standing beside him and on the point of saying something to him.

'How much do I owe you, my boy?' our hero asked in a quivering voice.

Loud laughter broke out all round Mr Golyadkin; even the waiters grinned. Mr Golyadkin realized that he had made another blunder and done something terribly stupid. Realizing it, he was so disconcerted that he felt obliged to feel in his pocket for a handkerchief, probably for the sake of doing something instead of just standing there; but to his own and everybody's amazement, instead of his handkerchief he pulled out the little bottle of medicine Christian Ivanovich had prescribed three or four days earlier. 'Get the medicine at the same chemist's as before,' the words echoed in his head. . . . Suddenly he started violently and almost shrieked in horror. A new light was dawning on him. . . . The dark, reddish, disgusting-looking liquid shone with an evil gleam in Mr Golyadkin's eyes. . . . The bottle dropped from his hands and smashed on the floor. Our hero cried out and stepped hastily back from the spilt liquid. He was trembling in every limb and the sweat started from his forehead and temples. 'So my life is in danger!' Meanwhile the room was full of movement and commotion; everybody pressed around Mr Golyadkin, talked to Mr Golyadkin, and some even caught hold of Mr Golyadkin. But our hero was dumb and motionless, seeing nothing, hearing nothing, feeling nothing. . . . Finally tearing himself away from the spot, he rushed out of the tavern, thrusting away all and sundry who tried to detain him, fell almost unconscious into the first cab that came along, and sped away to his flat.

In the entrance he met Mikheyev, the porter from the office, with an official envelope in his hand. 'I know, friend, I know all about it,' our exhausted hero said in a faint suffering voice; 'it's official business.' The envelope did indeed contain instructions to Mr Golyadkin, signed by Andrey Philippovich, to hand over all the business in his hands to Ivan Semyonovich. Mr Golyadkin took the envelope, gave the porter ten copecks, went into his flat, and saw that Petrushka had been getting together his things, all his bits and pieces, and piling them into a heap – evidently intending to leave Mr Golyadkin and go over to Katerina Ivanovna, who had enticed him into taking Eustaphy's place.

Chapter Twelve

PETRUSHKA came in with a swinging gait, a strangely off-hand manner, and an expression that combined servility with triumph. It was evident that he had formed some plan and felt completely within his rights, and he looked like an utter stranger, that is, like somebody else's servant, not Mr Golyadkin's at all.

'Well now, my good fellow,' began our hero breathlessly, 'what's the time, eh?'

Without a word Petrushka went behind the partition, returned and then in a rather insubordinate tone announced that it was nearly half past seven.

'Splendid, my dear fellow, splendid! Well now, my good fellow... if I may say so, my good fellow, all seems to be over between us.'

Petrushka said nothing.

'Well, now that all is over between us, tell me frankly, as you would a friend, where you've been, my boy.'

'Where I've been? To see some good people, sir.'

'I know, my friend, I know. I've always been satisfied with you, my good fellow, and I'll give you a reference. . . . Well, how did things go there?'

'What do you mean, sir? You know very well, sir. Everybody knows a good man won't give you bad ideas.'

'I know, my good fellow, I know. Good people are rare nowadays, my friend; value them, my friend. Well, who are they?'

'Don't ask me that, sir. . . . Only I can't stay in your service no longer, sir; you know that for yourself, sir.'

'I know, my good fellow, I know; I know how zealous and devoted you are; I have seen it all, my friend, I have taken note. I respect you, my friend. I respect a good and honest man, even if he is only a servant.'

'Well, of course, sir. Of course the likes of us is bound to look for good people, sir. Well, that's how it is. What can I do? Everybody knows, sir, it's impossible unless you've got a good master.'

'All right, my dear fellow, all right; I appreciate that. . . . Well, here's your money, and here's your reference. Now, my dear fellow, we must kiss and part. . . . Well now, my good fellow, I

want to ask you to do something for me, one last service,' said Mr
Golyadkin in solemn tones. 'You know, my good fellow, anything
can happen. There is sadness lurking even in gilded palaces, you
can't escape from it anywhere. You know, my good fellow, I think
I've always been good to you . . .'

Petrushka said nothing.

'I think I've always been good to you, my good fellow. . . . Well,
how much linen have we got now, my dear fellow?'

'It's all present and correct, sir. Linen shirts, six, sir; socks, three
pairs; four shirt-fronts; flannel vests, one; underwear, two pairs.
That's all, sir, as you know yourself. I haven't got anything of
yours, sir. . . . I look after my gentleman's things, sir. With you,
sir, I . . . well, of course . . . but I've never done anything wrong
sir; you know that for yourself, sir . . .'

'I believe you, my good fellow, I believe you. I didn't mean that
at all, my good fellow, not that at all; you see, my good fellow,
it's like this . . .'

'Of course, sir, we know that already, sir. You know, when I
was still in General Stolbnyakov's service, sir, they let me go,
because they were going to Saratov themselves . . . that's where
their family estate is . . .'

'No, my good fellow, I didn't mean that, I only asked . . . you
mustn't think, my dear fellow . . .'

'Of course, sir. Well, you know yourself, sir, it's easy to give the
likes of us a bad name, sir. And I've always given satisfaction
everywhere, sir. I've had places with ministers, and generals, and
senators, and counts, sir. I've been in service with all of them, sir,
Prince Svinchatkin, sir, and Colonel Pereborkin, and General Ne-
dobarov, he went away as well, sir, to his family estate. . . . Of
course, sir . . .'

'Yes, yes, my friend; all right, my friend, all right. You see, I'm
going away myself now, my good fellow. . . . Before every man lie
many different roads, and none can tell what path any man may
chance to tread. Well, my friend, lay out my things for me to dress
now; and put out my uniform coat . . . and my other trousers, and
sheets, and blankets, and pillows . . .'

'Shall I make them into a bundle, sir?'

'Yes, my friend, yes; a bundle will be all right. . . . Who knows what may happen to us? Well, my friend, now go down and find a carriage . . .'

'A carriage, sir?'

'Yes, my friend, a carriage, with plenty of room in it, and for as long as I want. And don't let your imagination run away with you, my friend . . .'

'Are you going a long way, sir?'

'I don't know, my friend, I don't know that either. I think you will have to put a feather-bed in as well. What do you think, my friend? I am relying on you, my good fellow . . .'

'Are you wanting to leave at once, sir?'

'Yes, my friend, I am! Things have turned out in that way . . . that's how it is, my friend, that's how it is . . .'

'Of course, sir; it was just the same when I was in service with a young officer, sir; at an estate in the country, sir . . . an elopement, sir . . .'

'Elopement? What, my friend? You don't . . .'

'Yes, sir, he eloped with her, and they were married at another estate. It was all arranged beforehand, sir. They were pursued, sir; then the Prince took their side, the late Prince, sir – and the matter was settled . . .'

'They were married, then . . . but how, my good fellow, did you . . .? How do you know, my good fellow?'

'Come, sir, everybody knows! The world is full of rumours, sir. We know everything, sir . . .; of course, which of us is perfect? Only I'll tell you something, sir, now; give me leave to say something in my blunt servant way; so long as things have gone so far, sir, let me tell you something, sir: you have an enemy – you've got a rival, sir, that's what it is, sir . . .'

'I know, my friend, I know; you, my good fellow, know. . . . Well, so I rely on you. What are we to do now, my friend? What is your advice?'

'Well, sir, look: if that's what you're up to now, sir, in a manner of speaking, well, you'll have to buy some things, sir – well, like sheets and pillows, and another feather-bed, double-bed size, sir, and a good quilt – and just here, sir, the woman downstairs; she's a shopkeeper, sir; she's got a good fox-fur coat, sir; you could have a look at it and buy it from her, you can slip down and have a look at it now, sir. You'll need it now, sir; it's a good coat, sir, satin on the outside, fox-fur, sir . . .'

'Very well, my friend, very well; I agree, my friend, and I rely on you, rely on you absolutely; perhaps even the coat as well, my good fellow. . . . Only quick, quick! for God's sake, quick! I'll buy the coat, only please be quick! Hurry, be as quick as you can, my friend . . .!'

Petrushka dropped the unfinished bundle of linen, pillows, blankets, sheets, and all sorts of oddments which he had begun to gather up and tie together, and rushed headlong out of the room. Mr Golyadkin meanwhile picked up the letter again, but could not read it. Clutching his aching head in both hands, he leaned against the wall in dismay. He could not think, he could not act, and he had no idea what would become of him. At last, seeing that time was passing and that neither Petrushka nor the fur coat had turned up, Mr Golyadkin decided to go himself. As he opened the door into the passage he heard from downstairs the noise of talking, arguing, and disagreement. . . . Several women were chattering, exclaiming, pronouncing judgement, arguing about something – and Mr Golyadkin knew very well what that something was. He heard Petrushka's voice, and then footsteps. 'Oh, God, they're bringing everybody in the world in here,' groaned Mr Golyadkin, wringing his hands in despair as he darted into his own room. Reaching it, he fell almost unconscious on the sofa, burying his face in the cushion. He lay there for a few minutes without moving, and then, not waiting for Petrushka, put on his galoshes, his hat, and his overcoat, seized his portfolio and rushed headlong downstairs. 'There's no need for you to do anything at all, my dear chap! I can do it all myself. I don't need you for the moment, and perhaps everything will turn out for the best then,' Mr Golyadkin murmured to Petrushka, meeting him on the stairs: then he ran out into the courtyard and away from the house. His spirits were low; he couldn't make up his mind how he ought to behave, what he ought to do, what steps he must take in his present critical situation.

'That's the point: what on earth am I to do? This just had to happen at this moment!' he exclaimed at last in despair, as he trotted along the streets at random, following his nose; 'it just had to happen now! After all, if it hadn't happened, if it hadn't been for just this one thing, everything would have been settled; it would have been settled at once, with one stroke, one clever energetic, determined stroke. I'll cut off my finger if it wouldn't. I even know just how it would have been settled. This is how everything would have been done: I'd simply have said, "Well, so and so, and such and such, and if you'll allow me to say so, my dear sir, it's nothing to do with me one way or the other; that's not the way things are done," I'd have said, "my very dear sir," I'd have said. "That's not the way to do things, and you won't get anywhere by imposture; an impostor, my good sir, is – well, he's no good, and he's no use to his country. Do you understand that, my good sir?" I'd say! That's how it would be. . . . No, though, why am I . . .? that's not it at all, absolutely not. . . . What nonsense I'm talking, like an utter fool! suicidal, that's what I am! Yes, I say, you're suicidal, things aren't like that at all. . . . Look, you degraded creature, look what's happening now! . . . What am I going to do now? What on earth am I going to do with myself? What good am I now? Well, you Golyadkin, you good-for-nothing creature, just tell me what you're fit for now! Well, what next? I must hire a carriage, she says, and bring it here; we'll get our pretty little feet wet, she says, if we haven't a carriage. . . . And who could possibly have imagined? Well, well, young lady, well, my fine young lady! A very well-conducted maiden you are, to be sure! our pride and joy! You've distinguished yourself, madam, you've distinguished yourself, I must say . . .! This all comes of being badly brought up; now that I've thought it over and got to the bottom of it, I can see it all comes of nothing but lack of morals. Instead of a bit of a whipping sometimes when she was little, they stuffed her with sweets and chocolates, and the silly old man slobbered over her: you're my sweetheart, you're my darling, he says, you're my pretty one, I'll marry you to a count . . .! And this is how she's turned out, she's shown her hand now; that's our little game, she says! Instead of keeping her at home when she was a child, they sent her away to school, to some little French madam, some *émigrée*, some Madame Falbala or other, and she learnt all sorts of things at Madame Falbala's – and it's all turned out like this. Come, she says, be happy! be under my window in a carriage, she says, at a certain time, and sing a touching Spanish serenade; I am waiting for you, and I know you love me, and we will run away together and live in a little wooden hut. But really, it simply can't be done; my dear madam – if things have gone as far as this – it's impossible, it's against the law, to remove an innocent and honest girl from her parents' house without their consent! And after all, why? what's the point? what need is there for it? Well, if she'd only marry the man she ought to, the man she's destined for, that would be the end of the matter. But I'm a civil servant, I can lose my job over this; I can end up in court, madam, that's how it is, if you didn't know! This is that German woman's doing! It all comes from that old witch, she's at the bottom of the whole mess. Slandering a man, making up a lot of old-womanish scandals about him, absolute lies, on Andrey Philippovich's advice – that's what it all came from. Otherwise, why is Petrushka mixed up in it? what's it got to do with him, the scoundrel; is it any of his business? No, I can't do it, madam, I absolutely can't, not for anything. ... You must excuse me this time, madam. It's all your fault, madam, it's not the German's fault, not her fault at all, but entirely yours, because the old witch is a good woman, the witch isn't to blame, it's you, madam, who are to blame for everything – and that's flat! You, madam, will be getting me accused of something I haven't done. Here's a man on his way to destruction, a man is losing his identity, and he can hardly control himself – and you talk about a wedding! And how will it all end? How will it be settled now? I'd give a lot to know.'

Thus our hero, in his despair, turned things over in his mind. Suddenly becoming aware of his surroundings, he found he was standing in Liteiny Street. The weather was abominable: there had been a thaw, snow was falling thickly and it was raining as well – everything exactly as it was in the middle of that terrible, never-to-be-forgotten night when all Mr Golyadkin's troubles had begun. 'What sort of journey is possible in this?' thought Mr Golyadkin, looking at the weather; 'everything's dead! Good God, how could I even find a carriage now, for instance? I think I can see something black over there on the corner. Let's go and investigate. . . . Oh God,' our hero continued, turning his feebly faltering steps in the direction where he had seen what looked like a carriage. 'No, I'll tell you what I'll do: I'll go and fall down at his feet, if I can, and make my humble entreaties. I'll say this, and that; I put my fate in your hands, I'll say, the hands of my superiors; Your Excellency, I'll say, give a man your protection and favour; thus and thus, I'll say, it's like this, the action is illegal; don't ruin me, I think of you as a father to me, don't desert me . . . save my pride, my honour, my name . . . and save me from a scoundrel, a depraved creature. . . . He is a different person, Your Excellency, and I'm a different person, too; he's an individual, and I'm a person by myself as well; really, a person by myself, Your Excellency, really; that's how it is, I shall say. I can't be like him, I shall say; transfer him, be kind and order him to be transferred – and put an end to this godless and wilful substitution . . . so that it won't be an example to others, Your Excellency. . . . I look upon you as a father; those in authority, of course, our benevolent superiors and protectors, cannot but encourage such actions. There is even something chivalrous about this. I look upon you, I say, my benevolent superiors, as a father; I entrust my fate to you, and I shall raise no objections; I put my trust in you, and I myself stand aside from the whole business . . . that's how it is, I shall say.'

'Well, my good fellow, are you a cabman?'

'Yes.'

'I want a carriage for the evening . . .'

'Will you be wanting to go far, sir?'

'For the whole evening, the whole evening, and to go wherever is necessary, my good fellow, wherever is necessary.'

'Perhaps you'll be wanting to go out of town, sir?'

'Yes, my friend, perhaps out of town. I don't know yet for certain, my friend, so I can't tell you exactly. You see, my friend, things may still turn out all right. Of course, my friend, you know . . .'

'Yes, sir, of course; I know. God grant they turn out well for everybody.'

'Yes, my friend, yes; thank you, my good fellow. Well, my good fellow, what will you charge me?'

'Do you want to go now, sir?'

'Yes, at once, or rather no, I want you to wait in a certain place ... just for a little, that is, you won't have to wait long, my good fellow.'

'Well, if you want to hire me for the whole evening, sir, I couldn't take less than six roubles, not in this weather, sir.'

'That's all right, my friend, and I shall know how to show my gratitude. Well then, my good fellow, take me now.'

'Yes, sir, get in; excuse me, I'll just set it to rights here; now please get in. Where do you want to go, sir?'

'To Izmailovsky Bridge, my friend.'

The driver clambered up on to his box, with some difficulty dragged his pair of lean nags away from their trough of hay, and got them moving in the direction of Izmailovsky Bridge. But all at once Mr Golyadkin pulled the cord, stopped the carriage, and begged the driver to turn back and go to another street instead of towards Izmailovsky Bridge. The cabby turned into the other street and in ten minutes Mr Golyadkin's newly-acquired carriage stopped in front of the house where His Excellency lived. Mr Golyadkin got out of the carriage, implored the driver to wait, and with his heart in his mouth ran up the stairs to the first floor and pulled the bell. The door opened and our hero found himself in His Excellency's hall.

'Is His Excellency at home?' Mr Golyadkin inquired of the man who had opened the door.

'On what business, sir?' asked the servant, looking him up and down.

'My friend, I ... well. My name is Golyadkin, I'm in the service, Titular Councillor Golyadkin. Say it's ... well, for an explanation.'

'You'll have to wait; you can't ...'

'I can't wait, my friend; my business is urgent, it allows of no delay.'

'Who sent you? Have you brought some papers?'

'No, my friend, I've come on my own account. Announce me, my friend; say it's to explain. I can't wait, it's impossible. ... You'll answer for this, my good man ...'

'It can't be done. My orders are to admit nobody; His Excellency has visitors. ... Please to come in the morning at ten o'clock.'

'Do announce me, my good fellow; I can't wait, it's impossible. ... You'll answer for this, my good man ...'

'Go on, announce him; what's the matter, are you trying to save shoe-leather?' said another servant, who was lounging on a bench and had not said a word until then.

'Shoe-leather be hanged! My orders is not to let anybody in, don't you know that? Their time is in the mornings.'

'Announce him. You haven't lost your voice, have you?'

'No, I've not: I'll announce him. But orders is orders, you know. Step in here.'

Mr Golyadkin went into the ante-room; there was a clock on the table. He looked at it: it was half past eight. He felt utterly cast down. He would have turned back, but at that moment the lanky footman standing on the threshold of the next room loudly proclaimed the name of Mr Golyadkin.

'What a din!' thought our hero, in indescribable anguish. 'He ought to have said ... well, this and that ... most humbly and dutifully presents himself to make an explanation, – and, well ... be good enough to receive him. Now the whole thing's ruined, all gone for nothing; however ... well, it doesn't matter. ...' There was, however, no time for thinking things over. The servant returned, said, 'Please come this way,' and led Mr Golyadkin into the study.

When our hero entered, he felt as though he had been struck blind, for he could see absolutely nothing. ... Then two or three figures flitted before his eyes, and it flashed through his mind that these must be guests. Finally he could clearly distinguish the star on His Excellency's black coat and then by degrees the black coat itself and at last he regained the power of steady vision ...

'Well, sir?' said the familiar voice above Mr Golyadkin's head.

'Titular Councillor Golyadkin, Your Excellency.'

'Well?'

'I have come to offer an explanation.'

'How ...? What ...?'

'It's like this. As I say, I've come to explain, Your Excellency.'

'But. ... Who are you?'

'M-m-mister Golyadkin, Your Excellency, Titular Councillor Golyadkin.'

'Well, what do you want?'

'As I say, it's like this: I look on him as a father; I stand aloof in the whole affair – and protect me from my enemy! There you are!'

'What is all this?'

'Everybody knows ...'

'What does everybody know?'

Mr Golyadkin said nothing; his chin was beginning to tremble slightly.

'Well?'

'I thought it was chivalrous, Your Excellency. ... There's something chivalrous about this, I said, and I look on my superior as a father. ... Well, I said, well, protect me. ... I b-b-beg you with t-t-tears in my eyes, and a-a-actions like this ought to b-b-be e-e-encouraged ...'

His Excellency turned away. For a few moments our hero's eyes could distinguish nothing. His chest felt tight. He was short of breath. He had no idea where he was. ... He felt somehow ashamed and dejected. God knows what happened next. ... When he came to himself, His Excellency was talking to his guests and seemed to be having a sharp and emphatic discussion with them. Mr Golyadkin recognized one of the guests at once: it was Andrey Philippovich. He did not know the other, and yet there seemed to be something familiar about the tall, heavy, middle-aged figure, with his thick bushy eyebrows and whiskers and his piercing and expressive eyes. An order hung round the stranger's neck, and he held a cigar in his mouth. He was nodding significantly as he smoked, and from time to time he glanced at Mr Golyadkin. Mr Golyadkin began to feel uncomfortable and turned away his eyes, and immediately saw another, and a very strange, visitor. In a doorway which our hero had until then taken for a mirror, as had happened on an earlier occasion, *he* had appeared – and we all know who it was, Mr Golyadkin's very intimate friend and acquaintance. Mr Golyadkin junior had in fact until that moment been in another small room, busily writing; now, evidently, he was wanted – and he appeared, with his papers under his arm, approached His Excellency and, while he waited for exclusive attention to be given to himself, very cleverly contrived to insinuate himself into the conversation and deliberations. He had taken up a position rather to Andrey Philippovich's rear, partly masking the cigar-smoking stranger. It was plain that Mr Golyadkin junior took a keen interest in the discussion, to which he listened with great politeness, nodding his head, fidgeting with his feet, smiling, and frequently glancing at His Excellency as if imploring him with his eyes to let him put in a word. 'The scoundrel!' thought Mr Golyadkin, and involuntarily took a step forward. At the same time His Excellency turned and came rather hesitantly towards Mr Golyadkin.

'Well, it's all right, it's all right; you may go. I will look into your case, and now I'll have you shown out.' Here the general looked at the stranger with the bushy whiskers, who nodded his agreement.

Mr Golyadkin felt, indeed clearly recognized, that he was being taken for something different from himself, and not looked on in the proper way at all. 'One way or another, I really must make myself plain,' he thought. 'It's like this, Your Excellency, I'll say. . . .' At this point he looked down at the floor in his indecision and saw to his extreme astonishment that there were large white patches on His Excellency's shoes. 'Can they have split?' Mr Golyadkin wondered. Very soon, however, he realized that His Excellency's shoes had not split but were simply shining with brilliant reflections – a phenomenon that was completely accounted for by the fact that they were of highly polished patent leather. 'Those are what they call *highlights*,' thought our hero; 'the term is used especially in painters' studios; in other places they are called streaks of light.' Here Mr Golyadkin raised his head and saw that it was time for him to speak, since it was highly possible that things would turn out badly. . . . Our hero took a step forward.

'As I say, it's like this. Some say one thing and some say another, Your Excellency,' he said, 'but impersonation won't work these days.'

The general made no answer, only tugged hard at the bell-pull. Our hero took another step forward.

'He's a degraded and wicked man, Your Excellency,' he said, almost beside himself and faint with fear, yet boldly and resolutely pointing at his unworthy twin, who was at the moment fidgeting about round His Excellency, 'some say this and some say that, but I am alluding to a certain person.'

A general stir followed Mr Golyadkin's words. Andrey Philippovich and the unknown figure began nodding their heads, and His Excellency tugged impatiently at the bell-pull with all his strength to summon the servants. It was then that Mr Golyadkin junior stepped forward in his turn.

'Your Excellency,' he said, 'I humbly ask your permission to speak.' There was a determined note in Mr Golyadkin junior's voice, and everything about him showed that he felt he was within his rights.

'Permit me to ask you,' he began again, anticipating His Excellency's answer in his zeal, and this time addressing Mr Golyadkin, 'permit me to ask you in whose presence you express yourself in that fashion, who it is you are standing before, and whose study you are in.' Mr Golyadkin junior was in an unusually excited state, flushed and glowing with anger and indignation; there were even tears in his eyes.

'The Bassavryukovs!' roared the footman at the top of his voice, appearing at the study door. 'A good aristocratic name, of Ukrainian origin,' thought Mr Golyadkin, and at that moment he felt somebody lay a hand on his back in the friendliest fashion; then another hand was laid on his back; Mr Golyadkin's infamous twin bustled forward to show the way, and our hero realized that he seemed to be being propelled towards the double doors of the study. 'Exactly like it was at Olsufi Ivanovich's,' he thought, and found himself in the ante-room. Looking round he saw beside him two of His Excellency's man-servants and one twin.

'Overcoat, overcoat, overcoat, my friend's overcoat! My dearest friend's overcoat!' twittered the obnoxious creature, snatching the coat from the hands of one of the lackeys and flinging it in mean-minded and nasty mockery straight over Mr Golyadkin's head. As he struggled from underneath it Mr Golyadkin senior distinctly heard the laughter of the two servants. But he was already walking out of the room without listening to them or paying any attention, and now he found himself on the brightly-lighted staircase. Mr Golyadkin junior followed him out.

'Good-bye, Your Excellency,' he called after the retreating Mr Golyadkin senior.

'Scoundrel!' said our hero, beside himself with rage.

'Scoundrel, if you like.'

'Infamous wretch!'

'And infamous, if you like,' answered the worthy Mr Golyadkin's unworthy adversary, looking from the top of the stairs, with his peculiar brand of vileness, straight into Mr Golyadkin's eyes without so much as blinking, as if challenging him to continue. Our hero spat with indignation and ran out on to the front steps; he was so shattered that he didn't even notice who helped him into the carriage, or how. When he came to himself, he saw that he was being driven along the Fontanka. 'So I must be going to Izmailovsky Bridge,' thought Mr Golyadkin. . . . There was something else that he was trying to think about, but he couldn't; it was something unaccountably terrible. . . . 'Well, it doesn't matter,' our hero concluded, and drove on to Izmailovsky Bridge.

Chapter Thirteen

THE weather really seemed to be trying to improve. The wet snow, that had been swirling down in great masses, began to fall more and more thinly and at last almost ceased. The sky became visible, with a few small stars twinkling here and there. It was now no worse than wet, muddy, raw, and stifling, especially for Mr Golyadkin, who had hardly recovered his breath yet. His sodden overcoat, heavy with wet, made his whole body feel un-pleasantly warm and damp, and its weight was almost breaking

his already exhausted legs. A kind of convulsive shiver sent sharp
pains shooting through his whole body, and exhaustion wrung a
sickly sweat from him, so that, suitable as the occasion was, Mr
Golyadkin even forgot to repeat with his usual firm resolution his
favourite sentiment, that maybe, perhaps, somehow or other, probably, certainly, everything would turn out for the best. 'However,
this doesn't matter, for the time being,' our hero, still sturdy and
undismayed, added as he wiped from his face the cold drops that
spouted in all directions from the brim of his round hat, which
was so sodden that it could absorb no more water. Adding that it
still didn't matter at all, our hero tried sitting down on a fairly
massive log lying near a pile of firewood in Olsufi Ivanovich's
yard. Of course, there was no question now of even thinking
about Spanish serenades and silken ladders, but it was absolutely
necessary to find a secluded corner that would at least offer some
comfort and concealment, if not much warmth. We may say in
passing that he had been strongly tempted by the idea of that
little corner between a cupboard and an old screen on Olsufi Ivanovich's landing, where previously, almost at the beginning of
this veracious history, he had stood for two hours among all the
domestic clutter, rubbish and worthless lumber. The fact is that
Mr Golyadkin had already been standing and waiting for a full
two hours this time as well, in Olsufi Ivanovich's courtyard. But
there were certain inconveniences attached to that secluded and
convenient little retreat that had not existed on the former occasion. The first was that the place had probably been marked, and
certain precautions taken, since the scandal of Olsufi Ivanovich's
ball; the second, that he must wait for a signal from Clara Olsufyevna, for some sort of signal there must certainly be. There
always is, and, as he said, 'We're not the first, and we shan't be the
last.' At this point he very opportunely remembered a novel he
had read a long time before, in which the heroine had given an
agreed signal to her Alfred in exactly similar circumstances by
tying a pink ribbon to her casement. But now, at night and in the
St Petersburg climate, so well-known for its humidity and change-
ableness, a pink ribbon was out of the question, and indeed, to
sum it up shortly, quite impossible. 'No, this isn't a case of silken

ladders,' our hero thought, 'and the best thing is for me to stay
here quietly out of sight. . . . I'd better stand just here,' and he
chose a place in the yard, opposite the windows and near the stack
of wood. Of course, there were always a lot of passers-by, like
grooms and coachmen, in the yard, and besides there were wheels
rattling and horses snorting and so on, but all the same it was a
convenient place whether he was noticed or not, and just now, at
any rate, it had the advantage that everything was more or less in
shadow and nobody could see Mr Golyadkin, while he could see
absolutely everything. The windows were brightly lit; Olsufi Ivanovich was having some sort of party. There was, however, no
music to be heard as yet. 'That means it's not a ball, so people
must have come for some other kind of party,' thought our hero,
his heart sinking. A thought struck him: 'Was it today? Is there a
mistake in the date? It's possible – anything is possible. That's
where it is – anything at all is possible. . . . It's possible that the
letter was written yesterday, and never reached me, and it didn't
reach me because that scoundrel Petrushka took a hand in the
game. Or it was written tomorrow, I mean I . . . that it was
tomorrow I was to do it, to wait with the carriage, I mean.' Here
our hero turned cold all over, and put his hand in his pocket for
the letter, to look at it again. But to his astonishment the letter
was not in his pocket. 'How is that?' whispered Mr Golyadkin,
half-dead with horror. 'Where did I leave it? Does this mean I've
lost it? – that's all I needed!' he groaned at last. 'What if it falls
into the wrong hands? (Perhaps it already has done!) Oh lord,
what will the consequences of that be? So bad that. . . . Oh, my
abominable luck!' At this point Mr Golyadkin began to tremble
like a leaf at the thought that his undeserving twin, having somehow got wind of the letter from Mr Golyadkin's enemies, had
flung his coat over his head with the express purpose of purloining it. 'What's more, he's purloining it as evidence,' thought
our hero, 'but why evidence?' After the first shock and stupor of
horror, the blood surged back to Mr Golyadkin's head. Groaning
and grinding his teeth, he clutched his burning brow, sank down
to his log, and began trying to think of something. . . . But there
was no coherence in his thoughts. Certain faces, and memories,

some vague and some clear-cut, of certain long-forgotten incidents, passed through his mind, and the tunes of certain foolish songs rang in his ears. It was anguish, unbelievable anguish! 'Oh God!' he thought, as he recovered a little, stifling a muffled sob, 'oh God, give me fortitude of mind in the unfathomable depths of my misery! There can no longer be any doubt: I am utterly lost, I am finished; and this is all in the nature of things, it could not have been otherwise. To begin with, I've lost my job, inevitably, of course I have. ... Well, let's suppose this other business gets settled somehow. Suppose the bit of money I have is enough for a new start; there'll have to be a new flat and a few sticks of furniture. ... But first of all, I shan't have Petrushka. I can get on without the scoundrel ... with the help of lodgers; fine! I can come in and go out when I like, and Petrushka won't grumble because I've come in late – that's it; that's why it's a good idea to have lodgers in the house. ... Yes, well, suppose all that's all right; only how is it I keep talking about the wrong thing, absolutely the wrong thing?' At this point the thought of his present position recalled itself to Mr Golyadkin's memory. He looked round. 'Oh my God! My God! What on earth am I talking about now?' he thought, utterly bewildered and clutching at his burning forehead ...

'Will you be wanting to go soon, sir?' said a voice from above Mr Golyadkin's head. Mr Golyadkin started; but it was only his cabby who stood before him, also wet to the skin and shivering all over; impatience at having nothing to do had inspired him to take a look at Mr Golyadkin behind the wood-pile.

'I'm all right, my friend ... soon, my friend, very soon; wait a bit ...'

The cabman walked away, muttering to himself. 'What's he mumbling about?' Mr Golyadkin thought tearfully. 'I hired him for the evening, didn't I? After all, I'm ... perfectly at liberty to ... that's what it is, I hired you for the evening and there's an end of the matter! Even if you simply stand all the time, it makes no difference. It depends on what I decide. I'll go if I want to, and if not, not. And if I am standing behind a pile of logs, that doesn't matter either ... and don't you dare say a word; as I say, if a gentleman wants to stand behind a wood-pile, he stands behind a wood-pile ... and he's not harming anyone's reputation – and that's that! That's that, madam, if you want to know. And in our day and age, I say, madam, nobody lives in a little wooden hut. That's that! and in our industrial age, my dear madam, you won't get anywhere without moral principles – a fact of which you now furnish a terrible proof.... You say I must become a justices' clerk and live in a hut by the sea. ... To begin with, my dear madam, there are no justices' clerks living on the seashore and in the second place, you and I won't get a job as a justices' clerk. Suppose, for example, I send in a petition, go to see them, and say, "It's like this ... well, to be a justices' clerk ... and protect me from my enemy...", they'll tell you this, madam: we've got plenty of clerks in the courts, and you're not at Madame Falbala's now, learning morals, of which you furnish a fatal example. Morality, madam, means staying at home, honouring your father, and not thinking about engagements until the time comes. Fiancés, madam, will come along in their own good time, madam. Of course, it is no doubt necessary to have acquired some accomplishments, such as playing on the piano sometimes, speaking French, knowing history, geography, scripture and arithmetic – but there's no need to go any further. Then there's cookery besides; cookery should certainly be within every properly conducted young lady's province! But as it is, what happens here? In the first place, my charmer, my fine young lady, you won't be allowed out, and if you are, there'll be a hue and cry after you, and you'll be put away in a convent. Then what, my dear young lady? what would you have me do then? Would you have me behave like somebody in a silly novel, come to some near-by hill-slope, dissolve in tears at the sight of the cold indifferent walls that imprison you, and finally follow the example of certain bad German poets and novelists, and die, is that it, madam? But first allow me to tell you, as a friend, that that's not the way things happen, and secondly you, and your parents too, would be soundly whipped if I had my way, for giving you French novels to read: for you learn nothing good from French novels. They are poison, rank poison, my dear madam! Or do you think, may I ask, do you think that, so to say, it's like this, we shall elope with impunity, and that will be all ...? You'll get your little wooden hut on the seashore, and we'll set to work billing and cooing and talking about our feelings, and live happily ever after; and then there'll be a little nestling, and we shall ... well, we'll go and say to our father, State Councillor Olsufi Ivanovich, "We've got a little one, so take advantage of this auspicious occasion to remove your curse and bless the happy pair!" – is that it? No, madam, once again, that's not the way things happen, and the first thing is, there won't be any billing and cooing, so you needn't expect it. Nowadays, my dear madam, the husband is the master, and a good, well-brought-up wife must try to please him in everything. And nowadays, in our individual age, madam, tender words are not in fashion; the days of Jean-Jacques Rousseau are past. Nowadays, for example, a husband comes home from work hungry and says, "What about a bite to eat, darling, a glass of vodka and a bit of herring?" and you'll have to have the vodka and the herring all ready on the spot, madam. Your husband will enjoy it heartily, and he won't even look at you, only say, "Slip into the kitchen, kitten, and see to the dinner," and perhaps once a week at most he'll give you a kiss, and a rather indifferent one at that. ... That's how things are in our days, my dear madam – and even then, as I say, the kiss will be rather indifferent! That's how it will be, if you come to think about it, if you've got far enough to look at things in that light. ... And what is it to do with me? Why have you dragged me into your little fancies? A kind-hearted man who is suffering for my sake and is dear to my heart in every way, and so on? But to begin with, my dear madam, I am not suited to you, as you know yourself, I'm not expert at paying compliments, I don't like making pretty speeches to the ladies, I can't stand languishing young ladies' men, and I must own my looks have never got me anywhere. You won't find false pride or false modesty in me, and I confess all this now in all sincerity. What I say is that I possess only a frank and open character and sound sense; I don't go in for intrigues. I'm no intriguer and I'm proud to say so. So there it is! I don't wear a mask among decent people, and to tell you the truth ...'

Suddenly Mr Golyadkin started violently. His cabby's red and dripping beard was again peering at him round the stack of wood.

'I'm coming at once, my friend; at once, you know, my friend; I, my friend, am coming this minute,' Mr Golyadkin responded, in a voice that quivered and almost died away.

The driver scratched his head, then stroked his beard, then took a step forward, stopped and looked mistrustfully at Mr Golyadkin.

'I'm coming at once, my friend; I, you see ... my friend ... I'll only be a little ... you see, my friend, I'll only be a second ... you see, my friend ...'

'Aren't you going anywhere at all?' said the driver at last, coming up to Mr Golyadkin with a determined and resolute step.

'Yes, my friend, I'm coming immediately. You see, my friend, I'm waiting ...'

'Yes, sir.'

'You see, my friend – what village are you from, my dear fellow?'

'We're serfs, sir.'

'And are your masters good ...?'

'All right ...'

'Yes, my friend; stay here a bit, my friend. You see, my friend, have you been in St Petersburg long?'

'I've been driving here a whole year.'

'And are you doing well, my friend?'

'All right.'

'Yes, my friend, yes. Thank Providence, my friend. You must look for a good master, my friend. Nowadays good people are getting rare, my friend. He will give you food and drink and washing, my friend, a good man will. ... But sometimes you see the tears flowing even through the gold, my friend ... you see a lamentable example of that; that's how it is, my friend ...'

The cabman seemed to have grown sorry for Mr Golyadkin.

'Well, if you like, I'll wait a bit, sir. Will you be waiting long, sir?'

'No, my friend, no; I, you know, well . . . I'm not going to wait, my friend. What do you think? I rely on you. I won't wait here any longer . . .'

'Won't you be going anywhere at all?'

'No, my friend; no, but I'll pay you for your trouble, my dear fellow . . . that's what I'll do. How much do I owe you, my good man?'

'Give me what we settled on, sir, please. I've waited a long time, sir; you won't be hard on a man, sir.'

'Well here you are, my good man, here you are.' Here Mr Golyadkin paid the cabby his six roubles, and having made up his mind in earnest not to lose any more time, that is, to leave before anything worse happened, especially as it was all over, and the cabman had been sent away, so that there was no more reason to wait, he walked out of the yard and into the street, turned left, and began to run, without a backward glance, panting but rejoicing. 'Perhaps it will all turn out for the best,' he thought, 'and this way I've steered clear of trouble.' Mr Golyadkin really did feel remarkably cheerful all at once. 'Oh, perhaps it really will turn out for the best!' our hero thought, although he had not much faith in his own words. 'Now I'll just . . .' he thought. 'No, I'd better . . . but on the other hand. . . . Or had I better do it like this?' Hesitating in this way and seeking for something to resolve his doubts, our hero ran as far as Semyonovsky Bridge and having reached it, very wisely, and once for all, decided to go back. 'That's the best,' he thought. 'I'd better approach it from the other side, I mean like this: I'll be just an . . . onlooker, an outsider and no more, and then whatever happens I'm not to blame. That's it! That's how it's going to be now.'

Having decided to return, our hero really did so, especially as he had by this happy inspiration established himself as somebody completely uninvolved. 'That's the best; you won't be responsible for anything, and yet all the same you'll see what follows . . . that's it!' That was, his calculations were correct and the matter was at an end. Reassured, he returned to the tranquil protection of his comforting guardian wood-pile and began watching the windows intently. This time he did not have to watch and wait for long. Suddenly a strange kind of bustle became visible in all the windows at once, curtains were drawn back, whole groups of people crowded into Olsufi Ivanovich's windows, all gazing out and looking for something in the courtyard. Secure in the shelter of his pile of logs, our hero in his turn watched the general commotion with curiosity, craning his neck to right and left in sympathy, as far, at least, as was allowed by the narrow patch of shadow that hid him. All at once he started and almost cowered, numb with shock. It had begun to seem to him, in fact he had completely realized, that they were not just looking for somebody or something in general: they were looking for him, Mr Golyadkin. Everybody was gazing in his direction and pointing towards him. It was impossible to run away: they would see him. Numbly Mr Golyadkin cowered as close to the logs as he could, and only then noticed that he had been betrayed by the treacherous shadow, which did not entirely cover him. If it had only been possible, our hero would most gladly have crept then and there into some little mouse-hole among the logs and crouched there in peace. But it was definitely impossible. In his anguish he began at last staring resolutely and directly at all the windows at once; that was after all the best thing to do. Then he grew hot with shame. He was definitely discovered, everybody had seen him at the same moment, they were all waving their hands, nodding their heads, and mouthing at him; now several windows were pushed open with a crack, and several voices at once were audible calling to him. ... 'I wonder they don't whip those girls when they're children,' our flustered hero grumbled to himself. Suddenly *he* (we all know who) ran down the steps without a hat or overcoat, out of breath, mincing, skipping, prancing, and perfidiously making a display of the most intense pleasure at seeing Mr Golyadkin at last.

'Yakov Petrovich,' twittered this notorious detrimental. 'You here, Yakov Petrovich? You'll catch cold. It's cold out here. Do come inside.'

'No, thank you, Yakov Petrovich. I'm all right, Yakov Petrovich,' our hero murmured meekly.

'But, Yakov Petrovich, you must; they're waiting for us, and they beg you, they respectfully beg you, to come in. "Do us the kindness of bringing Yakov Petrovich in." That's what they said.'

'No, Yakov Petrovich; don't you see, I'd better. .... It would be better if I went home, Yakov Petrovich,' said our hero, feeling as though he was being roasted over a slow fire, and yet at the same time cold with horror and shame.

'No-no-no-no-no!' the loathsome creature twittered. 'Not-not-not-not for anything! Come along!' he went on with the utmost determination, pulling Mr Golyadkin senior towards the steps. Mr Golyadkin senior would have liked to refuse flatly, but with everybody watching it would have been stupid to resist and make a fuss, and he went – although really he can hardly be said to have gone, since he had no idea what he was doing. Not that it would have made any difference!

Before our hero had had time to recover his senses, he found himself in the drawing-room. He was pale, tousled, and dishevelled; he looked dully at the people round him – oh horror! The drawing-room and all the other rooms were crowded to the doors. There were masses of people, a flower-show of ladies, all thronging round Mr Golyadkin, all pressing towards Mr Golyadkin, bearing Mr Golyadkin along with them, and he realized clearly that they were urging him in one particular direction. 'Not towards the door, though,' was the thought that flashed into his mind. And indeed they were urging him not towards the door but towards Olsufi Ivanovich's comfortable armchair. On one side of the chair stood Clara Olsufyevna, pale, languid, and melancholy, but magnificently dressed. Mr Golyadkin was specially struck by the little white flowers in her black hair, which produced a wonderful effect. Vladimir Semyonovich, in a black coat with his new Order in the button-hole, was on the other side of the chair. Mr Golyadkin was led into the room and, as we have said, straight up to Olsufi Ivanovich, escorted on one side by Mr Golyadkin junior, who had now, to our hero's inexpressible pleasure, assumed an extremely proper and decorous look, and on the other by Andrey Philippovich, with an expression of great solemnity. 'What can this mean?' Mr Golyadkin wondered. When, however, he realized that they were taking him to Olsufi Ivanovich he saw it all in a flash. The thought of the purloined letter came into his mind. . . . In indescribable anguish he came to a halt before Olsufi Ivanovich's chair. 'What shall I do now?' he thought. 'Put a bold front on it, of course, that is behave openly and like a gentleman; say this is how it is, and so on.' But what our hero distinctly feared did not happen. Olsufi Ivanovich seemed to welcome Mr Golyadkin with great amiability, and although he did not offer his hand, at least looked at him with a shake of his grey-haired and venerable head – a shake full of solemn melancholy, yet at the same time benevolent. So at least it seemed to Mr Golyadkin. It even seemed to him that a tear glistened in Olsufi Ivanovich's dim old eyes; he raised his own eyes and it appeared to him that a tear glittered on Clara Olsufyevna's lashes too, that there was something similar in Vladimir Semyonovich's eyes as well, that Andrey Philippovich's unruffled tranquil dignity was the equivalent of the general tearful sympathy, and finally the young man who had once seemed so like a high-ranking dignitary was sobbing bitterly, as his way of contributing to the present moment. . . . Or perhaps Mr Golyadkin only imagined all this because he himself had broken down and could distinctly feel the scalding tears running down his cold cheeks. Reconciled with the world and his fate, full of warm affection not only for Olsufi Ivanovich, not only for all his guests taken together, but even for his obnoxious twin, who now appeared to be neither obnoxious nor even his twin, but a mere bystander and a thoroughly agreeable person in himself, our hero, his voice shaking with sobs, made a touching attempt to pour out his heart to Olsufi Ivanovich; but he was too burdened with accumulated emotions to be able to express anything at all, and he could only point to his heart, in a silent and eloquent gesture. . . . At length Andrey Philippovich, probably wishing to spare the grey-haired old man's sensibilities, led Mr Golyadkin a little aside and then left him, apparently free to follow his own inclinations. Smiling and murmuring something inaudible, a little bewildered, but almost completely reconciled with mankind and destiny, our hero began to make his way through the thick crowd of guests. They moved aside for him, all looking at him with a strange kind of curiosity and an unaccountable enigmatic sympathy. Our hero went into the next room, everywhere attracting the same attention; he was dimly aware of a crowd following hard at his heels, observing his every step, furtively discussing something extremely interesting, shaking their heads, talking, reasoning, arguing, whispering. Mr Golyadkin would very much have liked to know what they were all talking and arguing and whispering about. Looking round, he saw Mr Golyadkin junior at his side. He felt compelled to take him by the arm and draw him aside, where he earnestly begged him to cooperate in all his future undertakings and not abandon him at a critical moment. Mr Golyadkin nodded with an important air and squeezed his hand. Our hero's heart was tremulous with excess of emotion. Besides, he was beginning to feel stifled, more and more closely hemmed in; all those eyes fixed on him seemed to be oppressing and crushing him. ... Mr Golyadkin caught a glimpse of the Councillor who wore a wig. The Councillor was looking at him with severe and searching eyes, in no way softened by the general sympathy. ... Our hero almost made up his mind to go straight to him, smile, and enter into an explanation with him, but somehow he did not seem able to do it. For a moment Mr Golyadkin almost lost consciousness; both memory and feeling left him. ... When he came to his senses, he saw that he was surrounded by a wide circle of guests. Suddenly Mr Golyadkin's name was called from the next room, and the cry was at once taken up by the whole crowd. All was noise and excitement, everybody rushing towards the drawing-room doors and carrying him along with them. The stony-hearted Councillor in the wig found himself side by side with Mr Golyadkin, and finally took him by the arm and placed him in a chair next to himself and opposite where Olsufi Ivanovich was sitting, although at a considerable distance from him. All the others who had been in either room sat down in several rows of chairs surrounding Mr Golyadkin and Olsufi Ivanovich. Everything grew hushed and still, everybody preserved a solemn silence, and all eyes gazed at Olsufi Ivanovich, who was evidently expecting something rather out of the ordinary. Mr Golyadkin noticed that the other Mr Golyadkin and Andrey Philippovich had placed themselves next to

Olsufi Ivanovich's chair and opposite the Councillor with the wig. The silence continued; something really was expected. 'Just like a family before somebody leaves on a long journey; all we need now is for somebody to stand up and say a prayer,' thought our hero. Suddenly there was an extraordinary stir, and Mr Golyadkin's train of thought was broken short. 'He's coming, he's coming!' – the words ran through the crowd. 'Who's coming?' wondered Mr Golyadkin, and a strange kind of feeling made him shudder. 'Now is the time!' said the Councillor, looking attentively at Andrey Philippovich. Andrey Philippovich for his part looked at Olsufi Ivanovich. Olsufi Ivanovich solemnly and authoritatively inclined his head. 'Shall we stand up?' said the Councillor, drawing Mr Golyadkin to his feet. Everybody stood up. Then the Councillor took Mr Golyadkin senior by the hand, and Andrey Philippovich did the same with Mr Golyadkin junior, and solemnly they conducted the two men, so completely alike in appearance, to the middle of the crowd, all with their eyes fixed expectantly on them. Our hero looked round in perplexity, but he was brought to a halt and his attention directed to Mr Golyadkin junior, who was holding out his hand. 'They want us to make it up,' thought our hero, touched, and he extended his hand to Mr Golyadkin junior, and then ... and then his cheek. The other Mr Golyadkin did the same. At this point it seemed to Mr Golyadkin that his perfidious friend was grinning and winking slily to the surrounding crowd and that there was something sinister in the worthless Mr Golyadkin junior's face, that he even made a grimace at the moment of his Judas-kiss.... There was a ringing in Mr Golyadkin's ears and darkness before his eyes: he imagined that an endless string of Golyadkins all exactly alike were bursting noisily in through all the doors of the room; but it was too late. ... The resounding treacherous kiss had been given, and ...

Then an entirely unexpected thing happened. ... The doors into the drawing-room were flung open with a crash, and on the threshold stood a man, the mere sight of whom froze the blood in Mr Golyadkin's veins and rooted him to the spot. The shriek died stifled in his breast. Yet Mr Golyadkin had known it all before and had already anticipated something like this. The unknown sol-

emnly and portentously approached Mr Golyadkin. ... Mr Golyadkin knew that figure very well. He had seen it before, seen it
very often, seen it that very day. ... The newcomer was a tall
solidly built man in a black frock-coat, with the cross of some
distinguished Order hanging round his neck and with a pair of the
blackest possible whiskers; he only needed a cigar in his mouth to
complete the resemblance. ... Yet the stranger's glance, as we said
above, froze Mr Golyadkin with horror. With a solemn and important air this terrible man advanced towards the pitiful hero of
our story. ... Our hero stretched out his hand, the stranger took
the hand and drew Mr Golyadkin after him. ... Our hero looked
round with a lost and beaten look ...

'This is Christian Ivanovich Rutenspitz, Physician and Surgeon,
your old acquaintance, Yakov Petrovich!' twittered somebody's
loathsome voice close to Mr Golyadkin's ear. He looked round: it
was the twin whose pernicious qualities made him so hateful.
Unseemly and sinister joy shone in his face; he was gleefully rubbing his hands, gleefully turning his head from side to side, gleefully mincing along past everybody, he seemed almost ready to
dance with glee; finally he leaped forward, seized a candle from
one of the servants and walked ahead, lighting the way for Mr
Golyadkin and Christian Ivanovich. Mr Golyadkin could distinctly hear everybody in the drawing-room come hurrying along
behind, all crowding and elbowing each other, and all calling
loudly after him, 'It's all right, Yakov Petrovich, don't be afraid;
after all, this is Christian Ivanovich Rutenspitz, your old acquaintance and friend.' At last they came to the brightly illuminated front stairs; there were many people on the stairs also; the
outer door was flung open with a crash and Mr Golyadkin found
himself outside on the porch with Christian Ivanovich. A closed
carriage was drawn up at the foot of the steps, its four horses
snorting with impatience. The gloating Mr Golyadkin junior
reached the foot of the steps in three bounds and himself flung
open the carriage door. With a commanding gesture Christian
Ivanovich invited Mr Golyadkin to get in. The gesture was quite
unnecessary, however; there were plenty of people to see him in.
... Numb with horror, Mr Golyadkin looked back: the whole

brightly lighted staircase was thick with people; curious eyes stared at him from all sides; Olsufi Ivanovich himself had appeared on the top landing, sitting there in his comfortable armchair and watching with attention and keen sympathy everything that went on. Everybody was waiting. A murmur of impatience ran through the crowd when Mr Golyadkin looked back.

'I hope there is nothing here ... nothing prejudicial ... or that might call for severity ... and public attention, concerning my official relationships,' said our hero, becoming flustered. A clamour of voices arose; they all shook their heads. Tears started from Mr Golyadkin's eyes.

'In that case, I am ready.... I have every confidence.... I put my fate in Christian Ivanovich's hands.'

As soon as Mr Golyadkin had stated that he put his fate completely in Christian Ivanovich's hands, a terrible, deafening, joyful shout burst from those close to him, and a sinister echo rolled through all the waiting crowd. Now Christian Ivanovich and Andrey Philippovich took Mr Golyadkin by the arms and began putting him into the carriage, while his double, in his usual nasty way, pushed from behind. The unhappy Mr Golyadkin took his last look at everybody and everything, and shivering – if the comparison may be permitted – like a kitten that has been drenched with cold water, crept into the carriage: Christian Ivanovich followed him at once. The carriage door slammed, the whip cracked, the straining horses jerked the carriage into motion, the whole crowd dashed after Mr Golyadkin. The piercing frantic yells of all his enemies pursued him by way of farewell. For a short time a few figures could still be seen flitting round the carriage as it bore Mr Golyadkin away, but little by little they dropped further and further behind and at last vanished altogether. Mr Golyadkin's unworthy twin held on longest of all. With his hands in the pockets of his green uniform trousers he ran on with a pleased expression on his face, jumping up first on one side of the carriage and then on the other; sometimes, grasping the window-frame and hanging on by it, he even thrust his head inside and blew kisses in farewell; but he began to grow tired, his appearances became fewer and fewer, and finally he too vanished altogether. Mr Golyadkin's heart ached dully; the hot blood throbbed in his head; he was suffocating, he felt like tearing open his clothes, baring his chest, plastering it with snow, pouring cold water over it. He fell at last into unconsciousness. ... When he came to himself, he saw that the horses were bearing him along an unfamiliar road. To right and left the forest loomed blackly; all around was silent and deserted. Suddenly his heart almost stopped beating: two fiery eyes were watching him in the darkness, and they shone with malignant hellish joy. This was not Christian Ivanovich! Who was it? – Or was it he? Yes! This was Christian Ivanovich, but not the same one, a different Christian Ivanovich, a fearful Christian Ivanovich ...!

'Christian Ivanovich, I ... I think I'm all right, Christian Ivanovich,' our hero began in a timid and trembling voice, trying to mollify this terrifying Christian Ivanovich, at any rate a little, by meekness and submission.

'You will haf official quarters, with firewood und *Licht* und service, which you do not deserf.' Christian Ivanovich's answer rang out like the stern and terrible sentence of a judge.

Our hero shrieked and clutched at his head. Alas! This was what he had known for a long time would happen!

1846.

READ MORE IN PENGUIN

In every corner of the world, on every subject under the sun, Penguin represents quality and variety – the very best in publishing today.

For complete information about books available from Penguin – including Puffins, Penguin Classics and Arkana – and how to order them, write to us at the appropriate address below. Please note that for copyright reasons the selection of books varies from country to country.

In the United Kingdom: Please write to *Dept. JC, Penguin Books Ltd, FREEPOST, West Drayton, Middlesex UB7 OBR.*

If you have any difficulty in obtaining a title, please send your order with the correct money, plus ten per cent for postage and packaging, to *PO Box No. 11, West Drayton, Middlesex UB7 OBR*

In the United States: Please write to *Consumer Sales, Penguin USA, P.O. Box 999, Dept. 17109, Bergenfield, New Jersey 07621-0120.* VISA and MasterCard holders call 1-800-253-6476 to order all Penguin titles

In Canada: Please write to *Penguin Books Canada Ltd, 10 Alcorn Avenue, Suite 300, Toronto, Ontario M4V 3B2*

In Australia: Please write to *Penguin Books Australia Ltd, P.O. Box 257, Ringwood, Victoria 3134*

In New Zealand: Please write to *Penguin Books (NZ) Ltd, Private Bag 102902, North Shore Mail Centre, Auckland 10*

In India: Please write to *Penguin Books India Pvt Ltd, 706 Eros Apartments, 56 Nehru Place, New Delhi 110 019*

In the Netherlands: Please write to *Penguin Books Netherlands bv, Postbus 3507, NL-1001 AH Amsterdam*

In Germany: Please write to *Penguin Books Deutschland GmbH, Metzlerstrasse 26, 60594 Frankfurt am Main*

In Spain: Please write to *Penguin Books S. A., Bravo Murillo 19, 1° B, 28015 Madrid*

In Italy: Please write to *Penguin Italia s.r.l., Via Felice Casati 20, I–20124 Milano*

In France: Please write to *Penguin France S. A., 17 rue Lejeune, F–31000 Toulouse*

In Japan: Please write to *Penguin Books Japan, Ishikiribashi Building, 2–5–4, Suido, Bunkyo-ku, Tokyo 112*

In Greece: Please write to *Penguin Hellas Ltd, Dimocritou 3, GR–106 71 Athens*

In South Africa: Please write to *Longman Penguin Southern Africa (Pty) Ltd, Private Bag X08, Bertsham 2013*